DESERVING ALASKA

The Refuge, Book 1

SUSAN STOKER

PROLOGUE

31 Years Ago

"Hi, are you new?"

Alaska Stein looked up in surprise at the boy who was standing next to her seat on the school bus. "Yes."

"Cool. I'm Drake. What's your name?"

"Alaska."

"That's a weird name," the boy said.

"So's Drake," she told him with a shrug.

To her surprise, instead of getting mad, he smiled. "I guess. When did you move here?"

"Last week," Alaska replied. She'd seen the boy at school and knew he was in fourth grade, a year ahead of her.

"This your first time riding the bus?"

Alaska shook her head. He'd walked past her on the bus four times this week, obviously without seeing her... which was already the story of her young life. Her mom

1

always said she should've named her Jane...as in plain Jane. She claimed her daughter could blend in with the walls. Being invisible had never bothered Alaska though. She was shy and didn't like when people stared at her.

"Oh, wait! I think you moved into the trailer a couple spaces down from mine. The brown and white one?" Drake asked.

Alaska nodded.

"Cool! Wanna play this afternoon? My friends and I are gonna play War."

Alaska scrunched up her nose.

"It's fun," Drake cajoled. "We split up into sides and the entire trailer park is our war zone. We try to get from Mr. Markle's trailer all the way down to Mrs. Benedict's without being shot."

"Shot?" she asked.

Drake nodded enthusiastically. "Not *really*, but pretend. You can be on my team. I'll teach you the best ways to sneak by the others. I'm pretty awesome at it."

Alaska found herself nodding. She wasn't sure she'd enjoy playing war, but this was the first time in her life she'd been asked to be on someone's team. Usually she was picked last.

"Cool!" her new friend said again, then he asked her about her teacher, where she came from, if she liked her new school, and a hundred other questions. He continued even after they arrived at their bus stop, keeping up a steady stream of chatter, and by the time they split off to go to their respective trailers, Alaska felt flushed with excitement. She couldn't remember the last time she'd had a friend.

She and her mom were constantly moving, and she wasn't the kind of girl who made friends easily. But her mom had promised this time they were here to stay. Alaska could only hope she wasn't lying. She had a good feeling about this school, this town. It hadn't even been a week, and she'd already been invited to play!

27 Years Ago

Alaska stood on the edge of the basketball court alone, watching her classmates dance and laugh with each other. She hated everything about middle school. If she'd thought she faded into the background before, it was *nothing* compared to now...when boys were becoming acutely aware of girls. But not Alaska. Her basic long brown hair was neither curly and lush nor straight and sleek. None of the current popular hairstyles looked right on her, so she kept it all the same length. She had no idea how to wear the makeup all the other girls experimented with and to top things off...she was on the plump side.

Put all that together, and it meant Alaska was overlooked more than ever. She had a few girlfriends...sort of...people she sat with at lunch and talked to between classes. But no one to talk to late at night on the phone, hang out with on the weekends, or to share her deepest secrets.

She'd come to the dance tonight simply because everyone else was going. No one had *asked* Alaska to go...no boy, that is. She met up with a few girls she knew at school and they'd hung out at the edge of the court for a while, gossiping and eyeing the boys. When a slow dance sounded over the speakers, the boys who'd come alone got up the nerve to ask the other single girls for a dance...and Alaska was left standing by herself.

"Hey, Al," a familiar voice said from her left.

Jolting in surprise, Alaska turned to see Drake standing there, leaning against the wall next to her. He bent a knee, putting a foot flat against the bricks behind them.

"Why aren't you dancing?" he asked.

That was the thing about Drake. In the four years since she'd met him, he'd never treated her as an outcast. Never let on that he was aware of how invisible she was...even if he didn't actually notice her in the way she *wished* he would.

They still sometimes hung out after school, but it wasn't to play War in the neighborhood anymore. Now it was to play video games in his trailer. Sometimes he had other friends over too, but he always picked her to play on his team. She'd gotten good at the military games he liked to play. It felt nice to be good at something...and to be wanted.

Alaska shrugged.

"Yeah, this is kind of lame," Drake agreed.

"Didn't you come with Bev?"

"Yep, but as soon as we got here, she saw Miles and Courtney fighting and made her move. She's always liked him better than me," he said with a shrug.

"You don't care?" Alaska asked, genuinely curious.

"Nope. I mean, girls are okay I guess, but when I

graduate from high school, I'm joining the Navy anyway. I'm gonna be a SEAL. I won't have time for girls."

"Really?" Alaska asked. "Isn't that super dangerous?"

"It is. But I don't care. I'm gonna be the best SEAL the Navy's ever had. I'm gonna kick terrorist ass." His voice dropped as he said, "Tim says I'm too small. That only big strong men can be SEALs, but I'll show him."

Alaska put her hand on Drake's arm. "You're gonna be amazing. You're the only one who never got caught when we played War. You were somehow always able to sneak by everyone without them seeing you. And no one has a chance when they play video games against you."

He stood up straight and grinned. "I know. I'm awesome."

Alaska laughed. One of the reasons she liked Drake so much was because he was so confident. In everything. School, girls, athletics...as if it was just a given that he'd excel at whatever he did.

"You wanna dance?" he asked nonchalantly.

Alaska's heart began to beat faster in her chest. She had no idea exactly when or why her feelings toward her friend and neighbor had changed. But one day at his place, as he shouted at the TV, frantically trying to get out of a sticky situation on the game they were playing, Alaska glanced over at him...and realized she liked Drake as more than a friend.

But she never held out hope that he'd ever return her feelings. She saw how the girls at school fawned over him. He was popular, and she was...just there. Not unpopular, but definitely not one of the cool kids either.

"Sure," she said after a long pause.

He smiled and pushed off the wall. Alaska followed, not knowing if she was supposed to hold his hand or what.

Just as he turned and reached for her, there was some shouting behind him.

Michael Jones was yelling at Miranda Brotherton and causing quite a scene. The two had been going together for most of the school year, but Alaska had no idea why. They didn't even seem to like each other much.

"I saw you staring at Julio!" Michael sneered, reaching out and shoving Miranda's shoulder as she cried, making her stumble back a few steps.

"I'm sorry, I've got to..." Drake said, gesturing toward the couple.

Alaska nodded and stood in the middle of the dance floor as Drake headed for the couple. He got up in Michael's face and told him pushing Miranda wasn't cool. There was a moment when Alaska thought they were going to fight, but eventually, Michael turned and left the dance floor.

Drake immediately went to Miranda, putting an arm around her shoulders and leading her away.

Realizing she was standing in the middle of all the couples dancing, Alaska bit her lip and slunk back to the wall she'd been standing in front of earlier. Regret filled her. That was probably the one and only chance she'd ever get to have Drake's arms around her. She wasn't surprised he stood up for Miranda though...that was just the kind of guy he was. And one of a hundred reasons why he'd make a great SEAL.

Alaska didn't get asked to dance by anyone else that

night. She smiled and chatted with her friends, but deep down, she couldn't escape the odd sense that something precious was slipping away. Drake would be switching to the high school next year, and she'd only get to see him on the bus. She was sad for herself, but happy for her friend.

23 Years Ago

Alaska's heart hurt. Drake was leaving to enlist in the Navy tomorrow. He was not only smart, but he'd also ended his high school baseball career with the most runs in a season *and* as the captain. She imagined he'd be an equally successful SEAL. The attention he got from teachers, girls, and all friends had only increased, people gravitating toward him naturally.

Still...he'd never forgotten about Alaska. They didn't get together as often as they once had, but every now and then he'd invited her over to his trailer, and they'd have dinner and play a video game for old time's sake.

His mom had thrown him a graduation party earlier today, before he left for boot camp. All his friends had been there, boys and girls. There were balloons, a cake, and everyone had brought presents. Alaska had felt weird giving him a gift in front of everyone else, so she waited until the party wound down before running back to her trailer to grab what she'd made for him.

Her mom had been drunk—again—and Alaska had to take the time to get her to bed. Her drinking had gotten out of hand and if it wasn't for Alaska, her mom probably would've starved by now. Alaska had taken it upon herself to make sure her mom ate dinner every night, since usually she got home from work and immediately started drinking.

By the time she was able to leave the trailer to go back to Drake's, it was later than she'd planned. Her heart dropped as she approached his home. No one was outside anymore...the party was obviously over. Alaska knocked on the door and held her breath.

Drake's mother answered. "Hey, honey. Did you forget something?"

"No, I went home to grab the present I got for Drake, but my mom needed me for a bit. Is he here?"

"I'm so sorry, he's not. He and his friends went out one last time before he leaves in the morning."

Alaska did her best to keep the tears in her eyes from falling. She'd missed him. He was leaving way early tomorrow, and she wouldn't see him before he left.

"Oh, honey...I'm sure he won't be out too late," Drake's mom said, obviously seeing Alaska's distress.

But she knew otherwise. She'd heard his buddies saying they weren't letting him go home until right before he had to leave...their way of "toughening him up." Their words, not hers.

"It's okay," she said with a small shrug.

"Do you want me to give him that for you?" his mom asked, gesturing to the gift.

Looking down at the messily wrapped present, Alaska suddenly felt ridiculous. She'd seen some of the other presents he'd gotten...expensive things. Clothes, electronics, money. She hadn't had any extra cash to get him a gift, hence the homemade offering. She was well aware that it looked awful. The thought of giving it to Drake now made her cringe.

She shook her head and said, "No. It's not a big deal. If you can please tell him that I wish him the best?" she asked. The words were as lame as her gift. There was so much she wanted to tell Drake, but not through his mom.

"I will. I'm sure he'll want to keep in touch."

Alaska smiled and nodded once more. Drake promised to send her his address once he got to boot camp, but she had a feeling he was going to be way too busy to write letters.

He'd been her best friend for years, even if he didn't realize it...and losing him felt as if she was losing a vital part of herself. She knew this day would come. When he'd walk away without looking back.

He was destined for greatness, and she was destined for...

Alaska didn't know what. Mediocracy? She had okay grades, completely average looks, and was hopeless when it came to athletics. She had no idea what she wanted to do when she graduated. She'd probably stay here and take care of her mom. Maybe take some classes at the community college. Get a boring desk job with a cubicle and slowly fade into the woodwork.

She backed away from Drake's mom, giving her one last wave as she headed back to her own trailer. On the way, she stopped at the trash can at the end of Drake's driveway, waiting to be picked up in the morning. Glancing back to ensure his mom was no longer in the doorway, Alaska opened the bin and threw the ridiculous present inside, the one she'd worked on for weeks, before trudging back to her own trailer.

As she lay in her bed, staring up at the ceiling, she whispered, "Good luck, Drake. But you don't need it. You're gonna be one of the best SEALs the Navy ever had. I know it."

15 Years Ago

Drake wasn't the kind of man who spent a lot of time thinking about his past. He had good memories from high school, but he was a completely different man than he'd been at eighteen. He'd seen and done a lot since then. Making it through the training to become a SEAL, living through harrowing missions, losing teammates.

But tonight, after attending the funeral of yet another friend who'd lost his life too soon, he was feeling nostalgic. The SEAL who'd been killed while on a mission had a family. A wife who was devastated and a little girl who was too young to have any real memories of her father.

It was that little girl, who'd sat on a chair way too big for her at the graveside service, swinging her legs and paying no attention to what was going on in front of her, who now had Drake remembering a childhood friend from the trailer park he'd grown up in. He had a regular reminder of Alaska Stein…but he hadn't thought of her so deeply in years. Tonight, he couldn't seem to get her off his mind.

Guilt and sorrow for a lost friendship inexplicably consumed him. He'd promised to write, but after arriving at boot camp, he'd been too busy making it from day to day to take the time. He'd been young, excited about life, figured he'd have time to connect with her later.

It wasn't until he'd finally become a SEAL, had been awarded his Budweiser pin, that he'd sat down and written her a letter. But it was returned to sender unopened.

When that letter had come back, he'd felt a sense of loss that he couldn't begin to explain. It was silly. He could've probably found her on social media, but that felt too...impersonal. He didn't like the idea of being one of hundreds of pseudo "friends" online.

Life stayed busy...meetings, missions, training. But every now and then, like tonight, his old friend returned to the forefront of his mind, making Drake wonder where she was, what she was doing. Was she married? Did she have children?

Did she ever think about her old childhood friend?

Maybe he'd ask his mom if she knew anything about Alaska, how to get in touch. His mother had always liked her, and unlike Drake, she was constantly on social media. If anyone could find his one-time friend, it would be his mom. He regretted losing touch with Alaska and hoped she was doing all right.

Sighing, Drake did his best to drag himself out of the doldrums. The Navy, and the world, had lost a good man today. He needed to get his head out of the past and concentrate on the future. Needed to train harder, to make sure he and the men on his own team didn't end up like his friend.

"Wherever you are, Alaska...I hope you're happy," Drake whispered before opening the folder on the table in front of him. He needed to study the intel on his upcoming mission...not think about what he'd lost.

CHAPTER ONE

4 Years Ago

Chaos. That was the first thing that registered when Drake "Brick" Vandine opened his eyes. The last thing he remembered was he and his SEAL team had been about to breech a house that was supposed to contain half a dozen HVTs—high-value targets.

Now he was lying under what felt like half a ton of bricks and cinderblocks.

He couldn't feel his legs, but he could hear Vader and Monster yelling. The ringing in his ears made whatever they were saying indistinguishable.

Brick attempted to free his legs, with no luck. When he didn't hear the voices of his other teammates —Bones, Rain, and Mad Dog—he struggled harder.

This mission had been fucked from the start. They'd realized after they were already in the middle of the op that the intel they'd received was faulty. That the area they'd been searching was *not* friendly toward Americans. Either something had changed overnight or whoever was gathering the information had been fucking drunk.

The civilians living in this part of the city were *definitely* not friendly. With every second he spent in the area, Brick's oh-shit meter rose higher and higher. He'd radioed back to base to request a termination of the mission, but had been denied because they were practically on top of the building where the HVTs were supposed to be located.

Brick had been last in line to enter the house—but he'd never gotten the chance. Mad Dog had taken the lead with Rain. Bones, Vader, and Monster were on their heels, with Brick taking up the rear.

He hadn't taken a single step inside the house before the entire thing fucking blew up.

Glancing around, Brick realized he'd been blown clear of most of the debris—but not all. Blinking the blood and dust out of his eyes, he tried to make sense of what he was seeing. Vader and Monster were trying to dig something out of the rubble...

Mad Dog. He recognized his friend and battle buddy by the picture on his helmet. His wife had painted the snarling and drooling German Shepherd on the Kevlar, and Mad Dog had worn it with pride. As Brick watched, Vader grabbed an arm that was reaching up through the bricks and pulled.

He immediately fell backward with the arm still in his hand...an arm not attached to a body.

Brick closed his eyes as nausea swirled in his gut. Then a sound caught his attention. It was unmistakable.

The whistle of an incoming mortar round.

He opened his mouth to call out a warning, to tell Vader and Monster to get the hell out of there, but nothing came out. He couldn't speak, couldn't call out to his teammates to let them know where he was.

One second he was watching his fellow SEALs attempt to rescue their battle buddies, and the next, all he could see were body parts flying through the air, along with more bricks, dirt, and debris. Brick opened his mouth to scream, but once again no sound exited his tight, burning throat.

Everything happened in seconds—from watching his friends get blown to pieces in front of him, to the large chunk of concrete flying through the air and hitting him in the face.

He was knocked unconscious instantly.

* * *

Everything hurt.

His face. His head. His legs.

Hell, even his hair hurt.

Brick had experienced his share of combat wounds during his time as a SEAL, but nothing had ever been as painful as what he was experiencing right now.

Even breathing sent shards of pain streaking down to his fingernails. He had no idea where he was or what had happened. The last thing he remembered was Vader pulling Mad Dog out of a pile of...

Shit.

Memory returned with a vengeance, and all Brick wanted to do was call out for his buddies. He tried to open his eyes but only saw blackness. When he attempted to speak, nothing came out. The steady beeping in the room sped up as he panicked.

"Calm down, you're okay, you're safe," a female voice ordered from nearby.

Brick could feel someone touching him but he jerked his arm away, not knowing if the person was a friendly or not.

"He's panicking," the woman said. "Knock him out."

"No!" Brick tried to say, but again, no words. He'd never felt so helpless in his entire life.

He felt the pull of whatever drug someone had given him and he tried one last time to find his teammates, to get away. He'd never been a prisoner of war and wasn't planning on becoming one now. But his body betrayed him. He felt as if he weighed a thousand pounds. He couldn't lift his head. Couldn't move his arms. Couldn't speak.

He succumbed to the drug he'd been given and in seconds, he was once again unconscious.

* * *

The next time Brick crawled out of the darkness in his mind, he lay as still as possible so as not to let anyone nearby know he was conscious. He listened intently, but all he heard was the beeping of whatever machine he was hooked up to. After several moments, he opened his eyes a fraction and was met with nothing but darkness. He was blindfolded.

When he tried to move his arms, he realized they were tied down.

Fuck.

He'd gone and gotten himself captured by the enemy. Bones was gonna be pissed as hell. His wife had just had their third kid, and all he'd been talking about was how much he was looking forward to going home and seeing him. And now he was a fucking POW.

Determination rose within Brick. He'd do whatever it took to get Bones and the rest of his teammates home to their families. He was the only single one, but he knew his mom would be taking his capture hard. After his dad had died, Brick was his mom's entire focus. She did her best to not bore her friends with every little thing he was doing, but it was almost impossible for her not to brag.

Brick heard a door open and tried to calm his breathing, slow his heartbeat. He needed information. Needed to know where he was, who was holding him and his team, and start formulating a plan to get the hell out of there.

"His stats seem good this morning," a man said—in English.

Brick would have frowned but moving any muscles in his face hurt, and he didn't want whoever had come in to know he was awake yet.

"He should be waking up soon. We've lowered the dose of meds enough for that to happen anytime now."

That was the same female voice he'd heard before.

She spoke without an accent...were they Americans who'd turned? Who were working for the terrorists?

"How's his breathing?"

"Amazingly good. The plastic surgeon did a remarkable job putting his face back together, but it'll be some time before those bandages come off and the swelling goes down."

"And you said he didn't speak the last time he woke up?"

"No. He opened his mouth like he wanted to, but it's possible we didn't give him enough time before he panicked, and we had to put him under again," the woman said.

"There's also a possibility he won't be able to for a long while. He took quite a blow to the throat."

"Of course. I'm hoping once the swelling goes down even more, he'll be able to speak."

"His other injuries?"

Brick finally understood the two people in his room, talking about him as if he wasn't right there, were doctors. They spoke perfect English with no accents. Confusion swam in his brain. Where was he? Was it possible he wasn't a POW? Where were his friends?

"Broken ankle and a few fingers, cracked ribs, and pneumonia from all the irritants he inhaled while he was under that pile of rubble."

"Infection?" the man asked.

"Yes," the woman said without elaboration.

"Right. Has his family been notified?"

"His mother, yes. But she was told to wait until he was transferred back to the States to visit him."

Wait—his mom had been notified?

Brick felt himself panicking again. He did his best to relax but it was too late. The infernal machine he was hooked to began to beep faster.

He felt a hand on his shoulder and could tell someone was leaning over him. "Can you hear me? Drake? My name is Doctor Benjamin Green. I'm one of several doctors who've been looking after you. You're safe. Understand? You're in an Army hospital in Germany."

Relief filled his entire body. But not for long. Panic once more threatened to overwhelm him. He tried to ask about his teammates, if they were okay, but still no words escaped his lips.

"Don't try to speak. Your throat was damaged. Your face also took quite a hit. Your eyes should be fine, but everything's swollen because of the repairs that had to be done. You're alive, son...that's what matters."

Was this man stupid? What mattered were his *friends*. His teammates. They were the ones with wives and children.

Deep down, Brick knew they were dead.

Memories of lying in that pile of rubble came back to him then. Of body parts. Of chaos. Of the men who'd had his back more times than he could count being blown to pieces.

His mind shut down. He couldn't process never seeing them again. Never hearing Rain's ridiculous laugh. Never seeing Mad Dog's grin when he spoke about his kids. Monster's corny jokes or Vader's exaggerated stories. Bones's ability to get the team out of just about any kind of fucked-up situation they'd found themselves in.

Except this one.

A sob welled up and escaped before Brick could control it. Why was he here when his friends weren't? He should've taken point and entered that house first. It should've been *him* blown to bits.

"It's okay, son, you're going to be okay," the man soothed.

But it wasn't going to be okay. Nothing was going to be okay ever again.

Brick began to struggle, knowing what would happen when he did.

Just as he thought, as soon as he smacked the man's hand away, the woman was ordering him to be sedated.

Good. He didn't want to feel. Didn't want to think.

This time when he felt the drugs overtaking his mind, he embraced the feeling. He wanted to go to sleep and never wake up again.

* * *

Time had no meaning for Brick. He'd wake up confused and hurting, realize where he was and what happened, and do something so the nurses would give him enough painkillers to knock him unconscious once more. He wanted to tell them not to bother when they gave him a sponge bath. Or when they turned him on the bed.

Brick knew there were discussions going on around him about when to move him back to the States, but he didn't care. He just wanted to be left alone. He'd failed to save his teammates and nothing could ever assuage the guilt swamping him.

If he was taken back to the US, he'd have to face his

mother. Maybe even his friends' wives. He couldn't do it. Couldn't look them in the eyes and see the disappointment and possible anger that *he'd* somehow made it out alive when their loved ones hadn't.

The bandages on his eyes had been removed, which was a huge relief to Brick. He could now watch as the doctors and nurses fussed around and over him. But he still felt dead inside. He could feel the pain of his injuries, but it was as if they didn't fully register. As if they'd happened to someone else.

A psychologist had come to talk to him one day and told him everything that had happened. How the terrorists had blown up the house and he'd been buried under debris. Apparently, he'd lain there for over twenty-four hours before he was found. A local civilian had notified the American base and he'd been rescued. His teammates hadn't been as lucky. They'd all been killed in the explosion or by the ensuing blast from the mortar round.

Brick didn't need the psychologist to tell him he was suffering from survivor's guilt. He wanted to turn to the man and say, "No shit, Sherlock," but he didn't. Had no idea if he even could, since he refused to speak. His voice had failed him when he'd needed it most, and Brick had no desire to use it now.

It felt as if he'd been lying there drowning in his own sorrow, guilt, and misery for weeks, when Doctor Green walked into his room one afternoon with a smile. Brick wanted to ask him what the fuck he was so happy about, wanted to rail at him for smiling when five of the best men he'd ever known were dead.

Dead.

But as usual, he didn't say a word.

"You have a visitor," the doctor said, his grin even wider.

Brick frowned. A visitor? He didn't want to see anyone. If one more volunteer came by trying to read to him, he was going to explode.

"Your fiancée is an extremely stubborn woman. She wouldn't take no for an answer when it came to seeing you. Even though she was told several times she wasn't allowed to visit, since she isn't a family member we have on record, she insisted. Very relentlessly."

Brick stared at the doctor. Fiancée? He wasn't engaged. Hadn't had a girlfriend for longer than he could remember. Who the hell would lie to get in to see him?

"We do need your approval for her to be admitted though," the doctor said.

For a moment, Brick considered saying no. He had no idea who the hell would be that insistent to see him —in Germany, no less. He'd been very careful not to get his few hookups over the years pregnant, so it couldn't be someone who wanted to get on the military gravy train. No matter how hard he racked his brain, he couldn't guess who it might be.

Curious enough to want to know, he nodded at the doctor.

"Great!" Doctor Green said with another huge smile.

Brick knew what he was thinking—that having a visitor would probably raise his spirits. Would help him heal faster. Would get him to talk.

The man was delusional. Nothing and no one could help Brick get over what had happened.

"I'll get her processed and sent up. If you need anything, just press the button. We'll give you two some space."

Then the doctor turned and left, leaving Brick to wonder who in the hell was about to enter his room.

CHAPTER TWO

Alaska was exasperated it was taking so long for her to be processed. From the moment she'd gotten the email from Drake's mom saying he'd been hurt and was being flown to Germany for surgery and treatment, she'd been on a mission to get to him.

It had been years since she'd moved out of the US. She'd gotten a two-year business degree from the local community college and immediately started looking for jobs overseas. She might not be cut out for the military, but she still wanted to see the world. So she'd taken the first job she'd been offered, as a secretary for a small company in France. Since then, she'd lived and worked in several different countries.

She'd quickly realized that being invisible wasn't just a US thing. No matter where she lived, she tended to fade into the background. She wasn't model-gorgeous, her hair wasn't the stuff of every man's dreams, she wasn't tall and svelte. She was simply too *basic* to stand out, no matter where she lived.

Alaska mused that if she went to Asia, she might not be quite so forgettable. But even then, she had a feeling she'd find a way to blend into the woodwork.

Over the years, she'd kept in touch with Drake's mom. Her own mother hadn't even blinked when Alaska told her she was leaving the country. Well, that wasn't quite true. She'd actually bitched about Alaska being ungrateful and moaned over how she couldn't possibly pay the rent on the trailer without her help.

Last she'd heard, her mom had moved to California. Alaska had tried to reach out a few times, but the old phone number she had for her was disconnected and all her emails had bounced.

She wanted to be sad about being estranged from her mom, but she couldn't manage to muster up the emotion. She'd been less of a mother and more of a burden with every year that passed. Once Alaska graduated from high school, her mother had spiraled deeper into drugs and alcohol than ever before. It was the main reason Alaska had gladly taken that first job overseas. She'd needed to get away before her mom sucked her down with her.

She was currently living in Germany—which was why she'd figured Drake's mom had contacted her. Over the years, it had been both a blessing and a curse to hear all about how Drake was doing from his devoted mother. He'd become a SEAL, like Alaska always knew he would. Not only that, but he'd apparently excelled. His mom didn't know the details of his missions, just that he was constantly being sent all over the world.

Just a few years prior, she'd actually gotten up the courage to send Drake an email. His mom had given her the address and insisted Drake would be thrilled to hear from her. Alaska hadn't been so sure about that, since it had been so long since they'd talked, but she'd been lonely enough to take the chance.

Surprisingly, Drake *had* seemed pleased to get her email. Since then, they periodically made contact to say hello and touch base, though not more than a couple times a year. Drake's emails were always full of exclamation points and babble about the various locales he was sent to for missions, bits and pieces about his teammates, how he kept busy during down time. And he'd asked her lots of questions about her life—questions that Alaska rarely answered.

What could she really say? That she was an anonymous worker at yet another large corporation? That she was a lowly secretary making any given country's lowliest wage? Her life was so dull compared to his, it wasn't even funny.

She should've stopped emailing him altogether, but she couldn't. Even after all these years, she still harbored a crush on the man. Alaska supposed at thirty-five, she couldn't really call it a crush anymore, but whatever.

She was constantly surprised when every email from his mom failed to mention an upcoming wedding, or how much she loved a soon-to-be daughter-in-law, or about how adorable her grandchildren were. Alaska had always assumed those emails would eventually come. But if Drake had gotten married sometime in the last twenty years, she didn't know about it.

When she'd gotten the latest email from his mom three days ago, Alaska had assumed it would be another chatty note bragging about her son and updating Alaska on all the hometown gossip. But instead, her words had tilted Alaska's world on its axis.

Drake had been hurt. Almost killed. He was in a hospital there in Germany, and the Navy had recommended she not make the trip across the world to see him, but to wait until he was transferred back to the US.

His mom had asked if it would be too much of an imposition for Alaska to go see him. Maybe email back and let her know how her baby was doing.

Alaska had no sooner finished reading the email when she was on the move. Without even bothering to check in with her boss, she'd bought a train ticket and was on her way to Landstuhl Regional Medical Center, the largest US military hospital in the country. She'd concocted an entire history for her and Drake before arriving, to increase the odds that she'd be able to see him. She'd even lied and said she was his fiancée.

It hadn't been easy, and Alaska had a feeling no one believed her, but now, finally, *miraculously*, she was being led toward his room. She hadn't slept in a day and a half, but she felt strangely energized. It had been years since she'd seen and talked to Drake, and even though the circumstances were devastating...she couldn't help the feeling of anticipation. She just hoped he wouldn't blow her cover story to smithereens the second she saw him.

"Your fiancé has suffered quite a few serious injuries," the doctor was telling her as they stood in the elevator. "Broken bones, infections, and he's had surgery on his face, and will likely have several more once he gets back to the States. The debris that hit his face did severe damage."

Alaska winced. She hated to think of Drake in pain.

"But what you really need to understand is that he hasn't spoken since he's been here. At first it was because he took a direct hit to the throat, but since the swelling has gone down, we expected him to be speaking by now. He isn't. He's suffering from an extreme case of survivor's guilt, and the psychologist believes his inability to speak is a result of him punishing himself for what happened."

Alaska had no idea *what* had happened, except that his entire team had been killed. She wanted to roll her eyes at the doctor and ask how *he* would feel if he was injured and all his best friends had been killed, but she simply nodded.

"Don't panic when you see him. He'll probably be more handsome when the plastic surgeons are done with him."

Alaska gritted her teeth at the insensitive comment. As if she cared what Drake looked like! She was just grateful he was alive.

"And when he doesn't talk to you, don't take it personally. He'll need to continue seeing someone when he gets back home. SEALs are the best of the best, but that doesn't mean they don't suffer from post-traumatic stress disorder."

Thinking about the always upbeat and congenial Drake Vandine suffering from PTSD made Alaska's heart hurt. She'd make sure to tell his mom everything the doctor had said, and insist he had the best help possible when he got home.

She nodded at the man. "I understand."

"Don't be upset if he's not thrilled to see you. Men

like him...they don't like their loved ones to see them hurt."

Alaska had a moment of doubt then. Would Drake be pissed she'd gone to such lengths to see him? She hoped not.

"If you need anything, just push the call button on his bed," the doctor told her as he opened the door to Drake's room.

Taking a deep breath, Alaska stepped inside.

The first thing she noticed was that the curtains were drawn and the room was dark. She frowned. Drake had always loved being outside. Adored the sunlight. And she could tell from his emails over the years, that hadn't changed.

Without hesitation, she walked over to the window and drew back the curtain, letting in the late-afternoon light.

A low growl sounded from the bed behind her, and Alaska took a deep breath as she turned to face the one man in the world she'd always admired.

By some miracle, she kept the distress at seeing him from showing on her face.

He looked like hell. There were bandages covering his face and head, except for his ocean-blue eyes. He was staring at her with an intensity that she remembered from when they were little. He always had a way of looking at her as if he truly saw her, even when no one else did.

No one else had *ever* made her feel the way Drake did simply by looking at her.

His chest was bare, and Alaska could see a snarling lion on his left biceps—his huge, muscular biceps. Her eyes traveled down the rest of his body, hidden by the sheet, and a small noise escaped her lips.

Reaching for the chair next to the bed so she didn't fall on her ass, Alaska sat with a small sigh. This man...good Lord. Despite his injuries, he was the most beautiful man she'd ever seen in her life. The tattoos, the muscles, even the obvious irritation shining in his gaze made her tummy do cartwheels. She hadn't seen him in nearly two decades, but it felt as if it was yesterday. And despite recent events, she saw obvious signs that time had been good to him.

Immediately, her thoughts made her uncomfortable. She was here because he was injured. Because he'd lost his teammates and friends. She shouldn't be ogling him. Shouldn't be fixated on his looks.

"Hi," she said quietly, after a moment.

He didn't respond.

Right. The doctor said he wasn't talking...which was probably to her benefit at the moment.

"It's me. Alaska. You remember me, right?"

She winced at the stupid question, but held her breath as she waited for any hint of a response.

When his chin dipped down a fraction, she relaxed.

"Good. I'm sorry about the fiancée thing. They wouldn't let me in to see you if I wasn't related in some way. I won't hold you to it though." She smiled awkwardly. "Right, okay...it's probably better that you aren't talking right now. I'm sure you'd order me to get the hell out and never come back."

He didn't move or otherwise make any attempt to communicate. His blue eyes just stayed pinned to her face.

"Your mom told me you were here. Probably because she knew I was working in Germany. I'm not actually that far away, in Stuttgart. Anyway, I got on the train and came straight here. Bet this isn't how you expected to meet up with me again, huh? Not that you *ever* expected to see me again. I mean..." She sighed. "Sorry, I'm being my usual awkward self. Clearly I haven't changed much since school. But...when I heard you were hurt, I had to come."

Leaning forward, she put a tentative hand on his forearm. "I'm so sorry about your friends," she said softly.

He reacted for the first time since she'd arrived. His eyes closed and he turned his head away from her. It was obvious the doctor was right. He hated that he'd survived, and his teammates hadn't.

"I'm not a doctor or psychologist," she said quietly. "I'm just a secretary...and not a very good one at that, if you listen to my former bosses. But I know with every-thing I am that your friends would be so thankful you're alive."

The noise that came from Drake's throat was a snort, or a laugh, or something. But it didn't deter Alaska from saying what she felt she needed to. "I'm serious. If the roles had been reversed, if it was one of your friends lying here, and you were watching from Heaven, you'd be pissed if they thought for one second they would've been better off dead. The world's a better place with you in it, Drake. What happened to them is devastating, and *nothing* I say will ease the pain you feel...but I know without a shadow of a doubt that they'd probably want to kick your ass for wishing you'd died and they hadn't."

Alaska had no idea what she was saying. She didn't know his friends. But she knew Drake. Or at least, she used to. He would never want someone to suffer on his behalf, and she had to imagine his teammates were similar.

Deciding she needed to lighten the mood, she squeezed his arm and said, "You know, I always had a feeling you were Deadpool, and this incident just confirmed it."

To her surprise, he turned his head again, eyes widening in disbelief.

She smiled slightly. "I know, Deadpool isn't the best comparison, but with your face all bandaged and all...it felt appropriate. Not to mention you were buried under all that rubble, and yet, here you are. It's like you're invincible." Alaska had a feeling she was totally bungling this, but she kept talking. "I liked the first *Deadpool* movie better than the second. Isn't that the case with most franchises? The first one is always the best. Okay, I think I liked the third *Jurassic Park* movie best, but the fifth one? No. Just...no."

Drake's eyes didn't move from hers as she spoke. So Alaska kept chattering about anything and everything. She had no idea what he was thinking, but he didn't turn his head away again, which she was taking as a positive sign. And his inability to speak kept him from ordering her to shut the hell up and get out of his room, for which she was grateful. Mostly because she didn't have anywhere to go. She didn't have excess cash to get a hotel room for several nights. She'd be okay for a night or two, but any more than that and she'd be scraping the bottom of her bank account.

She kept up the steady one-way conversation until two nurses entered the room a couple hours later. To her amazement, Drake hadn't dozed off once. He'd kept his surprisingly alert gaze on her the entire time.

"It's time for dinner and your bath," one of the men said.

"Oh, right. I'll just...I'll go find something to do," Alaska said awkwardly.

"There's a cafeteria on the ground floor if you want to grab something to eat."

She nodded. "Okay...then...I can come back up, right?"

"Of course. You want us to get a cot for you?"

"Yes, please." She was too chicken to look at Drake to see what he thought of that idea. He was probably sick of her and wondering why the hell she was still here. It wasn't as if they were close or anything. Not for many years. But the thought of leaving him before she knew for sure he was going to be all right was something she didn't think she could do.

"All right, give us about an hour," the other nurse said.

Alaska nodded. Then, figuring she needed to ensure they wouldn't become suspicious of her ruse that she was engaged to Drake, she leaned over the bed. She kissed his bandage-covered cheek gently and whispered, "Don't talk their ears off. I'll be back soon."

She gave him a small smile, then turned and headed out of the room.

* * *

Brick could've sworn he felt Alaska's lips on his cheek as she kissed him. It was impossible, considering how wrapped up he was. But he couldn't deny that he felt more alive right now than he had since waking in this hospital.

Listening to her chat about anything and everything had been surprisingly...invigorating. He was so sick of hearing staff tell him how well he was doing, saying they were sorry about what happened, telling him he would eventually accept what happened and be grateful he hadn't died.

Alaska hadn't done any of that. Well...she'd said she was sorry. But then she'd started babbling about random nonsense. Oddly, it seemed to be exactly what he'd needed.

She'd always been one of the few people who'd believed in him without reservation. Going to all his baseball games to cheer him on. Insisting he'd be an amazing SEAL.

And he suddenly couldn't get the graduation present she'd made for him out of his head.

Casting his mind back, he remembered his mom telling him Alaska had returned the night of his party to give it to him, and when he wasn't there, Alaska had thrown away the gift. Thank God Mom had fished it out of the garbage. Her gift had hung in every apartment he'd ever lived in. Every time he looked at it, he thought of Alaska's faith in him.

She hadn't changed much since high school. She had the same shoulder-length brown hair worn in the same simple style, the same shy awkwardness, and the same wide, guileless smile. But she was no longer a kid. Her curvy frame had filled out, became even curvier in all the right places. And there was a guarded maturity behind her eyes that told him her life hadn't necessarily been easy.

He'd realized quickly Alaska wasn't very forth-coming in their infrequent emails, was exceedingly adept at sidestepping his questions, but he'd gotten the impression that she worked hard for everything in her life.

Nothing could've shocked him more than seeing her walk through the door of his hospital room. He also couldn't believe she'd boldly claimed to be his fiancée, just to see him. But then again...he could. When she got something in her mind, he recalled she could be stubborn as hell. Always had been, at least when he'd known her. He realized he was grateful for that trait.

He also found himself overwhelmingly thankful for her presence. She had a quiet charisma and a realness about her that was refreshing compared to the rigidity of the Navy and the people he came into contact with while on missions.

To his surprise, it didn't seem to hurt quite as much as the nurses bathed him and rearranged his bedding. Dinner arrived, and he ate absently. Every time he opened his mouth, his face hurt, but he barely noticed. His mind was on the old friend who'd come to see him, instead of the pain.

Exactly an hour later, Alaska popped her head around the door and smiled. "Done?" she asked.

Since he was the only one in the room, he couldn't help but smile very slightly at the question.

"Right, sorry, stupid question again, huh?" she asked. She walked back to the chair she'd vacated earlier and put her hand on his forearm. The slight weight felt... nice. Comforting.

"You know, this place scares me."

Brick frowned.

"Not the people, per se. Just that I'm constantly afraid I'm going to say or do something wrong. The military is like this huge club I don't understand and definitely don't belong in, and it feels like any minute now, someone will point at me and shout, 'Infidel!' and escort me out." She giggled, then sobered. "Again, I'm sorry about lying to get in here, Drake. I'm certain they don't really believe me. I'm sure everyone's wondering what in the hell you'd see in someone like me." She shrugged, then winked. "But you can set everyone straight once you're back on your feet. Wouldn't want your reputation to suffer."

Brick opened his mouth to ask what the hell she was talking about, but she didn't give him a chance. She just went right into another long soliloquy about something she'd seen at her work the other day.

Eventually, she ran out of things to ramble on about. She yawned and apologized. "I'm sorry. I haven't slept in..." She looked at her watch. "Well, a really long time."

Brick gestured to the bed behind her. One of the nurses had set it up not too long ago.

"Right. Do you mind me staying?"

He shook his head. Surprisingly, he didn't. If asked just a day ago, he would've said he wanted to be alone.

But now that she was here, he couldn't stomach the thought of her leaving. He enjoyed her company.

"Okay, but if I snore, throw a pillow at me or something," she joked. She picked up the bag she'd dropped at the doorway when she'd arrived and disappeared into the small attached bathroom. She reappeared a couple of minutes later wearing the same clothes she'd had on all day and settled on the cot next to his bed.

"I truly am sorry about what happened, Drake. But I'm so damn grateful you're still here," she whispered. "I know we haven't talked much since high school, but I've thought about you pretty much all the time...and smiled, just knowing you were out there somewhere, kicking ass and taking names. I'm proud of you. Thank you for what you do."

Brick swallowed hard at her words. He'd been thanked more times than he could count over the years, but he'd always brushed aside the kind words. Somehow they carried more weight coming from Alaska.

She fell asleep almost immediately, and Brick lay there, watching her doze for most of the night. By the time the sun began to inch over the horizon, he'd made a decision.

To heal. To get home and become the kind of man Vader, Monster, Bones, Rain, and Mad Dog would expect him to be. He no longer wanted to be a Navy SEAL, had no desire to put on the uniform ever again. Though, he figured that probably wasn't an option anyway with his injuries.

He had no idea *what* he'd do, but he wanted to be a man Alaska could continue to be proud of. Somehow, some way, he'd pick up the pieces of his life and honor his fallen teammates...as well as his old friend who'd gone out of her way to be by his side when he was at his lowest.

* * *

Alaska was amazed at the changes in Drake over the next two days. He no longer simply lay in bed, staring at her. He ate all his meals, sat up for long stretches, and genuinely seemed interested in what was happening around him. A huge difference from the day she'd arrived, when all he'd done was stare at her or the ceiling as she rambled.

The doctors attributed his improved attitude to her being there, but Alaska didn't think that was the case. She wasn't the kind of woman to inspire such a difference in *anyone*, but whatever happened, she was relieved.

The third night, when she'd settled down on her cot, Alaska said, "It's probably time I got out of your hair."

She felt more than saw him turn his head to stare at her. His mattress was higher than hers, and she felt oddly safe with him being above her like he was. It was stupid; nothing was going to happen to her inside a military hospital. But she couldn't help but feel as if any minute now, the military police would burst through the doors and drag her away for lying about being engaged to Drake.

"Stay," he said quietly.

Surprised, Alaska sat up and stared at him. "Did you...Drake, you spoke!"

He smiled and said in a rusty voice, "Call the press, it's a miracle."

Moving back to the chair she'd been using for the last few days, she reached for the call button. "We need to tell the nurses!"

But Drake moved faster and grabbed her wrist, stopping her. "They'll figure it out tomorrow."

Alaska stared at him for a long moment before saying, "Something's very different."

Drake nodded.

"I'm glad," she said somewhat shyly. Now that he could speak, she braced herself for his questions. For him to lecture her for lying to the military.

Instead, he whispered, "Thank you for coming. I needed this. You."

She memorized those quiet words. Knowing she would bring them out again and again, anytime she was having a down day.

"I...They didn't deserve to die."

Alaska felt tears fill her eyes. "I know. Tell me about them?"

For the next hour, Drake did just that, regaling her with story after story of his fallen teammates. She laughed, she cried, and she mourned alongside him, for the loss of such amazing men and friends.

"I don't know what I'm going to do...but I'm going to find a way to honor their memories," Drake vowed.

His voice sounded rough. Probably from the trauma his vocal cords had suffered and from not speaking for so long. But every word was like a gift to Alaska.

"I know you will."

"You've always believed in me," he said.

Alaska could only nod. She had.

He stared at her for a long moment, then asked, "You gonna get shit for being here with me? For being away from your job for so long?"

She shook her head, knowing she was totally lying. She was *already* in trouble. Her boss had sent her a threatening email just that afternoon, saying if she wasn't back behind her desk in the morning, she wouldn't have a job to go back to. But she didn't care. Secretaries were a dime a dozen. She'd get another job. Being here with Drake was more important.

"Good," he said. "Once I talk to the doctor, I'm sure it'll be a matter of days before I'll be headed back to the States."

Alaska's stomach dropped, but she smiled at him anyway. "That's great."

"I'm not gonna be staying in the Navy," he said somewhat forcefully, as if he thought she might protest or something.

"Okay."

He grinned. "That's all you're gonna say about that?"

"Yup," she said with a shrug. "If you aren't a SEAL, you'll be something else equally amazing and wonderful and kick-ass."

He chuckled, then got serious. "Thank you for believing in me, Alaska."

"You don't have to thank me for that," she replied firmly. Then, before she got too weepy, she stood and went back to the cot. "You need to sleep," she said. "And not jabber all night." She grinned to let him know she was teasing.

Once she got settled on her bed again, she saw him turn to look down at her.

"Alaska?"

"Yeah, Drake?"

"I owe you one. If you ever need anything, and I mean *anything*, you let me know and I'll be there for you."

Tingles shot through her entire body. "Thanks. Code word 'fiancé,' right?" she joked, trying to lighten the mood.

But Drake didn't smile. "If anything goes south enough that you need a code word, sure. But I'm serious. You just may have saved my life. I'm in your debt."

She frowned at that. "You would've figured things out, Drake. I know it."

"Maybe, maybe not. But that doesn't change the fact that from here on out, I'm gonna be your pen pal. And more than one email a year. I want to keep in touch, Alaska. I...I *need* that."

"Okay," she agreed quietly. "I'll want to know all about whatever greatness is in store for you, anyway."

"And I want to know the same about you," he returned.

Tears filled her eyes again. There wasn't anything great about her life. It was just...there. She wasn't saving the world or finding a cure for cancer. She was simply going through the motions. But she was all right with that. She was seeing the world. Meeting new people. Experiencing new cultures. Maybe one day, she'd move back to the States. Maybe.

"Deal?" he asked.

"Deal," she agreed.

"Sleep, Al," he ordered. "Things are gonna get exciting in the morning."

She couldn't help but chuckle through her tears. Drake always loved surprising people, and his doctors were going to be extremely shocked when they found out he could talk...and that his attitude had completely turned around.

CHAPTER THREE

Present Day

Brick sat on the deck of his cabin in the mountains of New Mexico as he sipped his mug of black coffee. A memory of Bones rattling around in his head, repeating his favorite quote about coffee. *"It ain't worth drinkin' if it's not black."*

The memories of his lost teammates came just a little less frequently these days, and when they did, they were welcome more often than not. Brick didn't want to forget the men he fought with. They were worth remembering.

It had been a hard four years since they'd died. He'd been honorably discharged from the Navy, had endured several surgeries to put the bones in his face back in their proper places. It had been far more difficult to put his mind back together. The PTSD had been relentless.

It was after a long talk with his therapist, when he

finally accepted he wasn't the only one suffering repercussions because of the shit he'd been through in the military, that he'd hit on the idea of creating a place where people could go to get away from their worst memories.

He'd spent quite a few weeks camping after his discharge, trying to come to terms with his new reality, and it had helped tremendously. He figured if it helped him, maybe it would do the same for others.

So with Tex's help, he'd reached out to some men he'd met after he'd been discharged. Men who were going through the same thing he was, mentally. Struggling to find their place in the world without the military to fall back on.

Tex was a friend who had his finger on the pulse of the men and women who put their lives on the line for their country. He was a former SEAL, one who'd lost his leg—and dedicated every day since to watching over others. He'd even found the parcel of land for sale here in New Mexico, and Brick and the six others had met and camped out for several days, getting to know each other, talking about their visions for what they hoped to accomplish.

By the time they went their separate ways, The Refuge had been born. It was a labor of love...and they'd made it work.

Tiny was the only other SEAL in the group. He was six feet tall and all muscle. He had a pretty face, more than one guest claiming he looked like the lead male actor in that eighties movie, *Sixteen Candles*. The others laughed their heads off every time, much to Tiny's chagrin.

Tonka had been a member of the Coast Guard Deployable Specialized Forces. He was most at home working with the animals. Spike had been a Delta Force operative, Pipe was SAS—the British equivalent of a Navy SEAL—and Owl and Stone, who rounded out their group, had been Night Stalkers...the Army's legendary helicopter pilots. The latter pair had worked together, been POWs together when their choppers had gone down in enemy territory, and were now doing what they could to move on with their lives.

The Refuge sat on a few hundred acres near Los Alamos. The townspeople had been overjoyed when they'd bought the land, because the other interested party had been a developer who most certainly would've put in a subdivision with hundreds of houses. The Refuge had started out with a few yurts, and now had most of the things a luxury resort offered. Though the owners frequently referred to it as a "camp," since the majority of the mountainous acreage remained intact.

The main lodge was the hub of the property. There were comfortable couches in the lobby, where people could congregate and visit informally. The dining area was large enough to accommodate most guests at one time, and there were smaller rooms for therapy sessions and more intimate gatherings. The Refuge employed a chef, but meals were always laid-back and buffet style. Guests were welcome to visit the huge kitchen anytime for snacks, to gather what they needed for hikes or picnics, and even to bake, if that was what helped calm their PTSD.

There were a dozen cabins scattered around the lodge. They ranged from one-bedroom studios to three-bedroom suites. Each had a bathroom and shower, as well as a fridge and microwave. Housekeeping was offered every couple days to guests who wanted it.

A therapist came in three times a week to meet free-of-charge with guests who wanted to talk. They had a barn with horses, a cow, and goats. Cats roamed the property...and of course, Brick had Mutt. He'd found the injured stray not too long after he and the others had moved to the area to oversee construction. He was some sort of terrier-hound mix. His legs were long and gangly, he'd had an awful case of mange, but worst of all, his front left leg was completely mangled. The vet had no idea what had happened, but guessed he'd been in a fight with a wild animal and lost.

Brick hadn't wanted a dog. At the time, he was busy with all the paperwork and legal stuff that had to be done to get The Refuge up and running. But he couldn't resist Mutt. In the end, adopting him had turned out to be one of the best things he'd ever done. Only having three legs didn't slow the dog in the least. And late at night, when Brick couldn't sleep, having Mutt nearby kept him from sinking into a deep depression.

All in all, Brick was satisfied with his life. The Refuge had immediately proved to be a huge success, and it felt good to aid others. He and his friends had opened three years ago with the intention of helping military veterans, but quickly realized PTSD manifested itself in traumas of all kinds. Now they hosted women who'd escaped from abusive relationships, employees who'd survived workplace violence, even those who were struggling to recover from chemical dependency.

The Refuge was a place people could find the peace

and quiet they needed to continue their healing journey. Being here wouldn't cure anyone of their demons...but it was a place where they could shove those demons aside for a short while and just breathe.

Taking another sip of his coffee, Brick reached down and gave Mutt a pet. He was curled up in his usual spot, a pile of blankets on the deck next to him. He'd bought an expensive dog bed, but Mutt's preference was simple blankets or towels. Brick figured it was a throwback to his time on the streets.

As he lazily stroked Mutt, Brick allowed more memories of his battle buddies to surface. Vader and the others would've loved this place. It was as far removed from what they'd done as could be. His friends' families had open invitations to visit whenever they wanted—for free. The same went for the families of the men and women his co-owners had worked with.

The Refuge, and New Mexico in general, was peaceful...less populated than most of the states. Being in the middle of nowhere meant they didn't usually get random visitors. If someone came to The Refuge, it was intentional. No one accidentally stumbled upon them.

Which is how Brick and the others wanted it. A quiet and safe place where people could come to recenter themselves. To clear their minds. Get a break from all the noise in the world. They had Wi-Fi, of course, and cell phone reception was decent around the main property, but guests were encouraged to disconnect if they could.

Closing his eyes, Brick could admit he was pretty content. His life had taken a one-eighty-degree turn after he'd gotten hurt and lost his teammates. And while he'd had to work damn hard to get to where he was now, he was satisfied.

A part of him, deep down, mourned the fact he didn't have anyone with whom to share his life. He'd always figured he had plenty of time to get married, have kids, and settle down. He'd been so busy with his military career, everything else had taken a backseat. And now, while he was satisfied with helping others, he recognized that he was lonely.

He'd just turned forty, and while he knew it wasn't too late to fall in love, reality was, he simply didn't meet many single women. And those who visited The Refuge certainly weren't ready for relationships.

He'd recently had a long talk with Tiny about the subject. His friend was five years younger but felt much the same. Going into Los Alamos to the bars was always an option, but the small town wasn't exactly a hub of single women.

Inevitably, Brick's thoughts turned to the one woman who'd been on his mind frequently in the last four years.

When Alaska Stein had shown up at his bedside in Germany, claiming to be his fiancée, he'd been utterly shocked. Yes, he'd emailed her now and then the few years prior, and his mom had never really lost touch with her, updating Brick with the little she knew—she'd been only slightly less successful at sharing details with his mother. Those emails aside, he'd wouldn't have classified them as close friends any longer. Not since he'd left for the Navy.

But after Germany, that had changed. They emailed constantly, and sent messages over social media almost as frequently. He'd quickly learned that she traveled around Europe far more frequently than he'd imagined. She'd take a secretarial job, stay a couple years, then move on. She'd lived in more places in the last couple decades than most people visited in a lifetime.

Brick eagerly checked his messages every morning, hoping for a note from her. She made him smile just as often as she made him worry. Being a single woman in a foreign country wasn't dangerous, per se...but it wasn't exactly safe either. And Brick knew better than anyone how simply being American could make her a target for those who weren't happy with the United States' foreign policies.

He hadn't been thrilled when she'd told him three days ago that she was going to St. Petersburg in Russia to sightsee. He'd wanted to protest, tell her it wasn't a good idea, but she'd been so excited to see The Hermitage, The Peter and Paul Fortress, Palace Square at the Winter Palace, Peterhof Palace, to shop on Nevsky Avenue, and visit the Church of the Savior on Spilled Blood.

Her message this morning was full of pictures of her adventures the day before. She'd signed up with a private tour company and had spent the day with two other couples, visiting half the sights on her "must see" list.

Seeing Alaska's smiling face as she posed in front of various churches had made Brick's morning, despite his wariness about the trip. He was keenly aware that his old friend thought she was invisible. That she blended into the background. As far as he was concerned, she was wrong. Brick would choose someone with her loyalty and passion for life over a pretentious, perfectly made up woman any day.

He'd learned over the years that "average"—at least by Alaska's definition—tended to be much more satisfying in the long run than shiny and sparkling.

To him, Alaska stood out from the crowd. He could only hope she never stood out to the wrong sort as she traveled the world.

Today, she was supposed to head the thirty or so kilometers from the center of St. Petersburg to see the Peterhof Palace. Afterward, the plan was to swing by the Peter and Paul Fortress, which was the resting place of several Russian czars.

Brick had told her to message him when she returned to her hotel room. She'd agreed, but not before teasing him that he was paranoid and overprotective.

She wasn't wrong. He was definitely concerned for her safety pretty much at all times. But he couldn't blame his protective nature when he opened his email first thing every morning, eagerly awaiting her emails.

Even though they were a world apart, Brick thought about Alaska constantly. He knew she rarely dated. She insisted her looks were "boring"—brown hair, brown eyes, average height at five-eight, average build leaning toward curvy. But her laugh, her personality, her kindness, her genuine curiosity about the world around her... all of those things made her more notable than she realized. When he recalled their childhood, he remembered a girl who never minded getting dirty, laughing hysterically and tagging along when he suggested something not-quite legal...like letting the air out of the principal's tires late at night.

Brick couldn't really remember what his childhood had been like before her. Their relationship had evolved during those years. From War in their neighborhood, to marathon video-game sessions, to cheering in the stands at his baseball games, to listening when he bitched about his girlfriends. When he'd wanted to buy his then-girlfriend a huge bouquet of flowers in eleventh grade, and was short twenty bucks, Alaska had been the one to lend him the money.

They'd gone years without communicating at all. And now, even though they emailed and messaged more than they ever had in the past, Brick missed her terribly.

Having her with him in the hospital in Germany had changed things for Brick. Changed the way he thought of her. She was his friend, yes...but she was so much more now. She'd dropped *everything*—including her job —to get to him when he'd needed her most. Had lied to gain entrance to his room. Whatever it took to get to his side.

No one else had ever done something so selfless for him before...beyond the five men who'd died in the same explosion that had almost taken his own life.

Alaska was special. And while it was hard to believe he could miss someone he still barely knew in certain ways...there it was.

Mutt's tail began to thump on the wooden boards, and Brick looked up to see Stone coming toward him.

"Good morning," his friend called out.

"Morning," Brick returned. "Coffee's inside if you want a cup."

The seven owners of The Refuge had their own small cabins. They were set away from the rentals, surrounding the property on all sides. While they needed their privacy and space, they were all welcome at each other's homes anytime.

"Thanks," Stone said, giving him a chin lift and heading inside. He returned a minute later with his own cup of coffee. "It's gonna be a pretty day today," he said. "I overheard some of the guests saying they might want to go on a hike. Feel like going with?"

Brick nodded. "Sure thing." They all took turns showing the guests around if they wanted an escort. Since The Refuge had several hundred acres, the last thing they wanted was anyone getting lost. They'd spent significant time clearing and marking the trails, but there were some beautiful spots that weren't on the trails that Brick and the others loved to show off.

"We figured it would be good to get the guests out while the vet's here with Melba."

Brick winced. Melba was their resident cow. She was a sweetheart. Loved people. Loved being scratched under her chin. If allowed, she'd follow the guests around the property, rubbing her head against them and being an adorable pest. But one thing she did *not* like was a visit from the veterinarian. The sounds she made when she was being given an exam made it seem as if she were being tortured. The last thing their guests needed was to hear something that resembled a woman being taken apart one limb at a time. Anything they could do to prevent a flashback was a good thing.

"Right, so a long hike it is," Brick said with a smile.

Stone took the chair next to him and they sat in a comfortable silence for a while.

"We're booked solid for the next several months, right?" Brick asked.

Stone nodded. "Yeah. If reservations continue the way they are, the entire year will be booked within a few more weeks."

Brick was pleased, especially considering it was only spring.

"And before you ask," Stone said, "we're keeping the thirteenth cabin open for emergencies."

Brick nodded in satisfaction. They'd all decided from the start to always have a cabin open for those who needed an immediate place to stay. For POWs who'd recently been released, or anyone who needed an emergency place to heal.

"Although Becky did accidentally book it for a few different weeks later this summer," Stone said with a sigh.

Brick merely shook his head. They'd had a hell of a time finding someone competent who could answer phones, deal with customers, and who knew his or her away around a few simple computer programs. He'd thought it would be the easiest position to fill, but in the three years they'd been operating, they'd had almost twenty people in the job. Some didn't like the isolation, others felt nervous around the guests, considering some of their backgrounds. And some had flat-out lied about their abilities to multitask and get shit done.

The guy they'd had before Becky was the absolute

worst when it came to dealing with guests. He had the personality of a rock. It had been a disaster.

"I'm assuming everything got straightened out."

"Yup," Stone said. "Although, Pipe made her cry."

Brick frowned.

"He wasn't even that mean," Stone assured him. "He just kind of growled a bit and frowned at her, and Becky crumbled like a house of cards. But she *did* call everyone she'd booked into the cabin to apologize, and owned up to her mistake."

"Were they pissed?" Brick asked.

Stone shrugged. "Some, yeah. But most understood and simply picked other dates to come. Helped that we gave them a twenty-percent discount."

Brick was sure it did. The Refuge wasn't cheap. While POWs were invited to stay free of charge, others paid a considerable price for the rest and relaxation they found here.

"Good. Anything else going on other than Melba's imminent breakdown and Becky's fuck-up?"

"Nope."

Brick nodded again, relieved. Even though they were all co-owners of The Refuge, it kind of felt like his baby. It had been his idea, after all. "You good?" he asked his friend. They didn't talk about their personal demons a lot, but they all knew each other's triggers. Stone, like the rest of them, had some days that were harder than others.

"Yeah," his friend said quietly.

"The anniversary's coming up," Brick said.

"Five years. Sometimes it feels like a lifetime ago we

were drug through the streets and thrown into that cell, and other times it feels like yesterday."

"I know," Brick commiserated. He felt exactly the same way. On his bad days, he swore he could hear Mad Dog's voice, only to run outside and see a guest he didn't know standing there.

The two friends sat in silence for several minutes longer before Stone threw back his head and swallowed the rest of his coffee. He headed inside to return the mug, and when he stepped back out, gave Brick a chin lift before wandering off...probably to the lodge, to make sure breakfast was ready for their guests and everyone was happy.

Brick continued to sit, staring off into the trees behind his cabin, his thoughts turning back to Alaska. She should be back from her tour by now, since there was a nine-hour time difference between The Refuge and St. Petersburg. By the time he returned from the hike with the guests, he hoped to have another email with pictures from her day.

Standing, he took the time to pet Mutt, then entered his house. He needed to change into his hiking boots and different pants. Staying busy was the best way to keep his mind occupied. It would keep his demons at bay...and would get his mind off worrying about Alaska.

CHAPTER FOUR

Alaska smiled at Igor, the guide she'd spent the previous day with, as he entered the lobby of her hotel.

"You ready to go?" he asked.

She nodded, pushing away the uneasy feeling she'd had since yesterday, when she'd learned the two couples who'd been on tour with her weren't coming today. But Igor had promised she wouldn't be alone, that they'd be picking up some other tourists on their way out of the city to see Peterhof Palace.

She was only here for two days, and she wanted to see as much as possible. She'd splurged on the private tour, having been reassured that was the best way to see as much as she could in a short period of time. Yesterday was great. They'd even skipped the long lines at the Winter Palace, which was a huge plus.

But while Igor had been a knowledgeable guide, he also made her anxious for some reason. It wasn't anything about his looks; he was dressed impeccably in a pristine polo shirt and jeans. His dark brown hair was perfectly coiffed and he looked like any other person she'd met in the country.

She wasn't sure if her uneasiness came from the inordinate amount of time he spent on his phone, or the way every time she glanced his way, he seemed to be staring at her.

No one stared at her. She wasn't the kind of woman people found irresistible or intriguing. So finding herself the subject of his intense interest was discomfiting.

But she really did want to see the fountains at the Peterhof Palace, and she wasn't comfortable getting on a bus or boat to go out there on her own, since she didn't speak any Russian. So Igor and the private tour it was. She'd sent Drake a long email earlier with pictures from yesterday's outing, and also to give him her itinerary for today.

It was pathetic that she didn't really have any other close friends with whom to share her plans. She switched jobs too often to build close relationships with co-workers. She'd spent the last two decades moving around Europe, and had loved it. But in the last few years, she'd begun to crave home.

Alaska was well aware *why* she was suddenly having said craving.

Drake.

Ever since she'd gone to see him when he was in the hospital in Germany, he'd been a constant in her life. They talked on the phone every now and then, but mostly they messaged and emailed. Every day.

She was extremely proud of his progress over the last four years. He admitted that he still struggled with guilt, missing his friends, and with PTSD in general, but having The Refuge to focus on had been the best thing for him.

Alaska had looked up his "little venture," as he called it, and had spent quite a bit of time ogling all that he'd accomplished in such a short time. Every single review of The Refuge so far was positive. Guests raved over the accommodations, the food, the atmosphere... and a cow named Melba.

It was embarrassing, but Alaska had even saved the picture of Drake and the six friends who'd opened the retreat to her computer. The men were all gorgeous. But to her, Drake was the most handsome. There was just something about him that did it for her, even after so many years. The tattoos. The blue eyes. Even the frickin' veins in his arms and hands. He had a closely trimmed beard and mustache in the picture that he hadn't had in the hospital, and it really worked for him. Alaska could see the strength and determination in his posture, the way he held himself.

He was everything she'd always wanted in a man... and knew she'd never have.

It wasn't that she had low self-esteem; she was simply a realist. Men like Drake didn't look twice at women like her. They just didn't. But he was still the measure for every man she'd ever dated.

Not that she'd dated in a long while. It had been bad enough when all she had to compare was the memory of an eighteen-year-old kid she knew in high school, but since spending that time with him in Germany, it had been virtually impossible to date.

No one came close to Drake Vandine.

Talking to him, getting emails from him, was both exciting and excruciating.

She knew moving back to the States would make being his friend even more painful, but it was time. She was tired of living abroad, and being closer to Drake could never be a bad thing, even if he wasn't hers.

"You excited about today?" Igor asked, making her jerk in surprise, since she was so lost in her head.

Alaska chuckled slightly. "I think so. Are we going to be gone all day? I wasn't sure how long it would take to get out to the palace and back."

"It depends on the traffic. It's very awful around here. Too many cars and not enough road. But you trust Igor, I'll get you there safely. Watch your step," he said as he pointed to a hole in the sidewalk.

Gratefully, Alaska stepped over the troublesome spot as they headed for his vehicle. It was the same white mini-van they'd used the day before, and she climbed inside, sitting on the bench seat directly behind her guide.

Igor ran around and got behind the wheel. He started the engine and said, "We have two stops to make, then we'll be on our way."

Alaska nodded absently and stared out the window as they headed down the street. Almost everyone she'd met while in the country had been friendly, bending over backward to make sure she was satisfied and happy. Whether that was at the small café they'd visited or the restaurant where she'd eaten dinner the night before. Even the clerks at the hotel already knew her name and smiled at her as she came and went.

Igor pulled up in front of a hotel and hopped out. The sliding door opened and two men climbed into the van with her. Alaska gave them a brief smile, then turned her attention back to the window. She hoped the next guests Igor picked up included a woman. She wasn't sure she was comfortable being the only female in the group.

But to her dismay, at the second hotel, a third man joined them. He sat next to her on the bench seat—and strangely, the hair on the back of Alaska's neck stood up. She was two seconds away from telling Igor that she'd changed her mind and didn't want to go on the tour after all. But after a couple deep breaths, and when the man beside her just nodded politely, she told herself she was being ridiculous.

The van pulled away from the curb and into the increasing traffic. The temperature inside the vehicle was warm, and that, along with the vibrations of the motor, had Alaska dozing off as they got onto the road that led out of the city.

She wasn't sure how long she'd slept, but when Alaska woke and looked out the window...she knew something was very wrong.

"Where are we?" she asked.

Igor didn't acknowledge her question. He simply stared out the front of the van and kept driving.

Looking outside again, Alaska saw they were in some sort of industrial park, or...a train yard? There were Conexes everywhere she looked. The big shipping containers that were most often used on cargo ships. Trucks and forklifts were scattered here and there, transporting the huge containers from one place to another. The van seemed to be heading toward a large warehouse in the distance.

"Igor?" Alaska asked again as she leaned forward in her seat.

To her surprise, the man next to her thrust out an arm, pushing her back against the seat.

Her first instinct was to shove the man's arm away from her body, and when she reached up to do just that, two hands grabbed *her* arms from behind.

She was pinned to her seat by the men behind her.

Scared out of her mind now, all she could do was sputter, "What the hell?"

"There's been a change in the itinerary," one of the men said.

Alaska glanced over her shoulder, and the cold look in the man's brown eyes made her swallow the retort that was on the tip of her tongue. This wasn't someone who would take kindly to backtalking. How she knew that, she had no idea, but she knew to the bottom of her soul that he wouldn't think twice about hurting her. Badly.

"I like the silent ones," the man said with a chuckle. "To reward your self-control, I'll tell you what's happening. You now belong to *me*. At least for the moment. I've sold you to a friend who resides in China. He's a collector of sorts. And it's been a while since he's had an American. You're here on your own, no husband, no friends...so no one to think twice when you simply disappear."

Alaska's eyes widened in horror. She wanted to puke, but all she could do was stare at the man in disbelief.

"As soon as the money's been deposited into my

account, you'll be sent via train across Siberia, through Mongolia, to Beijing. If you survive the journey, I advise you to do what your new owner requests without question. He's not known for his patience."

The man laughed. The sound was so dirty, it sent shivers down Alaska's spine.

This couldn't be happening. Being kidnapped and sold into the sex slave trade happened in movies. Not in real life. And definitely not to someone like her.

Igor, who'd seemed genial enough a day ago, but had proven to be the devil himself, pulled the van up close to a door at the warehouse. The man next to her climbed out, then leaned over and wrapped a meaty hand around her biceps, all but dragging her off the seat.

Alaska almost fell to the ground, but as soon as her feet were under her, her other arm was grabbed and she was force-marched through the door into a bustling space. There were people going about their business everywhere, but no one turned to look at her. Not one person seemed interested in what was happening right in front of their noses.

But then again, why would they? They were all probably in on what was happening. On the kidnapping of women.

She was hauled across the floor toward what looked like an office.

The longer she was in the company of the two goons and the mastermind behind...*whatever* this was, the lower her chances of escape. Igor hadn't joined them inside, had probably already driven off to dupe some other poor unsuspecting tourist.

The office door slammed behind her, and Alaska was shoved toward a small couch. She managed to catch herself so she didn't smack her face against the nasty-looking cushions. Immediately turning, she stared at the three men. Were they going to rape her now? Beat her up? She began to shake with fright.

The man in charge sat in a chair behind a desk and began to type on a computer. Several minutes went by with no one saying a word. She might as well have been a piece of furniture for all they cared. But Alaska much preferred that to the alternative. Her heartbeat hadn't slowed since waking in the van and she felt sick with the amount of adrenaline coursing through her veins.

She had to do something. If she sat there like a scared little girl, she was going to be sent to China to be some man's sex toy.

"I'm married," she blurted suddenly, her voice sounding very loud in the too-quiet room. The whirring of machinery could be heard from out on the floor, but Alaska had a feeling even if she screamed her head off, no one would come to investigate what was happening. She was on her own, and it was a very scary feeling.

The man behind the desk smirked and leaned back in his chair. "No, you aren't," he said after a moment.

"I am," Alaska insisted.

"Then where's this husband of yours? Why would he let his wife wander around Russia on her own? Doesn't seem likely. You aren't wearing a wedding ring either. If I had a wife, she'd be at home where she belonged. How do you Americans say it...? Barefoot and pregnant?"

Alaska hated this man with every fiber of her being. But she knew turning into a shrew wouldn't help her right now. Especially given how he obviously viewed women.

"I didn't bring my jewelry to Russia because I didn't want it to draw anyone's attention or be stolen. And Drake's back in the States. He has a business there. I'm supposed to join him after I finish a job in Switzerland, where I work. I'd never been to Russia and had always heard such great things. So I decided to take one last trip before going home to him."

"I don't believe you," the man said, eying her intensely.

"I can call him. He'll pay double what the guy in China is to get me back."

That got the man's attention. "He'll pay two million American dollars for you?" he asked.

Holy shit. She was so screwed. Alaska's heart fell, but she nodded anyway.

"And what's this husband's name?"

"Drake. Drake Vandine. He owns a resort in New Mexico that makes a lot of money. He'll pay to free me. I guarantee it."

She had no idea what kind of money Drake made. She knew better than most that a business could look successful from the outside, while in reality, be barely scraping by. But Drake had told her if she ever needed him, all she had to do was ask.

Two million dollars was a hell of a lot to ask—but she was willing to take the chance.

The man in charge steepled his fingers under his chin and stared at her for a long moment. It was all Alaska could do not to squirm under his gaze.

"Why? You are not pretty. You're forgettable. Why would this man pay for you?"

The first thing that popped into Alaska's head was...*I have no earthly idea*. But she couldn't say that.

"He loves me," she blurted.

To her surprise, the man threw back his head and laughed. Hard. When he had himself under control, his gaze bore into hers. "Love doesn't exist," he said flatly. "It's a pathetic emotion men have used to control women for centuries. All we need is a hole to stick our dicks in and we're happy. And you have three perfectly good holes my client is eager to fill as often and in any way that he wants. You think this Drake will pay to get you back? Prove it."

Alaska's heart was pounding so hard, she was sure she was two seconds away from a heart attack, but she nodded anyway. "How?" she asked.

"Bring her here," the man ordered his henchmen.

Before Alaska insisted she could walk on her own, her arms were once more grabbed and she was hauled upright and brought over to the desk.

"What's his number?" the man asked. "This *Drake* who will pay two million dollars for pussy?"

"I...I don't know it. I mean, it's programmed into my phone in my purse, which I assume is still in the van." The skeptical look on the evil man's face nearly brought Alaska to her knees. She had to think fast. "But his resort in New Mexico is called The Refuge. There's a number. I can call that."

The man leaned forward and clicked buttons on the keyboard, obviously looking up The Refuge. Alaska hated that he'd now know where Drake worked, but it couldn't be helped. She mentally kicked herself for not memorizing his cell number. Relying on technology was too easy. She hadn't really had a reason to know his number by heart. All she had to do was click on his name. Stupid. So stupid.

The man reached over and hit a series of buttons on a phone sitting on the desktop. Alaska could hear the ringing through the speaker.

"You have four minutes to convince this Drake to pay up," the man told her.

Alaska nodded immediately. The vomit that had been sitting in the back of her throat threatened to come up once again and she ruthlessly swallowed it back. She didn't think the man would appreciate her puking all over his cheap wooden desk.

As the phone rang, Alaska tried to figure out what to say that would get her out of this situation. Before she'd decided, a female voice came over the line.

"Thank you for calling The Refuge. How can I help you?"

"I need to speak to Drake. It's an emergency."

"Drake? Who's Drake? Is he a guest?" the woman asked chirpily.

The smug look on the man's face in front of her made Alaska flush, but she didn't give him a chance to cut the connection.

"Brick. Drake is Brick. Please. Tell him it's his wife calling and I really, really need to talk to him immediately."

"Oh! Brick." The woman chuckled. "Sorry, no one around here uses the guys' real names. If you can hold, I'll find him for you."

"Thank you," Alaska said. Then added, "I'm calling from overseas so the faster you can get him on the line, the better."

"Will do, honey. Just hang on."

Then a Muzak version of "Beat It" by Michael Jackson began to play over the line.

To her relief, her kidnapper seemed to be willing to see how this ended. He leaned back once again and put his hands behind his head as he grinned. "This is kind of fun," he told her. "Now we wait to see how your beloved reacts to you asking for two million dollars."

Alaska would've already fled if she'd been able to. It didn't matter that she was in the middle of who knows where in Russia, didn't speak the language, and was surrounded by three of the scariest men she'd ever met. She would've attempted escape if she wasn't still in the grip of the two goons by her side.

She had nowhere to run. Nowhere to go. If Drake didn't come through for her, she was as good as dead.

* * *

Brick was chatting amiably with his guests. It was a good day with an equally good group. They'd been eager to hear stories about the land around them and content to hike at a sedate pace, the excursion lasting about four hours. More than long enough for Melba's routine vet appointment to be completed.

He had arranged for a light snack for everyone at one of the stops along the trail. The view was spectacular and everyone seemed to be in great spirits. They were about five minutes from the lodge when his phone began to vibrate with the emergency tone all the owners had programmed into their phones.

He immediately tensed. The last time he'd received an emergency alert was when one of the guests had locked himself in his cabin because he was having a flashback and thought he was about to be overrun by armed terrorists.

Looking at the screen, he saw the SOS message was from Pipe.

He turned to the guests, apologized for having to run off, literally, and told them to take their time getting back as he set off at a jog toward the lodge. He clicked on Pipe's name as he ran.

"Where are you?" Pipe asked when he answered.

"About three minutes away. What's happening?"

"Your wife is on the phone and wants to talk to you," Pipe said.

For a moment, Brick was confused. His wife? What the hell? He wasn't married. But the very next thought in his brain made him stumble on the path.

The only person who would dare claim to be his wife was Alaska. Although their code word had been fiancé, it was basically the same thing.

"Where is she? What's wrong?" he asked.

"You know who it is?"

"Yes," Brick said shortly.

"Right. Becky got a call from someone claiming to be your wife and needing to talk to you. She said it was an emergency and that she was overseas, and if you could hurry it would be good."

Adrenaline flooded Brick's system.

"She asked for Drake, and Becky didn't know who she was talking about until she clarified."

"Did Becky say that I wasn't married?" Brick asked.

"No."

"Thank fuck!" he muttered.

"She said she thought it was weird, but since we've told her that the customer is always right—which you and I know is bullshit, but whatever—she just went with it. Said she assumed it was someone trying to get to you any way possible. People don't usually call the commercial line asking to speak to any of us by name."

"It's Alaska," Brick told his friend. He could see the lodge now.

"How do you know without talking to her?"

"I know," Brick said. "And something's wrong. Very fucking wrong. Last I knew, she was in Russia. I'll be there in a minute."

"I'm here, and Tiny's on his way," Pipe said.

"The line's being recorded, right?" Brick asked.

"Of course. Like always."

"Good. Have someone call Tex. I have a feeling we're gonna need him."

"You don't know that. She might be calling to play a joke or something," Pipe said reasonably.

"No. Not Alaska. Something's happened, and I may need Tex to help fix it," he said without hesitation.

"Right. I'll get Owl to call Tex. I'm waiting by the back door."

"Thanks. Be there soon." Brick clicked off the phone and picked up his pace. He had no idea what was going on, but he knew without a shadow of a doubt, it wasn't good.

When he got to the lodge, he ran through the door Pipe was holding open for him and didn't slow down as he headed for a small office in the back. It wasn't used very often, but had a computer and phone that were both connected to the ones their admin used at the front desk.

He took a deep breath to calm himself. "Line one?" he asked Tiny, who'd arrived at the same time he had.

When his friend nodded, Brick put the phone on speaker then clicked the flashing light that said line one.

"Hey, honey! What's up?" he asked in a tone that was as laid-back and relaxed as he could muster. Meanwhile, his hands gripped the edge of the desk hard enough that his knuckles turned white. Pipe had a phone in his hand, holding it up so whoever was on the other end could hear what was happening. Brick prayed it was Tex.

"Drake?"

Alaska's voice was thready and he could hear it shaking.

"It's me," he told her. "How was your tour today?"

"Um...yeah, about that," she said. "I've found myself in a bit of trouble and need your help."

"Anything. You know that," he said, letting reassurance bleed into his voice.

"I need you to transfer two million dollars into an account as soon as you can, otherwise I'm gonna be sold to a guy in China."

Brick had expected something to be wrong, but this was...he didn't know *what* this was. Repulsive. Shocking. Horrifying.

He didn't doubt Alaska for a second. She wasn't the

kind of woman who would call him out of the blue asking for huge chunks of money. "Holy fuck, honey," he breathed, not even sure what to say at the moment.

"I know," she said with a small, very unamused laugh. "Crazy, right? You were right when you told me I shouldn't come to Russia on my own."

Brick felt awful. He *had* told her that. But in his worst nightmares, he couldn't have imagined this would happen to her.

"I'll get on it as soon as we hang up. What happens after I send the money?"

"I...I don't know. But they promised if you sent the money, they'd let me go."

"Okay, honey. Stay strong. I'm on this. Understand?"

"Yeah. And, Drake? I'm so sorry."

Fury rose hard and fast in Brick. There was no need for her to apologize. It shocked him that she felt as if she was in any way responsible for some piece of shit kidnapping her to sell for sex. "Is the person who took you there? Can he hear me?"

"Yes," she whispered.

"Please don't hurt my wife," he said, playing his role. What he *really* wanted to tell the fucker was that if he hurt one hair on Alaska's head, he was gonna regret it. He went on in as calm a voice as he could manage. "I want proof that you've set her free before I send you a dime."

He heard a deep chuckle in the background. Then a man spoke with a Russian accent. "Wrong. You send my money, then your wife is let go. Here's the account." He rattled off a series of numbers.

Brick didn't worry about writing them down. The call was being recorded.

"Got that?" the man asked.

"Yes," Brick said between clenched teeth. "It's going to take some time to get the money together and wired. I want your promise that nothing will happen to my wife in the meantime."

"I make no promises to anyone for anything," Alaska's kidnapper said. "But because you've both been so... accommodating...I'll give you some time. Don't fuck me over. If you do, she's as good as dead."

"I won't. Al, hang in there. No matter what, I'm gonna fix this... Alaska? Are you there?"

"The call's been dropped," Pipe confirmed.

"Fuck!" Brick yelled, then picked up the phone and threw it against the wall as hard as he could. Anger swam through his veins, impossible to control. He hadn't felt as helpless as he did right now in a long time —not since that day over four years ago, when he'd watched his battle buddies get blown to bits.

He turned to Pipe and thrust out his hand for the phone he was holding. "Tex?" he asked Pipe, as he took it from him. His friend nodded.

"I'm tracing the call," Tex said as soon as Brick put the phone up to his ear. "Since it took a few minutes for you to get to the office, there was time to trace it. Also got my computer working on that account number he gave you. We're gonna get her back."

"I want in," he said.

"Brick, you've been off the teams for four years," Tex told him.

"I don't have to be on the strike team, but I have to

be there. She's gonna need me," he told the older man. He couldn't explain how he knew that, he just did. Whatever Alaska was going through was bad. He felt it in his bones. Heard it in the tone of her voice. She was scared shitless. And there was no telling what would happen to her between now and when her kidnapper received the money. Even though the man had said he would wait for the money to appear, Brick didn't trust him, not one bit.

Tex sighed. "All right. I can make a phone call and get an extraction team on their way. They don't often work outside the US anymore, but they'll make an exception for this. If I get a plane to Los Alamos in twenty minutes, can you be on it?"

Brick didn't even ask how the hell Tex would be able to commandeer a plane, let alone getting it to the small town nearby in twenty minutes. "Yes. And Tiny will be coming with me."

Tex didn't argue. "Remember, you're both in the peripheral on this one. Got it? Support only."

"Ten-four," Brick agreed. He didn't care if he was the one to take down Alaska's kidnapper or not. He just needed to be there for *her*.

"That piece of shit won't get away with taking one of our own," Tex said. The conviction in his voice went a long way toward making Brick relax a fraction. "Twenty minutes. Be there." Then Tex severed the line.

Brick handed the phone back to Pipe. "Thanks," he said with a nod. He turned to Tiny. "You okay going with me?"

"Fuck yeah," he replied.

Brick was relieved. He'd picked Tiny to accompany

him because, one, he was in the room and already knew what was happening, and two, because he'd been a SEAL. He had nothing against the other men he worked with. They were just as deadly and competent. But there was a level of familiarity and comfort with Tiny simply because they'd both been SEALs.

The men ran out of the office, ignoring Becky, who was asking what was happening. They didn't have even one extra minute to explain. Alaska's life was on the line and it was going to take a bit of time to get to her. There was a good chance that whoever had kidnapped her would go ahead and ship her to China without waiting for Brick's money to arrive. If that happened, it would be almost impossible to find her—but Brick wasn't going to give up.

Tex would take care of the money transfer, making it seem as if the cash was on its way, that the transfer was pending when it actually wasn't.

Brick wasn't concerned about money. If Tex had to literally send the ransom for real, he'd gladly spend the rest of his life repaying the former SEAL. All that mattered was getting Alaska back safe and sound.

CHAPTER FIVE

When her kidnapper reached over and cut her connection to Drake in the middle of a sentence, Alaska wanted to scream. Wanted to cry. She did neither. She had to stay in control until Drake could get her out of this. He'd said she had nothing to apologize for, but he was wrong. She should've listened to him. He'd tried to warn her, but she'd been so sure of her safety, confident since she'd been traveling around Europe by herself for years.

"Now what?" she asked when the man didn't say or do anything.

"Now?" he said with a smirk. "Now we get you packaged up for your trip to China." He nodded at the men holding her.

Alaska struggled to get away, but they held her too tightly. "What? *No!* Drake's sending the money!"

"I certainly hope he does. Three million sounds a lot better than one," the man retorted.

Alaska fought like a wild thing as she was dragged out of the office and back into the warehouse. But no matter how much she kicked and writhed, she couldn't get herself out of the men's grasp.

"No! He's sending the money!" she shouted at the asshole still sitting in the office.

He merely called out, "I don't care!" as she was hauled away.

This time she didn't hold back as the men dragged her through the warehouse. She screamed at the top of her lungs. No one so much as looked at her. It was as if she really was invisible.

She opened her mouth to scream again, but one of the goons put his hand over her mouth...and her nose. It took a moment for her to realize that she couldn't breathe.

Panic set in. She viciously clawed at the guy's hand but he didn't let go.

The last thing she saw was the sick smile on his face as blackness overtook her.

When Alaska woke up, she was lying over someone's shoulder as if she were a sack of potatoes. She picked her head up slightly and looked around, realizing they were weaving through a massive amount of wooden boxes.

The man holding her, noting she was awake, dropped his shoulder, and she fell to the ground. She let out a grunt as she landed but immediately tried to spring to her feet.

The man was ready for her escape attempt. He grabbed her arm, in the same spot as before, and squeezed hard. He dragged her, once more kicking and fighting as hard as she could, toward the back end of a huge storage container. The same metal ones she'd seen in the yard through the window of the van.

Two men inside the container reached out and pulled her inside. They dragged her toward the back wall before throwing her to the metal floor. Alaska had a split second to look around, long enough to spot a bucket in one corner and a bottle of water attached to the wall above it, with a long tube coming out of the bottom—before everything suddenly went dark.

Startled, she turned back toward where the men had been only a second ago. Reaching out, her hands immediately made contact with a hard surface maybe a foot in front of her. Confused, she pushed on what felt like... a wall? The metal was cold against her palms, and she shivered.

For a moment, she was improbably relieved that there was somehow a wall between herself and her kidnappers.

Until reality set in, and her heart began to thump in her chest once again. She might be safe from assault by her kidnappers...but she was now locked inside a Conex container.

That wasn't good. It was really fucking bad.

She recalled the guy in charge saying she'd be put on a train headed to China—and that was when she full-on freaked out, screaming at the top of her lungs, kicking and punching the metal in the darkness. "Let me out!" she sobbed, hearing nothing but the sound of her own voice echoing around her.

How long she pounded on the metal wall, screaming for help, Alaska had no idea. But when she finally slid to her butt, wrapping her arms around her knees, she was exhausted and even more terrified. Tears ran down her face, her hands hurt from beating on the metal, and her ears were ringing from the sounds of her own panicked cries.

Now that she wasn't screaming, she could hear sounds on the other side of the metal wall. The voices were muffled and indistinguishable, but she could feel vibrations under her feet. Thumps, as if items were being dropped onto a floor. She remembered all the wooden boxes she'd seen before she'd been thrown in here.

Despair filled her. She'd obviously been put into a hidden section of the container, way at the back. And now the warehouse workers were packing the Conex with those boxes. She had no idea what was in them, but she figured it was something legal. Who would search a container full of perfectly legal goods?

No one.

She thought about the bucket she'd seen in her prison...was that where they expected her to use the bathroom? Bile rose up her throat yet again. Yes, they'd given her water, but how long would the air in her prison last? Were they going to starve her?

Alaska lay her head on her knees and cried. She was as good as dead.

Her captor had conned them. He was going to take Drake's money—and the money of the man who'd bought her—and she would disappear into thin air... probably like so many other women before her.

* * *

Brick's jaw hurt from clenching his teeth so hard. Everything was happening as fast as possible, but it was still too slow. A clearance issue saw the team leaving Colorado much later than scheduled, chipping away at Brick's sanity. He didn't even want to imagine what Alaska was going through right now. It took time to fly across the world, time he didn't think she had.

The men Tex had conscripted for the mission were currently planning their every step after they arrived in St. Petersburg. Tex had tracked the phone call to a manufacturing plant and rail yard not too far outside the city. They were heading straight there when they landed.

But would Alaska still be there? Would she be all right?

Brick had no idea. He doubted whoever had taken her planned to wait for the two million to be deposited into his account. He was probably counting on getting both the ransom money, as well as whatever price the buyer had paid.

Buyer.

Fucking hell.

Someone had fucking *bought* Alaska. It was unconscionable.

His expertise was with terrorists. Not men who were deviant enough to buy and sell human beings.

The group of men he was with, however, were well versed in that world. They were experts in tracking down and retrieving women and children from the sex trade. Tiny had talked to them quite a bit earlier, and had learned the leader of the group had successfully rescued his own wife ten years after she'd been taken.

While Brick was pleased for the man and his wife, the only thing that mattered to him was Alaska. He felt sick inside. She was there for him when he'd needed someone most, during his darkest moment. He couldn't stomach the thought of what the woman who'd slept by his side for days, in an uncomfortable hospital cot, might be going through right that second.

Tex had worked a miracle and gotten them approval to land on Russian soil. Brick had no idea how he'd done it or what markers he'd had to call in, he was just relived they didn't need to do a HALO jump from the plane. Not only that, but a team of *spetsnaz*, Russian special forces, would be joining them on their mission. Brick knew Tex had connections, but even he'd been surprised by Russia's agreement to cooperate on this level.

No one stopped them as they exited the plane onto the tarmac. They headed for a van parked nearby. The driver nodded as they approached and everyone filed in, not speaking as they began the journey, likely going over the plan in their heads.

Once at the warehouse where the call had originated, they'd enter fast and hard, and with a huge show of force. Brick just prayed she'd be there...alive.

He and Tiny would bring up the rear and have the other men's six. As much as Brick wanted to be at the front of the strike team, it had been years since he'd been on a mission. The last thing he wanted was to be a weak link and possibly get Alaska hurt or killed. So he'd stay in the background and let the mercenaries do what they did best.

As they approached the area under the cover of darkness, Brick was relieved to see almost no one milling about. There were no trucks moving storage containers from the storage yard to the trains. The cars on the rails were silent, waiting to be loaded with cargo. The few people he *did* see took one look at the caravan of trucks headed toward the main building and wisely slunk into the darkness.

When they pulled up near the warehouse—things moved with lightning speed.

Within seconds of the van pulling up near the building, swarms of camouflaged men surrounded the warehouse. Brick watched from a short distance as doors and windows were busted in and everyone—Russian soldiers and American mercenaries—swarmed inside.

All he could think of was Alaska. Hoping they'd find her and get her the hell out of there.

But when one minute turned to two, then to five, Brick's stomach twisted violently.

She wasn't here. He'd known it was a possibility, it had taken too long to get to her...but it still was a blow.

Reading his mind, Tiny said, "Easy, Brick. Don't jump to conclusions."

How could he not? If she was there, the Russian spec ops would've found her by now. Or the mercenaries would've brought her to him. With every tick of the clock, his hopes sank lower and lower.

He was too late. It didn't matter that he'd left as soon as he could. He didn't get to her in time.

Just then, several shots rang out inside the warehouse.

Tiny and Brick both went down on one knee and

brought their weapons up at the ready. There was shouting, both English and Russian, and Brick remained tense as they waited to learn what had transpired.

Within moments, one of the men from Colorado stuck his head out the door and nodded to them. "Situation's under control."

"Alaska?" Brick asked.

The man pressed his lips together and shook his head slightly before disappearing back inside.

"We're gonna find her," Tiny said as they stood, a hand on Brick's shoulder. It was all he could do not to fall to his knees. The sense that he'd failed the one person who'd been there for him—who'd *always* been there for him—fell heavy on his shoulders.

Without responding to Tiny, he entered the warehouse.

About three dozen employees had been corralled into a corner, being watched over by several members of the *spetsnaz*. Four of the mercenaries were standing by an office door, weapons drawn.

He made a beeline for them.

Ignoring the warning in Tiny's voice as he called his name, Brick didn't hesitate. At his arrival, the men parted, giving him space to get by and see what was happening inside the room.

A man, dressed in a three-piece suit, was lying on the floor with his hands wrenched behind his back. There was blood beneath him, spreading at an alarming rate. But he wasn't cowed. Wasn't begging for his life. In fact, when Brick stepped into the room, the man smirked.

"Let me guess. You're the husband. This...Drake person?" the man sneered.

Brick nodded once.

"Should've known the bitch had something up her sleeve. Are you even her husband?"

"Yes," he said shortly.

"She must be a fantastic fuck because she's dull as dirt," the man said.

Brick lunged forward to beat the shit out of the unarmed asshole, but the men on either side of him grabbed his arms, stopping him.

The *spetsnaz* operatives standing guard obviously didn't care for the man's words either, or maybe it was the tone of his voice. Whatever the case, both moved at the same time, kicking him on either side of his torso.

The man grunted, then coughed, blood spewing from his mouth to spray across the concrete floor.

"You'll never find her," he gasped when he could breathe once again. "She'll be fucked by hundreds of men across Asia. My client is generous like that. Doesn't mind sharing. Of course, that's because he gets paid a pretty penny by men who want a chance to do all the kinky shit they've dreamed about doing to a woman but haven't had the opportunity. He's fucking loaded. Always gets what he wants. And this time, he wanted an American for his stable."

Brick's throat burned with rage. He wanted to tell the man to shut the fuck up, but he knew as well as everyone in the room that the more the man talked, the more likely it was he'd let something slip that would lead them to their target.

No, not their target...to *Alaska*.

"She was so easy to dupe." The man laughed. "They always are. Stupid tourists, here to sightsee...all it takes is one day of buttering them up, lowering their guard. Then, boom—the next time they step into the van, they're ours." He laughed again, blood dripping from his chin. The sound grated on Brick's nerves.

"I'm dying. We all know it. But I *still* win. I've got operatives all over this fucking country. Government officials who are easily bribed to look the other way. Weak men who do my organization's bidding because if they don't, it'll be *their* sisters, mothers, daughters who will disappear. You might've caught me—but you'll never stop *us*. There's too much money in peddling pussy."

Brick couldn't hold himself back anymore. Wrenching out of the mercenaries' hold, he went down on one knee in front of the asshole, fisting the man's hair and tilting his head up. "Where is she, you mother-fucking piece of shit?" he growled in his face.

The man just smiled. An evil smile that made shivers shoot down Brick's spine.

"Gone. She'll be delivered to my client, nothing but a vessel for thousands of men to stick their dicks into."

Brick didn't hesitate. His arm moved without conscious input from his brain. He slammed the man's face into the floor as hard as he could.

Then he did it again. And again.

None of the men standing around made a move to stop him this time. It was obvious they knew the world would be a better place without this fucker in it.

It was Tiny who finally made him stop. He put a

hand on his shoulder and said, "Brick. It's done. He's dead."

Brick realized he was breathing hard as he let go of the man's hair and stood.

Never once, in all the years he'd been a SEAL, had he let his emotions get the better of him. But he'd never been in a situation like *this*. A woman he considered one of his oldest and dearest friends was missing, and the future awaiting her—the one this dead asshole had laid out so clearly—was abhorrent.

He heard the Russians talking amongst themselves but didn't know what they were saying. And it didn't matter.

Where was Alaska?

Frustration rose within him. Killing the piece of shit who'd kidnapped her felt good, but it didn't fix the problem.

Brick turned and strode out of the suddenly too-small office. He couldn't breathe. He needed air. He pushed past the men at the doorway and stopped once he was in the warehouse proper. He took a breath. Then another.

Before he knew it, he was panting. Breathing far too fast.

He looked at the men huddled in the corner, staring at him and the Russian special forces. They were terrified, that was obvious, but Brick didn't give a shit. They had to have seen something. Had to *know* something. There were no innocents here. Alaska wasn't the first woman who'd been abducted and brought here, that was clear.

Brick jumped in surprise when one of the *spetsnaz*

soldiers yelled from behind him. His voice echoed in the room and all of the employees' eyes flew to the man. A few more things were said to the group, and Brick prayed the words were threats.

None of the employees moved.

Brick's shoulders slumped.

The men clearly didn't want to talk—and he couldn't exactly blame them. The dead man lying in the office wasn't working alone. He had others who would most certainly take over his operation. If any of the employees spoke up, they'd be dead by morning. Or their loved ones would disappear, just as countless other women had.

Without a word, Brick headed for the door. He needed out. He'd failed Alaska—and it was taking everything he had not to break down right then and there.

He could sense Tiny following him but he didn't stop. He exited the warehouse and stared at the Conex containers all around him. There had to be hundreds... thousands. All waiting to be filled with the electronics being boxed up in the warehouse. They'd be shipped to who the hell knew where.

The thought of women being packed up along with the goods, delivered to deviants who'd paid for sex slaves, was the last straw for Brick.

He managed a single step to the side before emptying his stomach.

Throwing up didn't make him feel any better. He felt contaminated just standing there. Had Alaska stood in this exact spot? Had she known what was going to happen to her? She had to. He opened his mouth to puke again, stomach heaving. Nothing came out but bile.

"Brick!" an urgent voice called from the doorway. "Get in here!"

It was one of the mercenaries. Numbly, Brick headed back inside the warehouse, wiping his mouth with the back of his hand as he went.

"One of the employees broke. He saw Alaska," the man—Gray, his team called him— said quietly.

"What? Are we sure he's not lying?" Brick asked.

"As sure as we *can* be. He looks terrified. Said he has a sixteen-year-old daughter. Asshole claims she's being watched, and if he did or said anything about what was going on here, she'd disappear like so many others had."

"You think we can trust him?"

Gray snorted. "Do we have a choice?"

Brick pressed his lips together, knowing he was right.

"The *spetsnaz* promised him and his family protection if he cooperated. And if his info panned out."

"Where is she? What kind of intel did he have?"

"Like we thought—she was put into one of the containers."

"Which one?" Brick asked. That was the million-dollar question. Without knowing which box, or at least what train she was on, it would be impossible to find her.

"Four-two-one-seven. He said that's the number of the container. He wasn't sure where it was going, but he swears he saw an American woman being dragged inside before it was loaded, then placed on a railcar."

Brick's heart came back to life with a vengeance. It

beat so hard and fast it was physically painful. He looked around, as if the Conex would magically appear in front of him. "How long ago? Where is it?"

"Last night. The Russians are tracking it now."

Distress clawed at Brick. *Last night.* At least twenty-four hours. Even *one* hour was too long to be locked in a fucking container.

He needed to be moving. Doing something. If necessary, he'd track that damn box all the way across the country.

Time was of the essence. The metal Conex containers couldn't possibly have a lot of air. And did she have food? Water? Was she hurt? The sooner they found Alaska, the better her chances of survival.

Time seemed to slow. Seconds seemed like minutes. Minutes like hours. All Brick could do was pace, waiting, *praying* the *spetsnaz* would be able to locate the container.

Tiny had left Brick's side, watching and listening as the Russians went through files on the computer in the asshole's office. No one had moved him from where he lay on the floor, surrounded by blood. Brick wasn't sorry he'd broken the man's face and accelerated his death. Not in the least.

Then Tiny came out of the room. Brick tried to read his expression.

"They've got it," he said.

Adrenaline flooded Brick's system, making his hands shake. "Where?"

"It left the rail yard late this morning."

Brick's stomach heaved.

Tiny held up a hand. "But the authorities know where it is—and its destination is Beijing, just like the asshole hinted."

"Fuck!"

His friend grabbed his shoulder and practically shoved him toward the van that was pulling up at the door to the warehouse. "Come on, let's go get your lady."

Brick didn't need to be told twice.

* * *

It had taken way too fucking long for the Russians to get organized. But now they were in helicopters, flying across the Russian countryside. The train Alaska's container was on...allegedly...hadn't reached Moscow yet. The plan was to intercept before it arrived.

Brick couldn't help but pray the employee hadn't been fucking with them. If Alaska wasn't in container four-two-one-seven, she was as good as dead. Every single one of the mercenaries knew it. They knew better than *anyone* what happened to women who disappeared into the sex trade.

Brick kept his gaze trained on the ground several thousand feet beneath the helicopter. Every train they passed made his muscles tense, but so far the helicopter hadn't slowed.

In the distance, he caught a glimpse of yet another train—this one with container after container stacked along its length. It seemed far longer than any of the others they'd passed.

He heard one of the Russian spec ops soldiers talking to his comrades through the earphones. He didn't understand the words, but anticipation swam through his veins at the tone.

This was it.

The helicopters slowed, and Brick watched as the lead chopper lowered until it was hovering in front of the train. The pilot was absolutely amazing, avoiding hazards even as he turned the chopper sideways, allowing several members of the *spetsnaz* to point rifles at the large window of the engine car.

Brick felt as if he was watching a James Bond movie. He couldn't hear the train's brakes engaging, but quickly saw smoke rising from the rails as it slowed.

More words were exchanged by the soldiers over the headphones, likely trying to figure out which of the containers was their target.

It was obvious when they found it—Russians began to rappel out of the choppers, aiming for a train car nearly in the middle of the rest.

By the time it was Brick's turn to exit, the area was swarming with Russian special forces. Some had gone to the engine to secure the conductor. Others had taken up positions all around the target car. It was difficult to access the door at the back of the container because of its proximity to the next Conex, but eventually it was wrenched open enough to see inside.

Brick and Tiny crowded in behind Gray and the rest of his team, to see what was inside. He swallowed hard at the sight of wooden crates stacked from the floor to the ceiling inside the metal box.

"Jesus..." It was going to take a long time to empty

the container. Especially since they'd be doing it by hand. There weren't any forklifts to assist; they were literally in the middle of nowhere. Not to mention they weren't able to remove the container from the train car, making it easier to empty.

The decision was made not to wait for the train to get to a more convenient place to unload. Which was a good thing, as Brick would've lost his shit if Alaska had to wait one extra minute to be rescued.

All the men began to work in tandem. They formed an assembly line, removing the crates one by one. Luckily, most were small enough to be lifted by two people. It was taking too long, but Brick forced himself to keep calm. The men around him were doing their best to empty the container as fast as possible.

It wasn't until they were three-fourths of the way through the container when Brick began to panic again. There'd been no sign of Alaska. He was starting to wonder if she was actually *inside* one of the boxes they'd removed. If so, she would've had to be crumpled like a piece of fucking trash to fit.

He was contemplating opening up the larger crates after looking inside the Conex and realizing there were only a few boxes remaining. He ignored the looks of sympathy and frustration on the faces around him.

She isn't here. The employee lied...

No. Brick wouldn't believe it.

He'd seen the man. Seen the fear on his face. Had heard the sincerity in his voice when he repeated what he knew. Alaska was here. He felt it.

"What now?" Tiny asked. "Start opening the crates?"

Brick nodded, carefully studying the container...then

slowly tilting his head as something occurred to him. "Wait, no—the spacing is off in here. There are twenty panels on the outside of the container. I only count eighteen in here."

Each metal panel was about a foot wide. The inside of the container was two feet shorter than what it should've been.

"False wall," Brick and Tiny said together.

The Russians agreed, and soon were trying to figure out how to take down the sheet of metal at the back end of the container, which appeared seamless. It took everything within Brick to stand back and let them work. Alaska was behind that wall. He knew it.

One of the men let out an excited exclamation as he pried back a section of the false wall near the floor.

Instantly, a screech that sounded as if it had come from a wounded animal echoed around the space. Several of the men covered their ears, stumbling back— but Brick moved forward.

He *hated* the sound. The terror behind it made him want to both cry and fucking kill someone. Yet still, he reveled in it.

That sound meant they'd found Alaska.

Brick pushed a few men out of his way as he approached the opening. One of the Russians held a high-powered flashlight, pointing it into the twenty-four-inch gap between the false wall and back of the container. The light was so bright, it made Brick's eyes water—and he hadn't been kept in a dark, confined space for too fucking long.

"Turn it off," he growled, shoving the man's arm away from the hole. "You're fucking blinding her!"

Someone translated his words, and the beam of light cut off.

Brick got down on his hands and knees and stuck his head into the hole. He couldn't see a damn thing. "Alaska?"

"I'll fucking kill you if you get any closer!"

Her words were mere gasps. Her voice rough and scratchy. As if she'd been screaming for help...which she probably had.

"It's me, Brick. Drake. You're safe."

All he could hear for a moment was harsh breathing. Then, "No, you aren't. You're trying to get me to let down my guard. Fuck you! If you get your dick anywhere near me, I'll tear it off!"

Brick heard a few disbelieving chuckles behind him, but he wasn't amused. Not in the least. "It's really me, Al. Remember when we were around ten and playing War, and I had the bright idea to hide under old lady Harrison's trailer? I came face-to-face with that snake and it scared the shit out of me. But you calmly reached over and pulled it away from me. I think that was when I realized how brave and amazing you are. Every day since, you've continued to impress me."

"*Drake?*" she whispered.

"Yeah, honey. It's me. I'm going to come to you, okay?" The stench of body odor and human waste burned his nostrils, but Brick ignored it. His only concern was Alaska. She was alive—and he was so damn thankful. He also hoped she was unharmed...at least physically.

They'd deal with the mental ramifications of her captivity once they were home and she was safe.

A whimper sounded, and Brick took that as consent. His shoulders were almost as wide as the fucking space she was in, and he had to shimmy and squirm as he crawled toward her on his hands and knees. Brick was thankful that whoever was holding the bright-as-the-fucking-sun flashlight had turned it on again, pointing it at the floor of the space, giving him just enough light to see her huddling in the corner.

However, seeing Alaska was almost as painful as not knowing where she'd been. Her eyes were slits, as if even the minuscule amount of light coming from the hole was too much. She seemed smaller than he remembered...but it was the look of torment and devastation on her face that threatened to overwhelm him.

"I'm here," he said softly.

"You came," she whispered.

"Fuck yeah, I did," he replied in a low, trembling voice. "I told you that if you ever needed anything, all you had to do was say the word and I'd be there for you. I'm just sorry it took me so long."

"As soon as he hung up, he put me in here," she whimpered. "He told you he'd wait for the money to arrive."

"He won't ever hurt you again," Brick promised, one hand stretched toward her. He wanted to pull her into his arms, but he didn't want to do anything that would hurt or alarm her. He had no idea if she'd been assaulted or raped before she'd been put in this fucking box. The last thing he wanted to do was add to her trauma.

"He's not gonna be happy. He said the guy he sold me to is powerful."

"Shhh," Brick crooned. "I'm going to touch you now. Is that okay?"

"Yes, but...Drake...I'm dirty."

"Don't care," he said.

"I had to poop in a bucket," she said in a voice that he had to strain to hear.

"Still don't care." Brick touched her hand—and she jerked back so fast he heard her elbow hit the metal wall next to her. "Easy, Al."

He scooted as close as he could, then slowly took her face in his hands. Her skin felt cold against his warm palms, yet he couldn't help but relax a fraction when she tilted her head slightly, giving him some of her weight.

Her hands reached up and she gripped his wrists tightly, almost painfully.

"Your only job, from now until the moment we get on the plane back to the States, is to concentrate on *me*. No one else. Understand?"

"The stuff in my apartment..." she began.

The thought of dropping her off in some apartment in Europe, by herself, while dealing with the aftereffects of her ordeal was repugnant. He wouldn't do it. "We'll arrange for your things to be shipped," he said firmly.

For a second, he thought she was going to protest. He could feel her entire body shaking...but finally, she took a deep breath and nodded slightly.

"That'a girl," he praised. "There are a lot of people out there. But you don't have to be afraid of them. They're all here for you. To find you. But again—your only job is to keep your eyes on me. No matter what. Can you do that?"

"I'll try."

"Okay. I'm going to go backward. Keep hold of me and we'll do it together."

They slowly and awkwardly shuffled along the space, and when they got to the hole, Brick said, "I need to let go of you for a quick moment, but I don't want you to let go of *me*. Understand?"

She nodded.

Brick backed out of the hole on his hands and knees. He felt Alaska's hand on his wrist the entire time. He was crouched in front of the hole when he reached for her free hand. "You're doing really good, Al. Just a little farther."

He helped her crawl out of the hole and into the cavernous container. Her sensitive eyes closed against the comparatively brighter light.

"I've got you," he said, wrapping his arm around her waist and pulling her against him as he stood. They were plastered together, chest-to-chest. His six-feet height was only about four inches taller than she was, so they fit against one another perfectly. He felt her entire body trembling.

Her eyes opened into slits and she immediately turned her head to look around.

"No, Al. *Me*. Look at me."

Still trembling, she immediately obeyed.

Brick didn't want her to see the prison where she'd been kept. Didn't want her to be afraid of the Russian military all around them. He didn't want this rescue to add one iota of angst to her already battered psyche.

He backed up to the door of the container and was relieved when Tiny and Gray were there to help him out of the Conex, so he didn't have to let go of Alaska for even one second.

"It's so damn good to see you," Gray said quietly.

Brick felt her flinch at the other man's voice.

"Easy, Alaska. You're good. That's Gray. He's a friend. He and his teammates came all the way from Colorado to find you."

She nodded and kept her narrowed gaze on him. Fuck, he was so proud of her.

"Thank you for coming," she whispered, then pressed her forehead against him...and a funny feeling spread through his chest. Her immediate trust, after everything she'd been through, meant the world to him.

"The chopper's waiting. It'll bring us straight to the airport," Tiny said.

He felt Alaska's muscles tense against him once more.

"That's Tiny. He's one of the other owners of The Refuge," Brick told her.

"Which one? The biker guy, the one who wears glasses, the Ed Sheeran lookalike, Jake Ryan, or one of the other two?" she whispered.

Tiny burst out laughing. "Oh, I like her," he said.

Brick didn't laugh, but he did allow his lips to quirk upward. "Jake Ryan," he told her.

Alaska nodded against him.

At that moment, one of the Russian soldiers called out something to one of his teammates. Alaska jerked violently in his arms.

"You're okay. You're safe," he reassured her, bending slightly and picking her up.

Alaska clung to him as he carried her away from the

chaos toward a helicopter. It had landed in a field not too far from the train tracks. She didn't open her eyes, simply wrapped her arms around his neck and held on tightly.

"She's going to need to talk to the Russian authorities before we leave," Gray said, materializing next to them as he walked.

"No," Brick said.

"Okay," Alaska said at the same time.

Glancing down at her, Brick saw her eyes were slitted open once more. But her dark gaze remained on him, as he'd requested.

"If it will help other women from ending up where I did, I have to do it," she implored quietly.

Brick shook his head. "He's dead, Al. I promise you, he won't be selling any other women."

"But are all the people who worked with him dead? What about Igor?"

"Who's Igor?" Gray asked.

"The driver. The guide. I thought he was nice enough. But obviously that was fake. And the guys he picked up with me on that second day? The goons who restrained me and made sure I didn't run off? How about the guy who bought me? There are so many other people involved, Drake. If I don't tell them what I know, they could still be out there, kidnapping others."

She was right. Brick knew it. But he still hated the idea that she wouldn't have a chance to decompress before she met with the authorities.

"Okay," he reluctantly agreed.

"Will you stay with me?" she asked in a small voice.

"Wasn't planning on letting you out of my sight for a long fucking time." The answer was raw and rough. It was startling how much this woman had come to mean to him, despite the miles between them. Her constant emails and messages over the last four years had sunk into his psyche, giving him more strength than she'd ever know, and just the thought of her not being there for him to chat with, to be his daily anchor, shook him to the core.

Her eyes closed again and she lay her head on his shoulder. Brick's arms tightened around her and he sent a thankful prayer upward as he headed for the chopper. So many things had gone right for Alaska to be in his arms at this moment. All it would've taken is one piece of faulty intel and he would've lost her. She would've been across the border and living in hell.

He hadn't been able to save Vader and his other teammates, but he felt them watching over him now.

As he well knew, this was only the beginning of Alaska's journey. She might think as soon as she got back to the States, she could go back to her normal routine, but he and his friends knew better than most how difficult that might be. Brick *hoped* she'd be able to bounce back without much difficulty...but given the way she flinched every time someone spoke, the way she trembled nonstop in his arms, he had a feeling his brave friend was in for a rough road ahead.

Brick was more than thankful that he had the perfect place for Alaska to heal. Her mom wasn't in the picture, and she didn't have anywhere else to go, anyone else to turn to. He prayed that she'd find The Refuge as soothing and calming as he did. Once she'd worked through the demons in her head, she'd be free to go wherever she wanted.

He already hated to think about her leaving, but he'd never hold her back. His Alaska was a free spirit... and right now, his only goal was to help her return to the open, friendly woman she'd been before some asshole had tried to crush her under his boot.

CHAPTER SIX

Alaska couldn't stop shaking. It was ridiculous. She was safe. On a plane back to the United States. The meeting with the Russian officials had been hard. A lot harder than she'd expected. The only reason she hadn't ended up a hysterical mess was because of Drake. He hadn't left her side, his strong, warm hand constantly clasping her own, or resting reassuringly on her leg, or settled at the small of her back. He was literally the only thing that had held her together.

She hadn't thought it would be difficult to recount what happened. But as she was speaking, everything just hit her at once—hard. She couldn't deny that she'd been so close to becoming a statistic. Just another woman who disappeared without a trace, never to be found again. She would've been forced to have sex with who knew how many men. She would've been raped over and over...and no one would've cared.

She'd been able to hold it together until they'd stepped inside the plane taking them back to the

United States. It wasn't so much the plane that finally broke her, but knowing she'd be trapped inside for hours...just like she'd been in that container.

She'd hid her reaction from Drake, for which she was immensely relieved. She didn't want to seem weak to him. After all, she hadn't been raped. Hadn't been hurt. She'd been very lucky, really, and didn't feel as if she had any right to a meltdown.

But knowing all that didn't make her anxiety disappear. Instead, the longer she was inside the plane, strapped into a seat, crowded against the window without an easy escape route, the more panicked she became.

The private plane wasn't crowded. The seven men Drake had come to Russia with were there. As was Tiny. There were also around a dozen other men Alaska didn't know. Most spoke English, but a few were speaking Russian quietly amongst themselves. Drake swore she was safe...but Alaska had thought she was safe before being kidnapped too.

One second she was strapped in, staring out the window, trying to control her rising anxiety, and the next she was crouched on the floor in front of her seat, hands over her head, shaking and sobbing.

"Shit," she heard Drake say quietly.

That only made her cower more.

"Alaska, look at me," he ordered.

All she could do was shake her head and squeeze her eyes closed even tighter.

It took several minutes, but eventually she realized Drake hadn't moved. He was crouched on the floor next to her. It was a good thing there was more room between the rows of seats on this private plane than on a commercial flight.

He was talking to her in a low, calm tone. Reassuring her that she was all right. Safe. That he wouldn't let anything happen to her. That she was on a plane full of badass mercenaries and former Navy SEALs who would die before letting anyone near her.

"I can't breathe," she whispered, panting, trying to get oxygen into her lungs.

"Yes, you can," Drake countered. "It's your mind playing tricks on you. Open your eyes. Look at me, Al. You aren't in that container anymore. You're free. I'm here."

She tried, she really did, but she couldn't make her eyelids obey.

"It's okay, Al. When you're ready, I'll be here. Slow down your breathing a bit. Try to match mine...that's it. Good job. I know it's hard being on this plane. If I could've sailed you home, I would've. But that would take too long. Hang in there. Soon we'll be at The Refuge. Wait until you breathe the mountain air. I swear it's cleaner and fresher than anything you've ever inhaled. Our resident cow and pain in the butt, Melba, is gonna love you. Just know that if you give her too much attention, she'll never stop pestering you for more pets. And I can't wait for you to meet Mutt. My three-legged dog. He's amazing. He always seems to know when I need him. He wakes me up when I have nightmares, never leaves my side when the world seems to be crashing in on me."

Alaska heard Drake's words as if from the end of a long tunnel. After a while, his voice became her anchor.

She concentrated on the ebbs and flows of his tone, rather than the actual words.

Swallowing hard, she eventually forced her eyes to open. She didn't want to be a complete mess around him. She wanted to be strong.

How could she be anything else? After Germany, witnessing how Drake had been able to pull himself out of the dark place he'd been in after his best friends had been killed in front of him...she'd admired him so much. She wanted to be like Drake. Brave. Resilient.

"There she is," he said as she stared into his beautiful blue eyes. "That's it, keep looking at me. I'm here. No one's gonna hurt you again. Got it?"

She dipped her chin a fraction, and the smile he bestowed on her was almost painful to look at.

"I know this is hard. I *know*. But you can get through it."

"How?" she whispered.

"Because you're Alaska Stein, and you're the strongest person I know."

She snorted and shook her head.

"You are," he insisted. "I heard all about you from my mom after I left home. And of course, for the last four years, I've constantly been in awe of you. Traveling all over Europe by yourself. Taking jobs that aren't easy, especially when you don't speak the native language. You have a 'damn the torpedoes' personality that's refreshing and admirable."

"I don't feel like I'm the same person anymore," she admitted. "And nothing even happened to me! It's so ridiculous."

"Ah. Guilt. That's an emotion I'm intimately familiar

with," he told her. "You feel guilty that you're struggling to deal with what happened, when you weren't hurt," he said. It wasn't a question.

Alaska nodded.

"Don't," he said firmly. "You still experienced a trauma. I can't imagine what you went through in that container."

Alaska shivered and closed her eyes once more. It had been awful. The darkness, the sounds of the crates being packed around her, using the bathroom in that bucket, drinking water like an animal out of the contraption along the wall, the hunger pains, the fear of running out of air. All of it was horrible.

"It's okay, you don't have to talk about it yet. Eventually...you'll need to. Trust me, I know. But right now, all you have to do is exist. Don't think. Don't do anything. I'll get you home and then you can start to heal. Okay?"

She wanted to agree. Insist she could do this. But all she could do was shake.

When she felt Drake's palm gently cup her face, warmth spread through her, pushing back the coldness that had taken up residence in her body. She reached up and put her own hand over his, pressing his palm harder against her cheek.

"I'm not going anywhere, Al. I've got you."

She let herself lean on him, and even though they were wedged between seats, somehow Drake managed to pull her onto his lap. She snuggled close and let her mind go blank. She didn't hear others talking to him, barely felt it when they were pulled upward and Drake sat in one of the seats.

She clung to him as if she were a two-year-old child.

She didn't sleep though. Couldn't. The last time she'd fallen asleep while in a vehicle, she'd ended up in hell. As tired as she was, her body wouldn't shut down. Not completely.

The journey home was never-ending. They'd had to change planes once, and it took everything she had to walk onto that second plane voluntarily. The men who'd been with Drake were sympathetic and respectful. She'd vaguely noticed they all wore wedding rings. She was happy that they had someone waiting for them at home.

The trip from Colorado to New Mexico was a blur and, thankfully, short. Her head was pounding with a migraine from hell and her stomach was churning, even though she hadn't eaten much in the last three days. Drake had managed to get her to eat a little while on the plane from Russia to Colorado, but everything seemed to be sitting in her belly like a rock.

"She okay?" Alaska heard Tiny ask as if from a very long distance. She was once more snuggled up against Drake, as if he were the only thing that might keep her from breaking into a million pieces...and he probably was.

"Not really," was Drake's answer.

Alaska wanted to smile at that. Appreciated that he wasn't sugarcoating her condition.

"You need me to call Henley?"

"Not right now. She'll definitely need to talk to her, but I think she needs a few days to decompress."

She heard their conversation without the words really sinking in. She also had no idea who Henley was, but she got the gist that Drake wasn't going to make her meet with anyone right away. She was relieved.

"We're booked right now, but the POW cabin is open."

"She'll stay with me," Drake replied.

Tiny was quiet for a beat before he said, "Right. That's probably best."

"Al?"

She didn't respond. She simply kept her eyes closed.

"Alaska," Drake repeated, a little firmer.

"Hmm?"

"Can you open your eyes for a second?"

She shook her head against him. Felt more than heard his chuckle under her cheek, which was on his chest.

"Please?"

Sighing, knowing she couldn't refuse this man anything, Alaska opened her eyes slightly and tilted her head back just enough to see his face. His beard had grown a little in the short amount of time she'd been with him. She had the urge to lift a hand and rub his cheek, to see if the hair there was scratchy or soft, but she found she didn't have the energy.

"Your head still hurt?" he asked.

She nodded.

One of his hands came up, and he ran his thumb over her temple gently. "When we get to The Refuge, I'll have Pipe come and look you over. He was his team's medic, and the closest thing we have to a doctor."

Alaska didn't respond, too lost in her thoughts, trying to decide if his eyes reminded her more of the waters in the Caribbean or the blue sky over the Alps.

"Right...so here's what's going to happen. Tonka's picking us up at the airport, and he'll bring us back to The Refuge. While you're showering, I'll grab something for us to eat. We'll have dinner in my cabin, then you can rest. I'm sure you'll feel a lot better in the morning. I'll introduce you to the rest of the guys tomorrow. Okay?"

The only thing that registered was that Drake was going to leave her alone while he went to get dinner. The thought of being alone was absolutely terrifying. She could be grabbed, and she knew, just *knew* if she was taken again, she wouldn't be as lucky the second time.

She grasped his wrist with both hands and shook her head. Every violent shake made her migraine worse, but she couldn't care.

"Stop, Alaska," Drake ordered. "You're hurting yourself. What's wrong?"

"Don't leave me," she whispered harshly, suddenly afraid the Russian man would hear her. One part of her knew the man was dead; Drake had said so, and she could trust him. But another part was sure it was a ruse. That he'd tricked Drake and his friends. The evil monster was simply waiting until she was alone to make his move. She couldn't forget the determination in his gaze to get her to the buyer in China. How happy he was with the amount of money he was being paid to deliver her.

Drake stared at her for a moment, then nodded. "You'll be safe at The Refuge, Al. You think I'm gonna let anyone put their hand on you again? Not gonna happen. Not only that, but Tonka, Spike, Pipe, Owl, Stone, and Tiny won't allow it either. When you're in my cabin, you are absolutely safe, whether I'm there or not."

Alaska shook her head again. "I'm not! He'll find me. Put me back in that box!" she insisted. Her memories threatened to overwhelm her, but Alaska fought hard. She needed to make Drake understand.

"I can bring food to your cabin," Tiny said softly.

Drake didn't take his eyes from hers, just nodded. "Thanks. All right, Al, I'll stay while you get cleaned up."

"Clothes?" Tiny asked.

Alaska didn't pay attention to Drake's response. She was too relieved that he wasn't going to leave her. She *did* want a shower. Needed to wash the filth off. There hadn't been time between her rescue, her interview, and getting on a plane. She knew she smelled. She also knew she shouldn't care, given what she'd been through. But she did. She needed to get clean.

Her eyes closed once more, and when Drake's arms didn't drop from around her, she did her best to relax. Tomorrow she'd be stronger. Tomorrow, she'd put on her big girl panties and get on with her life. But for right now, all she could do was hold on to the one person she'd looked up to for decades.

For the rest of the trip, Alaska kept her eyes shut, trusting Drake to get her where she needed to go. When she stumbled after exiting the plane, he picked her up. The feeling of being carried was foreign. She wasn't a small woman. She wasn't exactly large either. She was simply average. None of the few men she'd dated had ever picked her up like this. They weren't strong enough. But of course, her Drake was.

Deep down, Alaska knew she shouldn't be thinking of him as "hers." Eventually she'd be back to her normal self, and she'd have to get down to the business of figuring out her life. Getting her stuff sent from overseas back to the States, finding a job, opening a bank account...all those mundane little things. For the moment, she was content to let Drake take over.

She felt the vehicle moving under her as they made their way toward The Refuge, but again, Alaska felt disconnected. She had a feeling she should be worried about her current apathy, but she couldn't muster the energy. She was tired, so damn tired, yet she couldn't sleep. She'd be too vulnerable. The Russian or his buyer could get to her if she let down her guard.

The car stopped, and Alaska heard voices around them when Drake exited the vehicle, still cradling her in his arms.

"Is she all right?"

"She will be."

"What do you need from us?"

"Pipe, can you come with us to my cabin? Her head hurts, and I think it's just everything catching up to her, but I want to be sure."

"Of course."

"Everything okay with the guests?"

"Yeah."

"Good. Where's Mutt?"

"He's been staying with me at night, but morosely sitting on your deck during the day. He's gonna be thrilled you're home."

"You want me to call Henley?" an unfamiliar voice asked.

"Tiny's got it. I'm going to play things by ear. See how she is in the morning."

"If you need anything, we're gonna be pissed if you don't tell us."

"I will. Promise. Right now, she just needs sleep. And to feel safe."

"She's safe here."

Alaska didn't know the men who were talking, but she could hear how relaxed Drake was as he spoke to them. He didn't tense up, didn't sound apprehensive in the least. If he trusted them, so could she. Besides, she'd looked at the picture of Drake with his friends and fellow Refuge owners so many times, she could picture them all in her mind as they spoke. She didn't know who was who, of course, but it was still a comfort to feel as if she somehow already knew them.

"She looks done in," the man with the English accent said.

Absently, Alaska realized it must be Pipe speaking. He'd been in the SAS, the British equivalent of special forces. She'd looked up his branch on the internet and had been impressed with what she'd read.

"She is. I'm gonna take her home now," Drake said.

"I'll be there in a few with something to eat," Tiny offered.

"Appreciate it."

Then they were moving again.

"She also seems out of it," Pipe observed as they walked. "How long has she been that way?"

"Most of the trip. The plane...wasn't good. We found her in an eight-foot by two-foot space behind a hidden wall in a Conex container. All that was in there was a fucking bucket to piss in and a contraption on the wall that held water, and she had to drink out of a tube like a damn gerbil," Drake growled.

Alaska tensed at the anger in his voice.

"Sorry, honey," he soothed in the calming tone she'd come to crave.

"Right, so she's probably hungry, dehydrated, and I'm guessing after all that time in the dark, her eyes hurt."

Alaska had the fleeting thought that Pipe was probably a damn good medic. He'd known her for minutes, and after hearing very little about her ordeal, had accurately summed up her condition.

"Yeah," Drake agreed.

The men didn't speak for a long moment, the only sound their footsteps on the ground as they walked. Then a dog barked.

"Hey, Mutt! I know, buddy. I'm home. I need to get Alaska inside and comfortable before I can pet you. Hang on..." He chuckled, and Alaska felt what had to be Drake's dog sniffing her legs as she was carried into his cabin.

She tensed, waiting for Drake to put her down, for his arms to let her go, but to her surprise, he sat on something and kept her on his lap. The cushion next to her sank, and she felt a wet tongue sweep across her cheek.

It was impossible to keep her eyes closed after that, so she opened them slightly, relieved that the lights in the cabin hadn't been turned on. It was still light enough outside to see just fine, but no sunlight shone through the many windows all around them.

She was on a couch, sitting sideways on Drake's lap, and she had time to see a TV, a coffee table, a recliner, and a bookshelf before the dog put his face in hers once more.

It was impossible to tell what kind of dog Mutt was, but Alaska got an impression of long legs, a happy sort of smile, and lots of white and tan fur before the dog had somehow wormed its way between her and Drake. Mutt was probably around thirty pounds or so, not huge, but definitely not a little lap dog either.

To Alaska's surprise, the dog didn't turn to Drake, trying to commandeer his attention. Instead, he turned toward *her*, putting his head on her shoulder.

Alaska's arm fell from Drake's neck to close around the dog. She still gripped the material of Drake's shirt in one hand, even as she held the dog with the other. She could feel Mutt's fast heartbeat against her chest and his warm doggy breaths against her neck. He didn't move, seemed content to simply snuggle against her.

Emotion clogged Alaska's throat but she ruthlessly held back her tears. She couldn't fall apart. Not again.

"So that's how it is, buddy?" Drake asked with a small chuckle. "I guess I can't blame you. She's pretty amazing."

It took Alaska a second to realize he was talking about her. She wasn't amazing. She was a *secretary*, for crying out loud. One who never held a job longer than a couple years. She didn't talk to her mother anymore. Hell, didn't even know where the woman was right now. And she'd somehow managed to get herself kidnapped by a lunatic who'd wanted to sell her into sexual slavery.

She definitely wasn't amazing. Not even close.

Alaska shook her head and lowered her chin, burying her nose in the soft fur of Mutt's neck. He smelled like…outside. Dirt, pine, and hound. It shouldn't have been a comforting smell, but still was.

Somehow, Pipe managed to give her a cursory exam even as she sat on Drake's lap and with Mutt in her arms. He declared her to be dehydrated, but with sleep and food, should feel more like herself in a few days.

Alaska allowed herself to fall back into the fog that had enveloped her earlier. It was easier to let Drake take care of everything and not worry about having to think. She vaguely heard Pipe leave, and for another few minutes, Drake sat on the couch with her in his arms, not moving or speaking.

But all too soon for Alaska's liking, he said, "We need to get you in the shower. Mutt, off."

The dog in her arms turned his head, gave her ear a lick, then jumped down.

"Come on, Al, you'll feel better after you get clean."

She wasn't sure about that, but since it was Drake asking her to move, she did. He kept an arm around her waist as he walked her down a short hallway to a bathroom. He sat her on the toilet, reached over, and turned on the water in the shower. He grabbed a towel from a small cabinet and put it over a rack on the wall. Then he pulled open a drawer and took out a toothbrush still in a wrapper. He opened it and placed it on the counter. Finally, he squatted in front of her.

"Al?"

She stared at him. Alaska felt as if she was watching herself from somewhere high above.

"Are you with me?"

After a moment, she nodded.

"I need you to get in the shower. Wash your hair. Use my soap. I'll grab some sweats of mine you can put on afterward. Is that okay?"

She nodded again.

But Drake didn't move from his spot in front of her. He reached out and put his palm on her cheek. He was warm, and the calluses on his hand felt familiar and comforting. "You're safe here. Okay?"

She nodded a third time.

Drake sighed. "Are you gonna drown if I leave you on your own?"

Alaska frowned slightly and shook her head.

"Good. I'll be right outside the door if you need me. But I know you can do this. You'll feel so much better afterward. I swear."

Alaska watched him stand and leave the room. For a split second, she panicked. She hadn't been alone since her rescue from that metal box. Her breathing sped up and her heart began to beat out of her chest.

Drake returned with a pile of clothes. He put them on the counter next to the toothbrush and silently held out his hand.

Alaska knew she was falling apart at the seams—and hated it. She put her hand in his and let him pull her to her feet.

"You're killing me, honey. You're stronger than that asshole thought you were. He picked the wrong woman to fuck with. You outsmarted him by calling me and using our code. I'm sorry I didn't get there faster—but you won, Al. *You won*. He's dead, and he can't kidnap any other women. Okay?"

His words penetrated the layer of ice that seemed to surround her. She needed to be stronger. Needed to be like Drake had been when he'd lost all his friends on that mission all those years ago. She nodded.

She liked seeing the relief in his eyes at her agreement. Licking her lips, she said quietly, "I've got this."

"Damn straight, you do," Drake said. Then he leaned in and kissed her forehead. His lips were warm against her skin, and it was all Alaska could do not to throw herself back into his arms. But then she took a deep breath...and smelled herself. Her nose wrinkled.

"Again, I'm not leaving you. I'll be right outside. Tiny should be here soon with something for us to eat. Then you can get some sleep. You'll feel better in the morning."

Alaska wasn't so sure about that, but she nodded anyway.

Then she was alone in the bathroom once more.

She picked up the toothbrush and began to brush her teeth, the mundane task calming her. When she was done, she felt a surprising eagerness. She liked the fresh, clean taste in her mouth. Wanted the rest of her to be just as clean.

She stripped off her clothes slowly, leaving them in a heap on the floor and stepping into the shower stall. The hot water immediately soaked her hair and body. It felt good. Really good.

How long she stood there, letting the water pound down on her, Alaska didn't know, but eventually she roused herself enough to pour some shampoo into her hand. She lathered up her shoulder-length brown hair and a familiar smell filled her nostrils. Drake.

She'd recognize his scent anywhere.

She rinsed out the soap and washed her hair again. Then did it a third time. It felt as if she'd never be able to wash the stench of fear, captivity, and the tangy scent of metal out of the strands. She poured some liquid soap onto a washcloth and was immediately rewarded with more of Drake's scent. Woodsy, a bit of citrus, and earthy. It felt as if his arms were still around her, even though she was alone.

After scrubbing her skin nearly raw, Alaska once again stood under the spray with her face tilted up. A sob worked its way through her throat and escaped, but once again, she forced her tears back. She wrenched off the water and reached for the towel Drake had left. The sweats were too big, but being surrounded by more of his scent, and that of freshly laundered cotton, felt like heaven.

She cautiously opened the bathroom door, aware of the cloud of steam that rolled out of the room. She did her best not to panic when she didn't immediately see Drake. She took three steps into the hallway and sighed in relief when she saw him in the kitchen. Tiny had obviously been there and left, because there were several bags on the counter.

Mutt saw her first and his nails clicked on the wood under his paws as he rushed toward her. When he reached her side, he leaned against her leg, and Alaska could swear he was smiling as he stared at her.

"Come here, Alaska. Tiny brought us a little bit of everything. We've got soup, some bread our chef made this afternoon, some green beans, sliced turkey, and mashed potatoes."

He placed a heaping plate of food on the small two-person table in his kitchen and held out a chair for her.

Alaska wasn't hungry, but she obediently walked over and sat. She didn't want to do anything to irritate him. To make him ask her to leave. She stared down at the food, nausea rolling in her belly.

"You don't have to eat it all. Just a little. Your body needs the nutrients, Al. Please."

She picked up the fork and nodded. She'd eat a little bit. For him.

She didn't remember actually tasting anything, but she must've been hungrier than she'd thought because by the time Drake pushed his chair back from the table, half the food on her plate was gone.

"Proud of you, Al. Good job," he said as he picked up her plate.

Alaska stared at the table in front of her. That floaty feeling was returning. He was proud of her for eating food? God, she was pathetic.

Then Drake was back. He pulled her to her feet and led her past the couch, back to the hall. He passed the bathroom and headed into a bedroom. She saw a queen-size bed with a large wooden headboard and a navy blue bedspread before her eyes closed of their own accord.

"Climb up, Alaska," he said.

She obeyed, and soon was enveloped in Drake's masculine aroma once more. It was much stronger here in his bed. On his sheets. And the mattress felt amazing under her sore body. Sitting and lying on the hard metal of the box she'd been locked in had been uncomfortable and painful.

After pulling the covers over her, Drake turned to

leave the room—and Alaska couldn't stop a whimper from escaping.

He turned back, studied her for a long moment, then slowly walked to the other side of the bed. He got under the covers without saying a word and pulled her close.

Alaska *hated* how weak she felt. How many times had he reassured her that she was safe? That the Russian was dead? She knew it, but deep in her psyche it felt as if, left on her own, she'd somehow be taken again.

The mattress at her feet dipped, and she realized Mutt had followed them into the room and had jumped onto the bed. She was on her side, Drake on his back, and she felt the dog's weight settle in the crook of her knees. She was surrounded by warmth.

For the first time in days, she finally felt safe.

"Sleep, Al," Drake said softly. "I've been where you are. I promise after you get some sleep, you'll feel better. But you don't have to be Wonder Woman. You've survived something horrific. Your freedom was taken from you. You were threatened with some pretty horrible things. But you're all right. You're safe. I'm so sorry about what happened to you, but I'm so damn grateful you're still here. The world's a better place because you're in it.

"You said that to me...remember? Back in the hospital, in Germany. I haven't forgotten it. When shit gets heavy, when I feel as if I can't go one more day, when the guilt of surviving overwhelms me, I think about those words. And they make me feel better. Just knowing you're out there somewhere, happy I'm alive, gives me the strength to keep going."

This time, it was impossible to keep the tears from leaking out of her eyes, down her face, and soaking into the material of his shirt.

"I'm serious. If you hadn't come to me in Germany... I don't want to think about where I might be. The Refuge, my new friends, my ability to function...it's all because of *you*. I'm sorry about the reason you're here, but I can't be sorry that you are. Sleep, Al. We'll figure things out one day at a time. Okay?"

Gah. That was...she didn't know what that was. All she knew was that she'd never heard more beautiful words in all her life. And Drake—*Drake*—had said them to *her*.

They hadn't talked much about when she'd gone to visit him. They'd sent messages and emails back and forth about countless other things, but not about that dark time in his life. To know that her visit had truly helped him, made her need for him now seem not quite so...lopsided.

She closed her eyes, but couldn't seem to stop the tears. They fell as if someone had turned on a faucet. But Drake didn't seem to mind. He simply tightened his hand on the arm that she'd slung across his belly and turned to kiss her forehead once more.

CHAPTER SEVEN

Brick hated feeling helpless. He'd spent most of his career as a Navy SEAL in charge of any situation he'd been put into. Except for *that* day. When he'd been as helpless as he'd ever felt in his life. Since then, he'd worked hard to never be put in that position again.

Until now.

As he lay in bed, holding Alaska, feeling her tears on his shoulder, helplessness swamped him. He wasn't sure he knew what to say to make her feel better. She was crying in her fucking *sleep*, for God's sake. It was obvious she was terrified to be left alone.

He'd been worried about the blankness in her gaze. But this was worse. As relieved as he was that she was finally showing some emotion, it still clawed at his gut.

Mutt whined deep in his throat as he lifted his head and stared at Alaska.

"It's okay," he whispered. "She's safe." He wasn't sure if he was saying it for his sake or his dog's. But Mutt seemed to be comforted by his words and rested his head on Alaska's drawn-up knees.

She eventually stopped crying, but sleep didn't come easy for Brick. He had no idea why Alaska's pain affected him so deeply. Yes, he'd known her for most of his life, and he'd respected and liked her before now. But knowing how close he'd come to losing her, of never receiving another email or text from her ever again...it hit him hard.

She'd been the first one he'd told about buying this land with his new friends. She'd been so excited. Ooh'd and aah'd over every picture he'd sent. She'd even given him some suggestions about where to put the guest cabins. Even though they were thousands of miles apart, she'd been there for him. Mentally, if not physically.

The fact that she was here—in person—was a miracle. He knew it. His friends knew it. And he had a feeling she knew it too.

Brick desperately wanted to help Alaska get back on her feet. To recover from her ordeal. He didn't want to do anything that might fuck that up. Though, he had a feeling the longer she was here, the more time she got to spend with him, the harder it would be to let her go once she recovered. She was a grown-ass woman, and when she was finally feeling more like herself, she could decide to go back to her nomadic—and probably more exciting—life in Europe.

He dozed on and off the rest of the night, and when he woke up the last time, just as the sun began peeking over the horizon, he and Alaska—and Mutt—were in the exact same positions they'd been in all night. Alaska was plastered against his side, using his shoulder as a pillow. Mutt was curled into a ball in the space her legs made as they were drawn up against him.

It felt cozy. Warm. Intimate.

As much as he didn't want to move—and didn't want Alaska to wake up alone—he needed to use the bathroom. Needed to touch base with his friends and make sure all was well with The Refuge. He'd been gone for a few days, and while he knew they could handle anything that came up, this place was still his baby.

"Stay, Mutt," he said softly.

His dog lifted his head, then lowered it again with a sigh.

Smiling, Brick carefully shifted out from under Alaska, replacing his shoulder with a pillow. She grumbled a bit, shifted on the bed, but didn't open her eyes. He was relieved. Brick had no idea if she'd gotten any real sleep while locked in that Conex container, but her body certainly needed to recharge after all the stress and terror she'd experienced.

Four hours later, after hearing for himself that their current guests were all good, and after eating breakfast and talking to Henley McClure, the therapist who met with guests who might need or want her services, Brick was getting a little worried that Alaska still hadn't woken. She'd slept for over twelve hours now, and from experience, he knew that excessive sleeping could be a sign of depression.

Mutt had come out of the bedroom about two hours ago, and Brick had let him out to do his business. Most days the dog wandered off and spent his time exploring the land around The Refuge, but today he came right back inside and, after eating, returned to the bedroom and snuggled up against Alaska once more.

When Brick couldn't stand it any longer, he headed down the hall to check on her. Quietly opening the door, he saw that she was awake. She was sitting up in bed, absently petting a delighted Mutt, her stare locked on the wall opposite the bed.

Turning to see what she was looking at, Brick couldn't help but smile.

"It's been on my wall in every place I've lived since I was eighteen," he told her.

Alaska jerked and turned to look at him.

"Sorry, I thought you heard me come in," he apologized. Then nodded to the five-by-eight cross-stitch on the wall. "I wanted it to be the first thing I saw when I woke up. In those early days, it spurred me on to finish my SEAL training. To earn my trident. In my twenties, it reminded me of who I was. And now...it reminds me of my lost friends. How I might no longer be a SEAL, but what I did, the lives I saved...it mattered."

"I...How in the world did you *get* that?" she asked quietly.

"After you left my house the night of my graduation party, my mom saw you throw whatever you'd brought for me into the trash. She went out and got it and gave it to me the next morning, before I left for boot camp."

"It's awful," she said softly. "The stitches are uneven, and it's hard to even tell what that gold blob is."

"I knew the first time I saw it that it was the SEAL trident. And seeing those words...Navy SEAL Drake Vandine...knowing you had no doubt that one day I'd actually *be* a SEAL...I got goose bumps when I opened it."

"I can't believe you've carried that thing around all these years."

Brick walked into the room and sat on the edge of the mattress. Not crowding her, but wanting her to understand exactly how much her long-ago gift meant to him. "My name might be crooked, the color of the Budweiser might be off, but you made that from your heart, Alaska. You put your time and energy into making it for me. It meant more than you'll ever know. *Means* more."

She closed her eyes and sighed.

"Al?" he asked softly. Not even sure what he was asking with that one word.

"I feel weird," she admitted without opening her eyes.

"How so?" Brick asked, alarmed. "Do I need to call Pipe? Shit, I should take you into town and have the doctor take a look at you."

She shook her head and finally opened her eyes and looked at him. "No, not physically. Just...weird. Like I don't belong in my own skin. I'm nervous and jumpy, and the thought of leaving this house, this room...this *bed*...makes me want to cry. It's not me—and I loathe it."

"I hate to say this, honey, but that's normal. After going through what you did...wanting to hole up and protect yourself is a natural reaction. When I got out of the hospital, I felt the same way."

"How long did it last?" she asked.

Brick wrinkled his nose. "Longer than I wanted. But you know what helped?"

"What?"

"Coming here. Looking up at the sky. Knowing there were people like you out there who I could lean on if I needed it."

Alaska stared at him for a long moment. "I've never been an outdoorsy girl," she finally said.

Brick laughed. He couldn't help it. "This coming from the girl who calmly grabbed a rat snake? Who used to crawl in the dirt and grass while we played soldier?"

Her lips quirked up in a wry smile. "I only did that because of you," she said quietly.

The admission settled deep in Brick's bones, and it took him a long moment to respond. "Let my mountain heal you," he finally said. "I promise you won't have to crawl in the dirt, and I don't need you to save me from snakes anymore. We'll take things one day at a time. Go for hikes. Eat good food. Laugh with good friends."

"Drake, I can't stay here for long. I need to figure out my life. I don't have a job anymore. I need to find one. I have to get my stuff from my apartment, get new IDs and a bank account here in the States...and speaking of money, I certainly can't afford to stay here."

Slight indignation rose inside him. "You think I'm going to charge you to stay with me?"

She eyed him for a moment, then said, "You should. This place is fabulous. And I'm well aware that you're always booked in advance. You and your friends have made this into one of the best places people can come to when they need a break from their stressful lives.

And I know about the POW cabin too. You're all generous, damn good businessmen, and decent human beings to boot. I don't want to take advantage of that."

Brick leaned forward, pleased that she'd researched The Refuge. "It *is* one of the premier places to heal, which is why I want you to stay. I don't give a shit about money. This is about me returning the favor you did for me four years ago. If you want it, that POW cabin is yours. For as long as you wish. Free of charge."

He held up his hand before she could protest. Somehow knowing what she was going to say.

"And before you tell me you weren't a POW, you're wrong. You were taken against your will and held captive. There's a war going on in the world today against sex trafficking, and you were definitely a casualty of it. But you aren't going to let that Russian asshole win. No way. I know you too well. You'll eventually beat back that weird feeling you've got. I know it."

Brick didn't like the look that crossed her face as she silently contemplated his offer.

"What? What was that thought?" he asked.

"I don't...Being in that cabin by myself..." Her words faded off before she finished her thought.

"You can stay here with me," he said without hesitation.

"I can't," she protested.

"Why not?"

"Because! It's your *home*."

"And I'm inviting you to share it with me. You think I don't get lonely, Al? You think I'm not still fighting my own demons? I am. They're not as strong as they used to be, but they're still there. Always will be. I hate to bring that up now, when you're feeling...off...but it's true. You can learn to live with those demons and not give them the energy to take up much space in your head, but they'll never go away. Let me help you shrink them. Stay. Let the land and this place heal you."

He waited with bated breath. The truth was, having her here, in the cabin with him, would be one of the hardest things he'd ever done. The more he was around Alaska, the more he wanted her to stay. When it came time for her to move on, it would hurt. Losing her would hurt almost as much as losing his battle buddies.

But...what if she didn't leave?

What if he could convince her to stay?

His mom had told him years ago that it was obvious Alaska harbored a crush on him. A woman didn't put energy and time into a gift like the cross-stitch she'd made if she didn't have more than friendly feelings toward him. But back then, he'd been on a mission. To be a Navy SEAL. To make a difference in the world.

Sitting next to her now, he knew with sudden clarity that there was another reason he'd kept her gift all these years. A reason why it was one of his most treasured possessions. A reason why he'd panicked so badly upon hearing Alaska was in danger.

She'd managed to do what no other woman had... she'd gotten under his skin.

Brick's days were better when he heard from her. His mood lighter when he got to talk to her on the phone. It should've been obvious, but it wasn't until right this moment, with his friend right in front of him...

He was attracted to Alaska.

The revelation didn't concern or shock him. Instead, it was as if a heavy, four-year weight had been lifted from his chest.

Could the feelings she'd had for him once upon a time be resurrected? Did they have a shot at possibly making a relationship work?

Brick wasn't sure...but now that he'd identified what he was feeling, he wanted to try. Slowly. When Alaska was ready.

"It won't be hard to get you IDs and a bank account and transfer your money," he told her, knowing his first task was making her feel comfortable and safe. "And I'm sure you can find some kind of job in Los Alamos. When you're healed and ready...you can move on to bigger and better things."

Those words were tough to say, but the last thing Brick would ever do was hold her back.

"Are you sure?" she asked softly. "I feel as if I've barged into your life and you didn't have any say whatsoever."

He chuckled. "You're wrong. From the moment I heard someone was on the phone, calling me their husband, I knew it was you. And I knew I'd do anything possible to help you. Want to know why?"

"Why?"

"Because I've always felt a connection with you. *Always*. From the first time we met on the school bus, to when I saw you in Germany, to when I heard your voice on that phone line, scared out of your mind but being smart and doing what you had to do in order to help yourself. I didn't need to go to Russia, honey. In fact, I'm sure the team would've preferred if I stayed here and let them do their thing without tagging along. I didn't need to bring you back here—I *wanted* to. You didn't barge into my life, and I knew exactly what I was doing."

Alaska took a deep breath. "Okay," she whispered.

"Okay," Brick agreed, more relieved than he could put into words. "How about another shower, then we'll sit outside on the deck while we eat lunch?"

"Lunch? It's that late?" she asked, surprised.

"Yup. You needed your sleep. I'm sure the guys will trickle over to meet you, now that you're not practically comatose. Don't be alarmed if you feel like sleeping a lot over the next few days."

"Let me guess. That's normal?" she asked with a small smile.

Seeing the grin on her face made Brick sigh in relief. "Exactly," he told her. "Now, how about getting your butt in gear...I've got some more sweats you can wear until we get you some clothes."

"Are you gonna go all Navy SEAL on me?" she asked. "What?"

"You know, like yelling orders, telling me to 'hurry up, maggot, faster, get a move on,' things like that."

Brick chuckled. "Maybe. You can take the man out of the SEALs, but you can't take the SEAL out of the man."

The smile she gifted him then made his stomach tighten.

"We'll get you some appropriate bath stuff soon," he said, trying to cover up how that smile made him feel.

"Oh, I...it's okay. I like yours."

"You like smelling like me?" he couldn't help asking.

Her simple, honest answer proved just how strong this woman was. "Yes."

Brick's cock twitched, startling him so much, he abruptly stood and headed for the door. "I'll see what I can scrounge up for lunch. Take your time," he told her as he left the room.

He wanted to kick his own ass for leaving so abruptly, but the hunger suddenly swimming in his veins, the desire that came out of nowhere after hearing she liked *smelling like him*, made it impossible to sit next to her without possibly doing something that would scare the shit out of her.

She'd almost been sold into sexual slavery. The last thing she needed, or probably wanted, was his erection all up in her face.

Still...he couldn't get the image of her clinging to him yesterday and last night out of his mind. She hadn't calmed until he'd held her. And he hadn't missed the way she'd buried her nose in the crook of his neck.

Brick forced himself to think about something else —about the plumber that was coming later to check out a leaky pipe in one of the cabins, the menu for next week that he needed to review...about *anything* other than his sudden desire to turn around and go back to the woman who'd grabbed hold of his heart without even trying.

* * *

Yong Chen glared at the messenger standing in front of his desk, shifting nervously as his eyes darted from Yong to the door and back again. The news he'd brought wasn't good. Not at all. Yong had expected the man to inform him that his newest acquisition had arrived at the rail yard and was in the process of being transported to his home.

Instead, he'd learned that it was gone.

She was gone.

"Get out," Yong barked between clenched teeth.

The young messenger didn't hesitate to obey. He fled the office as if he'd made a lucky escape...and perhaps he had.

Yong couldn't remember when he'd last been as angry as he was right this moment. He'd been so excited, anticipating his newest plaything. And when he got tired of her, his plan, as always, was to rent her out to others to recoup the money he'd spent.

He'd shelled out almost seven million *yuan* for the bitch—and what did he have to show for it? Nothing.

That was unacceptable.

Yong leaned over and picked up the phone. He'd get his money back from that fucking Russian if it was the last thing he did.

Thirty minutes later, Yong was even more furious than he'd been upon learning the woman he'd ordered was rescued before she'd even left Russia.

His contact was dead...the money he'd given him gone.

Enraged, Yong picked up the heavy stapler on his desk and threw it as hard as he could across the room. It hit the wall and shattered on impact, sending pieces flying around the room. The satisfying display did nothing to curb his fury. For days, he'd been looking forward to having the American. It was easy to get

Russian, Indian, Chinese, and even Korean pussy. Americans, though...they were a bit rare. And Yong had expected his to be delivered as promised.

He sat and stewed for quite a while. None of his staff dared disturb him. Word would have gotten out that the newest "guest" to their household would no longer be arriving. Humiliation swamped him. He'd bragged about the woman. Had promised his friends and clients they'd get their turn once he was done with her, once she'd been sufficiently trained. He'd so looked forward to that training. It was his favorite part of acquiring new product.

They were always so defiant when they first arrived. But it rarely took more than a few sessions with him before they were eager to spread their legs and do whatever he ordered.

The thought of his American slut being rescued, thinking she was safe, that she'd somehow outsmarted him...made his gut churn with bitterness.

He'd paid a million American dollars—and he wanted what was rightfully his.

Nothing would keep him from claiming his property. She'd beg for Yong himself to keep her after a few sessions with his rougher clients.

That would be her punishment. He'd immediately give her to others...while he watched.

But first, he had to get her.

Finding her would be easy enough. He already knew the name of the man she'd called for help. The Russian broker's second-in-command had told him everything he wanted to know, likely scared Yong would go somewhere else for his women.

The man's name was Drake, and he claimed to be her husband. Owned some sort of business in New Mexico called The Refuge. Yong had no doubt his pussy was *there*, mistakenly assuming she was safe, now that she was in the United States.

She was so wrong.

Yong would take care of retrieving her personally.

For the first time in hours, he smiled. This would be fun. It had been years since he'd retrieved an acquisition personally, but he still remembered the thrilling rush of adrenaline the moment a target realized she'd been deceived.

He had some logistics to work out. He'd have to obtain a forged visa and paperwork in a false name to get into the US. He needed a cover story to get close to this Drake asshole. Once he'd studied the lay of the land at that Refuge place, he'd make his move. Bring his seven-million-*yuan* pussy back home and break her.

No one fucked over Yong Chen. He might not be able to kill the Russian who'd screwed him over, then stupidly got himself shot—but he could still get what he'd bought and paid for.

CHAPTER EIGHT

Alaska hadn't yet found the courage to venture far from Drake's cabin. They'd sat on the back deck for lunch. Chili that was perfectly spiced and tasted amazing. But as soon as she'd finished eating, she found she couldn't keep her eyes open. She apologized profusely, knowing Drake wanted to introduce her to his friends, but he brushed away her regrets and helped her back inside.

When she'd lain down to nap on the couch, he'd left the screen door open. The sound of the wind and the birds in the trees, and the feeling of fresh air, was as different from her Conex prison as possible. But unlike the night before, she slept fitfully, plagued by nightmares.

She finally forced herself to get up. She and Drake once more sat on the back porch for dinner. She was still wearing his sweats and had no motivation to go anywhere or meet anyone.

Drake had casually mentioned that he'd thrown away the clothes she was wearing when she was rescued, which was more than all right with Alaska. She had no doubt simply seeing them would bring back way too many bad memories. At some point, she'd need to buy new clothes. Find the energy to do more than eat, sleep, and sit around...but tomorrow was a new day.

Mutt had been her constant companion, as if he knew she needed him more than Drake did at the moment. When she wasn't petting him, he had his head on her thigh if he was sitting next to her. His presence somehow calmed her, for which she was grateful.

After she'd insisted on helping with the dinner dishes, they'd retreated to the deck once more. The sun was setting, and for some reason, Alaska wasn't worried about the vast darkness of the forest spread out in front of her.

"This place is amazing, Drake. You should be very proud," she said as she ran a hand down Mutt's back. The dog had jumped into her lap the second she'd sat down. Drake had attempted to make him get down, but Alaska enjoyed the animal's slight weight. He was also very good at keeping her warm in the slightly chilly air.

"You know, when I got the idea for The Refuge, I envisioned it being this laid-back, small operation. Where I'd invite mostly people I'd met in the service to hang out and camp for a while. It ended up so much more than that."

Alaska nodded. "I'd say. I've followed your success since you opened and you've got far more than just a vacation spot. The men and women who've visited have nothing but complimentary things to say about their stay. How it felt like for the first time in ages, they could let down their guard and truly relax."

"I think that's more the area, and not as much The Refuge itself," Drake said with a shrug.

"You're wrong," Alaska retorted. "You and your friends have created a place that caters to people who are struggling with the things they've seen and done. From the therapist who comes to talk, the way the meals are set up, the animals that are certainly therapeutic, to the cabins themselves. It's incredible, Drake."

She suddenly felt his gaze on her, and she glanced over. "What?"

"It's just...you really *have* been following our progress."

Feeling a little self-conscious, Alaska shrugged. "I was worried about you," she admitted. "When you left Germany, I'd *hoped* you'd be able to get through what happened, but I couldn't stop wondering how things were going, outside of our emails. So...I may or may not have kind of internet stalked you."

Drake laughed. The sound was low and rumbly, and it made Alaska's stomach do flip-flops.

"If anyone else had told me they'd kept such close tabs on me, I'd probably be concerned. But knowing you cared enough to want to keep your finger on the pulse of what I was doing feels good. And while we're sharing secrets...I hope you don't take this the wrong way, but I'm glad—so very glad—I get to return the favor you did for me four years ago. I hate *why* you're here, but I'm still so happy you're here, Alaska. Even though we haven't spent more than a few days together since we graduated, I consider you one of my closest friends."

Tears sprang to Alaska's eyes, and she dropped her

head to look at her hands, which were still petting Mutt.

"Every day of my life, the first thing I see when I wake up is that gift you made for me. Knowing someone out there believed in me with such conviction when I was just a kid gave me the confidence to push through the hard times. And believe me, there have been a lot of those over the years. I'm gonna do every-thing in my power to help you get through this. I won't lie, fighting your demons can be excruciatingly hard... but I believe in you. I know you can do it."

He was killing her. To hide how much his words meant to her, Alaska joked, "You gonna make me a cross-stitch?"

Drake chuckled. "I just might. We can add it to our schedule here at The Refuge. Craft night. You can be our teacher."

Alaska rolled her eyes at that. "Right. I hate to tell you this, but that's the one and only thing I've ever cross-stitched. And it's awful."

"It's the most beautiful thing I've ever seen," Drake countered.

Alaska looked over at him, surprised at his tone, and froze at the look in his eyes. He was staring at her intently.

She'd never been the subject of such focused atten-tion before, least of all from men.

She'd read lots of books where women went on and on about seeing the lust and want in a man's eyes, but she'd never experienced it herself. Most of the time, men looked *through* her. If they bothered to see her at all, it was because they wanted something. Either sex or something related to the many places where she'd worked.

For a long moment, they stared at each other. Alaska held her breath as she waited for Drake to say something else. When he did nothing but continue to drink her in with those intense blue eyes of his, she finally dropped her gaze back to the dog in her lap.

Being the center of anyone's attention was uncomfortable. As much as she might sometimes resent always being in the background, it was what she was used to. Having Drake look at her, as if he truly *saw* her, was somewhat scary.

As if he knew he was making her uncomfortable, he leaned back in his seat and closed his eyes. "So, tomorrow...I thought we'd head over to the lodge for breakfast. Our chef does a great job of having something for everyone. From yogurt and fresh fruit, to pancakes, bacon, and omelets made to order, if you prefer. It's served buffet style, so everyone won't be there at the same time."

Alaska wasn't sure she was ready to leave her safe bubble at Drake's cabin yet, but she couldn't pretend she was simply on vacation. She had stuff she needed to do to get on with her life.

Drake continued, "Then I thought we could go down to the barn, and I'll introduce you to Melba. I think she gets more social media time than anything else here at camp. We could have the most beautiful sunrise or sunset you've ever seen, or someone could finally have a breakthrough and leave feeling a hundred times lighter than when they got here...and yet Melba will be the one thing they post pictures of and talk about when they get home."

Alaska had indeed seen a ton of pictures of the resident cow. She had huge brown eyes, a brown and white hide, and seemed to simply love humans. She also had as much of a traumatic history as most of the guests. She was rescued shortly after Drake opened The Refuge. So that connection between the cow and humans seemed to be more special as a result.

Alaska was surprised to feel anticipation snaking through her. It had been a while since she'd looked forward to something like she was looking forward to meeting a docile cow.

"Then we can play the rest of the day by ear," Drake said. "If you're tired, we can come back here and you can take a nap. Or if you want, I could show you around. You can see where the offices are in the main lodge, we could take a short hike, or we could come back here and sit on the deck and do nothing."

"You don't have to babysit me," she told him. Alaska loved that he was saying "we" and not "you," but she also felt guilty. He had a business to run. "I'm sure you have better things to do."

"I don't," he said, turning his head and pinning her in place with another look. "One of the reasons there are seven of us who own this place is so there's always someone to pick up the slack when needed. We all have our issues," he said solemnly. "Sometimes we need to disappear for a while. Head off into the forest to regain our equilibrium. Or we need to go see our families, or friends who are struggling more than we are to acclimate into society. If one of us needs to take time off, it's fine. The Refuge won't collapse. We can all do every job, and we understand the need to get away sometimes. Taking time to be with you, to make sure you're okay, is perfectly fine with everyone. And there's nothing I'd rather do than show you my pride and joy and see her through your eyes."

"Okay."

He grinned. "Okay, what, Al?"

"Okay, we can do what you suggested tomorrow."

His smile didn't dim. "Good. The guys'll all be around. Tonka never eats at the lodge, but he stops in. If not, he'll be down at the barn for sure. He's our resident animal expert. I'm not sure why Mutt here took to me instead of him. He's like an animal whisperer."

"Mutt knows a good thing when he sees it," Alaska told him. Then she bit her lip and contemplated how to phrase what she needed to bring up. She'd been too out of it last night, and she hadn't figured out a way to talk about it today. But now the sun was setting and she was running out of time. "Drake?"

"Yeah, Al?"

"Um...about last night..."

When she didn't continue, he asked, "What about it?"

"I was really out of it, and I didn't mean to...I don't..." Her voice faded, and she could tell her face was bright red. This shouldn't be as embarrassing as it was. She was almost forty years old. Blushing was ridiculous. "Where should I sleep tonight?" she finally blurted. "I can't take your bed. It's not right."

"It felt pretty damn right to me," Drake muttered.

Then he turned to face her. "You slept like a rock last night," he told her.

Alaska nodded. He wasn't wrong. Of course, that was probably because she hadn't really slept at all while locked inside that metal box. And the entire trip to the States had been fairly traumatic. But she didn't need to say any of that. Drake knew.

"Were you uncomfortable?" he asked.

"No." She wouldn't lie to him.

"Then what's the issue?" he asked.

"Drake, I don't make it a habit to sleep with men casually like that," she said, a touch exasperated. "I can sleep on the couch."

"No fucking way," he said with a firm shake of his head. "I'm happy to take the sofa. But, Alaska...it's too soon."

She frowned in confusion. "Too soon for what?"

"For you to be alone. You know, in that hospital in Germany, I hadn't slept more than an hour at a time until you arrived—unless I was knocked out with drugs. But knowing you were there, that I wasn't alone, allowed my brain to finally shut down. Before that, the only thing I could see when I closed my eyes was my friends' body parts flying through the air. Then you were there, and every time I woke up, I immediately turned my head and saw you sleeping soundly. Safe. It meant...*everything*. After what you went through, I think the worst thing you can do it sleep alone for a while."

She wanted to protest. Tell him that of course she could; she'd been sleeping alone her entire life. But deep down, she knew he was right. Even when she'd napped earlier today, she'd tossed and turned and hadn't fully allowed herself to rest.

Drake reached out and took her hand in his. "You can trust me, Al. Nothing's gonna happen. We're just going to sleep. I'll watch over you, and you can watch over me. Okay?"

"This isn't normal," she sighed.

Drake merely shrugged. "What the hell is 'normal' these days? We're all fucked up in our own way, and if sleeping next to a friend is what it takes to allow us to make it through the night without losing our minds or having nightmare after nightmare...who cares? If you're worried about what the rest of the guys will think, don't be. It's obvious to them that you're important to me. They'd do anything for me, and now you, by extension."

One part of her wanted to continue to protest. But she couldn't deny that sleeping next to Drake was comforting in a way she couldn't explain. "Okay," she whispered. "But if at any time it gets old, and you want your space back, you have to promise to tell me. I'm sure there are hotels in Los Alamos. I can always go there."

"Not a chance in hell, Al. You tired?"

She shrugged. "A little."

"How about we head inside? I've got some paperwork I need to look over, logistics stuff, and you can read, or watch TV, or whatever until you're ready to go to sleep. Mutt, off," he ordered.

The dog groaned, but did as Drake ordered. He leaped off Alaska's lap and stretched. His one front leg extended as he arched his back.

"Go do your business, Mutt. It's bedtime."

The dog ran off into the darkness, and Alaska frowned. "Aren't you afraid he's gonna run off and never come back?"

"I was at first. I'd never had a dog before. But Mutt knows how good he's got it. Besides, I think whatever happened to make him lose his leg scarred him as much as it did everyone else around here. He's never far from someone's side."

As if to prove his point, Mutt came running back toward the deck, stopping right by Drake, sitting and looking up at him with an expression so adoring, it was all Alaska could do not to burst out laughing.

Drake smiled at her. "Come on, let's get you settled."

They walked in the house together and Alaska watched carefully as Drake locked the sliding glass door, put a wooden rod against the bottom for added protection, then went to each of the windows and the front door to make sure they were all locked.

She'd never been all that worried about locking up in the past. But that was then, this was now. She appreciated his attention to security.

She headed down the hall ahead of him, and he gestured to the bathroom. "Go on, I need to grab my laptop and stuff."

Alaska didn't protest, going into the bathroom to get ready for bed. She felt a little awkward when she emerged and went to the bedroom. Drake was already sitting on the bed, his legs stretched in front of him, his feet bare, his laptop on his lap. He smiled at her when she entered and put the computer aside. "Be right back," he said, then exited the room.

Alaska climbed under the covers and sighed once more in appreciation of the piney masculine scent that enveloped her.

Drake returned and settled in his former spot. She lay on her side and watched him for a long moment. He turned his head and asked, "You good? Can I get you a book or something? I can turn on the TV."

Alaska shook her head. "No, I'm good. Is this where you sit when we talk on the phone?" she asked.

"Sometimes. Either here, on the couch, or on the deck."

Alaska nodded. She liked seeing his home firsthand.

He turned back to his computer and began to type something. After a while, his lips twitched and he looked back over at her. "Are you just going to lie there and stare at me while I work?"

Alaska nodded. "It's fascinating."

"It's really not *that* interesting," he said dryly. "Renewing the laundry contract and making sure the bills get paid isn't all that exciting."

"It's just...I always pictured you as a go-go-go kind of guy. It's nice to see you doing something incredibly mundane as working on a computer." As soon as the words were out of her mouth, Alaska regretted them. What if he took her comment the wrong way?

But to her relief, he chuckled. "Yeah, being a Navy SEAL was always much more physical. But there were plenty of reports and other paperwork we had to fill out as well."

"I know, I just..." Alaska shrugged.

He smiled, then turned his attention back to the computer screen.

There was something oddly intimate about lying in bed next to Drake as he got caught up on paperwork. Alaska wasn't sure when she began to drift off, but as soon as she did, she jerked as her unconscious mind refused to completely shut down.

"Shhhh, Alaska. You're all right. You're safe."

Her eyes popped open and she saw Drake, still on the bed. Then, to her surprise, he scooted over until he was right next to her. He picked up one of her arms and draped it over his lap. His hip was right next to her face, and her arm was between the edge of his laptop and his belly. He placed his hands back on the keyboard, his wrists resting on her forearm.

"Better?" he asked.

Surprisingly, being able to touch him was much better. Alaska nodded.

"Good."

The fact that he didn't make a big deal out of her irritational—or at least, what she *felt* was irrational—fear went a long way toward making her relax.

"It'll get easier. I promise, honey," he said softly. "Is the light from the screen going to bother you?"

She shook her head, her nose almost brushing against the thin cotton of the pajama pants he wore. She'd almost commented on them when he'd come into the room. Seeing a hard, badass former SEAL like Drake wearing a pair of soft knit pants to bed seemed incongruous. Whether he always wore them to bed, she didn't know, but she appreciated that his bedtime routine was so...*normal*.

Alaska was still wearing the sweats she'd had on all day. They were really the only thing she had to wear, and fortunately they were extremely comfortable. Drake had given her a T-shirt to wear to bed, instead of the sweatshirt she'd borrowed this morning.

Closing her eyes, Alaska moved a fraction until her forehead rested against Drake's hip. She inhaled deeply, comforted by his scent once more. There was not one hint of metal in her nostrils now. No creaking of the hard container. No muffled Russian conversation in the background.

This time, when Alaska fell asleep, she went under deep. She didn't dream. And she felt safer than she'd felt in a very long time.

Brick had finished up the work on his computer, but he didn't dare move. Alaska's arm was trapped between his wrists and his thighs. Her face was smooshed up against his hip. She'd even moved so her knees were pressed against the length of his leg.

When was the last time he'd slept with a woman...? He couldn't remember. Before the fucked-up mission that had killed his friends, he'd had sex occasionally, but never stayed the night with anyone. He enjoyed sex, but hadn't felt the need for more. Alaska was right—his life was all go-go-go at the time. Even though Bones, Rain, and the others said he was missing out, that finding a woman to share his life with changed everything, he hadn't truly understood.

And after that awful day, he'd been too messed up, too busy healing to even think about a relationship. The

Refuge had become his mistress, and he hadn't wanted any other.

Now, sitting there next to Alaska, witnessing how his presence affected her, how she was able to relax once she was physically touching him...he began to understand what Mad Dog and the others were trying to tell him all those years ago.

The Refuge might be his mistress, but she'd never given him the satisfaction Alaska had in such a short period of time.

Moving slowly, Brick shut the laptop and moved it to the table next to his bed. Then he slowly shifted downward until he was lying on his back. He kept hold of Alaska's arm, and when he was situated, it was draped over his midsection.

She sighed and snuggled into him. His arm went around her shoulders, and he pulled her closer.

"Drake?" she mumbled.

"It's me," he reassured her.

"You get your work done?" she asked sleepily.

"Yeah."

"Good."

"Sleep, Al."

"'Kay."

Almost as soon as the word escaped her lips, she was once more breathing deeply and soundly.

He hadn't missed the way she'd inhaled deeply when he'd first scooted closer. He *loved* that she enjoyed his smell. That fact did something to his insides that he couldn't even begin to explain. He also couldn't deny that every time she came out of the shower with his scent all over her, he felt an uncommon rush of possessiveness.

Many people would insist he was falling hard and fast because of some sort of savior complex—but they'd be wrong. Alaska Stein had always been just there...forever in the background...but there nonetheless. And now that he was getting to know the little things about her, as an adult? Her likes and dislikes, how unpretentious she was, how she tried to hide her fears and uncertainty from him?

Yeah. This woman could ruin him for all others.

He felt her jerk next to him, as if she'd seen something in her dreams that scared her. Brick tightened his hold and turned to kiss the top of her head.

"Shhhh, you're safe, Al."

To his immense satisfaction, she immediately relaxed.

Mutt raised his head as if to check on them both, then lowered it again to rest on Alaska's calf.

Brick had come so damn close to never experiencing this. To not having her next to him right this second. The reoccurring thought was abhorrent and unacceptable. If she hadn't been smart enough to convince the Russian to let her call him...if she'd been a weaker person, someone who couldn't survive that fucking coffin she'd been put in... If he hadn't immediately acted, if the warehouse worker hadn't come forward to tell them the number of the Conex she was in...

There were so many things that could've gone wrong, and Alaska would've been lost to him forever.

Brick wasn't a very religious man, but he sent up a prayer of thanks that she'd been spared. That he'd been able to bring Alaska here, to his mountain, to heal. She didn't have an easy road ahead of her, but she'd make it. Brick had no doubt.

He fell asleep with the weight of Alaska's head on his shoulder and the deep knowledge that he was right where he was supposed to be.

CHAPTER NINE

Once again, Alaska woke up alone in bed, though as she stretched, she felt amazingly refreshed. It was surprising how well she'd been able to rest, all things considered, but also a relief. And for the first time, she was excited to see more of The Refuge. She was still coming to terms with everything that had happened, but now...she wanted to explore a bit.

Sitting up, she saw the lopsided cross-stitch she'd done for Drake on the wall and shook her head. She still couldn't believe he had that thing, or how much it apparently meant to him.

She headed out of the bedroom and saw Drake sitting on his back deck with Mutt. He was absently scratching the dog's head as he stared off into the woods. His other hand held a mug of coffee.

Alaska ducked into the bathroom and wrinkled her nose at her reflection. She was still looking rough. Her hair was a mess, her cheeks paler than normal, and she didn't have to look under her clothes to see the bruises she could still feel on her body.

But she'd been lucky. Very lucky. And it was time to start living again...one baby step at a time. The thought of moving to an apartment by herself was scary as hell, but for today, she could explore The Refuge with Drake at her side.

Wishing she had some clothes that fit, Alaska headed out of the bathroom after using the toilet and brushing her teeth and hair. She made a detour to the kitchen to pour herself a mug of coffee before heading toward the deck.

Drake must've heard her coming, because he turned and smiled at her before she'd even opened the door.

"Morning," he said easily.

"Good morning," she returned, then took a seat in what she kind of considered "her" chair. They didn't speak for a long moment as Alaska took in the land around her. The air was chilly, and when she shivered, Drake stood and went inside the cabin. He returned a moment later with a fluffy throw blanket. He placed it over her lap, gave her another small smile, then sat back down and picked up his coffee.

"Thanks."

"Welcome."

"You aren't cold?" she asked.

"Nope."

Another comfortable silence fell between them. Then Drake said, "Tiny stopped by this morning with some clothes for you. They're on the couch inside. He wasn't sure what size you were, so he got some leggings with elastic waists and a couple different-size T-shirts.

We need to get you some boots that fit, but in the meantime, he grabbed some slip-on sandals."

Alaska swallowed hard at the emotion that threatened to overwhelm her. It was an incredibly considerate gesture. She'd come here with nothing but the clothes on her back...and she never wanted to see those again. She didn't mind wearing Drake's sweats, but the thought of wearing something that might fit was appealing for sure. She didn't even know Drake's friends, and yet they'd treated her better than the so-called friends she'd made over the years.

They finished their coffee then she headed back inside to get ready to head over to the lodge for breakfast. The leggings fit perfectly, and she chose the pink T-shirt that said *Los Alamos* in big block letters. The flip-flops were a little big but she didn't mind.

As they walked over to the large building in the middle of the resort, Drake said, "All twelve cabins are currently occupied at the moment. Not everyone comes to breakfast, but it'll probably be pretty full. We can eat inside at the large dining table, or in the sitting area, or even outside if you prefer. We try to give guests a variety of choices as far as eating goes. Some aren't comfortable around strangers, others need a wall at their back, and still others are somewhat claustrophobic and prefer to eat outdoors. When it's really cold, we've got propane heaters so they don't freeze to death while they're eating."

Alaska had read up on The Refuge, but she hadn't realized how many small details Drake and his friends had to focus on, due to their clients' needs. Most business owners didn't have to think about providing so many different options when it came to something as simple as eating.

"We'll play this by ear," he told her.

She frowned. "Play what by ear?"

"Where you want to eat."

She wanted to insist she was fine. That eating wasn't a big deal, even after what she went through. He must've seen the impending protest on her face, because he continued.

"Al, you pretty much haven't been around anyone but me since you were rescued. There's no telling what might trigger your residual fears. Maybe nothing will, and that would be great. But if something *does* upset you, don't be embarrassed about it. Every single person here, and most of the animals as well, are dealing with the consequences of whatever shit life has thrown their way. You just have to figure out how to deal with your specific demons and go from there."

Alaska didn't like that. Not at all. She'd always prided herself on her independence. Was proud of the fact she'd lived overseas alone. That she'd seen more of the world than most people ever would. But now she wondered if that independence was part of her past. If she'd end up a scared and lonely old woman who was afraid to step outside her apartment.

"Shit. Now you're thinking too hard," Drake muttered. He stopped and put his hand on her forearm. "All I'm saying is to go with the flow. If you get in there and anything makes you uneasy, we'll deal with it. Okay?"

"My shit isn't your shit," she said.

"What?"

"I just...I think I'll be fine after a few days, but the *last* thing I want is you having to worry about what's in my head, on top of what's in yours."

Instead of getting upset, Drake grinned.

"Why are you smiling?" she asked.

"You know, I've been on the receiving end of your lectures in the past. Over the phone. In emails. You always fuss about me. Tell me I'm working too hard. Worrying that I don't take enough vacations. But I've never gotten to see that wrinkle in your brow while you're scolding me." He reached out a finger and gently brushed over the frown mark between her eyes.

Sparks shot down her entire body, straight to her toes, from the simple touch.

"It's cute," Drake informed her with a wink, before reaching for her hand, wrapping his fingers around hers, then continuing their trek toward the lodge.

"Seriously, Drake—" Alaska started to say, but he interrupted.

"You can tell me not to worry about you until you're blue in the face, but it's not going to make a lick of difference. You're literally my oldest friend...there's no way I'm *not* going to watch out for you."

Ouch. She'd just been friend-zoned. That sucked. Big time. But she supposed being Drake's friend was better than the alternative. Besides, while she'd crushed on *him* from afar since she was fourteen, it wasn't as if being around her for a day or two would suddenly make Drake see the light, so to speak, and fall at her feet to declare his love.

She didn't get a chance to respond because they'd arrived at the lodge. He opened the door for her and she walked inside, mourning the loss of his hand around hers. But she told herself not to get used to that kind of thing.

Looking around, she was once more super impressed with everything that Drake and his friends had built. They entered into the massive open room of the lodge. There was a huge fireplace on one side, with comfortable-looking leather couches and chairs placed around it. There were bright rugs on the hardwood floors and the exposed rafters made the room look even bigger than it already was. The smells coming from the kitchen made her stomach growl.

Drake smiled when he heard it, and took her elbow in his hand and urged her to the left, toward a dining area. There was a large table, big enough to fit at least sixteen people, and a smaller one that had four chairs around it. Nearby was a long rolling buffet table, filled to the brim with breakfast food.

She could see the outdoor eating area Drake had told her about through the windows. There were several picnic tables with umbrellas and a few propane heaters scattered around the patio. A door from the dining room gave guests easy access to the additional eating space.

There were half a dozen strangers sitting at the large table, eating breakfast and talking in low voices. When she and Drake arrived, they all glanced over and greeted them warmly.

Alaska smiled back...but it wasn't until Drake stepped closer and wrapped his arm around her waist that she realized she'd stopped moving.

"You're okay, honey. Just breathe."

She let out the breath she'd apparently been holding with a whoosh. She tried to figure out what it was about the casual scene that had gotten to her.

"All right, I'm thinking we'll sit over at the smaller table. Come on," Drake said, urging her to walk around the guests to the four-seater table.

She vaguely worried about the others thinking she was rude, but couldn't seem to muster the mental fortitude to force herself to sit and interact with them.

Drake pulled out a chair and she sat automatically. He pulled over another chair so close to hers, their thighs were touching. "Look at me, Al."

She turned her head. As soon as she focused on his familiar blue eyes, she relaxed a fraction.

"Are there too many people in here?" he asked.

"No," she said immediately.

"Is it that you don't know them?"

Alaska shook her head.

Drake studied her for a long moment before asking, "Then what do you think is bothering you?"

Alaska closed her eyes and took a deep breath. "I don't know. I guess I...I was remembering that morning. The people sitting around the communal tables and chatting reminded me of the breakfast I had before... before I was taken."

She felt his hand rest on her cheek.

"The first flashback's the hardest. Some things will get easier, others not so much. But you're doing really, *really* well, honey."

Alaska opened her eyes to look at Drake, to try to see if he was blowing smoke up her ass or if he was telling the truth.

As soon as she met his gaze, he said, "The first time I heard thunder after I got home, I had a meltdown. I dove under a table at the VA hospital and started yelling for everyone around me to take cover." He shrugged as if he wasn't embarrassed in the least about sharing what had to be a difficult memory. "So trust me when I tell you that you're doing an amazing job. Okay?"

"Okay," she whispered.

"Hey," a deep voice said softly.

Turning, Alaska saw Pipe standing nearby. He was the one she'd dubbed "the biker guy." He had tattoos covering almost every inch of his arms and what she could see of his chest. He also had longish hair, and a much longer beard than any of the other guys. If she'd met him in a bar, she probably would've been wary, but since he was one of Drake's friends, she relaxed.

"You good?" he asked Alaska.

"Yeah."

"Want me to grab you something from the buffet?"

Oddly soothed by his British accent, Alaska opened her mouth to decline, but Drake beat her to it. "Thanks, man. I'm thinking a little bit of everything? I'll eat anything she doesn't."

Pipe nodded. "No problem. Be back."

The second he turned, Alaska frowned at Drake. "I'm not an invalid. I could've gotten my own breakfast."

"I know. But there's no need to prove to any of us around here how tough you are. We're already well aware."

Alaska wanted to argue. But when she started to, Drake put a finger over her lips.

"Let me...let *us*...pamper you a bit, Alaska. There will be lots of opportunities to exert your independence. But this is your first foray back into the world. Sometimes it's better to take baby steps than charge back into life."

Alaska swallowed the retort that had been on the tip of her tongue. It actually felt really good to be taken care of by Drake and his friends. From the clothes, to Pipe looking after her health when she'd first arrived, to him offering to get their breakfast.

She nodded and was rewarded with Drake's smile. "Thanks, Al."

He hadn't taken his other hand from her face the entire time they were talking, and when he finally sat back in his chair, Alaska had to hold back the sigh of disappointment that he wasn't touching her anymore.

She'd never been the kind of woman to crave human contact. In the years before she'd left home, her mom had basically stopped touching her with affection at all. She was either too drunk or high to even remember she had a daughter, much less give her hugs or tell her how much she loved her. And other than a few boyfriends she'd had over the years, she was never really touched by anyone, even casually.

Drake seemed incredibly demonstrative, touching her more than she'd been in years. It felt good. Too good.

"Here you go," Pipe said.

Alaska was so lost in thought, she jerked in surprise, and Drake put a hand on her thigh and murmured, "Easy, Al."

Swallowing hard, she looked up at Pipe and offered a

small smile. But it quickly morphed into an open-mouthed stare at the two plates the man had placed on the table in front of her and Drake.

"Holy crap! You can't truly expect us to eat all that."

Both Drake and Pipe laughed.

"Didn't know what you'd prefer, so like Brick asked, got a bit of everything. Don't worry, anything you guys don't finish will be fed to the goats. They love it when people's eyes are bigger than their stomachs."

"Will you sit with us?" Alaska invited tentatively.

"Sure. I'll be back," he said as he turned to go fill a plate for himself.

"You don't have to be polite," Drake said when he was out of earshot. "If you need to eat by yourself, everyone here will understand."

"I don't. Besides, I've met Pipe...and you trust him. And I know I'm not in that hotel in St. Petersburg."

"No, you aren't. But if at any time you need space, just let me know. Or *don't* let me know, and just get up and head outside. I'll figure it out."

Pipe returned with one of the other owners of The Refuge at his side.

"I'm Owl. May I join you?" the newcomer asked.

Both Drake and Pipe looked at her to answer his question.

"Of course," Alaska told him.

Owl sat, then said, "There's no 'of course' about it. It's impossible to know what might trigger someone. The color of my hair could set you off if it reminds you of someone else," he said with a shrug.

"It doesn't," Alaska reassured him. But she under-stood what he meant. Once again, she was impressed by how incredibly intuitive these men were. They weren't just running a resort, they were truly doing everything possible to help other men and women who'd been through difficult traumas.

The other owners of The Refuge trickled into the room at different times as they ate. They all made a point to come over, introduce themselves to her, tell her how glad they were that she was all right, and to check in with their buddies. It was obvious how much the guys liked and genuinely respected each other.

After the others sat at the big table with the guests, Owl turned to Alaska and said, "You don't seem to have a problem remembering our names."

She shrugged. "I've always been pretty good with names and faces. It kind of goes hand in hand with being an admin assistant. You know, so I can greet customers by name...and so I can remember who was a pain in the butt in the past, in order to be extra saccharine sweet when I talk to them again."

"I'm not sure that completely explains how you know who everyone is. This is the first time you're meeting Stone, Spike, and Owl. I know I told you their names when you asked, after seeing that picture in my cabin from our opening day, but still," Drake said.

Why did he have to be so observant? Alaska knew she was blushing. "There's that picture of all you guys on The Refuge's website," she said as nonchalantly as possible.

Both Drake and Pipe's mouths curled upward.

"So you stalked us," Pipe said.

"No! Of course not," Alaska protested. "I just have a good memory." No way was she admitting she'd saved the picture—going so far as to print it out and tack it to the wall behind her computer.

"Well, I'm impressed," Drake said.

Alaska snorted. "It's not like you're hard to remember. For starters, Pipe, you don't exactly look like the others with your biker-guy vibe going on."

"And you said that Tiny reminded you of that guy in that eighties movie," Drake reminded her.

"Yes. And of course, I already know *you*," Alaska said with a nod to Drake. "Stone's the one with glasses, and Owl reminds me of Ed Sheeran. That only leaves Tonka and Spike. I *do* kind of get them mixed up, even though Tonka was our ride from the airport. I wasn't at my most...aware," she finished feebly.

All the men made murmured sounds of assurance.

"But mostly...you're all memorable. I mean, you guys aren't exactly hard on the eyes," Alaska said as she poked at the eggs on her plate. "I wouldn't be surprised if women wanted to come here just so they could get a glimpse of the hot owners."

Drake, Owl, and Pipe all shared looks, and it was Alaska's turn to smile. "Let me guess. That's happened."

Pipe shrugged. "Maybe. But it's not like any of us are looking for a wife. The women who *have* arrived with high hopes left pretty disappointed."

"We made an agreement to never get involved with a guest," Drake told her.

"It could get messy, and we vowed never to let our private lives interfere with the business," Owl added.

Alaska nodded, but deep down, the hope that she might somehow be able to get Drake to look at her as something more than just an "old friend" died a fiery death.

"For the record," Drake said nonchalantly, "you aren't a guest."

Alaska's gaze flew to his. Drake stared right back.

"Right," Pipe finally said with a grin. "You're his wife."

Alaska choked on the bite of egg she'd been in the process of swallowing.

"Right, Brick?" he said, still grinning.

"Pipe was the one who contacted me when you called," Drake told her.

Ah. Right. "It was the only thing I could think of to alert you that something was wrong," she explained quietly.

"It was perfect, and so smart," Drake reassured her. "I immediately knew it was you on the phone and that you needed me."

"That's right. Brick told us how you got in to see him in Germany by telling everyone you were his fiancée," Owl added.

Alaska swallowed. "I'm sure they were wondering what the hell was wrong with Drake when they saw plain ol' me," she said, blushing furiously.

"There's nothing plain about you," Drake countered.

"Agreed," Pipe chimed in. "From your chestnut hair, to that spark of intelligence in those big doe eyes, to that backbone of steel...I'd say you're as far from plain as someone can get."

Alaska shook her head. She appreciated them trying to make her feel better. But she knew what she was and what she wasn't.

Just then, a loud crash sounded on the other side of the room, making her jump. There was a flurry of movement, and she realized two of the people sitting at the guest table had stood up so fast, their chairs hit the floor behind them with a bang. Another had fallen into a crouch next to the table...and the woman who'd dropped a plate of food was looking down at it with a horrified expression on her face.

"I've got the woman," Pipe said quietly as he stood.

Stone and Spike were already talking to the two people who'd knocked over their chairs. Both looked on edge, and it seemed to Alaska that if they'd had weapons, they would've been shooting by now. Tonka was kneeling by the man still crouched behind his seat.

Drake put a comforting hand on her leg once more. "You okay?" he asked.

Alaska looked at him. "Why wouldn't I be?"

"Loud noises like that can set some people off. Aggravates their PTSD."

She nodded in understanding. "I'm fine."

"Good," Drake said with a nod. "You want to go down to the barn and meet the animals and take a walk?"

"You don't need to stay?" she asked, gesturing to the room behind him with her head.

"No, the others have things under control. We try not to make a big deal out of it when something like this happens. I'm betting the guests will bounce back quickly. Unfortunately, they're kind of used to reacting like this...at least here, they won't get stared at and treated as if there's something wrong with them."

He wasn't wrong. Even now, the guests who'd had the bad reactions were sitting back down at the table.

"Then yes, I'd love to meet this Melba I've read so much about online," Alaska told him.

Drake nodded and picked up their breakfast plates. He brought them over to a small table near the doorway and scraped their uneaten food into one bin and put the plates in another.

Tiny was now cleaning up the broken dish and spilled food. They ran into Tonka on their way out the door.

"We're headed to the barn," Drake told him.

"I'm just going down to feed them," Tonka said. "You want to help?" he asked Alaska.

She smiled and nodded enthusiastically.

"Warning, the goats will try to eat anything they get their mouths near. The food, your fingers, your shirt..." Tonka told her.

"Thanks for the warning."

The three of them headed toward the barn. It was as large as the lodge itself. Painted red and boasting a large fenced-in area behind it. Since Alaska had read up on the place, she knew they offered trail rides with the horses, and they'd gotten Melba when a large fire had broken out at a nearby farm, and her owner no longer wanted her after it was obvious she had some trauma after being rescued from the burning building. The goats had been taken in when the ranch they were living on was sold, and they'd been left behind to starve. All the various cats had either been dumped in the area or been brought in to help control the mouse situation in the barn.

Drake seemed content to let her and Tonka talk about the animals and their routines. But he was never farther than inches away. Instead of feeling suffocated, Alaska felt safe. She knew there was no way she would've if she'd been out here by herself. Even with Drake so near, she couldn't help but think of all the places someone could hide, then jump out and grab her. It was stupid. She wasn't in Russia anymore. No one was lurking around, trying to kidnap her. Still, she couldn't seem to shake the feeling.

But with Drake there, she managed to keep the panic at bay.

Refusing to think about what would happen when it came time to leave and get on with her life, Alaska did her best to concentrate on the feeding instructions Tonka was giving her on the various animals.

CHAPTER TEN

Brick kept a close eye on Alaska. For the most part, she seemed to be enjoying herself with the animals. She giggled when Melba laid her big cow head against her shoulder and moaned as Alaska scratched under her chin. She cooed over the goats...until they started to nibble on her shirt. Most of the cats kept their distance, but the horses were happy for the extra carrots she offered with a smile.

He also noted the way her eyes were constantly on the move. Constantly scanning her environment for danger. He couldn't blame her. Brick still did the same, even years after the explosion that had ended his SEAL career and killed his friends.

But he didn't like seeing the fear in her eyes every time her gaze darted around the space. He knew from experience that would fade with time, but for now, he'd do what he could to help calm her fears.

After spending two hours in the barn with the animals, it was time to leave Tonka to his chores. He'd been surprisingly patient with Alaska, which Brick appreciated. His friend wasn't known for being all that friendly with the guests. He was amazing with the animals, far more comfortable with them than people. But Tonka hadn't seemed irritated with Alaska's questions, and was far more verbose than normal. He'd even let her help with a couple chores, which was extremely unusual.

Alaska seemed to have a way with people *and* animals.

All of his friends had known about her prior to her ordeal. Knew she was one of Brick's dearest friends. He'd told them the story of how she'd barreled into his hospital room in Germany, how she'd done wonders for helping him get his head on straight as he began his new life, post-Navy SEALs. He supposed all the stories he'd told about her over the years made them feel as if they knew her a bit. And Brick was thankful. He loved seeing the men he respected most in this world getting along with his Alaska.

"You want to go for a walk?" he asked as they exited the barn.

She nodded, then scrunched up her nose and looked down at her feet, holding one up. "I'm in flip-flops though."

"Shit. I forgot. You think you're up for a trip into town to pick up some things? There isn't a mall or anything like that, but they've got a few shops that sell hiking gear, and we can go to the box store and get some other stuff to tide you over until your things arrive."

"Until my things arrive?" she asked in confusion.

"Yeah. I'm not sure how long it'll take for your stuff to get here, but there are people at your apartment packing up as we speak."

"There are? What the heck, Drake?"

Brick loved that she called him by his real name. Pretty much only her and his mom called him Drake. "I haven't had a chance to tell you," he told her with a shrug.

Alaska put her hands on her hips and frowned. "What if I didn't *want* my stuff packed up? What if I wanted to go back to my job?"

"Do you? Want to go back, that is?" he asked calmly. Inside, his heart was beating abnormally fast as he waited for her answer.

She sighed and dropped her hands from her hips. She looked anywhere but at him as she said, "No. But that's not the point."

Brick reached out and put a finger under her chin and gently turned her face so she had no choice but to look at him. "I just thought you'd be more comfortable if you had some of your own things around. I'm not trying to take over your life. You're a grown woman who's been making her own decisions for a very long time. But you've also been through something harrowing. Let me help you, Al. There are no strings to my assistance. When the time is right, and you're ready, I'll help you go wherever you want. If that's back to Europe, then fine. But I have a feeling you haven't ever really slowed down. Take this time to reflect, relax, and simply breathe."

He stared into her expressive brown eyes and held his breath. He'd never been the kind of man who liked taking care of others. He liked independent women. Those who weren't clingy and didn't come with a lot of baggage. But he was finding that he liked taking care of Alaska. A lot. She was independent, for sure, but with a vulnerability that reached into his chest and took hold of his heart.

She nodded slightly.

Brick let out his breath on a long sigh. "Good. So... shopping? Then a short hike? I'd love to show you Table Rock. I don't know what the official name of it is, if it even has one, but that's what we've started calling this huge rock along one of the trails. It's not too far from here and the view is amazing. We can either grab lunch while we're in town or pilfer something from the kitchen when we get back and take it with us."

"Sounds good," she said quietly. "Drake?"

"Yeah, Al?"

"Thanks. For everything. I mean it. I would've been in big trouble if you hadn't figured out where I was and gotten me out of there."

"You're welcome," he said simply. Then, not wanting her to get bogged down in bad memories, he said, "You want to drive?"

Alaska blinked in surprise. "Really?"

"Nope. No one drives my baby but me," he said with a grin.

She rolled her eyes. "You're such a guy."

"I am," he agreed. Then he reached for her hand and headed for his cabin. He really didn't give a shit if she drove his Rubicon or not. It had more scratches and dents than he could count. But it was reliable and fun to drive, especially in the summer when he took the doors and top off.

He squeezed her hand lightly; it felt good in his. Familiar. As if he'd held her hand every day of his life for the last twenty years. Which was crazy, as he couldn't remember ever really touching Alaska before Germany.

Despite the circumstances, Brick couldn't deny he loved having her here, was enjoying getting to know her better. And even though they'd grown up together, there was so much more he wanted to discover.

* * *

The trip to town was difficult for Alaska. They'd stopped to get her a quality pair of boots, and Brick had insisted on throwing in some pants and shirts as well. Then they'd gone to the larger big box store for toiletries, underwear, and some other clothes to tide her over until her belongings arrived. That was where things had gone downhill.

In the much larger store, Alaska was jumpy and couldn't stop looking around nervously as they shopped. Brick recognized the signs of an impending breakdown and cut the trip short. He'd managed to grab the necessities for her, but anything extra would have to wait.

He was kicking his own ass for rushing her. He knew better.

The trip back to The Refuge was made in silence. When they returned to his cabin, he said, "Go on and get changed, then we'll head to the lodge and grab stuff for lunch before we head out."

She only nodded as she disappeared into the bedroom with her new things.

It wasn't until they were finally on the trail and headed for Table Rock that he brought up the trip to town. "I'm sorry," he told her. "I rushed you. I should've just gotten your sizes and sent one of the guys to town instead."

But she shook her head and said, "No, it was good for me. I can't hide away forever. I just...I swore I kept seeing the guys who took me. I know it's impossible for them to be here, but my brain kept telling me they were waiting behind every rack or in the next aisle to grab me again."

"For what it's worth, that's not abnormal," Brick said softly.

"Maybe. But I hate it."

"That feeling will fade," he told her. "Promise. I used to feel the same way. Anytime I saw someone carrying a bag, I was convinced it was full of explosives and they were about to blow up whatever place we happened to be in. For me, it was entering buildings that was always the hardest. Basically, I relived the moment that house blew up every time. As soon as I'd step toward the threshold, I'd panic...thinking the entire thing was about to explode in my face."

Alaska looked over at him shyly. "Really? You aren't saying that just to make me feel better?"

"Really," he said. "Still to this day, I sometimes have to close my eyes as I step through a door." Brick realized she was the first person he'd admitted that to, other than his therapist. But instead of embarrassing, it felt freeing.

"The brain is an amazing thing. It can help us solve complicated mathematical equations and play intricate musical pieces, but it can also be our worst enemy. It can take a split second of our lives and replay it over and over, and no matter how much we try to forget, or retrain our brain, sometimes that never happens. But you'll learn to make it work *for* you. I'm not saying you'll never be able to walk into a crowded store without constantly looking over your shoulder, but at the same time, maybe being a little more aware of your surroundings isn't a bad thing.

"I've been able to train my brain to allow me to walk into a building without panicking but...like I said, sometimes I have to do it with my eyes closed." Brick shrugged. "It is what it is. And it could be worse. I hate that my friends are no longer here to enter *any* building, but I accept my life the way it is now. Even if sometimes it's fucking hard."

Alaska didn't say anything for a few long minutes as they walked. Brick didn't push her. She needed to come to terms with her kidnapping. He was so damn grateful he'd found her before something even worse had happened. If they hadn't been able to locate the Conex, Brick would've expanded his search to Beijing. He wouldn't have stopped looking for her. But the woman he eventually found wouldn't be the same Alaska he'd always known.

It would've taken a lot more than a trip to The Refuge to put her back together if the person she'd been sold to had gotten his hands on her.

His thoughts had turned morose, and when she spoke, Brick jerked in surprise.

Shit. He couldn't think about the what-ifs. Alaska was here now, and she was going to be fine. Eventually.

"I think it's more that I thought I was safe back in Russia. You know? The first day of the tour was good. Igor was funny, even if he was constantly texting on his phone. So when the second day came, and I felt uneasy because the other guests weren't taking the tour, I told myself that I was being paranoid. I knew the guide, and even though I was the only woman and wasn't thrilled with that, I didn't think my life would be in danger. I was too trusting. I actually fell asleep," she admitted softly. "The vehicle was so warm and the ride so quiet, I fell asleep in the damn van. I thought we were on our way outside the city to see that palace. And instead, when I woke up, I had no idea where I was and the guys in the van grabbed me so I couldn't struggle. And Igor drove away without looking back once."

"You had no reason not to trust him," Brick said.

"Maybe, maybe not. But when I was in that store today, I kept thinking about that. How one side of me said I was perfectly safe. That I was doing what everyone else was...going on a normal shopping trip. But the other side kept pointing out that I'd thought I was safe in that van in Russia. How it was a normal sightseeing trip. And look what happened. So I couldn't stop looking around to see if anyone was following me. It was discomfiting. I couldn't turn my brain off to concentrate on shopping."

He hated that for her. "I know," he said. What else *could* he say?

Then Alaska took a deep breath. "It'll get better," she said firmly.

And Brick swore that was the moment he fell in love.

She could've been utterly bitter. Enraged at her circumstances. Angry at the world. But instead, she was pulling herself up by her bootstraps. Because she was strong. Brave. Resilient.

She was exactly the kind of woman he wanted by his side. The kind he wanted to be with for the rest of his life. Someone who wouldn't crumble if the car ran out of gas or if dinner was burned. A woman who would shrug and get on with life.

But she kept talking, so Brick didn't have time to do or say anything about his startling epiphany. Which was just as well, because if he blurted out that he loved her, she'd probably laugh in his face.

"This forest is beautiful. When my mom first moved to California, back when she was still talking to me, she bitched that the drive across New Mexico was boring as hell and there was nothing but dry plains."

"Well, there are those, but there are also beautiful mountain ranges, especially here in the northern part of the state," Brick said. "You and your mom still aren't talking?" he asked.

Over the last four years, he'd learned bits and pieces about Alaska's family, such as it was. She'd never known her dad, and after Brick left for the Navy, Alaska had pretty much taken over responsibility for her mom. After high school, she took classes at the community college, worked a full-time job, and then had to pick up her mom at two in the morning when she called for a ride home from a local hole-in-the-wall bar. When she didn't call, Alaska had to spend her mornings trying to find her, to bring her home.

After obtaining her degree, Alaska had accepted a job overseas...and her mom only gave a damn because she wouldn't be able to afford the rent on the trailer without Alaska's contribution. She'd called her daughter ungrateful, then informed her that she was moving to California with a friend.

"No," Alaska answered his question. "The last I heard from her was two years or so ago. I didn't have her number or email address. She somehow found mine, emailed and told me how great things were. Then she asked for money." She sighed in disgust. "She hasn't changed. I used to hope that maybe she'd get her head out of her ass and figure out she was wasting her life. But at this point, I've realized she probably won't. And regardless, I can't be responsible for her choices."

"Surely she'd want to know what happened to you, and that you're safe," Brick suggested.

Alaska merely shrugged. "I doubt it. I'm not sure I want her to know I'm back in the States. I have a feeling her emails asking for money would come more frequently. And while I haven't sent her any money for a long while now, it's still hard for me to ignore her. So I'd rather her think I'm still in Europe."

"Okay, honey." Brick suspected she would probably always struggle over the relationship with her mom. It pissed him off that the woman cared so little for such a selfless daughter.

"What about *your* mom? Is she good?" she asked.

Case in point. Alaska never failed to ask about his mom. She literally hadn't seen the woman in over twenty years, and yet she still cared about her well-being.

"She's good. I talked to her last week. She was getting ready to head out to play bridge with one group of friends, and after, she was going to a gay bar with another set of friends to dance."

"Your mom's a lesbian?" Alaska asked, her eyes wide in surprise.

Brick laughed. "No. But she says she likes going to the gay bars more than the regular ones because the music's better, everyone's so friendly, and she doesn't have to deal with 'old wrinkly guys'—her words, not mine—hitting on her."

Alaska laughed, the happy noise echoing in the trees around them, and Brick couldn't ever remember hearing a better sound. "Your mom's awesome," she said, when she'd gotten control of herself.

"She is," Brick agreed.

"I'm sure she's so proud of you," Alaska went on.

"Yeah. For a long time, I thought I'd let her down. After I got out of the hospital I was kind of lost. But she didn't pester me to find a job or to pull myself together. She was always there with a positive word, cheering me on. She cried her eyes out the day I signed the papers with the other guys to buy this place. Back then, it was nothing but a piece of dirt. But she told me she knew I'd make it special. You remind me of her."

"Me?" Alaska asked.

"Yeah. She's always believed in me too. No matter what, she had no doubts I'd achieve whatever I set out to do."

"You're the kind of guy who's easy to believe in. You ooze confidence, Drake."

"Thanks. Although, I haven't always been confident. You should've seen me in SEAL training. I was *this* close to ringing that bell and quitting during hell week." He held up his hand, his thumb and index finger almost touching.

"What made you keep going?" she asked.

"My stubbornness. My idiocy. The thought of the cross-stitch in the bottom of my bag with my name and 'Navy SEAL' on it."

Alaska stumbled and looked over at him, her brow furrowed.

"Not lying," he said, easily reading her disbelief. "I knew if I quit, I'd have to look at what you made me and know I'd failed you. I couldn't do it. So thank you for always being there to give me a kick in the butt and to cheer for me when I needed it."

"You're welcome," she said quietly, not meeting his gaze.

Brick could see the red filling her cheeks and thought it was adorable. But because he didn't want her to be any more embarrassed than she was, he turned his attention back to the trail.

The second they rounded the next bend, and Table Rock came into view, Alaska gasped in appreciation.

"Oh my gosh, this is beautiful!"

She wasn't wrong. The rock overlooked a small canyon. There was a fairly steep drop-off near the rock and trees as far as the eye could see. It was nature at its finest.

Brick got them situated on the massive flat rock and

pulled out the lunch he'd put together. It wasn't anything special—turkey sandwiches, potato chips, bottles of water, and apples—but eating it there, with Alaska, it tasted like the best meal he'd ever had.

After a moment, as they continued nibbling on their sandwiches, he asked, "So...you got your college degree. You have a graduation party? My mom mentioned that you didn't have one when you graduated from high school."

She glanced at him with a look he couldn't interpret.

"I didn't even go to the ceremony," she said after a moment. "I'd planned to, but I got a call from our neighbor that my mom was passed out on the lawn in front of our trailer. I had to go home and get her inside, and she was...difficult. I missed the ceremony."

"Oh, shit. I'm sorry."

Alaska shrugged. "It's okay. Not a big deal."

It *was* a big deal, and they both knew it. But Brick didn't want to continue talking about such a hurtful memory.

"I took my first overseas job not too long after that," she told him.

"You obviously liked living in Europe," Brick said.

A smile formed on her lips. "I did, for the most part."

They spent the next forty-five minutes or so talking about some of the places she'd lived and the interesting people she'd met over the years.

By the time they got back to The Refuge, it was nearing dinnertime. "You want to eat at the lodge or make something at the cabin?" he asked.

"Would you mind if we make something ourselves?

I'm not super hungry, and I'm not sure I'm ready to be around a lot of other people yet."

He was proud of her for not only knowing that about herself, but being able to verbalize it. "Of course not," he said. "Anything you're in the mood for?"

"Nope. I'm happy with a bowl of cereal, honestly. It's kind of my go-to meal."

He grinned. "I think I can do better than that."

"Okay...but I hope you know you don't have to cook for me."

"It's kind of nice. I tend to eat here more than over at the lodge, but I like cooking for two rather than just one." He didn't add that he actually liked taking care of her, making sure she got something healthy into her while she healed both mentally and physically. He hadn't missed how stiff she was, after their short hike, and how she was moving carefully. It made him want to go back and kill the Russian a little more painfully, but since he couldn't, he'd channel his efforts into making sure Alaska healed as fast as humanly possible.

"In that case, I'll let you. I'm not much of a cook," she told him with a smile.

He smiled back. Being with Alaska was comfortable —and comforting. Brick didn't feel the need to keep up a steady stream of conversation; she knew more about him than just about anyone other than his mom, anyway. Having her around felt...right.

Thinking about her heading back into the world without him was painful, but if that was what she eventually needed, he'd let her go with another smile and without holding her back...by letting her know how much she was starting to mean to him.

CHAPTER ELEVEN

Alaska smiled serenely into her mug of coffee as she sat on Drake's back porch. She'd been at The Refuge for just two weeks and was already feeling better. Stronger. She'd even been back to Los Alamos, and didn't feel quite as much need to check every few seconds that no one was preparing to grab her from behind while in the store.

She'd gotten better at being alone too. She still didn't feel completely comfortable, but Mutt helped. A lot. Whenever Drake had to go off and do something related to running The Refuge, he made sure Mutt stayed with her.

With every day that passed, Alaska felt a little more normal. As far as she was concerned, this place was a miracle. It truly was a refuge, where she could regain her equilibrium and the confidence to face the world again.

But not quite yet. She was perfectly happy to hang out here and simply exist.

The more she got to know Drake's friends, the more she liked them. They had very different personalities, but still similar in that they were protective, a little bossy, and kind. Alaska wasn't sure she'd ever met a group of men who were more growly and intense, or such overachievers. All of them were dedicated to making The Refuge the best it could be, wanting each and every guest to leave feeling better than when they'd arrived.

And speaking of making things better...Drake was currently over at the lodge. He had a meeting with the rest of his friends about an overseas investor. The man had apparently heard about The Refuge from acquaintances who lived in Los Alamos and worked at the government's top-secret research facility located nearby. He'd gotten a hold of Drake through the contact link on the website, and after a week of emails back and forth, The Refuge owners had agreed to meet with him via video conference.

Drake hadn't said much more than that, but Alaska could tell he was curious about what the potential investor had to offer. The man must've been very convincing, because Drake and his friends were already savvy businessmen.

Mutt had climbed into her lap and was perfectly content to lie there and be petted as Alaska enjoyed her mandatory cup of coffee, soaking in her surroundings. She loved the sweet dog. Though honestly, everything about The Refuge appealed to her. The cabins, the lodge. The employees were all extremely welcoming and nice...even the guests had been low-key and respectful. She and Drake had checked out a few more of the hikes, and even being in the forest somehow calmed her.

She'd never really been an outdoorsy kind of person. The last twenty years had been spent in various cities. She hadn't even owned hiking boots until Drake had bought her that first pair a couple of weeks ago.

Now she could identify a few different kinds of mushrooms, and even poison ivy. Okay, that wasn't terribly impressive, but for someone who'd never been within ten feet of the vine before, she thought it was a good first step.

Her things had recently arrived from overseas, and Drake had rented a storage unit for her. It was weird to see her entire life, things she'd last seen before she'd left for vacation, all neatly packed in a relatively small number of boxes. She didn't even want to *think* about someone touching her underwear as they packed it away. Which was stupid; they probably didn't blink. But she'd make sure to wash everything before she wore it anyway.

Drake's cabin was now a little more full than it had been when she'd first arrived, but he hadn't complained even once. He'd insisted on putting up some of the pictures she'd hung on her own walls in his living area. One afternoon, when they'd gone back to Table Rock, he'd also taken a selfie of the two of them, then framed it and added it to the collection of knickknacks on his bookshelves.

Everywhere she looked, Alaska saw things from her life mingled with Drake's. It gave her a warm feeling. However, though he'd never mentioned her finding a job and moving on, she couldn't help but keep that in the back of her mind. Living with Drake was a dream come true, literally, and while she cherished every minute she got to spend with him, she wasn't counting on theirs being a permanent arrangement.

The problem was, the more time she spent with Drake, immersed in his world, the more she wanted to stay.

She knew she couldn't. Eventually, she'd have to get on with her life. Alaska had no idea where she'd go next, but she *had* made the decision not to go back overseas. While she was doing better, she didn't think she'd be able to handle leaving the US.

Bad things happened here in the States. She knew that. It wasn't as if she was safe simply because she was living in her home country. But living in a country where she didn't speak the native language worried her now, even if it hadn't before. Perhaps it was because she couldn't stop thinking about what would've happened if she hadn't been found. If she'd been successfully smuggled into China. She wouldn't have been able to communicate. Wouldn't have been able to ask for help...if anyone she came into contact with even wanted to help her.

The thought of being so vulnerable again scared her to death.

So, she'd stay here. Maybe head to the northeast. Maine sounded good...

It was about as far from Drake as she could get while still in the US.

Being near him and not being able to have him was painful. More so each day. Putting distance between them was the best thing for her. She wouldn't be even further tempted into thinking they could be more than friends.

She'd loved every second of being with Drake over the last two weeks. They'd laughed, she'd cried, they'd talked, they'd sat together in complete silence. He'd cooked for her and she'd returned the favor. He was incredibly easy to be around, and to live with...and with every day that passed, Alaska fell harder for him.

There had even been moments when she was sure Drake felt more for her than just friendship. But the last thing she wanted to do was say or do something that would prove her wrong. So she simply soaked in his affection and did her best to enjoy the time she had with him so when it ended, she'd have memories to last a lifetime.

A tinny noise from inside the cabin caught Alaska's attention. Then she remembered Drake telling her that every cabin had intercoms that could be activated in case of an emergency. She hadn't asked what kind of emergency would warrant such a thing, but hearing someone speaking through the radio in Drake's cabin made her heart race.

She quickly got up, apologizing to Mutt as she disturbed him, and entered the house. She caught the tail end of what was being said.

"...you there?"

She went over to the wall and pushed the button to respond. "Hello?"

"Alaska?"

Frowning, she recognized the voice as Robert's...the lodge's chef. "Yes, it's me. What's wrong? Is Drake all right?"

"He's fine. But he and the rest of the guys are still in that meeting. The shit's hitting the fan here, and I need help."

"What's happening?"

"Reservations for next July opened today...which means the phone has been ringing off the hook. We're always booked solid for the weeks around the Fourth. You know—people trying to get away from all the fireworks set off in their neighborhoods. They're a big trigger. Anyway, there are also people here to check out and others to check in—and Becky quit."

Alaska blinked. "What?"

"Yeah. Said she couldn't handle the stress anymore and simply walked out. I've got a lobby full of people, the phone won't stop ringing, and I'm in the middle of making lunch."

"I'm on my way," Alaska told him.

"I really just need someone to keep everyone calm until the guys are done with their meeting," Robert said.

"All right. I've got this. I'll be right there."

"Thank you so much! I wouldn't have asked if I wasn't desperate."

"Any chance you can whip up a batch of your amazing chocolate chip cookies?" she asked.

"You think that'll help?" Robert asked.

"It certainly can't hurt," she returned.

"You're right. And yes, I'll get on that."

"See you soon."

Alaska turned and headed down to the bedroom— where she and Drake were still sleeping together every night. As friends. Not as anything else.

Refusing to look at the mussed covers and fall back down the friend-zone rabbit hole, Alaska went to the closet, where she'd put some of her clothes that had arrived from Europe. Most of her "work clothes," as she called them, were in the storage unit, but there had been a few slacks and dressier blouses packed into the boxes with her casual clothes. It was too much trouble to bring them back into Los Alamos and store them away, so she'd just hung them up next to Drake's clothes.

Grateful now that she had something more professional to wear, Alaska quickly changed out of her leggings and into a pair of tailored black slacks. She chose a professional-looking white blouse to go with it, but donned her boots, because they were both comfortable and practical for the area's terrain.

She headed toward the lodge at a slow jog. Mutt pranced at her side, and Alaska couldn't help but smile.

The dog headed toward the barn when she arrived at the back door of the lodge, and Alaska took a deep breath before entering. She could hear people milling around in the great room, but she took the time to stick her head into the kitchen.

"I'm here," she told Robert. When he'd been introduced, he'd told her in no uncertain terms that his name was Robert and that was what he liked to be called. Not Bobby. Not Rob. *Robert*. He was in his sixties, with long grayish hair he kept pulled back in a ponytail at the base of his neck. He had Native American blood and took great pride in his heritage. His skin was dark and wrinkled, and he frequently wore chunky turquoise jewelry.

He was a bit eccentric—and made some of the best food Alaska had ever eaten.

He glanced over and she could instantly see the relief on his face. "I know I should've let the boys know, but I could tell they were all excited for their meeting. I didn't want to do anything that might make this investor decide not to give money to The Refuge, if he knew about the chaos going on right now."

"It's okay. We'll get it figured out," Alaska soothed. The truth was, she didn't know if she could figure out *anything*, but she'd do what she could to calm the guests.

She rushed into the lobby and was immediately bombarded with negative vibes from unhappy guests and the sound of a phone ringing off the hook. She walked behind the counter where she'd seen Becky sitting countless times in the last two weeks. When she took in the phone system, she breathed a small sigh of relief. She was familiar with it from one of her past jobs.

The first thing she did was hit the mute button on the ringer. Then she took a deep breath and turned to face the dozen or so people in the lobby.

"I'm so sorry for the confusion. Our admin had a personal emergency and had to leave, but I'm here now. I'm going to do my best to get you all on your way as soon as I can, if everyone could extend just a bit more patience. Those who are checking out...do any of you have to catch a flight?"

To her relief, everyone shook their heads.

"Okay, great. As you know, lunch isn't included on check-out day, but I think we can make an exception this afternoon. Please help yourself to the buffet while you're waiting. Robert is working hard in the kitchen to make sure there's plenty of food for everyone. And I'm sure you can also smell that he's making a batch of his super-awesome chocolate chip cookies. They're so good warm."

She took a breath before continuing. "I need about fifteen minutes to dig into the computer system and make sure everything is good to go. For those of you waiting to check in, feel free to help yourself to lunch as well. Or if you prefer, you can wander down to the barn. I promise you Melba, our resident cow, will greet you with open arms. She loves being scratched under her chin. But watch the goats—they'll try to make you think they're starving to death by eating your shirt, your pants, and anything else they can get their teeth on."

Alaska smiled at the group. To her relief, the majority seemed to be relaxing a fraction. She knew from experience that, most of the time, all people needed was for someone to take charge. To organize the chaos.

"This isn't a very good start to my trip," one man grumbled. "I thought this place was supposed to be relaxing. I'm not feeling very relaxed."

Without pause—and hoping Drake wasn't going to flip out on her—Alaska nodded sympathetically. "I understand your frustration. I'd feel the same way if I was you." She'd learned a long time ago that the best option when faced with an unhappy customer was to empathize, make them feel as if their opinion was important...and give a discount when possible. "As a small apology from The Refuge for the confusion, everyone here will receive fifty dollars off their bill."

Upon hearing that, most of the guests actually

smiled. Even the man who'd verbally voiced his displeasure.

When everyone left the immediate area around the desk, Alaska sat down and held her breath as she wiggled the mouse to wake the computer. To her relief, Becky had left so quickly, she hadn't bothered to lock it. It wasn't smart, but since it was working in her favor, Alaska couldn't be too upset.

Over the years, she'd had to learn more than a dozen different administrative programs. One of her best skills was an ability to quickly figure out computer systems. She clicked around for ten minutes, until she was fairly certain she'd be able to check guests in and out, as well as print receipts and input credit cards. She was relieved when it was fairly easy to apply discounts, as well.

Taking a big breath, she went to the dining area to find her first customer to check out.

* * *

Brick clicked off the computer and turned to his friends. "So? What do we think?"

"If he's legit, it sounds good. Really good," Spike said.

"Agreed," Pipe said.

"I mean, it's a little weird that someone all the way over in China wants to invest, though, right?" Tonka asked. He was the skeptical one of the group, which wasn't a bad thing. It was smart to have someone who saw it as their job to present alternate opinions.

"Maybe. But he's looking to invest in the US, which isn't uncommon. And he mentioned his local friend who told him about The Refuge, who thinks it has potential to be so much more than it is now," Owl said.

"But do we *want* it to be more?" Tiny asked with a shrug.

His friend had a point. Right now, they had a dozen cabins, a chef, and several men and women who came to clean the rooms, take care of the landscaping around the cabins, the maintenance on the guest rooms and the lodge...it was a fairly big operation as it was.

The potential investor, a Mr. Choo, was proposing adding another dozen cabins, a larger main building—which would hold thirty hotel-like rooms—more hiking paths, and even a few walk-in campsites, as well.

"The thought of being able to help more men and women with PTSD is tempting," Brick said. "But at what cost? One of the best things about The Refuge is its exclusivity. The peacefulness of the place."

"We wouldn't have to implement everything, though, right? We could add more cabins and the walk-in campsites, but not the hotel building. That would allow us to work with an investor but not change the vibe of the place," Stone suggested.

"But doubling the number of guests would still mean a lot more work on the back end," Spike said.

Brick held up his hand. "I suggest we all take some time to think about this. We don't have to decide anything right this second. Even if he does end up coming out here to check out the property, he might change his mind after seeing it. Even if he doesn't, we can still decide not to move forward. Yes, the money would be welcome, but when we first signed the paperwork for this place, we all agreed we weren't in it to get rich, right?"

Everyone nodded their heads.

"Right, so we'll let his proposal digest. I think we'd be stupid to turn down the amount he mentioned without at least considering it. There are things we all want to do to improve The Refuge, and having that kind of money in the bank would certainly make it easier. For now, just think on it, and we'll come back and discuss the pros and cons in a few days or so. Agreed?"

Once again, everyone nodded.

As his friends began to file out of the room, Brick looked down at his watch. Damn, they'd been in the video meeting for three hours. He hadn't meant to be gone so long. While Alaska was making great strides in her recovery, it was obvious she was still nervous to be alone for significant stretches of time.

Whenever he thought about what she'd been through, Brick got angry all over again. No one deserved to be treated as a piece of meat. Or property. And anyone who had anything to do with the sex trade should rot in hell—especially those who did the actual kidnapping.

Brick was gathering up the graphs he'd used to give Mr. Choo details about their operation, and all his notes, when Spike stuck his head back into the room.

"Um...I'm thinking you need to get out here, Brick."

His friend's odd tone immediately made him tense. "Why? What's going on?"

"You'll see. Come on."

Brick left the papers on the table and headed for the

exit. The second he stepped out the door, he smelled the unmistakable scent of cookies. Which was odd, because Robert usually only made cookies in the evenings. Something about that small change in the chef's routine made Brick tense up even further as he entered the great room.

At first, he didn't see anything out of place. There were a few guests milling around, but everyone seemed at ease, which was a relief. Sometimes newly arrived guests were tense because they didn't know what to expect with a change of environment. Their PTSD could get the better of them.

"Look behind the desk," Spike finally said, with a small chuckle.

It took Brick a moment to understand what he was seeing.

Alaska was in Becky's spot behind the computer, handing an old-fashioned key to a man in his mid-twenties.

Without hesitating, Brick quickly walked toward the desk in time to hear Alaska say, "Please enjoy your stay. If there's anything you want, all you have to do is ask. Henley, the therapist, will be here tomorrow if you feel a need for her services. Meals are buffet-style and breakfast is from eight to nine-thirty. The rest of the times are on the schedule I gave you. The Refuge is happy to welcome you, and I think you'll find your stay is both rejuvenating and relaxing. I know I have."

She gave the young man a huge smile as he nodded at her, smiled back, then turned to head off to his cabin.

"What in the world is going on?" Brick asked.

Alaska turned to him. "Oh—hi, Drake. Is your meeting over?"

"Yes. Alaska, what are you doing? Where's Becky?"

"Apparently she quit."

"*What*? Seriously?"

"Uh-huh. Robert used the intercom thingy to contact me and I came to help. Things were pretty crazy for a while, but I think we're good now. And I should tell you myself before you find out later—I gave about ten people fifty-dollar discounts. I can pay it back though."

Brick waved off the crazy offer. "You aren't paying it back. But why?"

"Well, half the guests were pissed they couldn't check out, and the other half were irritated they couldn't check in. I could tell they were all nervous, either about traveling home or because their vacation wasn't starting off well. I've learned after years as an admin that discounts are the fastest way to make people happy."

She wasn't wrong.

"Oh, I also let the departing guests have lunch. And I asked Robert to make his awesome, ooey-gooey cookies. Nothing like a discount *and* amazing baked goods to make people happy. So I got everyone checked in and out, but I haven't even touched the phone lines."

Alaska frowned down at the phone, and Brick could see both lines were blinking with incoming calls. The message light was also blinking.

"Shit. July Fourth reservations opened today," he remembered with a groan.

"Yup," Alaska said. "Now that I've cleared the lobby,

I can start checking voice mail and calling people back in the order they left a message," she said, sitting at the computer.

Brick stared at her blankly. "Why would you do that?"

"Because it needs to be done?" she replied with a confused furrow of her brow.

"You're a guest here," he protested.

"No, I'm not. I mean, I *am*, but I'm not paying. I've taken advantage of your generosity long enough. I want to help. And for the record, I don't think you're charging enough. Yes, this place is in the middle of nowhere, but it's still a full-service resort. You offer food, entertainment, even therapy sessions free for anyone who's staying here. I think you could easily add a hundred bucks a night to the cost of the rooms and people would still gladly pay. That would help cover the POW cabin as well. Oh! You could also put a donation button on your website and let people send money in for that cabin, as well as to raise money for people who can't afford to come stay, but really need what you're offering here at The Refuge!"

Brick could only continue to stare.

She frowned again. "What? Oh, shoot—I'm over-stepping, aren't I? I just wanted to help. I'm so sorry, Drake. I'll just—"

"Holy crap, Brick, I just spoke with that guy who rented cabin ten—you know, the grumpy old dude who wasn't happy with anything?" Owl said. "He just bent my ear for a full five minutes, complimenting us on how The Refuge handled the chaos today. He was particularly happy to get lunch before he left, since he has to drive quite a distance today and didn't want to stop. And you would've thought we'd reimbursed him for the total cost of his stay rather than just fifty bucks." Owl turned to Alaska, smiling broadly. "You're amazing!"

She blushed fiercely. "Thanks. And now that you mention it, I think regularly offering lunch to those leaving, who might want it, wouldn't be a bad thing. It wouldn't cost that much more, would it? And it'll leave departing guests with a good feeling and a full belly."

"I agree," Owl said. "Although, we should probably check with Robert."

Brick walked behind the desk and grasped Alaska's arm. "Can you take the desk for a minute?" he asked his friend.

Owl grinned. "Sure thing. But please don't make me answer the phone."

"I'll do it when Drake's done with me," Alaska assured him.

"If he yells at you, ignore him," Owl ordered.

"I'm not going to yell at her," Brick growled as he steered Alaska away from the desk toward the back door. She didn't speak as he led her outside or during the entire walk to his cabin.

He ushered her in, and as soon as the door shut behind them, she said, "Drake——"

He didn't give her a chance to say anything else. He backed her up against the wall and did what he'd been thinking about for the last two weeks. He kissed her.

She froze for a split second as his tongue teased along the seam of her lips...then she let out a sigh and melted into his arms.

Brick hadn't planned this, but when he saw her at

the desk, heard how she'd taken over without a second thought when they needed her, he'd been overwhelmed with gratitude, gratefulness, and love.

This woman was...

She was everything. He'd never met someone so selfless. Not only that, she'd somehow instantly learned a computer system it had taken Becky weeks to comprehend. She'd managed to turn around a situation that could've equaled extremely bad reviews for The Refuge. People who'd been inconvenienced actually left with smiles on their faces.

She didn't have to help. Brick hadn't *expected* her to help, in fact. But she still had.

The last two weeks had been both the best of his life—and the most frustrating. The more time he spent with Alaska, the harder it was to keep himself from showing her how much she meant to him. He'd loved watching her slowly relax. When she laughed, it made his belly do somersaults. She got along with his friends as if she'd known them for years.

And the nights...God. Holding her was a dream come true. He hadn't realized how intimate sleeping with someone could be. They weren't having sex, but their emotional intimacy...it was so much more powerful than anything he'd ever felt. Knowing she trusted him not to hurt her, or take anything she wasn't willing to give, was a heady feeling. Knowing that each day, she was slowly healing...it made his longing worth it. The frustration of being around her but not telling her how much she meant to him.

He'd been holding back his feelings for two weeks,

and it wasn't possible to do so any longer. Not after finding out what she'd done for The Refuge...and him.

To his relief—and excitement—she kissed him back just as enthusiastically, her tongue caressing his own again and again. One of his hands went to the back of her head to hold her still as he devoured her. A small moan in the back of her throat only served to turn him on more.

It wasn't until he felt her fingernails digging into his sides and her leg hiked up against his that he realized what he was doing.

This woman deserved more than a quick fuck against the wall. While the image of doing just that appealed, this wasn't the time or place.

Brick pulled his lips from hers with difficulty, but he didn't let her go. He moved his hand to her nape and rested his forehead against hers. They were both breathing hard, and with every breath, her tits brushed against his chest. Brick's cock was hard against her belly, but she didn't seem to mind, and he literally couldn't pull himself away from her if his life depended on it anyway.

"Drake?" she whispered.

He took a deep breath. "I...I don't have the words to explain everything I'm feeling right now," he admitted.

"Are you mad?" she asked.

"*Mad?* Not in the least. I'm overwhelmed. I'm proud. I'm pissed at Becky for leaving like she did. And I'm turned way the hell on."

"I can tell," she whispered.

Brick chuckled, then lifted his forehead just enough to stare into her eyes. "For the record? The discount, lunch, and cookies were a brilliant idea. I'm not sure why Robert contacted you instead of interrupting our meeting, but he did the right thing."

"He knew how important your thing was, and he didn't want to do anything that might put a possible investment in jeopardy. If that guy realized chaos was erupting in the lobby, it might've turned him off."

"Maybe. Maybe not. But you were great with everyone. And Robert too. He can be moody."

Alaska shrugged. "He's not so bad. Besides, I think he's allowed to be moody since he's such an amazing cook."

"Agree. Now...about us."

She stiffened against him.

"I want you," he said bluntly. "I don't want to pressure you. Or do anything that will scare you. But I want you so bad, Alaska. I like everything about you. The more time I spend with you, the more time I *want* to spend. But I value our friendship too much to fuck it up. If you don't want this, don't want *me*, that's okay. Nothing between us will change. You can still stay here for as long as you want and need to."

Brick couldn't read the expression in her eyes, but he held his breath as he waited for her response.

"Drake, I...are you sure?"

"Yes."

"But you can have anyone you want. I'm not...I'm nothing special."

"I don't want anyone else, and the hell you aren't."

"I'm totally plain," she said firmly, almost accusingly. "Average. *Boring*. You deserve so much more than someone like me."

"Wrong. I deserve someone *exactly* like you. Someone generous. Fun. Easy to be with. Someone who knows my deepest fears and regrets, and isn't afraid of them. I don't need a supermodel on my elbow, Al. I need someone who likes me for who I am. Who believes in me. And I can't think of anyone in the world who believes in me more than you. I've got a cross-stitch on the wall to prove it."

Alaska closed her eyes, and Brick tensed.

"It's okay if you say no, Al. Like I said...nothing will change."

She opened her eyes and met his gaze. "All I've ever wanted is you," she admitted softly. "I've compared every man I've dated to you, and they all come out lacking in one way or another. I want this. If I can only have you for a month, a week, a single night...I'll take it. All I ask is that when you're ready to move on, please go easy on me."

"And if I'm never ready to move on?" he asked.

Her eyes filled with tears, and she shook her head. "Don't. I'm okay with having a fling with you, because my entire life I've dreamed of you looking at me the way you are right now. But don't lead me on. Don't let me think this can be something permanent."

Brick frowned. It seemed unfathomable this woman didn't know her own worth. But he had plenty of time to make her see it. "Okay," he agreed quietly.

He had no intention of letting her out of his bed, ever, now that she was in it. But if she needed the reassurance that he would tell her if he wanted out of the relationship, he'd give it to her. He had no plans of ending anything. She'd realize that eventually.

"How about a kiss to seal the deal?" he said as he lowered his head. He didn't give her a chance to agree or disagree.

She clearly wouldn't deny him. In fact, she went up on her tiptoes and kissed him back just as passionately.

Brick felt more energized than he had in years. He'd been excited when The Refuge opened, but having Alaska agree to be his felt as if it opened up possibilities he'd never dreamed of.

They were both breathing hard again when he pulled back a second time. "Now, can we talk about how the hell you know how to use our computer system?" he asked, doing his best to ignore the way her breasts filled out her blouse—and how badly he wanted to drag her down the hallway to the bed they shared every night.

"It's not that hard," she said with a shrug.

"It took Becky two weeks just to learn how to check people in and out."

She frowned. "It did?"

"Yes."

"Wow. Well, the system is a lot like one I used when I worked in France. And the phone is *exactly* like one I used back in Finland. There are minor differences, of course, but I took ten minutes and clicked around in the system and figured out how to do the easy stuff. Reports usually take me a bit longer to learn."

"So...Becky quit. It'll take us a while to find someone to replace her. Will you—"

"Yes," she said, not letting him finish.

"You don't know what I was going to say," he replied with a grin.

"If you were going to ask me if I would help out, the answer's yes," she told him.

"Thank God. I can't tell you how much we all hate working the desk. And we're not that good at it either."

"I doubt that. All the guests I've met have loved you guys."

"That's because we aren't trying to work the computer," he said with a grin. "And I'll talk to the others about the prices of the rooms. And the donation button is a great idea. We'll pay you, of course."

Alaska was already shaking her head. "I've been staying here free for two weeks. I don't need money."

"Yes, you've been here as my *guest*—and you'll continue to stay as my guest," he added firmly. "This isn't negotiable. If you do admin work for us, you'll get paid."

"All right," she agreed quietly.

"And you'll only work four hours a day."

"But, Drake—"

"I mean it. You're here to heal, not work like a dog," he said sternly. "I'm thinking you can get what needs to be done in that amount of time. I'm guessing you're twice as efficient as Becky was, anyway."

"What about guests who need to check in late?" she asked.

"I'll get Tiny to handle that. He's our go-to guy when it comes to the late arrivals."

"Okay."

"Okay," Brick agreed. His eyes raked over her face.

"What?" she asked, a blush forming on her cheeks.

"I'm just still pinching myself that you're really here. Ever since we reconnected in Germany, I've thought about you constantly. Felt as if I was missing something. *You*, Alaska. I was missing you."

She pressed her lips together tightly and he saw tears form in her eyes.

"Don't cry," he ordered. "I can't handle when you cry."

"They're good tears."

"Even so. I'm not going to fuck this up," he said, more to himself than her.

"I'm going to do my best not to either," she said.

"Right. So...you think there're any of those cookies left?"

Alaska smiled. "Well, I made sure to nab a few. They should still be at the desk—unless Owl's found and eaten them all by now. But I'm guessing Robert wouldn't mind making another batch if I asked him to."

"It doesn't surprise me in the least that you've got Robert wrapped around your little finger." Brick kissed her once more. A short, hard kiss, then twined his fingers with hers and turned toward the door.

They were halfway back to the lodge when she asked hesitantly, "Is this weird, Drake?"

"No," he answered without having to think about it. "I like you, you like me, we're already sleeping together...what's weird about it?"

To his relief, she giggled. "Right. What could possibly be weird about this?" she asked rhetorically.

When they stepped back into the lodge, it was obvious Owl had filled in the others on what had happened. Everyone profusely thanked Alaska for her help.

Spike eyed their clasped hands and raised an eyebrow. Brick figured it was best to address that now.

"Alaska and I are dating," he said baldly. "She's also willing to take over the admin stuff until we can hire someone, but only four hours a day. Tiny, if you can manage the late check-ins, I think we'll be good."

"What about the July Fourth reservations?" Stone asked.

"If Owl can stay on the desk, I'll check the messages and start returning calls," Alaska said.

"Deal," all the guys said at once.

"We hate the phone," Pipe added with a grimace.

"Alaska's had some suggestions I think we should consider, as well," Brick told his friends.

"It's nothing that needs to happen immediately," she protested.

"Color me curious," Spike said.

"Me too," Owl agreed.

"We can discuss them when we get back together to talk about the meeting we had this morning," Pipe suggested.

Everyone nodded their approval and began to wander off. Tonka had apparently already escaped to the barn.

"You sure you're good?" Brick asked her.

"Yeah. If I have any questions, I'll ask Owl," she reassured him.

"It's weird to be both pissed off and thankful for that day so long ago," Brick said quietly, referring to when he'd gotten hurt and his teammates had been killed.

"Drake," Alaska protested softly.

"I'm gonna go talk to Robert, make sure he's good," he said, not letting her dwell on his words. "I'll bring you some cookies later."

"Thanks."

Brick was equally thankful, but not surprised, that his friends hadn't said a word about his and Alaska's updated relationship status. He'd caught their questioning and speculative glances over the last two weeks, but he hadn't explained his decision to move her into his cabin, beyond reiterating that they were friends. Their non-reaction over his declaration was as good as an approval.

He leaned in and kissed her on the lips before squeezing her hand and heading toward the kitchen. It felt incredible to be able to kiss her the way he'd longed to for days now. He'd be an idiot to let Alaska slip through his fingers—and he was anything but an idiot.

Smiling, and feeling lighter than he had in a long while, Brick went in search of more cookies.

* * *

Yong Chen smiled as he stared at the blank screen on his computer. He'd spent the last few hours lying his ass off, and he felt really good about his progress. He was getting closer to getting what he wanted.

His new plan was even more exciting than his original one. Yes, having his plaything already with him in China so he could break her, sell her to his faithful clients, would've been preferable. But snatching her right out from under the nose of the man who'd saved her would be even better. Because of his vast connections on the dark web, he already had over a dozen men in the US interested in taking a turn with his acquisition...after he'd had *his* turn, of course.

He would take the bitch to California and spend a few weeks with her there. A friend he'd met years ago, who had similar sexual interests, had offered his basement playroom. He already had a soundproof setup with restraints and every conceivable device Yong might need to...play.

When he was done, when she fully understood she hadn't escaped her fate after all, he'd pocket the money he'd make from renting her out—much more than he'd paid for her in the first place—and head back to China.

He had a new girl on order. He'd return home just in time to collect her.

His clients in Beijing would be disappointed they hadn't gotten to play with the American they were promised, but he had a feeling they'd like the next one even better...she was younger, slimmer, and had natural blonde hair. A novelty in China.

Smiling, Yong stood and adjusted his cock in his pants. Soon. His time was coming soon.

CHAPTER TWELVE

Alaska had to pinch herself to make sure she wasn't dreaming as the days went by. She spent her mornings with Drake on his back porch, as usual. They drank their coffee and talked about the upcoming day. Then she spent a few hours over at the lodge, checking guests in and out and answering the phone. In the afternoon she, Drake, and Mutt hiked around the property. She looked forward to the exercise and getting to know the land around the lodge. And she was happier and more content than she'd been in a long time.

She also learned more about The Refuge every day. She'd always known they welcomed more than just military personnel suffering from PTSD. Anyone who'd experienced a trauma was welcome with open arms. But one of the more interesting discoveries was that if someone was scheduled to arrive who might have danger following them—a stalker, or an ex with a grudge, for example—everyone at The Refuge was notified. Staff *and* guests. While weapons weren't allowed on the property, Drake explained that anyone on the premises could be vital in keeping a guest safe and, of course, needed to be alerted for their own safety, as well.

If someone didn't want to be involved, if their PTSD made it impossible for them to be comfortable in that kind of situation, they were given a refund, plus a free stay equal to what they'd originally booked. To Alaska's surprise, only one person in three years had ever taken the offer. Every other guest had been willing and eager to keep watch over the more vulnerable visitors.

That alone reaffirmed Alaska's faith in humanity.

There was also a lockdown procedure. If something happened that put guests in danger, everyone was notified via the intercom system and they'd be expected to hunker down in their cabins or in the lodge. The security procedures Drake and his friends had put in place were impressive, and Alaska assumed they went a long way toward making everyone feel reassured.

Drake had initially been worried Alaska might be alarmed over some of the things she was learning about the behind-the-scenes operation of The Refuge, but in reality, the knowledge made her feel even more proud— and safer—than before.

Though she was thrilled to learn more about the business, that was eclipsed by spending time with Drake, himself. Since declaring them dating, they'd spent their evenings much the same as before, reading, watching TV, but with the added benefit of making out —a lot.

And every night, when they crawled into bed, she

held her breath hoping *this* would be the night. The night he'd do more than simply hold her.

She couldn't deny she was nervous to have sex with the man she'd wanted for years, but her excitement overrode any trepidation. She wanted to be good enough for him—in bed and out—even if she still thought she'd never live up to all that was Drake Vandine. But she hadn't lied; she'd take any time with him she could get.

He'd had another long meeting with his friends and they'd decided to invite the potential investor to The Refuge, to see if his interest still held once he saw the place. Drake had been concerned about her reaction when she learned the man was Chinese, but Alaska assured him she wasn't upset. Yes, some anonymous person in Beijing had bought her from the sex trafficker, but she hadn't even made it halfway to Asia. She would hardly hold the male population of an entire country responsible for her ordeal.

Whoever that buyer was, she assumed he was lying low to ensure he wasn't caught up in the backlash from her rescue. Besides, it was unlikely he would know who she was, or even where she'd disappeared to after the rescue. The man who'd called The Refuge that fateful day was dead.

This morning, Drake had been called away from their lazy coffee on his porch to cut up a tree that had fallen over one of the more popular hiking trails on the property. She had the hour before work to herself, and had planned on spending it relaxing, but then she'd remembered that Henley McClure was going to be at The Refuge that morning.

The therapist came to visit guests three times a week. Alaska had been avoiding the sessions. She wasn't sure why. Maybe because she wasn't ready to talk about what happened. Maybe because she was embarrassed at how easily she'd been duped.

But for whatever reason, this morning, Alaska was ready. At least to sit in on a group session and see how things went.

Being alone had gotten easier. She no longer jumped at every strange sound and the nightmares had faded away almost completely. Of course, she had a feeling the latter was due to spending every night cuddled up with Drake, but still.

Now that she was working at The Refuge, Alaska felt a duty to know more about what the therapist did, so she could more accurately inform the future guests of their options.

So, after finishing up her second cup of coffee and giving Mutt extra pets, she headed out of Drake's cabin toward the lodge. There was a room off the dining area that Henley usually used for sessions. If a guest indicated that he or she wanted a more private conversation, arrangements were made for that to happen.

Most of the guests were new since Henley's last visit, and Alaska knew that meant the session might be fuller than normal. Robert was just cleaning away the breakfast buffet when she arrived. The chef gave her a welcoming smile as she headed for the therapy room.

Alaska had *thought* she was ready—but the second she walked into the room, sudden nervousness almost made her turn around and leave.

She was *fine*. She didn't need this. Nothing actually

happened to her. She wasn't raped. She wasn't even really all that hurt. Not like most of the people she'd met who came here to heal.

She'd just taken a step backward when a deep voice sounded next to her.

"You okay?"

Jerking and quickly sidestepping away, Alaska looked behind her.

Tonka was standing nearby, frowning at her reaction.

"Sorry," she said, looking down. Tonka was nice. All the men who ran The Refuge were. She'd spent the least time around him, because he was always at the barn, dealing with the animals. He didn't tend to hang out with the others at the lodge, and she rarely saw him eating a meal there. The animals seemed to calm him like nothing else did.

"No, I'm sorry. I shouldn't have come up behind you like that," he said easily. "It's not too late to leave, you know. Hell, even after Henley gets started, you can still leave."

His words were enough to make Alaska's resolve harden. "No. I need to know what goes on here so I can better tell the guests what to expect."

Tonka stared at her for a long moment. He was tall, a few inches taller than Drake, so she had to tilt her head back to look into his eyes. His dark hair was well groomed, as was his beard. Out of all Drake's friends, The Refuge's owners, Tonka seemed to be the most...wounded. He seemed to be wound tightly and he didn't mingle with the guests, preferring to spend his time in the barn with the myriad of animals who now made the ranch their home.

It was the emotion she saw swimming in his eyes that caught her attention. The anguish she saw swimming in their depths made her heart hurt. Like the others, this man had been to hell and back. She didn't know his story, and Drake had admitted *he* didn't either, but it was obvious whatever had happened to him, it had far-reaching repercussions.

"You remind me of the squirrel who lives behind the barn," he said quietly.

"Um...thanks?" Alaska said.

Tonka's lips twitched. "The first time I saw him, he was pretty much just days from dying. Skinny as hell, two of his feet were missing, and his tail didn't have any hair on it. He was ugly as hell...and so damn pathetic, it would've been in his best interest for me to put him out of his misery."

Alaska inhaled sharply. "Um...ouch?" she said with a wrinkle of her nose.

"Sorry, you in no way remind me of that squirrel because of your looks. I was just trying to set the scene."

His words made her feel a little better. He went on.

"I went inside and got a handful of almonds I'd planned on eating with my lunch. I sat against the side of the barn and talked to him. Threw him a few of the nuts, and eventually the little guy got up the courage to come closer. I'm guessing that was because of his belly growling and not because of my witty conversation," he said with a wry grin.

Alaska was fascinated. This was the most she'd heard him say at one time since she'd arrived.

"Anyway, the little guy was obviously terrified, but so damn determined at the same time. I don't know what happened to him, why he was in the condition he was in, but even though he was clearly scared to death of me, of the new experience he was having, he didn't run away. That's why you remind me of him."

Staring at the man, Alaska relaxed a fraction. She *was* scared. It was ridiculous, really. There was nothing to be afraid of. She didn't even have to talk during the session if she didn't want to. She'd read the notes on what happened at group therapy. Henley would lead the conversation and anyone who wanted to contribute could do so.

"Is he still around?" she asked after a moment.

Tonka smiled again, and it changed the entire countenance of his face. "Yeah. I built him a squirrel condo. It sits against the base of a tree behind the barn. He's now got a girlfriend and they had babies this year. The hair on his tail grew back, he's fat and happy, and doesn't seem to mind that he can't climb trees."

Alaska grinned. "I'm glad."

"Me too. So...you staying or going?" he asked.

Straightening her shoulders, Alaska said, "Staying. You?"

Tonka shrugged. He tried to make it seem nonchalant, but Alaska could sense the tension in him. "Staying."

They walked into the room together and took seats side by side. The chairs were surprisingly comfortable. They weren't simple folding chairs. Drake and the others had splurged, wanting the men and women who came to the sessions to be as relaxed as possible, and that meant not sitting on cheap, hard metal seats.

Six guests joined them, along with Henley. The therapist was petite, around five-four, somewhere in her mid-thirties. It looked as if she had some Native American ancestry. Her thick brown hair was held back in a long braid down the length of her spine. She wore a loose, floor-length purple skirt and a flowy white blouse. The blue of her turquoise necklace stood out against the pale material.

She was absolutely beautiful—which made Alaska feel dowdy in comparison. Of course, she felt that way around a lot of women, so it wasn't a new feeling.

But as soon as Henley began talking, Alaska relaxed. She had a low voice, soothing, and she welcomed the group as if she was genuinely pleased to be there. After everyone introduced themselves, Henley began talking about trauma. How it affected people in different ways.

After several minutes, one of the guests, a man who looked as if he was in his mid-fifties or so, said quietly, "No offense, but how can someone like you possibly know what I've been through? Have you ever been in the military? Have you had to kill or be killed? Have you ever had to look into the eyes of another human being right before you blew their head off?"

His words were harsh, even if his tone was mild, and Alaska kind of understood his point. How could this woman empathize with the guests at The Refuge? She looked as calm and self-assured as anyone Alaska had ever seen. Then again, spending time at this place, she'd learned that how people projected themselves didn't necessarily speak to their experience with trauma.

She felt Tonka stiffen next to her, and Alaska turned her head slightly to look at him. He was clenching the arms of the chair, hard. A muscle in his jaw ticked and his lips were pressed together tightly. Alaska couldn't actually tell if he was seconds away from beating the shit out of the guest, or if he agreed with him.

"I think you'd all agree that there's no way of telling what traumas someone has endured simply by looking at them. Humans have gotten very good at hiding what they perceive to be imperfections from the world. It's a survival mechanism. We think if others knew how broken we feel inside, they'd probably run away screaming. The reality is, even the most put-together person may have their demons."

The man snorted lightly. "You trying to tell us *you* have demons?"

Henley leaned forward in her chair and pinned the man with a calm gaze.

For some reason, Alaska braced for her response.

"Yes. When I was ten, I was at home on the reservation with my mom. My dad was working at the casino. It was late, probably around midnight or so. I woke up to my mom's screams. I leapt out of bed and ran to my door. For some reason, I didn't throw it open, but instead peeked through the crack. I saw my mom in the living room fighting with two men. They had her pinned on the floor, and one man was cutting off her clothes, not caring if he hurt her in the process. For just a second, our eyes met—my mom's, that is—she didn't stop fighting the men, but she mouthed *hide* to me.

"I was trapped in my room, the only way out was through the living room, where the men were hurting my mom. The window in my room was nailed shut to keep out the cold and dust. I crawled under my bed, between the boxes that were stored there, and curled into a ball. A second later my door flew open, and I heard one of the men telling the other that the room was empty.

"The two men dragged my mom inside, threw her on the bed, and raped her. Over and over. Right above my head. I heard every scream, every cry, every slap of their skin against hers as they violated her for hours. When they were finally done, I heard them stab her. Once. Twice...Fifty-seven times. They laughed as they killed her. Told her she was nothing but Indian trash who didn't deserve to exist. They bitched that her daughter wasn't home, so they couldn't have fun with her too.

"After they left, I stayed where I was, frozen in terror. I didn't hear a sound from my mom, but her blood began to seep through the mattress. I watched as the stain above my head slowly grew as she bled out."

"Holy shit," one of the guests exclaimed quietly.

Alaska agreed wholeheartedly.

Henley had recited her story almost emotionlessly, and Alaska guessed this wasn't the first time she'd told it. She'd been working at The Refuge for at least two years, and had probably been in similar situations where she'd recounted her personal trauma to clients unconvinced she could ever understand what they'd been through. It was heartbreaking...and her willingness to share her pain awe-inspiring.

"My dad came home around the break of dawn. He found his wife dead on my bed and frantically searched the house for me. I didn't come out until the police came. Only then did I move the boxes aside and crawl from under that bed. I didn't speak for five years. So... yes, I have demons," Henley finished. "I'm guessing my demons might even make some of yours seem like nothing. But comparing whose story is worse isn't what these sessions are for. They're to help you understand that you aren't alone. You aren't the only one who's been traumatized. You aren't the only one who feels as if your skin is too tight sometimes. You aren't the only one who feels guilt."

"Guilt?" a woman asked. "You can't possibly feel guilty about what happened!" she exclaimed, her voice filled with empathy.

"Can't I? I didn't do anything," Henley said. "I didn't even try to get help. Maybe if I'd come out from under that bed, they would've turned their attention to me and my mom could've grabbed the knife and fought back."

"You were a kid," a man said.

Henley shrugged. "Guilt doesn't care how old you are. It just is. The human brain will come up with a hundred 'what-if' scenarios. What if we did this differently? What if we did that differently? What if we didn't stop for that cup of coffee? What if we'd listened to our gut? The reality is, what happened to us *happened*. We can't go back and change it. Maybe if we did do that one thing differently, the outcome would've been altered. But we didn't. And here we are. The only thing we can do is move forward. Come to terms with our current reality and put one foot in front of the other."

The room was silent, and Alaska closed her eyes as she pondered Henley's words. She was right. There were so many things she wished she'd done differently that day...but none of them changed where she was at now.

"For as many what-ifs, there are just as many things you did right," Henley went on. "It might be hard to admit them to yourself, because it's much easier to think about all the things you think you did wrong. In my case, the right thing to do was hide. To stay quiet. If I'd come out from under that bed, it's likely I'd be dead along with my mother. And I would've been raped. At ten. I'm not sure I would've been able to come to terms with that if I lived.

"No matter what your situation is, what you did, what happened...No matter how many times you wish you'd done things differently, the truth is...you did a lot of things right. Things could always be worse. I truly believe that."

Again, Alaska had to agree. She'd had the presence of mind to get her kidnapper to call Drake. If she hadn't done so, she'd most likely be dead...or wish she was.

"Does anyone else want to share? If you can't think of anything you did right, I'm sure as a group we can all help with that. It's much easier to look at a situation from outside it," Henley said.

Slowly, people began to share their stories. The reasons behind their visit to The Refuge. Alaska listened attentively. The things the guests had been through were all heartbreaking. But Henley was spot-on; as a group, they were able to point out things that each person had done right.

Alaska remained silent. Her problem wasn't that she couldn't figure out what she'd done right that day, it was more that she didn't feel as if she had a right to be as messed up as she felt sometimes. Guilt that she hadn't suffered as much as others around her.

Tonka didn't speak either. And his grip on the arms of the chair hadn't lessened. He seemed just as tense now as when Henley had first started telling her story. She didn't know if he was upset because he was thinking about whatever had happened to him...or because he was furious about what happened to *Henley*.

She doubted this was the first time he'd heard her story. But if it made him that upset to hear it, why did he attend the group sessions?

She was still trying to figure that out when he abruptly stood and quietly headed for the door.

For just a moment, Alaska caught a look of sorrow—and intense longing—in Henley's eyes, before she blinked and turned her attention back to the woman who was speaking.

She had a feeling Tonka's reaction was personal. He'd come to the therapy session, but hadn't spoken up. Hadn't shared his story. Was he there to support Henley? To torture himself? Alaska had no idea. But she didn't miss the way Henley's shoulders dropped just a bit after he left.

Alaska also suspected she'd seen something neither Henley nor Tonka had wanted anyone to know. They had some sort of connection...but for whatever reason weren't ready or willing to act on it.

Alaska got up and excused herself soon after Tonka left. Even though she hadn't participated in the conversation, she felt oddly lighter. She'd done some stupid things when she was in Russia, but she'd also been doing what thousands of other tourists did every day. She should've been able to trust Igor, a guide who'd come recommended. And when her situation turned dangerous, she'd been able to get a hold of the one person she could trust to help her. And he had.

Her thoughts remained on Drake as she headed back to the cabin to get ready for her administrative shift. Things were still very busy. The Refuge was completely booked through August of next year, and there weren't a lot of open spaces in the remaining months either. Not only that, but after discussing it with the others, Drake had increased the nightly rate for the cabins, and Alaska had helped add a donation button to the website, sharing a few stories from the POWs who'd benefited from being able to stay for free.

They'd already netted ten thousand dollars in donations in just the last week.

Lost in thought, Alaska let out a yelp of surprise when Mutt appeared as if out of nowhere by her side and nuzzled against her hand.

"Mutt, heel," Drake said firmly from behind.

Turning, Alaska saw Drake coming toward her from the tree line.

Without thought, she closed the distance and wrapped her arms around him. To her relief, Drake immediately held her tightly.

"What's up? Are you okay?"

He was always so concerned about her. For someone

who'd gone years and years without anyone truly caring about her well-being, it felt good.

"I'm just so grateful I'm here. That you came for me," she said softly.

Drake's arms tightened. "You don't have to be grateful for me coming when you needed me."

"I do," she insisted. "If you hadn't believed me. Or if you'd hesitated. Or if you didn't have the connections you do...I wouldn't be here right now."

"What's brought this on?" he asked softly.

"I sat in on Henley's session this morning," she told him.

She could feel his muscles tensing. He shifted until he got a finger under her chin and lifted her head to see her eyes. "And?"

"And nothing. It was good. Just made me think. The best decision I made that day was convincing that guy that I was married and that you'd pay twice what he was charging his client to get me back. Of course, he was an asshole who'd planned to take your money *and* the other guy's too, but still...it was a good decision on my part."

"Yes, it damn well was. I can't think about what would've happened if you hadn't," Drake admitted.

Alaska shuddered, then shook her head. "But I'm here now. And I'm okay. I'm thinking I might always have problems with small, dark spaces, but I can handle that. Because the alternative would've been a hell of a lot worse."

"You heard Henley's story then?" Drake asked.

Alaska nodded. "I guess you have too?"

"Yeah. We all have. She's amazing."

"I think she and Tonka have something going on," Alaska blurted.

Drake's brows shot up. "Tonka and Henley? I don't think so."

Alaska shrugged. "I kind of got the impression that they might like each other more than either of them is willing to admit."

"Shit. Tonka's...he's not in a place to be in a relationship. Not sure he ever will be."

"I think she knows that. But the heart wants what the heart wants," she replied quietly. "Even when the brain knows it'll never happen, it doesn't stop the heart from hoping."

Drake's expression gentled. "I feel as if I've missed so much," he whispered. "So much wasted time."

Alaska shook her head. "Neither of us would be the people we are today without our experiences."

He sighed. "I know you're right, but if I could go back in time and prevent what happened to you, I would."

"I know. And I'd do the same for you."

They both knew how ridiculous that was. It wasn't as if she was a SEAL, and she certainly would never have been in that small town at the same time he was when a bomb went off.

"Thank you," Drake said softly.

"You're welcome."

"No, *thank you*...for being strong. Smart. For being here. For helping with the admin stuff. For being incredible."

Alaska blushed. "You're welcome," she repeated. "Although I should be the one thanking you again."

"We'll thank each other then," he decided as he tucked her against his side and led them toward his cabin at a brisk walk.

"What's the hurry?" she asked.

"The hurry is that I want to kiss you. And I want privacy because I'm gonna take my time. Gonna show you exactly how thankful I am that you're here. That for some reason you haven't been scared off by my bouts of moodiness and how much I work. I want to make sure you realize how important you are, not only to me, but to all my friends too. You've become a part of The Refuge so fast, I can't imagine you not being here."

His words made her melt...and turned her on so much she thought she was going to die if he didn't get his lips on hers in the next ten seconds. They'd been taking things slow. Making out a lot, yes, but nothing more. If he'd wanted to have sex, she would've agreed without hesitation. But as it was, she felt as if they were dating. Even though they were living together, the excitement she felt when she first started spending time with someone, learning about their likes and dislikes, and that fluttery feeling in her belly...those things were still there.

She didn't want this to be a one-time fling. A short-term relationship. She'd wanted to belong to Drake her entire life, and she was scared to death she'd do something to mess it up. So as much as she wanted to sleep with him, she'd let him set the pace.

And if he wanted to get her inside so he could kiss her, she was completely all right with that. The truth was, she loved every second of the time she spent with him...even when he was moody. It made him real.

Besides, she was plenty moody herself. One second she'd be happy, the next she'd be back *there*, in that dark box.

He walked her to the cabin and as soon as they were inside, he backed her against the wall next to the door. He kissed her long and hard. And this kiss felt different. It was as passionate as always, but it was more...*emotional* as well. Maybe it was because of the stories Alaska had just heard. Maybe it was because her own ordeal was at the front of her mind. She wasn't sure, but she did know that she liked it a lot.

Just when things were moving from making-out territory to something deeper, Drake pulled away.

One of Alaska's hands was shoved down the back of his jeans and the other had snaked under his shirt. His nipple was hard against her fingers, and she couldn't stop the moan that left her mouth when he stopped.

One of his own hands was around the back of her neck, and the other was at the small of her back, under her shirt, holding her flush against him. He was breathing just as hard as she was, and Alaska could feel his erection against her belly.

"I want you," she blurted.

"Damn," Drake groaned. "I want you too."

She waited, but he didn't move. "Drake?"

"I just came in for a break," he said. "I'm supposed to take a group on a hike out to Table Rock, and beyond if they're up for it."

Alaska sighed. "And I need to get to the lodge to check out two guests and to greet the new ones coming in today."

"This is happening," Drake said.

Alaska furrowed her brow. "What is?"

"Us. It might've taken me twenty-two years to see what was in front of me all along, but I see you now, Al. And I might be slow, but I'm not dumb. I'm going to make up for the time we've lost."

"Okay," she whispered, loving the sound of that.

"Okay," he agreed.

Neither moved.

Drake smiled. "You're gonna have to let go of me, honey."

"And you're going to have to let go of me," she retorted.

His grin widened. "I had no idea it could be like this."

"What could?"

"Being with someone. Having a girlfriend. Loving someone." Then he leaned down, kissed her nose, and let his fingers slide out from under the hair at her nape.

Alaska wasn't sure she was breathing. Did he really say that? No, he couldn't have actually meant it. Just because she'd loved him forever didn't mean he felt the same after...what...a few weeks? No, he must've just been talking in generalities.

"I'll catch up with you after lunch," Drake said.

"Don't you have another meeting with that Mr. Choo guy this afternoon?" Alaska asked.

Drake frowned. "Damn. I forgot. Yes. We're finalizing his visit to The Refuge."

"I could make us dinner here...if you wanted," she suggested.

"Okay. If you don't mind."

"I don't."

"Sounds like a plan. Alaska?"

"Yeah?"

"Tonight, when we go to bed...?" He paused.

Goose bumps sprang up on her arms. "Yeah?"

"We're gonna do more than sleep. You ready for that?"

She couldn't keep the huge smile off her face. "Yes."

"Good." Then he stepped back toward her as if he couldn't stay away. He pulled her against him, hard, and kissed her once more. Long, slow, and so passionate, it was all Alaska could do not to melt into a puddle right there on the floor.

He pulled back, staring at her for a long moment before opening the door. He looked back once, licked his lips, then was gone.

It took Alaska a little longer to feel confident enough to move. She pushed off the wall and headed to the bedroom to change into the more professional clothes she wore when she was working.

Yong Chen felt the adrenaline coursing through his veins. This was finally happening. The owners of The Refuge had been tougher negotiators than he'd anticipated. He'd figured they would jump at the chance to have extra money poured into their rustic camp. But instead, they'd balked at the expansion he'd proposed. Of course, he wasn't going to be paying them a dime, but they didn't know that. The idea that they wanted to keep their business small was ridiculous. He also thought it was ludicrous that they were bothering to help all the crazy people in the world.

PTSD was nothing but a weakness of the mind, as far as he was concerned. He'd seen more than his fair share of people break, once in his lair. It was amusing to bet on how long it would take the women he bought to beg for their lives. They nearly always started out defiant, but after a few customers had their way with them, they changed their tune.

And once they were broken completely, he disposed of them. When the challenge was gone, they were no longer fun. Yong loved the ones that fought...and still lost.

But the men he was toying with were worthy adversaries. They did and said many smart things when it came to business. If he was anyone other than who he was, if he was truly interested in investing in their backwoods camp, he'd be impressed. But since he was only getting close to them to reacquire his property, he didn't care what was happening in the woods in New Mexico, USA.

And the closer he came to his departure for the States, the more excited he got. He'd arranged for yet another ten customers to spend time with his acquisition. That brought his profit up to a cool two million US dollars. There was something so satisfying about the entire operation that Yong was considering branching out his *own* business.

His Chinese customers were loyal. Nowhere else could they play out their deviant sexual fantasies than with the women he bought for them. But it was more than obvious there were men like him everywhere. And since he never kept a woman for more than a few weeks, two months at most—by then, they were completely useless—the risk was minimal. He had men who disposed of the bodies for him, but he'd learned a thing or two over the years. Yong had no doubt he'd be able to get rid of any bodies without detection in the US...or any country around the world, for that matter.

His cock hardened at the thought of traveling to India, England, Mexico, and other countries to obtain a plaything. He'd collect his fees from the men he contracted through the dark web, dispose of the evidence, and leave a much wealthier man than when he'd arrived.

The more he thought about the idea, the more he liked it. New Mexico and the woman who got away would be his test. If he could pull it off there, he could do it anywhere.

Anticipation swam through his veins. He wanted to get started now...but he had to have patience. The best news he'd learned today from his meeting with the owners of The Refuge was that his target, Alaska Stein, was there. Right where he thought she'd be.

The man she'd called had led Yong straight to her.

Drake Vandine had mentioned his admin assistant would be emailing an itinerary of his visit to The Refuge. They'd discussed what he'd see, who he'd meet when he was there, but Yong hadn't really been listening. All he cared about was that he wouldn't have to travel all over the country to reacquire his property. She was there. Just waiting on him to collect her.

And collect her he would. He'd make certain she understood that the punishment she'd receive was going to be ten times worse than what she would've experienced if she hadn't ruined his plans.

She felt safe now. Hiding in the middle of nowhere. But soon, he'd feed on her terror and horror. And her pain. He couldn't wait to see her bleed.

Yong stood. He needed to pack. He had a trip to take.

CHAPTER THIRTEEN

Brick was having trouble concentrating. All he could think about was getting back to his cabin...and Alaska. He was kicking himself for not seeing what was right in front of his face for years. He blamed it on the many miles between them and their very different lifestyles up until now, but those were excuses.

He knew she was special back when he was eighteen years old. Why else would he still have the cross-stitch she'd given him on his wall? Why else would he feel warm and fuzzy inside when he looked at it? Why else would he feel a heightened sense of anticipation when his phone rang, or when he was notified of an incoming email or message?

Deep down, his subconscious had to have known she was meant for him. It sucked that it had taken such shitty circumstances to get them together. But now that he'd spent almost every waking moment with her for weeks, Brick didn't want to lose her.

The other morning, he'd had a long talk with his

mother. He'd briefly mentioned the circumstances that had brought Alaska to The Refuge, and without prompting, without any hint that she'd begun to mean a great deal to him, his mom had let out a long, relieved sigh and said, "It's about time."

Surprised, he'd asked her what she meant.

His mom had gone on to remind him that she'd known Alaska had a crush on him since they were teenagers. It was one of the reasons why she'd gone out to the trash bin to pull out the present she'd made for him.

When Brick had tentatively asked his mom what she thought of Alaska, he was immensely relieved when she declared in no uncertain terms that if he let her slip through his fingers, he was an idiot, and not the smart man she'd raised.

It was safe to say his mom was a big Alaska Stein fan.

"Brick, you paying attention?" Spike asked.

He hadn't been, but he looked over at his friend and nodded anyway.

Spike had asked for a quick meeting before they all went their separate ways for the day.

"Can't blame him," Owl said with a smirk. "If I had a woman like Alaska in my cabin, I'd be scatterbrained too."

"Shut up," Brick said, picking up a pen and throwing it at his friend. Everyone chuckled.

"But seriously, man. I think it's great," Owl said. "Seeing one of us successfully having a normal relationship gives me hope."

The others nodded.

"I'm not sure I'd call what Alaska and I have normal," he said honestly. "We're both navigating our way through two decades of friendship, trying not to fuck that up, while also dealing with our own PTSD issues."

Tiny shrugged. "I don't know. I'd say you two have the most important thing when it comes to a relationship."

"What's that?" Brick asked, genuinely curious to hear what his friend had to say.

"A foundation. When we found her in Russia, you were the only person who was able to get through her panic and calm her down. You were the first person she thought to call when she needed help. And when she heard about you in that hospital in Germany...she did what needed to be done to get to you. You guys are perfect together. It's easy to see."

Tiny wasn't wrong. And his words made Brick feel good. "She's...a good person through and through," he said after a moment. "And I can't say that about most people I meet. She doesn't have a mean bone in her body, which makes it all the more horrific what almost happened to her."

"You gonna keep her?" Stone asked.

Brick couldn't help but chuckle. "It's not as if she's a stray, like Mutt."

"You know what I mean," Stone said with a shrug.

"If she wants me, yes," he said simply.

"Good. The Refuge needs her. She's a hell of an admin," Pipe said.

Brick's good mood took a small hit. "I don't want

her because she's good with the guests and paperwork," he growled.

Pipe held up a hand. "Whoa! I didn't mean to imply that at all. But seriously, you can't help but be a little relieved that she seems as invested in this place as we are. It would suck if she hated it here."

Brick did his best to rein in his temper. Pipe had a point.

"Right, so now that we all know Brick is serious about Alaska, and we've given him our support...hopefully he won't fuck it up. In the meantime, I wanted to get together real fast and talk about Choo's visit. Are we ready?" Spike asked.

No one said a word for a long moment.

Spike sighed. "That's what I suspected. I've been thinking...maybe we got overexcited about the fact that someone wanted to invest in this place. That we might be able to expand, help more people. But now that this guy is actually coming next week, I have to admit I'm having second thoughts."

Brick looked around the table and saw his friends nodding. "I'm not sure we can back out of the visit now. Choo's paid a lot of money to set everything up," he said.

"He's not coming just for us though, right?" Stone asked. "He's got some other meetings and things planned, I thought. He mentioned he's going to be in the States for a month and a half or so."

"That's what I understood, from what he told us," Spike agreed.

"So, we still meet with him—but we need to tell him

that we haven't made a final decision," Tonka said, speaking up for the first time.

"I agree," Spike said. "I just wanted to make sure we were all on the same page. I mean, I'd love to get more money to make this place even better, but I'm not sure doubling the number of cabins *would* make it better. I don't know about you guys, but as long as we're not losing money, I'm satisfied with what we've built here."

Everyone agreed.

"So, what? We just entertain Choo, then say, 'sorry, we changed our minds'?" Tiny asked. "That would make us look like assholes, not to mention possibly hurt any chance in the future of us getting another investor if we wanted one."

Everyone was silent a moment. Then Brick said, "We were going to have Tex look into this guy if we decided to go forward, right?"

"Yeah. Why?" Spike asked.

"This might sound completely asshole-ish, but what if we requested he look into him now? Before he gets here? That way, if he finds anything hinky, we'll definitely know we're doing the right thing by declining the partnership."

"I'm not sure that will make it any easier to say no," Pipe said with a shrug. "I mean, it's not like we can just come out and say we had him investigated and didn't like what we found."

"Why not?" Brick asked. "We'd be stupid not to have a foreign investor, someone we don't know, checked out."

"True. Or we can simply say that after discussing it, we decided to go in a different direction," Tonka said with a shrug. "Keeping it simple is always better than mucking up the waters."

"He's right," Spike said. "But it still won't hurt to see what Tex can find. I'll give him a call today."

"Last I heard, he and his wife were going on that two-week vacation to Maine," Tiny said.

"Shit, I'd forgotten about that. What about that other woman he works with all the time?" Spike asked.

"Elizabeth," Owl supplied.

"Yeah, that's her. Maybe I'll give her a call."

"I've heard she's scary good," Brick said. "Her expertise is the dark web. If there's something to be found on anyone there, she finds it."

"Well, here's to hoping she doesn't find anything on our friend Mr. Choo," Spike said.

"I'll second that," Stone said. "The last thing we need if he's involved in something shady is to have the Chinese Communist Party breathing down our necks."

Brick frowned. The more they talked, the more uneasy he felt about the investor's visit. Truthfully, he'd been uncertain from the beginning, but he'd hoped it was just paranoia. He didn't want to unintentionally jeopardize the future of the camp, and the niggling feeling wasn't something he could be certain of, anyway. That said...he was a big believer in the idea that nothing was a coincidence.

And he couldn't dismiss the fact that a guy from China contacted them out of the blue, wanting to invest in The Refuge, just days after Alaska's rescue.

Again, it wasn't the first time he'd thought it, but he figured he was overreacting because of his deepening feelings for Alaska.

He snapped out of his troubling thoughts when he realized the meeting with his friends was over, as Tonka got up to head back to the barns, as usual, and the others followed suit.

"You okay?" Tiny asked Brick as they headed out of the room to start their day.

"Yeah, I guess," he said with a shrug.

"I'm glad Spike said something. I've been thinking about this a lot lately."

"Same," Brick agreed.

Tiny slapped him on the back and said, "For the record, I'm fucking thrilled about you and Alaska. I really like her. She's...relaxing. She doesn't get ruffled when shit goes sideways with the guests. She's able to keep everyone calm and her problem-solving skills are phenomenal."

Brick agreed one hundred percent. "She mentioned that she's learned a lot from all the places she worked overseas. I think being exposed to so many different cultures and nationalities helped her look at situations in a different way, made her more tolerant."

"I agree. And she's good for you."

"In what way?" Brick asked.

"You aren't so jumpy. You seem more relaxed around the guests."

Brick thought about his friend's observation and had to agree. "I don't know if it's that I've changed, or that I'm just always happy about getting back to my cabin and seeing Alaska again," he admitted.

"Not a bad thing, my friend," Tiny replied, slapping his back once more. "Have to say, I'm kind of jealous. Not that I want Alaska; it's clear she only has eyes for you. But that you've found someone who makes you happy. Who soothes you. What else could washed-up old military grunts like us want? Anyway, you need a hand with the hike today? Two of the guests are apparently really struggling with their demons."

"If you wouldn't mind, I'd love company," Brick told him.

As they met the group of guests who were gathering for the hike, Brick couldn't help but think about Tiny's comments. And those of his other friends. He hadn't been looking for a life partner. But it was seriously impossible to think about his life *without* Alaska in it. Even though she'd only physically been with him for a short period of time, she'd gotten under his skin.

And speaking of skin...he couldn't wait to get home tonight and show her just how happy he was that she was here, with him.

* * *

As it always happened when he had somewhere he wanted to be, the world seemed to conspire to keep Brick from getting home. The hike with the guests had started out well enough, but some of the more out-of-shape hikers started falling behind. Which irritated two of the younger, more fit guests.

Tiny had taken the younger men ahead while Brick stayed behind with the other four. They'd made it to Table Rock and had a nice leisurely lunch, but then one of the women had a flashback and refused to budge, certain an enemy was lurking in the trees, ready to ambush them.

Brick couldn't in good conscience send the other three guests back to the lodge by themselves, so he used the radio he always carried to get in touch with Pipe, requesting he come out and assist. Luckily, Henley was at The Refuge doing an individual session, and she'd agreed to come with him to help with the guest.

Four hours later than he'd planned, Brick had finally made it back to the lodge. He'd needed to reassure the other men and women, who'd heard about what happened, that everything was fine. That the guest who'd had the bad episode was much better and wasn't leaving, that she was determined to stay. Which had led to an impromptu kind of group session over dinner, where everyone shared some of their worst setbacks.

By the time Brick was able to excuse himself, he was grimy, exhausted, and irritated that his plans had gone so sideways.

As he approached his cabin, Brick stopped outside the door. The sweet smells coming from inside made his belly growl. He'd sent a message to Alaska that he wouldn't be home for dinner, and why. He'd invited her to join them at the lodge, but she'd declined.

He'd worried about her all evening. Wanted to go to her, make sure she was all right with the change in their plans, but he hadn't been able to leave. The guests seemed to be extra needy, as they occasionally were, and the last thing he wanted to do was make them feel as if he'd abandoned them.

But from the delicious scent coming from his cabin, Alaska hadn't been idle.

Pushing open the door, Brick made plenty of noise to let her know he was home. He'd learned from experience that surprising someone with PTSD wasn't a good thing.

Mutt's nails clicked on the floor as he ran toward him. Smiling, Brick leaned over to pet his dog. "Hey, boy. Did you have a good night? You must really like Al, huh? I don't think you've missed a meal at the lodge in a long time." The dog's butt wiggled as Brick spoke, showing him nonverbally how happy he was that his master was home.

Brick stood and looked over to the kitchen, and saw Alaska standing by the table, smiling at him.

"Hey," she said softly.

"Hey," he returned, moving quickly. He strode up to her, and as she backed up against the counter, he blocked her in by resting his hands on the granite. She rested her own on his chest as she tilted her head back to look at him.

"It smells good in here," he told her.

Alaska shrugged. "I made myself a salad for dinner, but then thought maybe you'd appreciate some double chocolate cupcakes for dessert. I'm sure they aren't up to Robert's standards, but they aren't half bad either."

"If they taste half as good as they smell, they'll be the best cupcakes I've ever eaten," he said with a small smile.

She returned it, then her brows furrowed. "Everything okay? I mean, that woman...she's okay?"

"Yeah. It was tough there for a while, but Henley was amazing with her. And the other guests were too. No one told her she was being irrational, or to suck it up, and we were able to get back to the lodge without too many issues."

"People actually say that? I mean, what the heck?"

"Oh, yeah, they do...and worse. It's impossible for those who have never suffered from a flashback, or experienced the fear that comes from hearing a certain sound or seeing something that reminds them of the trauma they've been through, to understand how hard it can be to pull yourself out of that dark place."

Alaska raised a hand and put it on his cheek. "I'm sorry," she said softly, understanding shining in her gorgeous eyes.

Brick took her hand in his and turned his head to kiss the palm.

"You look tired," she observed.

He shrugged. "I'm okay."

"Why don't you go take a long, hot shower. The cupcakes should be cool enough for me to frost while you're in there. We can relax and watch a few episodes of *Scrubs* when you're done."

Brick eyed her for a long moment, then sighed. "This isn't how I wanted tonight to go."

"I know. But life happens," she said sensibly.

"I want you so much," he said bluntly. "I want to bury my head between your legs and feast. I want to watch you suck me off. I want to feel you come around my cock as you fly over the edge. I want to be inside you more than I've ever wanted anything in a very, very long time."

Alaska's face turned bright red as he spoke, but she didn't look away.

"But right now, I don't think I can give you the attention we both deserve," he finished a little reluctantly.

"Let me take care of *you* for once," Alaska said. "And for the record, I want all that too, but not when I know you've had a hard day and are exhausted."

Brick closed his eyes and rested his forehead against hers. He stood there, breathing her in, letting her calmness seep into his soul. He had no idea why simply being next to her made him feel so grounded.

"Shower," she said after a while. "Hot. I'll have cupcakes, blankets, and the show queued up when you're done."

"Okay," he agreed. Brick lifted his head, but tilted her chin up with a finger. He stared into her deep brown eyes for a moment before closing the distance slowly.

She met him halfway, and the kiss was long, leisurely, and loving. She was the first to pull back. Brick could see the passion and longing in her gaze, but she merely licked her lips and put her hands on his hips to turn him toward the hall. "Go, Drake. I have cupcakes to ice."

He went.

But before he'd gone too far down the hallway, he turned around. Alaska had turned her attention to the cupcakes cooling on a rack on the counter. He watched her for a beat. Realizing how at home and *right* she looked in his cabin. When he'd picked the floor plan for his place, he hadn't been thinking about a wife and kids. He'd wanted simplicity. A large living area, a functional kitchen, two bedrooms, one bathroom. He hadn't needed anything more.

But he'd been wrong.

He'd needed this.

Her.

Alaska.

Puttering around his home as if she was born to be there.

She was right, she wasn't the flashiest woman in the world. She much preferred to fade into the background. Didn't like being the center of attention. But to Brick, she stood out simply because of her personality. He'd come so close to losing her. To not understanding how loving someone could completely change his life.

With that thought in his head, he entered the bathroom. He turned the water on in the shower, stripped off his clothes, brushed his teeth, then stepped into the shower. As the hot water pounded his shoulders, Brick spared a thought for his long-lost battle buddies. Vader, Monster, Bones, Rain, and Mad Dog would've loved The Refuge. Of course, if they hadn't died, The Refuge wouldn't exist.

Give and take.

The world was full of it.

Over the last four years, their wives had gotten remarried, had more children...moved on with their lives. At first, Brick hadn't understood it. Couldn't comprehend how they could betray their husbands like that. But he got it now. Life changed. People changed. And when you found someone who felt like the other half of your soul, you'd do anything, *anything*, to keep that person.

Loving Alaska had changed his life. She'd changed it twenty-two years ago when she'd made that cross-stitch. She'd changed it four years ago when she'd had the courage to lie to the Navy and show up at his bedside.

And she'd changed it when she'd convinced her kidnapper to call him.

Life was a big fucking game of dice. Sometimes you got lucky and threw doubles, and other times you got nothing. It was how you played, what you did when you were close to losing that mattered. How you appreciated what you were given when you got lucky.

And Brick knew he was damn lucky. Other men in Alaska's life might not have seen the absolute gem they had in her, but he did. And he wasn't idiotic enough to let her slip away. She made him a better man, and he knew it. She thought she was nothing special, which was equal parts frustrating and part of her charm. Brick would show her how much she was appreciated and loved every day for as long as he'd be privileged enough to be by her side.

She'd not go another day without knowing how he felt about her.

An idea sprang to mind then. Something he could do for her that was way too late in coming. It was something she'd never think to do for herself.

Exhaustion still pulled at him, but now anticipation swam through his veins as well. He had a lot of planning to do, but Brick had no doubt his friends would help.

* * *

Alaska sat on the couch next to Drake and stroked his hair over and over. He was fast asleep against her, his deep inhalations telling her without words just how tired he was. Drake didn't sleep well. She'd noticed it in the hospital, and he'd mentioned it a time or two since.

But at the moment, with his head in her lap, one arm curled around her thighs, Mutt snoring in the crook of his knees, he was *out*.

It felt good to be able to give this to him.

She couldn't deny she was a touch disappointed that they weren't currently naked in his bed, making love, but this was almost as good. In many ways, this was more intimate.

It had been a long day. Alaska had a feeling Drake would deny it, but helping others through their traumatic reactions took a lot out of him. Brought back his own not-so-good memories. Being here for him now, allowing him to let down his guard and veg on the couch without having to think too hard about anything, felt good. She felt needed.

So much of her life, she'd been on her own. No one really cared if she came or went. But seeing Drake's appreciation for the sweets she'd made him, for not being upset about their change in dinner plans, for her willingness to sit on the couch and watch mindless TV... It was everything.

But it was getting late. Her leg was falling asleep where Drake's head lay. And tomorrow was going to be a long day for both of them. For her, because she was working on revamping The Refuge's website, and for Drake because he'd most certainly want to keep a closer eye on the guests after what happened today.

"Drake?" she said softly.

He didn't stir. But Mutt lifted his head to look at her.

Alaska knew the dangers of waking someone with

Drake's past from a deep sleep. She wanted to get him to bed, but wasn't sure how to go about it.

Mutt took the decision out of her hands. He jumped off the couch, then circled back and began to lick Drake's face as he slept.

It was all Alaska could do not to laugh. At first, Drake kind of mumbled in his sleep. But when Mutt didn't stop licking him, he groaned and brought up a hand to push the dog away.

Mutt persisted, licking Drake's fingers, wrist, then his face again when he could reach it.

"Damn dog," he mumbled. "I'm awake."

Alaska knew she was smiling like crazy, but she couldn't help it.

Drake lifted his eyes to hers, and she stilled. She couldn't interpret the emotion she saw in his gaze, but it made her belly clench with longing.

"What time is it?" he asked, the intense moment passing.

"Twelve-thirty or so," she told him.

"Shit. I didn't mean to fall asleep on you."

"It's okay. I was trying to wake you up so we could go to bed when Mutt decided to help."

"Good boy," Drake said, reaching out a hand and ruffling the fur on top of the dog's head. "I didn't teach him to wake me up like that. He figured out on his own it was better for me to wake up slowly than be surprised with an alarm."

"Yeah, I didn't know exactly how to wake you up without startling you."

Drake sat up, and to her surprise, she saw a mischievous look cross his face. "I could think of a few ways," he said.

Alaska couldn't stop herself from glancing at his lap. Even as she watched, his dick seemed to grow in his sweats.

"Yup, that's one way," he said, without sounding the least bit embarrassed. He stood. "I'll let Mutt out if you want to head on to bed."

Things between them were so...easy. So domestic. Alaska had thought living with a guy would be so much more awkward. But nothing about her days or nights with Drake had been uncomfortable, ever. He always let her use the bathroom first. Gave her plenty of time to get changed without her having to worry if he'd barge in on her. He cleaned up after himself. Was constantly looking out for her. Making sure she had enough to eat, that she was warm enough, that she wasn't bored.

He made her feel special. Which was a new thing for Alaska.

By the time she finished in the bathroom, Drake and Mutt were back inside. She headed into the bedroom with the dog while Drake visited the bathroom. She was crawling under the covers when he returned.

While he always gave her alone time to change before bed, Drake had no problem getting ready in front of her. Probably because he had not one thing to be shy about when it came to his body. Tonight, Alaska didn't even pretend she wasn't watching as he stripped off his shirt.

His biceps were large enough that she didn't think she'd be able to get both hands around them at once.

The yowling lion tattoo on his left arm rippled as he moved, and even from where she was lying, Alaska could see the veins in his forearms. Why that was so sexy, she had no idea, but the thought of those hands and arms around her made her squirm.

Next, Drake shucked his sweatpants. His ass in those boxers was rock hard, and his thighs were huge. He was a big man...all over. That wasn't something she could miss. And tonight, she let her gaze linger on the front of his boxers as he walked around the bed to the side he slept on.

"Like what you see, honey?" he asked as he crawled under the sheet.

Alaska's nipples were hard under her sleepshirt, and she could feel the wetness between her legs. Instead of being embarrassed about her perusal of his body, she felt emboldened. And she instinctually knew Drake wouldn't make her feel shame in her *own* body. Wouldn't think her boobs were too small or her nipples too big. He wouldn't make her feel weird about how wet she got when she was super turned on. And she had a feeling he'd have no problem whatsoever with her taking control.

She might not be the most sexually experienced woman in the world, but she liked what she liked...and she definitely liked Drake.

"Yes," she said simply.

"Good. Because I *more* than like you looking." He reached for her waist and pulled her against him, into her usual sleeping spot against his side.

Alaska snuggled into him, nuzzling his shoulder as she got comfortable.

His hand, which usually rested against her back, gripped her shirt and tugged upward. He pulled on the material until his hand could get under it. He rested his palm on the small of her back, holding her to him.

Alaska didn't usually wear more than panties and an oversized shirt to bed, so her bare legs and even her belly brushed against his equally bare skin. And she couldn't stop thinking about how close his fingers were to her butt. Her nipples actually hurt as they pressed against his side.

"You feel so good against me. I don't think I've told you that before," Drake said softly.

Alaska shook her head. "And you feel good against *me*." She ruined her attempt at seduction by yawning, hugely.

Drake chuckled and gave her a quick hug. "It's late. Sleep, Al."

She wanted to protest that she was too turned on to sleep, but her eyes seemed too heavy to keep open all of a sudden.

Drake ran his fingers up and down her arm, which she'd wrapped around his belly. She could feel and hear his heartbeat under her cheek.

"Thank you for tonight. It was exactly what I needed," he said after a moment.

Alaska fell asleep with the feel of Drake along every inch of her body, the sound of Mutt snoring behind her, and the knowledge deep in her bones that this was where she was meant to be.

CHAPTER FOURTEEN

Alaska was having the *best* dream.

She'd had ones like it plenty of times in the past, but this time it seemed much more real. She was in bed with Drake, and he was looking at her as if she was the most beautiful person in the world...which was how she knew she was dreaming. He eased down her body, then spread her legs slowly and began to lick her clit. And he wasn't just going through the motions. It was as if he honestly enjoyed what he was doing, not going down on her as a precursor to getting to the "good stuff," so to speak.

It wasn't until Alaska tightened her hold on his hair that she realized she wasn't dreaming at all.

Every muscle in her body stiffened as she opened her eyes and lifted her head.

She was on her back in Drake's bed. It was still early, the sun hadn't come through the window yet, but enough light shone from outside that she could clearly see the twinkle in Drake's eyes as he lifted his head slightly from between her legs. He'd somehow removed her underwear without waking her, and she was completely bare from the waist down.

"Morning," he said huskily, before going back to what he was doing.

Alaska wasn't awake enough to form words. Her body was overloaded with pleasure. In her dreams, Drake always seemed to know exactly where to touch her to make her feel good, but the reality was so much better.

"Drake," she breathed as his thumbs caressed her inner thighs while he feasted.

"Mmmm," he hummed, and Alaska jerked as the vibrations shot through her clit to her nipples.

She could feel him smiling against her as he continued to lick. It was a weird feeling, but not unpleasant in the least.

"What are you doing?" she managed to gasp.

He chuckled again, and this time when he lifted his head, one of his hands took over and began to play in the wetness between her legs. "If you don't know, I'm not doing it right," he teased.

"You are. I mean, I can see and feel what you're doing, but...why?"

"After last night, when we talked about the best way to wake someone up so you didn't startle them...I couldn't resist. You were sleeping so soundly, I didn't want to scare you, so I decided to try this. You like?"

"Um...duh," she said.

"I thought so. You're *really* wet," Drake breathed, dropping his gaze to watch his finger slide into her body.

But Alaska stiffened at his words. He wasn't making fun of her, she knew that. But she'd been told the same thing in a derogatory way too many times.

Drake immediately looked up, obviously feeling the change in her reaction. "What? What'd I say?"

"Nothing, I...maybe I should—"

She didn't get to finish her statement. Drake shifted forward a fraction and put one of his forearms over her belly, lightly pinning her in place. She could move if she really wanted to, but honestly, her body was still humming from what he'd been doing before she so stupidly decided to have a little chat.

"You should tell me what I said wrong, so I can either fix whatever misconception you've got going on in that head of yours, or I can kick my own ass for saying something hurtful."

"I...you... It's not normal...how wet I get," she blurted. "I can't help it though."

The smile that spread across Drake's face was so breathtaking, Alaska couldn't look away. "You think being wet is a turn-off? Oh, honey—it so isn't."

"But it's messy. And I'll get the sheets all yucky."

"It *is* messy," Drake agreed. But before she could respond, he went on. "And so damn sexy, you don't even know. If we have to change the sheets every day for the rest of our lives, so be it. I don't give a shit. Besides, you don't think when I come, it won't be messy? You gushing around my fingers the second I get my tongue between your legs is fucking *awesome*." His finger slid inside her again, and she couldn't help but lift her hips toward him.

"And knowing I won't hurt you when I get inside

251

here is a relief. I'm a big man, honey. This just proves you were made to be mine. Don't be ashamed of your body's reaction to me, Al. It's beautiful. *You're* beautiful. Now...take off your shirt. I want to see those nipples that have tormented me every night."

Alaska hesitated a beat. Was this really happening? She'd thought after last night, they'd wait until at least this evening. Maybe even a few more nights. But she wasn't opposed to Drake making love to her. Not at all.

She wiggled a bit, attempting to get the shirt over her head without pulling away from Drake at the same time. After she threw the shirt to the side, she looked down at him.

"Jesus, honey," he said, almost panting. "I don't know what I want more...to keep tasting you here, or to suck on those beauties."

Looking at herself, Alaska saw her nipples were sticking up even more than they usually did. They were so hard, they almost hurt.

"Are they sensitive?" Drake asked almost nonchalantly as he reached for one.

The second his fingers closed around her nipples, Alaska's hips bucked against the finger still buried deep inside her.

"Oh, yeah, they're sensitive," Drake whispered. "Damn, I feel as if it's Christmas and my birthday all wrapped into one." Then he lowered his head once more as his fingers continued to play with her nipple.

The double stimulation was almost too much. Alaska writhed under him as his fingers and lips brought her closer and closer to a monster orgasm. It had been so long since she'd felt sexual, that Drake's attention hurt...in a good way.

It wasn't long before she felt herself on the verge of exploding. She reached down and grabbed Drake's wrist, his fingers still playing with her breast, and squeezed tightly, her other hand gripping his hair.

Her muscles began to shake and her body curled toward him.

Drake must've felt she was close because he began to fuck her harder with two fingers now, even as he sucked fiercely on her clit.

"Drake!" she cried as she tumbled over the edge.

Her world went dark for a moment as pleasure coursed through her body. By the time she came back to herself and realized where she was, Alaska's body was still humming. Usually after orgasming, she was replete. Finished. But right now, she felt like a live wire.

Forcing her fingers to let go of the death grip she had on the man's hair, she did her best to remember how to breathe.

She watched as Drake scooted forward. He lowered himself to one hip, and for a second, Alaska couldn't figure out what he was doing. When his boxers went flying off the side of the bed, she inhaled deeply.

She couldn't take her eyes off his cock as he moved forward, spreading her legs farther apart as he went. He *was* big. Thick and long.

Alaska's mouth watered. She liked sex. But she hadn't been with many men, and certainly none built like Drake.

"You keep looking at me like that and this isn't going to last," he warned.

Alaska's gaze swept up his flat stomach, past his hard nipples and up to his face. His hair was mussed, probably from her hands. His tongue came out to lick his lips and he said, "So damn delicious."

He leaned over and pulled open a drawer next to the bed. When he came back to his knees, he was holding a condom in his hand. Without fanfare, he ripped open the wrapper with his teeth and rolled the rubber down his length.

Then he focused his gaze between her legs once more.

Alaska appreciated his willingness to protect them both without bitching about it. As much as she wanted to feel him inside her bare, this wasn't the time or place to have that discussion.

Her ass lifted off the mattress without any input from her brain, but not before she could feel how wet the sheet was under her. For a moment, embarrassment swept through her, but then Drake's cock brushed against her folds, and she couldn't think about anything other than getting him inside her.

"Yes..." she said.

"You sure? Once I have you, I'm never letting you go," Drake warned.

Alaska wanted to snort. As if that was a deterrent.

"I'm sure," she breathed.

* * *

Brick was two seconds away from coming. He grabbed hold of his cock at the base and squeezed hard. Seeing Alaska spread out under him, smelling her arousal on his beard, seeing how wet she was...nothing had ever turned him on so much. He wanted this woman more than he could remember wanting anyone, ever.

She was sensual and so damn beautiful, it made him physically hurt. When she'd orgasmed earlier, her juices squirted all over his hand. He'd heard of women being able to do that, but hadn't experienced it for himself. Until now. It was unbelievable that she was embarrassed about something so fucking erotic.

Even now, he could see her thighs glistening with her release. His cock grew even harder, which seemed impossible.

Looking down at her, she seemed so tiny compared to him. He had a moment of doubt that he'd be able to fit. When he'd been finger-fucking her, she'd squeezed his fingers so tightly, Brick had almost come just imagining how she'd feel around his cock. But now he worried. He didn't want to hurt her.

"Drake?" Alaska asked in concern. "Is something wrong?"

"No," he said immediately. "You are just so precious...I'm memorizing this moment."

She smiled up at him, then reached down and brushed his hand away from his cock. To his amazement, she lifted her hips and notched his mushroomed head between her pussy lips. "Please," she whispered. "I'm so empty."

Brick felt a burst of precome escape the tip of his cock and he moved without thought. He buried himself to the hilt with one hard push.

The pleasure that he experienced at the feel of being inside her made his fingers tingle and his balls draw up in preparation for a monster orgasm. He held his breath and prayed he could control himself. The last thing he wanted was for this to be over before it even began.

"Drake!" Alaska exclaimed. "You feel...oh my..."

She squeezed him then, and Brick lost control. He planted his hands on the mattress next to her and pulled his hips back, before thrusting forward. He'd never been so glad in all his life that a woman could get so wet. She was taking him as if she was made for his cock...and as far as Brick was concerned, she was.

"Can't. Stop," he grunted as he continued to pump in and out of her body.

But Alaska wasn't lying docilly beneath him. She was raising her hips to meet each and every one of his thrusts. The sound of their skin slapping together was loud in the quiet morning, and it only served to make Brick burn even hotter.

He'd rarely met a woman who could take everything he had to give. Not only take it, but demand it. Alaska was everything a man wanted in his woman. Sedate and polite on the outside, and a fucking wildcat in bed.

When one of her hands crept to her chest and she began to play with her nipple, plucking at it and pinching it between her fingers, Brick lost control completely.

"God, that's it. Harder, Al. Fuck yes! You're so damn hot. You gonna come on my cock? Going to squirt all over me? I want to feel you on my balls. Yes...just like that. You want more?"

Brick had no idea where the dirty talk was coming from. All he knew was, with every naughty thing out of his mouth, Alaska clenched harder around him. His cock felt like it was in a vise. A tight, warm, wet vise that was doing all it could to squeeze the life out of him. His balls physically hurt...in a good way. He was going to come harder than he'd ever come in his life.

And it was all because of the firecracker writhing under him. He'd loved her when he thought she was meek and mild, but witnessing the passion she hid inside made him love her even more.

Putting his weight on one hand, Brick thrust one last time inside her body, then pulled out, ripped off the condom, not even feeling when it pinched as it came off, and jerked his cock rough and hard until he exploded.

He couldn't explain why he needed to see her covered in his seed. It was a visceral reaction, one that, when he could actually see again, sent pleasure shooting through him when he saw his come all over her belly, her tits, and even on her neck.

But he wasn't satisfied. Wouldn't be until she came again. He reached for her clit and roughly thumbed it. She groaned and tried to shift her hips away, but Brick wouldn't let her. He felt like a caveman and wanted to see her come again.

"Let go," he ordered. "Let me feel you come on me." He didn't let up, and when he felt her began to tremble under him once more, a smile of satisfaction curled his lips upward.

"That's it, Al. Do it. Fucking come all over me."

She jerked once, and he was rewarded with a spurt of come from between her legs. It splashed onto his cock and dripped down to his balls. It wasn't as much as earlier, but just as satisfying. Just the thought of giving her a G-spot orgasm sometime very soon, and seeing how much she could squirt, was erotic as hell.

Not giving her a chance to be embarrassed or to flee, Brick lowered himself on top of her. He could feel his warm come on her chest, smearing into his own, but it didn't turn him off. Not even a little. Nothing about what they'd done made him uncomfortable. On the contrary, their lovemaking just reassured him that he was making the right decision. That she was perfect for him.

He studied her face as she came down from her orgasm. Her heart rate slowed and the fingernails she'd dug into his biceps finally eased their grip. He was ready to reassure her. To soothe any embarrassment she might feel. To convince her that what they'd done was not only perfectly normal, but the best sex he'd ever had in his life.

Instead, when she opened her eyes, Brick saw nothing but deep satisfaction.

"You okay?"

"If you mean am I boneless with pleasure and want to do that again as soon as possible, then yes."

Brick smiled. "Yeah, me too."

"You, um...you know that when you wear a condom, that usually means you can come while you're inside, right?" she teased.

Fuck, Brick loved this woman.

And on the heels of that...another thought struck him. He knew without a doubt that if she'd been delivered to whoever the Russian was sending her to, she would've been irrevocably changed. Her natural sexuality would've been suppressed and smashed to smithereens. The thought of this woman, this sensual, beautiful woman, experiencing something so horrifying when she so obviously enjoyed sex, was abhorrent.

He pushed the thought away viciously. He'd found her. She was safe from that asshole and he'd do everything in his power to keep her exactly how she was right this moment. Sated, satisfied, and comfortable with her sexuality.

"I know," he said belatedly. "But the thought of seeing you covered in my come was too much to resist."

This time, she did blush. "Um...you were right...sex is messy." She wrinkled her nose.

Brick laughed, then got serious. "I've never...that was... *Damn*, woman. You're amazing."

She gave him a small grin. "You aren't so bad yourself. It really doesn't bother you that I, you know...get super wet?"

"Did anything I do make you think that I was bothered?" he asked.

She shook her head.

"I have to say, I'm actually relieved. Because I didn't exactly give you time to adjust to me. If you weren't as wet as you were, I could've hurt you. You were made for me, Al. It took me twenty fucking years too long to figure it out, but now that I have? I'm yours."

The smile on her face made his cock twitch between them. "I thought men usually liked to say it the other way around. That the woman is theirs."

"I'm not like most men," he said with a shrug. "Besides, I like the thought of belonging to you more. Women take better care of their belongings. And I'm definitely okay with you showing me off. I'm proud to be yours, Al."

For a second, Brick thought he'd fucked up. That he'd said something wrong. But then Alaska took a deep breath and nodded.

"Out there?" he said, gesturing to the window with his head. "You can be whoever you want. Shy, reserved, subdued, professional administrator, hard-ass customer service rep... I don't care. But in here, in our bed...I want you to be exactly who you just were. A woman who knows what she likes and goes after it. Be uninhibited. Tell me what you like and what you want. Take control if you need to. Both sides turn me on, Al. I respect and love every single facet of who you are."

"I, ah...I like sex," she admitted softly.

"I think I got that, honey," Brick said.

"But with you...I love it," she told him.

"That's good. Because I have a feeling we're gonna be having a lot of it. Come on, we need to shower before one of the guys comes to check on us," Brick said as he got up onto his knees. He couldn't help but stare down at her. She was so damn beautiful, it was hard to believe he was actually here with her like this. Her gorgeous chest still blotchy from her orgasm. Her nipples still hard. And his come was smeared all over her body, giving her flesh a decadently shiny look.

"Are you sure you want to go shower?" she asked, looking down at his hardening cock.

"Damn. It hasn't done that for years. Get hard so fast after an orgasm, that is."

When Alaska reached a hand toward him, Brick moved out of her grasp quickly. "None of that," he scolded. "We really do need to get going. I'm sure Tiny or Spike or someone will be knocking at the door if we don't."

Alaska pouted, and it was all Brick could do not to throw himself back on top of her.

"Woman, have mercy," he mumbled, before standing next to the bed and holding out a hand. She grabbed it, and he helped her to her feet.

The shower wasn't as quick as Brick had planned because as soon as they stepped inside the stall and he'd closed the curtain, Alaska was on her knees and had his cock in her hand. The enthusiastic way she'd given him head far surpassed her technique. Brick had never had a better blow job.

He reciprocated by grabbing her around the waist and pulling her against him so her back was to his chest. He used his hand to get her off once more, loving how she squirmed and thrashed in his arms, and how she clung to him when she finally exploded.

Once they finally reached the lodge, it must've been obvious that their relationship had moved to the next level. Every single one of his friends—except for Tonka, who was still down at the barn with the animals— slapped him on the back and gave him huge, shit-eating grins.

But the best part was that Alaska didn't seem embarrassed in the least. She simply rolled her eyes, said, "men," then took up position behind the desk in the great room to start her day.

CHAPTER FIFTEEN

Alaska had literally never been as happy as she was right now. It was strange that it took such a horrific event to make it possible for her lifelong dream to come true. If it hadn't been for her getting kidnapped thousands of miles away, she'd still be toiling at some administrative job in Europe, and dreaming longingly of the boy who would never be hers.

But now here she was, with said boy...now man...and loving every minute of her new reality.

Ever since they'd first made love that morning a week ago, during the day she took care of their guests, and at night, she and Drake made love in every position possible. They'd done away with the condoms after Alaska told him she had an IUD, and the first time he'd come inside her, they'd both moaned from the heavy emotion of the moment—then grinned like complete idiots.

She loved that she could be herself with Drake. He didn't think her desires were weird; in fact, he encouraged her to tell him all the things she wanted to do with him. They'd done them all—and then some. If Alaska thought she got wet with a normal orgasm, it was nothing compared to how much she'd squirted when Drake had experimented with giving her a G-spot orgasm. The first time, she'd been horrified and thought she'd peed on him, but he'd reassured her that she hadn't—then proceeded to fuck the worry right out of her.

Poor Mutt had started sleeping out on the couch in the other room. Alaska felt bad, but Drake quickly made her forget about the dog by giving her an orgasm simply by sucking on her nipples.

Yes, it was safe to say she and Drake were fully compatible when it came to the bedroom. But it was more than that. Even when they weren't in bed, they seemed to be able to read each other remarkably well. One afternoon recently, he'd been moody and short with everyone, and Alaska had encouraged him to take Mutt and go on a long hike, by himself.

When he'd returned, he seemed more settled. And that night, he'd admitted that he'd gotten an email from Mad Dog's former wife, mentioning she was pregnant with her new husband again. He'd thanked her for being understanding, and she'd held Drake a little tighter as they fell asleep.

Over the last three days, the guys had been getting ready for the visit from the investor from China...and were all acting strange. At least, Alaska *assumed* that was why they weren't acting like their normal selves. Drake was constantly pulling one or more of them aside and having private conversations. It wasn't that she felt left out—she didn't need to know every little thing Drake talked about with his friends and co-owners of The Refuge—but it still felt odd nonetheless.

It was three o'clock in the afternoon, and she'd just finished checking in the new guests and returning all the phone messages for the day when Drake appeared at her side.

"Hey, hon. Everything go okay?" he asked.

"Of course. The new guests have been briefed on all the things, they're aware of dinner tonight, I made twenty new reservations today, and we've gotten three thousand dollars in donations since yesterday. Everything's great."

"Good." Drake leaned down and kissed her, but it seemed he was distracted. "Can you come to the therapy room with me for a sec?" he asked.

Alaska frowned. She had no idea what was wrong, but if he wanted to talk to her in there, it had to be something big. She nodded and stood up, her legs shaking slightly.

Was this it? Was he thinking they were done? Had he and his friends hired someone new as an admin? It had only been a week since she and Drake had been *together*-together. Was he already tired of her? Had she done something wrong?

All sorts of worst-case scenarios were flying through her head. She hated that she was so unsure, but she'd never been as happy as she'd been in the past week...and she didn't want anything to ruin that.

She was still lost in her head, trying to figure out where she might go and what she was going to do if he asked her to leave, when Drake reached the door to the room they used for meetings and therapy sessions. He held it open as she walked in first.

Alaska stopped dead in her tracks at the sight in front of her.

Everyone was there. All the guys—including Tonka —Robert, Henley, a few of the women who cleaned the cabins. There were even several guests inside, as well. The table had been pushed against one wall, and there were maroon and white balloons all over the room. Someone had even taped strands of streamers from one side of the room to the other.

"What in the world?" she muttered, right before Tiny counted down from three and, on one, everyone yelled, "Happy Graduation, Alaska!"

Alaska gasped in realization—maroon and white were the colors of the community college she'd attended after high school.

"You didn't get a graduation party back then, so I thought I'd throw you one now," Drake said into her ear from behind.

She felt his hands at her waist, but all Alaska could do was stare at the table by the wall. There was a punch bowl, and a huge cake in the shape of a diploma. She walked toward it in a daze. When she got close enough, she could see her name written in icing on the top in perfect cursive letters. Robert had outdone himself, because the cake looked exactly like the diploma she'd received once upon a time...and had lost in one of her moves.

Drake brushed past her and grabbed something from the table. He brought it to her and opened the padded folder, showing her what was inside.

"Is that...oh my God, Drake. That's my diploma!" Alaska said.

"Yup. After you told me you'd lost yours, I called my mom, and she went to the registrar's office and ordered a replacement for you."

Alaska wasn't a crier—but she burst into tears.

Drake immediately pulled her into his arms. She could hear everyone's murmured whispers, wondering if she was okay, but she couldn't seem to pull herself together enough to reassure them.

"I just...no one's...this is..."

Drake chuckled against her. "It's okay. I understand."

Alaska took a deep breath and looked up at him. "I don't think you do. I haven't had *anyone* who's cared about me like this in a very long time...maybe ever."

"You do now," Drake said simply. "Now how about you dry your tears and smile before my friends beat the shit out of me because they think I've truly upset you."

She knew he was teasing, but she immediately wiped her face and took a deep breath. She leaned up and kissed Drake firmly. "Thank you. You have no idea what this means to me."

He smiled. "I love making you happy," he said, then turned her to face their friends. "She's good," he informed them.

"Awesome. Can we eat now?" Pipe asked. "That cake's been calling my name for *hours!*"

Alaska laughed. "Go for it."

"We got you presents too," Spike informed her, gesturing to the pile of gifts under the table that she'd somehow missed.

"You guys," she protested. "That wasn't necessary."

"Just as you stepping in to help us when we needed you the most wasn't necessary," Tonka told her with a slight shrug.

"Exactly!" Stone agreed.

An hour later, Alaska's face actually hurt from smiling so much. Everyone had gone above and beyond with her gifts. Some were silly, some were useful, but the one that meant the most was from Henley. She'd snapped a picture of her and Drake from behind. They were standing outside, and Alaska had an arm around Drake's lower back as she snuggled against his side. He was leaning down and kissing her forehead as she stared at him lovingly. With the trees in the background, and no buildings in the shot, it looked as if they were the only people on earth.

It was perfection. Alaska couldn't remember what they were talking about when the picture was taken, but it didn't matter. She'd treasure the photo forever.

By the time everyone had indulged in cake and punch and had wandered out of the room to do their own thing, Alaska was practically overwhelmed with emotion.

"I think that went well," Drake said with satisfaction.

"Well?" Alaska asked. "It was awesome!"

Drake snatched her closer, and she let out a small *oof* as she hit his chest. "*You're* amazing," he said, before lowering his head.

Alaska eagerly met his lips and did her best to show him without words just how much she appreciated all he'd done for her.

"Damn, woman," he said after a moment. "As much as I wish I could continue this...I've got some last-minute shit to take care of for Mr. Choo's arrival tomorrow."

Alaska smiled. "And I need to clean this stuff up."

"I'll help," Drake told her.

"Nope, you've done more than enough."

"But it's going to take you several trips to get everything back to our cabin."

Hearing him say "our" cabin made shivers go through Alaska's body. "It's a beautiful day," she said with a shrug. "And I think I can handle walking back and forth a few times."

"Are you sure?"

"Of course. I'm not helpless, Drake. I didn't even have a car back in Europe. Whenever I went shopping, I had to lug everything home by myself."

He stared down at her for a long minute.

"What?" she asked.

"This place isn't very exciting compared to what you're probably used to. We're out here in the middle of nowhere. Our idea of excitement is to stare up at the full moon. Hell, because The Refuge doesn't have a liquor license or allow alcohol on the property, we can't even celebrate with a glass of champagne at a time like this." He frowned.

Alaska put a hand on his cheek. "I don't need museums, festivals, alcohol, or city life to be happy," she said softly. "I've traveled a lot, saw some amazing places, but none of them felt like home. I've been more content here in the so-called 'middle of nowhere' than in any city I've lived in for the last two decades. Because... *you're* here."

As soon as the last three words left her lips, Alaska's nerves kicked in. It was too soon to be saying stuff like that. Yes, she and Drake were very sexually compatible, but they hadn't talked about anything long term. There was no way he'd be satisfied with her forever. She wasn't exotic. Wasn't exciting. Wasn't sophisticated. She preferred sitting on his deck and staring at the stars than going out on the town. If given the choice, she'd choose to make dinner at home than be at the lodge around the guests. It wasn't as if she couldn't make small talk; she just liked not having to worry about what others thought of her or saying the wrong thing.

"No," Drake told her.

Alaska frowned. "No, what?"

"You can't take that back. I can tell you wish you hadn't told me that. But, honey, you have to know I feel the same. I've always loved The Refuge. The first time I camped on this property, I knew this was where I wanted to live. It's far enough from the world that I don't have to worry about saying or doing the wrong thing or being triggered by something I see or hear. The other guys feel the same way. I've always felt at peace here...but since you arrived? It feels more right than ever."

Alaska pressed her lips together and closed her eyes. All her life, she'd felt as if she was living on the sidelines. Watching everyone else get what she wanted... namely, someone to love, and who loved them back. And for the first time she felt as if maybe, just maybe, she'd finally found what she'd always been looking for.

"We're going to sit down and have a long talk after Mr. Choo leaves," he said.

She stilled, her brain automatically going to a black place, thinking maybe he'd want to tell her things were moving too fast.

She mentally shook her head. No. He'd given her no indication of that; actually, he'd done the opposite. She had to stop thinking the worst when it came to guessing Drake's intentions.

"To put your mind at ease," he said as if he could read her mind, "I don't want you to leave. I want you to *stay*. Here. With me. At The Refuge. You're the best admin we've ever had, but that's not why I want you to stay."

Alaska swallowed hard. The look in Drake's gaze was full of affection. He was looking at her in the way she'd always dreamed he would.

"It took me twenty years too long to see you, Al, and I can't let you go now. I learned the hard way what it's like to have regrets. What it's like to lose those I love...I can't, and won't, do it again."

"You aren't going to lose me," she said gently.

"I'm going to do everything in my power to make sure of that. Do you think, someday, you might be able to love me back? I can be rough around the edges, and there are plenty of times I get lost in my head thinking about the past, but I'm getting better. I swear. I don't have a lot to offer, but everything I have I'll gladly share with you. 'Refuge' means to be safe or sheltered from pursuit, danger, or trouble. And that's exactly what this place started out as for me...somewhere to hide away from the world, to hunker down, lick my wounds and figure out how to go on with my life. But now I see it as so much more. It's not only my safe place, but with you by my side, it's a new beginning as well."

"Drake," Alaska whispered.

"I know I'm not being fair," he went on. "I'm taking advantage of what happened to you. Of you being in a vulnerable position. But honestly? I don't care. I'm yours, Alaska. I've never felt this way about *anyone* before."

Tears dripped down Alaska's cheeks. It was hard to believe this was actually happening. She'd daydreamed of hearing a man say these things to her, but for it to be *Drake*...she felt like she had to pinch herself.

"Drake," she repeated, but he kept talking, as if scared about what she might say.

"I can slow down. Or back off. I don't want to scare you away. I know this is fast, but I've always gone gung-ho after something I want. And I want *you*. So much. I feel like an idiot that it's taken me so long to get here, but I also suspect that if we'd gotten together before now, it wouldn't have worked. I was too engrossed in my career. You were in Europe and I was in the States. But—"

Alaska grasped the back of his neck and pulled him toward her. She shut him up by kissing him soundly, then drew back. She had a feeling her face was splotchy, and her eyes red from all the crying she'd done that afternoon. But Drake looked at her as if she was precious.

She'd never felt beautiful before in her life. But right now? Listening to Drake say such incredible things and as he gazed down at her with his heart in his eyes...how could she not believe him?

"I don't think I'll be able to love you someday," she started. His lips pressed together and every muscle in his body stiffened, but she went on before he could pull away from her. "Because I've loved you since I was fourteen years old."

It was scary to admit that. To throw her biggest secret out there. But when he took a huge breath and closed his eyes, even as his arms banded around her like a vise, Alaska tightened her grip on his nape.

His eyes opened, and he whispered, "You love me?"

"Yes," she admitted without hesitation.

"I'm not sure I deserve it—but I'm going to do everything in my power to never make you regret loving me," he said.

"I haven't regretted it in the last twenty-five years, I'm not going to start now," she said.

"Hey, are we having this meeting or what?" Pipe called out as he stuck his head inside the room.

"Keep your pants on!" Drake told him. "I'm having a moment with my woman here."

"You want me to put the Do Not Disturb sign on the door so you can have your moment in peace?" Pipe quipped, his accent pronounced with his amusement.

Alaska giggled, even as Drake let out a dramatic sigh.

"No, I'll be right there," he said.

When they were alone again, Drake stared at her for a long moment.

"What?" Alaska asked nervously.

"I'm just memorizing this moment. I'm forty years

old...I kind of thought it was too late for me to find my other half. But you've been there all along."

"Yeah," Alaska said with a small nod, because what else could she say? She *had* always been there. Not as close as she would've liked, but there all the same.

"After my meeting, which hopefully won't take too long, do you want to take a walk with me to one of my favorite places at The Refuge?"

"Yes." It was an easy question to answer. She'd follow Drake anywhere he wanted to go.

"So damn sweet," he murmured before lowering his head. It was several minutes before they finally broke free.

"I can ask Robert to help you with all your gifts if you want," Drake said.

"It's okay. Don't bother him. I've got it."

"Are you sure?"

"Yes."

"Okay. I'll go to this meeting, then I'll be home. If you feel up to it, you could make us some sandwiches for dinner. It's about a three-mile hike to get to what I want to show you. Is that all right?"

"Yeah...as long as it's worth my while," Alaska teased. That was another thing about Drake; she'd never felt comfortable or sexy enough to tease a man as much as she did him.

He grinned. "Oh, I'll make it worth your while, Al. You can count on that."

Her nipples hardened under her shirt.

"And now I really have to go. The guys are gonna give me shit as it is."

Alaska bit her lip. "I'm sorry."

"I'm not," he said with a grin. Then he closed the small gap between them and kissed her hard and fast once more. "Can't get enough," he said, backing away.

He gave her one last smile, then strode toward the door.

Alaska watched him go with a matching smile on her face.

It was hard to believe everything that had just happened. Drake Vandine loved her. And she'd finally admitted that she loved him back.

She hugged herself for a long moment then turned to look at the remnants of her graduation party. It was silly, she'd long since forgotten that day she'd had to miss her ceremony. But Drake loved her enough to want to celebrate it twenty years after the fact. And her new friends...they didn't have to get her gifts, but they did. Alaska felt all warm and fuzzy inside.

Did it make her a sick person to be glad for what happened to her? To be *thankful* she'd been kidnapped? Man, that was such a horrible thing to think. But if she hadn't been taken, she never would have called Drake. Wouldn't be here with him.

She thought back to when Drake had told her about lockdown procedures, and the possibility of someone dangerous following a guest to the camp. A violent incident at The Refuge could definitely be a trigger. So she'd asked why, if everyone was struggling to control their various forms of PTSD, no one seemed overly concerned about the possibility of danger. Why they all seemed eager to help, in fact, if something *did* happen.

Drake had explained that while former military men and women, and even first responders, had seen and experienced awful things, the people they worked with frequently made their jobs worthwhile. He'd admitted that even knowing what he did now, he still would've chosen to become a SEAL. That there was nothing like the comradery of working with people who had your back, no matter what.

And also, helping others was like a drug. It made *everything* worthwhile.

So even though a violent event at The Refuge would suck, Drake and all his co-owners, and even the guests, had no problem stepping up and doing what needed to be done to protect each other...even at the expense of their mental health.

It made sense to her now. Did she want to ever be kidnapped again? No. Hell no. *But*, if it was the only way she could be with Drake, her answer would definitely change. If it meant Drake was safe? If it meant saving some other woman from the same fate? Then yes, she'd do it all again.

Taking a deep breath, Alaska forced her mind away from that dark thought. She wasn't going to be kidnapped again. That Russian asshole wouldn't be able to take any other women because he was dead. She was safe here at The Refuge. And Drake loved her.

With that unbelievable thought, she got to work stacking her gifts to bring them home.

CHAPTER SIXTEEN

Brick couldn't help but look over at Alaska as they walked. The meeting with the rest of the guys went as well as expected. They hadn't gotten an update from their expert, Elizabeth, on Mr. Choo. She'd been searching the dark web for any trace of him, but so far hadn't had any luck. Which was actually a good thing. But Elizabeth was a lot like Tex...stubborn and not willing to quit just because she hadn't been able to find any dirt on the prospective investor the first time she looked.

From what Brick understood, the computer genius had been through her own kind of hell. She was now married and apparently blissfully happy living in San Antonio with her firefighter husband. But being happy didn't wipe away bad memories. It helped dim them, but didn't get rid of them altogether, as Brick had learned.

Elizabeth hadn't asked for any payment in return for her help. She'd claimed she liked ferreting out the untrustworthy, especially assholes who needed to be stopped from hurting others. So Brick had told her that she was welcome to come to The Refuge anytime they had an opening, free of charge. She'd immediately accepted the offer, saying she'd heard amazing things about the place and she wasn't about to let the opportunity to experience it for herself pass by.

Mr. Choo was scheduled to arrive after breakfast tomorrow. He'd spend the morning touring the camp, the cabins, and seeing some of the trails. Then they'd have lunch, sit down for more discussion about his possible involvement and improvement ideas, and he'd head out in the late afternoon. The day after was left open in case he wanted to come back or if their discussions weren't completed.

While Brick and the rest of the owners had pretty much agreed they weren't really interested in bringing Choo on board as an investor, they still wanted to meet with him and make sure their decision was the right one. There was no doubt the money he could bring to the table would be welcome, but the question was whether or not it was truly needed. Brick and his friends didn't think so. But they were willing to be open-minded enough to go forward with the meeting.

At the moment, Brick was tired of thinking about business. He was ready to spend some time with the woman he loved—who loved him back. He was still pinching himself. It didn't feel real. But then again, the warmth of Alaska's hand in his felt plenty real as they walked together along the trail.

"What are you thinking about so hard?" she asked after a while.

"You," Brick told her.

"Wow, you must be bored out of your mind," she quipped.

"On the contrary, you fascinate me," he retorted.

"I don't know why. I'm boring as hell."

"No, you aren't," he countered. "I was thinking about how brave you were to move to Europe for that first job. Not many twenty-year-olds would've done that."

"Actually, I think that's when most people *would* do that kind of thing. They're single, curious about the world, and have no problem staying in hostels and other low-cost hotels while they're traveling."

"Okay, good point. But that's not why you went."

She shook her head. "No. I was running. You already know about my mom. I just needed to get away. And that was as far as I could get. When I saw the job come up online, I jumped at the chance. You actually had a lot to do with that decision, you know."

"Me?" Brick asked. "We hadn't talked since I left."

"I know. But by then, you were well on your way to becoming a SEAL. I knew you'd be traveling to all kinds of exotic places. Meeting new people. Experiencing new things. You weren't afraid to put your life on the line, to step outside your comfort zone, and I wanted to be like you." She shrugged a little self-consciously.

"I'm honored you thought of me that way," Brick told her. "But I have another question."

She turned toward him and raised her eyebrows in query.

"Why'd you have so many jobs over the years? I

mean, I'd think that once you found a company you liked, in a city you liked, you'd stay."

Alaska looked away from him then, and Brick found himself wary of the expression on her face as she did so.

"Well, secretaries are a dime a dozen. And I didn't exactly fit the mold of what a lot of my bosses thought their admin should look like."

"What does that mean?" he asked in a low tone. He had a feeling he wasn't going to like her answer.

"I wasn't tall, blonde, and beautiful," she said. Brick could hear the hurt in her tone. "I also didn't flirt with the men who called or came in. I did my job—very efficiently, I might add—but that didn't matter. What mattered was that I wasn't pretty, outgoing, or special enough to be an asset."

"That's bullshit!" Brick exclaimed.

Alaska didn't seem fazed by his outburst. "It's the truth," she countered. "The world is run by pretty people...at least on the outside. Those of us who aren't blessed with good looks, or who have disabilities, or who look different from what's deemed acceptable—whether that be the color of our skin, our size, how we sound, or our gender norms—have to work twice as hard to be accepted than everyone else. I can't tell you how many times I was let go because of 'downsizing' or because I just wasn't 'working out.' I knew it was bull-shit, just as my boss did, but there wasn't anything I could do about it because I was an at-will employee. They just made up reasons to get rid of me."

"I'm sorry. That sucks."

"I think the only time I was legitimately fired was

when I went to see you in Germany," Alaska said with a smile.

Brick frowned. "What? You were fired?"

"Yup," she said, almost cheerfully. "I didn't call my boss to let him know where I was or what was going on. I just didn't show up one day."

"I'm sure that happens all the time," Brick argued. "People get sick or in accidents and can't get to a phone, or they aren't thinking about calling their boss."

"Yeah, but it was on a day my boss had a huge meeting. I was supposed to bring in his notes and set up his presentation...basically do all the work for him. I had it done, of course, but in my panic to get to you, I forgot to email everything to him. I guess he looked like an ass in front of his potential clients and they passed on the opportunity to work with the company." She shrugged. "It was worth it though. I would do the same thing all over again if it meant being able to help you."

This woman. He *didn't* deserve her, but he was going to spend the rest of his life doing everything he could to try to be the kind of man who did. He brought their clasped hands up to his lips and kissed the back of hers.

"Anyway, I was glad to leave that job, and not just because my boss was a jerk. I'd been in Germany for a couple years and wanted to experience somewhere else. I just couldn't get the hang of the German language. It's hard."

"So how many languages do you speak now? I mean, you lived in so many places, you had to have picked up some of the native languages here and there."

"One. English."

Brick smiled. "Seriously?"

"Seriously," she told him. "Some people are language savants. They're speaking like a native after only a week in a country. Me? I can say please and thank you in several different languages, but that's about it. I'm hopeless."

Brick couldn't stop the burst of laughter that escaped.

Alaska wrinkled her nose at him. "And now you're making fun of me."

"No. Okay, maybe a little. It's just...you lived in Europe for decades and you didn't pick up *any* languages?"

"Nope," she said with a smile. "I was completely inept. But lucky for me, the people were generally really nice. I'd break out my guide book and say hello, then butcher a simple request for a loaf of bread or something, and they'd switch to English for me. It's amazing how many people know some English. Enough for us to communicate, with lots of hand signals, that is."

Brick simply shook his head. He liked that she could laugh at herself. "By the way," he said. "You should know that the guys are never going to let you leave either. Even Tiny's impressed with how organized you are, how many great ideas you have, and when he needs to check people in after hours, how seamless it is because you've already got everything ready for him. You're really good at what you do, Al. We wouldn't care if you had three heads and a tail...we'd still want you to stay."

She smiled at him. "Thanks. I know it's probably not cool to admit that I like being a secretary. Admin. Whatever. But I do. There's something soothing for me to take files that are completely messed up and fix them. Consolidating and organizing them into some semblance of order. And while I'll never be an IT person, I seem to have a knack for figuring out small issues with a computer and websites too."

"Our website already looks so much better since you've been here," Brick praised. "More professional. And those updated pictures of the cabins you took have made a huge difference."

"I love the guest testimony page I added most, I think. It's important to have real people's thoughts and not bogus crap on there that most people can tell is made up."

Brick agreed. Their talk stayed business related for the rest of the way to the spot he wanted to show her. She was smart and had great insights into every aspect of running The Refuge. He made a mental note to talk to the guys about the possibility of making her a more permanent partner. Any decisions they made on that wouldn't be dependent on them staying together, although he prayed that would never be an issue.

As they neared their destination, Brick stopped in the middle of the trail. It was somewhat overgrown, as it was a lesser-used trail on the property, which was more than all right with him. "We're almost there. Do you trust me?"

"Yes."

Her response was immediate and made his belly do somersaults. There were very few people he trusted with his life...and this woman was definitely on the short list. He'd seen firsthand how loyal she was when she'd lied to get to him in Germany...and he hadn't known even the tip of the iceberg of how incredible she was back then.

"Close your eyes," he told her.

She did so immediately, and he loved the small smile that formed on her lips. He pulled her closer and wrapped her hand around his arm. She snuggled against him as he started walking again. Brick made sure to avoid the roots in the path as they made their way forward.

He steered her off the trail through some tall grass. It took about another two minutes to get to where he wanted to go. A large rock seemingly placed strategically at the optimum spot.

"Sit here," he said quietly as he led Alaska to the rock. It was curved on one side, creating a short backrest. He'd always mentally called it the Sitting Rock. Once she was seated, he shrugged off the backpack with their dinner and eased himself down next to her.

"Can I open my eyes yet?" she asked impatiently.

Brick smiled. "Yup."

Instead of looking at the view in front of them, Brick kept his gaze on her face. Alaska blinked a few times, trying to get her eyes to adjust to the light, but then her mouth dropped open.

"Holy crap, Drake. This is amazing!"

It was. The view from this spot was unparalleled. The forest seemed to open up in front of them. They were on a ridge, and could literally see for miles. The view from Table Rock was nice, but this outdid it four hundred percent. There was nothing to see but trees. Thousands of acres of wilderness. The first time he'd found this spot, Brick had been amazed there was still a part of the country that was uninhabited like this. As if it was completely untouched by humans at all.

Of course, he knew there were probably houses out there. Pockets of civilization. But he liked to think of it as virgin territory. Where animals could roam freely, where the Native Americans reigned not so long ago. Out there, men weren't fighting wars. Weren't doing horrible things to one another. There were no drug problems, no rapes, no men and women getting killed by illegal firearms.

It was a fantasy, Brick knew that. But sitting here, looking out at the land, breathing in the fresh air, he could easily imagine it. And seeing Alaska's reaction to his favorite place to hide when he was struggling was everything he'd hoped it would be.

He took hold of her hand and they sat there for long minutes, soaking in the view, listening to the sounds of the forest around them, and simply being in the moment.

"Thank you for showing this to me," Alaska said quietly after a while. "It's...it makes me feel as if my problems are so small. That the world is so much... bigger than me. And believe it or not, that makes me feel better."

"Same," Brick said.

She lay her head on his shoulder and they sat there for a few more minutes in silence before he asked, "Hungry?"

Just then her stomach growled, and they both chuckled.

"Guess that answers that." Brick grabbed the backpack he'd put on the ground earlier, and they ate their sandwiches while enjoying the pristine view.

When the sun started to sink lower in the sky, he said, "We should probably get back so we aren't hiking in the dark."

"You have a flashlight?" she asked.

"Yes."

"Then I'd love to stay and watch the sun set completely," she said. "If you think it's safe."

"It's safe," he said without hesitation. He wanted to say more. To explain exactly *why* she was safe on their property...but he and his friends had made the decision not to disclose all of the resort's secrets to anyone.

"I know," Alaska said with a nod. "I'm with you, so I know it's safe."

A love so intense it was almost painful swept through Brick. He needed this woman. Now. More than he could put into words.

Luckily, the rock they were sitting on was long and wide. Not quite long enough to fit his entire body, but he didn't care. He set aside the backpack and turned, stretching out on his back next to her. He undid his belt and the zipper on his pants, lifted his ass and shoved them down so his cock sprang free.

Alaska licked her lips as she stared at him.

"Fuck me, Alaska. I need you."

She didn't protest, simply reached for her own belt.

She straddled him, keeping her feet flat on the hard rock under them to protect her knees, and balanced herself by putting a hand on his belly.

Having her take him like this, on top, the last of the

sun's rays enveloping them in their warmth as it sank behind the trees on the horizon, Brick felt almost primal. How many other men had made love to their women in the forest beyond their perch above the trees?

He was about to open his mouth, to tell Alaska to touch herself to make sure she could take him without pain, but his woman was way ahead of him. She used one hand to rub her clit and the other to grasp his cock in her tight grip and stroke.

It didn't take long before they were both ready. When Alaska finally sank down on him, it was all Brick could do not to blow right then and there. Her gaze alternated between looking into his eyes, down at where they were joined, and to the beautiful setting sun. But Brick couldn't take his eyes off his woman.

He could understand how someone might think she was plain at first glance; Alaska actively avoided any kind of attention or spotlight. But to anyone looking, her beauty shone from within, so clear and vivid. It was in the small sounds she made as she moved on top of him. How she cared about her job. How she always had a kind word to say to Robert, or the women who cleaned the cabins, or his friends. The light within her was so bright, sometimes it amazed him he could look at her and not be blinded by its brilliance.

He didn't need coifed hair or painted fingernails. A perfect body and flashy clothes. He just needed *her*. Exactly how she was. A woman who accepted Brick fully, with all his faults.

"Drake," she breathed. "This is...I'm close!" Her voice quivered. Thigh muscles bunched as she used them to pump herself up and down on his erection.

He didn't rush her. Simply let her set the pace and find her release in her own sweet time. He was enjoying watching the way the orange of the setting sun flirted with her hair, bouncing around her shoulders as she moved on him. He loved hearing the gasps and moans that escaped her lips. Watching a sunset would never be the same. Ever. He'd remember this moment for the rest of his life.

Being at this spot had taken on a new meaning as well. It was no longer simply a place he'd run to when his demons overwhelmed him. It was the place where he and Alaska were together for the first time after declaring their love for each other.

As soon as her muscles tensed around his cock and she leaned toward him, Brick moved. He grasped her hips tightly and began to pound into her from below. She bounced precariously in his grip, but there was no way he was going to let go, no way she'd get hurt when she was with him.

He fucked her hard and fast, pushing through her tightening muscles as she orgasmed around him. Each thrust felt as if she was strangling his cock, and the sex was raw. Intense.

As the last rays of the sun disappeared, Brick thrust once more and filled the woman he loved to the brim. It felt as he would never stop coming. He could even feel his release leaking out of her and onto his balls as he held himself inside her as far as he could get. She crumpled onto his chest as if boneless, and Brick held her tightly as they both tried to catch their breaths.

"Holy crap," she breathed after a few minutes had passed. "That was..."

"Perfect," Brick finished for her.

"Exactly. I can't say outdoor sex was ever on my bucket list, but it should've been."

Brick grinned. He couldn't help but feel a little cocky. "Your legs feel okay? That position had to have been a little awkward."

"Legs? I have legs?" she quipped against his throat.

This time when he chuckled, his cock slipped out of her warm heat. She moaned.

Brick agreed. There was no place he loved being more in the world than buried deep within her body.

As much as he wanted to lie there and bask in the most amazing sex he'd ever had...now that the sun had set, it would get chilly. And dark. It got *really* dark on The Refuge. And he'd much rather be holding Alaska in their nice comfortable bed instead of on this piece of rock.

"Give me a second and I'll grab you something to clean up with," Brick told her, sitting up with her still in his lap.

He held her against him as he fumbled for the backpack and extra napkins.

Alaska relaxed on his lap and didn't try to assist. Brick couldn't help but grin. "Where'd the woman go who's always so eager to do her part? Who wants to help even when I want to spoil her?" he asked.

"You fucked her into submission."

Brick could feel her smile against his shoulder. He laughed. "That's all it takes to make you do what I tell you to?"

"Maybe," she told him.

Without a word, he reached between them and ran the napkins between her legs.

That got her moving. She sat up and leaned back. "I can do that," she told him.

"I got it," he said, brushing her hand aside. "It's only fair."

To his pleasure, she let him. This was more intimate than anything he'd ever done with a woman, and with Alaska, it felt natural. He did his best to wipe away his come and her own juices before putting the used napkins in a plastic bag and shoving it back into his backpack.

"Is my underwear around here somewhere?" Alaska asked, looking around. "I think I might've thrown it in my haste to get you inside me."

Spying the blue strip of cotton nearby, Brick leaned over and snagged it. Then he helped Alaska to her feet and stood next to her, keeping a hand on her arm so she wouldn't accidentally slip and fall. They got dressed without any fuss and when he had the backpack on, she leaned into him.

"Thank you for showing me your special spot."

"It's our special spot now," he said easily.

The smile she gave him was beautiful, just like her. "I love you," she said a little shyly.

"I love you too, Al. So much, it almost scares me."

"I've had longer to get used to the feeling," she said.

Brick would never cease to be amazed by her. "You ready to head back?"

"No, but yes."

He totally understood. "Okay, stay close. I've got the

light but the trail needs some repairs. The tree roots can totally blend into the shadows."

Alaska nodded and they set off toward home.

Home.

The Refuge had always been a place Brick loved. A place of peace. Of healing. But now it was more than just a cabin. A business. It was truly a home. Because Alaska was there with him.

He'd do everything possible to keep it that way. To make her happy. To keep her safe. The thought of anything happening to her now that she was his...it made Brick a little crazy. He made a vow right then and there, with Alaska's hand in his, her scent in his nostrils, the vision of her lost in pleasure still fresh in his mind— he'd kill before that kind of evil ever touched her again.

He hadn't spent his life as a Navy SEAL to fail the one person who'd always believed in him.

Brick knew he was feeling a little bloodthirsty at the moment, but he put it down to the carnality of making love to his woman in the open air. Like he was a conqueror of old. That was all it was.

It wasn't the niggling at the back of his neck that spoke of pending trouble.

No, he was just being paranoid that his happiness, their happiness, might be snatched away before it could blossom. A natural fear, he guessed, considering he'd never been in love before.

He deserved to be happy. Deserved Alaska. Nothing and no one would take her away from him.

* * *

Yong Chen was bursting with impatience. He was finally here. In the United States. In New Mexico. Hours from claiming what was his. What'd he'd paid good money for. He deserved to be as happy as the next person...and what would make him happy was breaking Alaska Stein.

He didn't usually bother to learn the names of his acquisitions. It didn't really matter what they were called; all that mattered was how fast they opened their legs and did what he ordered them to do.

But Alaska was different. She was the one who got away...the only one. But not for long.

It was all Yong could do not to break from the role he'd been playing and ask about her. But that would have been strange. For an investor to show even the slightest amount of curiosity toward a secretary. Tomorrow, he'd finally see her in the flesh. He hoped he'd get a chance to talk to her. To play the friendly visitor, so she'd let down her guard. So when it came time to snatch her right out from under the noses of the so-called soldiers she worked with, she'd be more trusting and would go with him without making a scene.

Yong had read all about the seven assholes who owned the crappy camp on the mountain. That was basically what it was, no matter what they called it or how they tried to make it seem as if it was more. If he *was* an investor, it would be the last place he'd choose to spend his money.

First, it was surrounded by miles and miles of nothingness. Dry desert terrain on one side and forested mountains on the other. Close to Los Alamos, which was miniscule. Not nearly enough people for his liking.

He much preferred Beijing. A massive, thriving metropolis where a man could blend in...hide his actions.

Second, The Refuge was a place for the mentally deficient. Weak men and women who couldn't handle what life threw at them. They were like babies who wanted to be coddled, and Yong didn't tolerate weakness in any form.

It was going to be a piece of cake to take back what was his. Yong hadn't been this excited in years. He could almost thank the Russian for fucking up their transaction. Almost.

Tomorrow, he'd get the lay of the land. Play his part. Then he'd figure out what his next move should be. Sneak back in at night and take Alaska? Wait until the next day and cause a distraction so he could stealthily move in and grab her? See if he could get her to come with him willingly? There were so many possibilities, each with its own level of risk, but Yong had no doubt he'd be victorious. He had three million dollars riding on his success. Three dozen men now who were willing to pay, and pay handsomely, for a chance to fulfill their every sick fantasy with the woman.

His plans for the American might have changed over the last few weeks, but the outcome would be the same. She'd be his plaything until he tired of her, then he'd triple his investment before going back to his life in China. He always got what he wanted.

Always.

CHAPTER SEVENTEEN

Alaska slept better than she had in what seemed like years. And that was saying something, because she'd slept pretty good in Drake's arms the last few weeks or so.

But something had happened out there on that rock. She and Drake had connected in a way that was almost spiritual. He'd been sexy and alpha, but she hadn't missed the way he'd still protected her. The way he'd put himself between her and the hard rock. How he'd tenderly cleaned her afterward. Held her close as they made their way back to the cabin in the pitch darkness.

No one, not one person, had treated her as if she was the most precious thing in their life. Alaska couldn't even remember her mom doing that when she was little. She'd been allowed to wander their various neighborhoods as late as she wanted from a young age. Her mom never asked where she'd been when she came home. Anytime she'd gotten hurt, it had been up to Alaska to clean and bandage herself.

When she was with Drake, she felt loved. He sought her out the second he stepped into the lodge—and when their gazes met, gave her a small, private smile. Always made sure she wasn't too tired, too cold or warm. Checking to see if she'd taken a break or grabbed some lunch. The list went on and on. She felt as if she was always on his radar. That he was constantly reassuring himself that she was good.

She'd been fairly pessimistic about them working out for a good while, but she was beginning to think they might just go the distance. It felt unbelievable.

Alaska knew part of her pessimism came from his background, from the fact he'd lost his best friends. She now understood more about PTSD, how everything could be going great, then the smallest thing could send you into a tailspin. Drake had a better handle on his demons than most...but still, life was full of ups and downs, and the downs always seemed to have more of an effect on a person's long-term attitude and actions than the ups.

She'd seen the same in herself. Alaska wasn't as trusting as she used to be. She took stock of her surroundings more. Was on watch. She didn't particularly like that, but when she'd talked to Drake about it, he'd pointed out that her watchfulness wasn't a bad thing. She agreed, but still missed the mostly carefree person she used to be. She'd been independent for so long. Now, just the thought of traveling on her own made her break out in hives.

But she had no intention of going anywhere anytime

soon. Life at The Refuge was idyllic. She loved her job. Got along great with the other men who owned the resort. Found the guests fascinating. And of course, there was Drake. She had to trust that even when he succumbed to his demons, he'd have the strength and fortitude to wrestle them back into submission. Maybe even with her help.

She'd been ready to continue their lovemaking when they got home from their hike last night, but Mutt needed attention, and she needed to empty the backpack of their trash and leftovers. Then Drake wanted to check his email, since he had to get up early in the morning to go into Los Alamos and pick up Mr. Choo. By the time they crawled into bed, they were both tired. So Drake had simply pulled her against him in their usual sleeping positions and they'd been dozing within minutes.

Drake had gotten up early, kissed her and told her to sleep in, said that he'd see her later. He and his friends would be busy most of the day as they showed Mr. Choo around the property and had a meeting about the future of The Refuge.

Because she was feeling lazy, Alaska did as he ordered and snuggled into the bed that seemed far too empty when he wasn't in it with her.

Later that morning, she wandered into the lodge and greeted the guests that lingered there. While some of the men and women who visited the resort chose to spend the majority of their time in their cabins or hiking the property, others enjoyed hanging out in the lodge. There was always someone reading, eating, or relaxing on the leather couches in the great room.

Alaska greeted two men who were talking quietly in the sitting area as she entered, and headed toward the desk in the corner. She booted up the computer and got to work answering emails and phone messages as she prepared to check out the three guests who would be leaving later that morning.

Around lunchtime, Drake entered the lodge with Spike and Pipe and a man who could only be Mr. Choo. He was around Alaska's height, with a round face, short black hair, hooded eyes and his golden skin looked a little sallow, as if he didn't spend a lot of time outdoors. He wore a pair of pressed black pants, a short-sleeve yellow polo shirt, and had an air of superiority he didn't bother to hide.

Alaska instantly felt guilty for thinking the latter when she'd yet to even meet the man.

Drake headed straight for her, and she stood. With one look, she could see he was stressed. His movements were slightly stiff and the small smile he gave her didn't quite reach his eyes. He leaned down to kiss her briefly, and she whispered, "Are you okay?"

And just like that, he relaxed a little. "I am now that I've seen you," he told her quietly. Then added, "It's just been a stressful morning. I'll be okay."

Alaska nodded, hating that he was so tense.

The others had approached the desk by that time and Drake turned to them. "Bolin, I'd like to introduce Alaska Stein. She's our admin, and we don't know what we'd do without her. Alaska, this is Bolin Choo."

"It's nice to meet you," Alaska said politely, holding out her hand.

Mr. Choo took her hand in both of his and bowed over it slightly, drinking her in with dark eyes.

For some reason, the hair on the back of Alaska's neck stood up, and she stilled. The man's grasp was cold and clammy. Just the feel of his skin on her own made her want to wipe her hand down her pants to try to remove the feel of his fingers. It was an odd reaction. She couldn't count the number of strangers she'd met in her lifetime...but not one of them had given her this kind of feeling.

Luckily, he let go quickly, and it was all Alaska could do not to follow through and wipe her hand on her clothes. She tried to convince herself that her reaction was simply because this was the first Asian man she'd seen since her ordeal. How many times had Drake warned her about being triggered? The man didn't deserve her distrust.

She swallowed hard and forced herself to smile. This was good for her. All a part of healing and moving on with her life.

"We're going to head into the therapy room for lunch," Drake told her.

Alaska nodded. "Do you want me to tell Robert you're here?" she asked in as normal a tone as she could muster, praying he'd agree so she could have an excuse to leave.

"That'd be great, thanks," he said. "But tell him to give us twenty minutes or so. The others will be joining us soon."

"Okay.'"

"Thanks, hon," Drake said. He leaned down and

kissed her temple before turning back to his friends and guest. "Shall we?" he asked.

The three men turned to go to the therapy room, but Drake lingered for a moment.

"What's wrong?" he asked, his brows drawn into a frown.

For a moment, Alaska was tempted to tell him that she did *not* like Mr. Choo, but she quickly reconsidered. Drake was under enough stress as it was. The last thing he needed was to be worrying about her when he was in the middle of an important negotiation. Even though he'd already told her that they were leaning toward turning down Mr. Choo's offer, it wasn't a done deal. He and his friends might change their minds after this visit. Alaska didn't want to ruin the chance for Drake to expand The Refuge. He loved this place, and she wouldn't stand in the way of helping more people if she could help it.

"Nothing," she said with a forced smile and a small shrug. "I'm just worried about you. You look tired and stressed."

"I am," he said. "But not because things aren't going well. On the contrary, they're going better than I thought. Mr. Choo has some good ideas and he loves what he's seen so far."

Alaska understood. "Which makes the decision whether to turn down his offer or not all the more difficult."

"Exactly," Drake said with a nod.

"I'm sure you and your friends will make the right decision," Alaska told him.

He smiled, and it seemed a bit more relaxed than

moments ago. "The money on the table would definitely be welcome," he admitted. "But we're in no way ready to pull that trigger yet. We have a lot to discuss this afternoon...and we're waiting on a phone call from a friend with more information about Mr. Choo. So we won't make any decisions until we have all the info we need."

"More information?" Alaska asked.

Drake shrugged. "Yeah. We're just being cautious and want to know everything there is to know about the man before we go into business with him."

"Oh, so like a background check," she said.

"Something like that. It's taking longer than it might have otherwise, because so far he's squeaky clean... which is a relief," Drake said. "Enough about that. You had lunch yet?"

Alaska smiled at his concern. "Yeah, I took a break right before you got here."

"The guests get checked out okay?"

"Yep. There's a new couple coming in around one, and then the last new guest should be here right before I go off duty, around three or so."

"Good. If you need anything, just let me know."

"Drake, I'm not going to interrupt you in the middle of your meeting. If something comes up, I'll handle it."

He smiled. "Yeah, you will, won't you?"

"It's what you pay me for," she quipped.

"You're amazing," Drake said.

Alaska rolled her eyes. She wasn't amazing, she was doing her job...something the other admins they'd hired hadn't been able to do very well, but still. She couldn't imagine ever interrupting such an important meeting. If something happened, she'd deal. It was what she did.

"Go," she told him. "Kick some butt."

Drake grinned. "Yes, ma'am. For the record...I'm going to be peopled out by the time this meeting is over this afternoon. You want to go for another hike with me? Or are you too sore?"

"I'm not sore," she told him. At least not in the way he was asking. She could still feel him between her thighs—he wasn't exactly a small man—but her leg muscles didn't hurt from the hike last night. She'd gotten in much better shape over the weeks she'd been here.

"All right. Maybe just a short hike this time. We can grab dinner when we get back, if that's all right."

"Of course. I'll grab a snack before I head to the cabin to wait for you."

"Perfect." Drake reached up and wrapped a hand around the back of her neck. "I don't deserve you," he said.

"Yes, you do," she countered. "We deserve each other."

He gave her a small smile, then leaned down and kissed her. It was a passionate kiss, but not long. "I'll see you later."

She nodded and watched him walk away, licking her lips. Alaska could still taste him.

That she was here, that this was her life, was so wild. She'd thought about Drake so much over the years. Wondered where he was, what he was doing. And after he'd left the Navy and started The Refuge, she'd been relieved he wouldn't be putting his life on the line anymore, but she'd still worried about him.

And now she was here. With him. *With* him. It was a dream come true.

The years had been good to Drake. He was more handsome now than when he was an eighteen-year-old boy, and his maturity made him more attractive to her, not less. In twenty more years, he would definitely be a silver fox. She'd always be plain, would always fade into the background, but with Drake at her side, she realized she didn't care. The only person's opinion she cared about was his.

And he'd made it more than clear that he didn't think she was plain. That he loved her exactly how she was. It was a heady feeling.

"Excuse me?" a woman asked from next to her.

Alaska nearly jumped out of her skin, but chuckled as she turned to the guest. "I'm sorry, I wasn't paying attention. What can I do for you?"

"I didn't mean to scare you...but I don't blame you for being distracted. If I had a man like him, I'd have all my attention on his ass as he walked away too."

Alaska laughed without taking offense. How could she? The woman wasn't wrong. "He's as beautiful from the back as he is from the front, for sure," she agreed. "Now, how can I help you?"

"I was wondering if you could recommend one of the trails for my friend and me? I'm not the best hiker and don't want anything too strenuous, but this place is just so beautiful, I don't want to sit around and do nothing all day."

Alaska smiled and did her best to turn her attention

away from Drake. She was still worried about him and his friends. They were stressed, and she hated that for them, but Mr. Choo's visit should be over soon and they could relax once again.

* * *

Brick sighed in relief as Owl walked Mr. Choo out of the room. He'd volunteered to take their visitor back to his hotel in Los Alamos. Brick had been with the man all day and it was a huge relief to pass the responsibility off to someone else.

"So?" Stone asked. "What does everyone think?"

There was silence in the room for a long moment before Tiny spoke. "He's got some really good ideas. And while I think we could pull most of them off without his money, it would take several years before we'd be able to implement any of them."

The others all nodded in agreement.

"I was ready to not like any of his suggestions, but he seems to be an astute businessman," Spike agreed.

The next twenty minutes was spent going over the pros and cons of the improvements and expansions they'd discussed with Mr. Choo.

Tonka had been quiet throughout the conversation, much as he had all day. The man was frequently silent, preferring to let others talk when he could get away with it. He wasn't so reticent around the animals. When he thought he was alone, he talked up a storm to Melba, the goats, and the other animals in the barn. No one was offended, they knew it was just who he was...that all their pasts affected them in different ways.

But he spoke up now.

"I don't like him," Tonka said resolutely.

"Why not?"

"It's just a feeling," he replied.

Brick felt a weight lift from his shoulders. There was something about the man that didn't sit well with him either, but he didn't know what it was. He hadn't said or done anything inappropriate in the hours Brick had spent with him. He'd been polite, curious, and enthusiastic about The Refuge in general.

But there was a niggling voice in the back of his mind that said something was off about the man. And he hadn't missed Alaska's reaction when she'd met him either. She'd insisted it was worry for Drake. Now he wasn't so sure.

If his friends had been in a normal boardroom anywhere other than at The Refuge, they might've dismissed Tonka's words as paranoia. But they'd all been in situations where a gut feeling had saved their lives.

"I agree," Brick said after a moment.

"Have we heard back from Elizabeth?" Spike asked no one in particular.

"No," Tiny said. "Last I heard, she still hadn't found anything on the man."

"Which is a good thing, right?" Stone asked.

"Well, yeah. If she hasn't found anything, then there's a better than average chance he's legit. But Elizabeth wasn't ready to quit. She said the more evil the person, the better they could hide their tracks. She was determined to know with one hundred percent certainty that he was exactly who he claims to be...a man who's interested in growing his investments in the US."

The room was quiet for a long moment.

"I can't speak for you guys, but I'm beat," Pipe finally said. "I don't know what it is about being 'on' that drains me, but there it is."

"Same," Tiny agreed.

"Choo's coming back tomorrow after lunch to meet with us once more. How about if we take the rest of the afternoon and evening to think about everything. Tomorrow morning, we'll get together and discuss what we want to do when we're fresh and rested. We can let him know when he arrives what our decision is," Tiny suggested.

Everyone agreed and stood to clean up the room and head out.

Tonka and Brick were the last ones in the room, and Brick stopped his friend by asking, "What is it about Choo that makes you uneasy, do you think?"

Tonka shrugged. "I'm honestly not sure. On the surface, everything seems great. But he's almost *too* perfect. Every single thing we suggested, he agreed with. If we didn't like one of his ideas, he immediately backed off. He didn't push us—at all. That didn't sit well with me. Not from a man supposedly interested in profiting from an investment."

Brick realized he was right. "I hadn't noticed at the time. Now that you've pointed it out, it's obvious."

"But it's more than that," Tonka said. "I watched the guy as you gave him a tour of the grounds. He said all the right things, but his eyes never stopped moving. Taking in everything."

"Isn't that what he should've been doing?" Brick asked.

"Yes, but this was...not normal. It was as if he was casing the place."

Brick frowned.

"Remember when we first got Bubba? He'd been abused horribly and was way underweight. He wanted nothing to do with me or any other human."

"I remember," Brick said. "You were amazing with him. Taught him first to trust the other horses, then got him to trust not only you, but everyone else too."

"Right, but in the meantime, when he was in the corral, I watched him. He was constantly on alert for an escape route. His eyes scanned the area looking for a weak spot in the fence. He was desperate to escape a situation he likely thought was exactly like the one he came from. I saw that same intense interest in Choo's eyes today."

"What do you think he was looking for?" Brick asked.

"I have no idea. But it made me uneasy."

Brick sighed. His head was throbbing. In the past, he would've been desperate to be by himself for a few hours. To take some time to get his equilibrium back. But today? All he wanted to do was see Alaska. She was his rock. His safe place.

"I appreciate you speaking up. I felt the same way, but didn't really realize it until you said something."

"I've learned the hard way that it's more important to speak up when I have misgivings rather than to stay quiet and go with the flow," Tonka said in a somewhat monotone voice.

Not for the first time, Brick wondered what the hell his friend had been through, but he knew when—or if—he was ready to share, he would. Brick wouldn't push him.

"Again, it's appreciated."

"And for the record?" Tonka went on.

Brick waited for him to continue. It had been a while since he'd heard Tonka say as much at one time as he was right now.

"Alaska...I like her. She's good for you. For The Refuge. She fits this place perfectly. She fits *you*."

Brick's heart swelled. He didn't need his friend's approval, but he definitely wanted it. "She fits me perfectly," he agreed.

Tonka nodded at him, then abruptly turned and headed for the door. "Melba's probably eating her stall about now," he muttered. "Need to get her fed."

He turned at the door, and Brick braced for whatever he was about to add.

"Be careful," Tonka warned. "Choo has an agenda, but there's no telling what it is."

Brick nodded, though his friend had already turned around and left. He stared after him for a long moment. A foreboding swept through Brick, making him shiver even though the room wasn't cold in the least. Not knowing why he suddenly felt so claustrophobic and anxious made him desperate to get out. Of the room, the building, and into the land that had always soothed him.

He considered calling Alaska and telling her that he was going to take Mutt and head off into the forest on his own, after all. But he swiftly rejected the idea. He wouldn't be able to hike as hard or fast as he would by himself, but he didn't want to leave her behind. He didn't have a good reason why, except that he enjoyed being with her and didn't want to leave her alone.

So taking a deep breath, Brick headed out of the room. He did his best to give a friendly smile and nod to the guests relaxing in the lodge as he walked toward the front door. Deciding to put Choo, the investment decision, and everything else out of his mind for now, he made his way toward his cabin. Toward Alaska.

* * *

Yong paced his hotel room impatiently. He'd changed into black cargo pants, a black shirt, hiking boots, and had readied the pistol he'd picked up from a contact when he'd arrived in the United States. It was so easy to get firearms here, it was ridiculous. But since it suited his needs, he wasn't complaining.

He wasn't actually planning on shooting anyone, if it could be avoided. The gun was just to make sure Alaska went along nice and quietly. And after this afternoon, he was doubly glad he had it. Yong hadn't missed the protective looks Vandine had shot her way. He already knew the man wasn't her husband, as she'd told the Russian. One of the other men let it slip that none of them were married. It was still a complication that she was fucking her rescuer, but not exactly unexpected.

If he'd been in Vandine's shoes, he would've taken advantage of the situation and started fucking her too. Women were predictable and easy. Alaska was probably so overcome with gratefulness, she'd spread her legs for him before they'd even arrived back in the US.

But Vandine's feelings toward her didn't matter. Neither did *her* feelings. Alaska was his. *His*, dammit! He'd paid for her, fair and square. She'd be coming with him tonight, one way or another.

When he'd finally gotten a chance to touch her today, he'd almost blown his cover. He'd wanted to claim her as his own right then and there. Her hand was so soft, and the way it had trembled in his grip turned him on so much, it was all he could do to hide his erection.

Deep down, she knew she was his. That he was her master. He reveled in her fear, and it would ramp up so much once he had her where he wanted her. She'd fight at first, there was no doubt, but before too long, she'd submit. They all did.

Vandine might be a problem, but not one Yong couldn't handle. Today's visit had been perfect. He'd been able to study the area without raising any suspicions. He knew which cabin Alaska was staying in, knew where the other cabins were, and discovered the animals on the property weren't a concern. They were docile as could be and wouldn't raise the alarm if they spotted him wandering around.

He needed to wait until it was dark, then he'd make his move. He had a vehicle he'd borrowed from a man who'd paid a staggering amount to have first crack at Alaska...after Yong, of course. The man who'd provided the car had even scoped out the property. There was a dirt road, some sort of old logging road, off the main thoroughfare that led to Los Alamos. Yong would park there, hike through the forest, execute the diversions to keep everyone busy, then retrieve his property.

And if absolutely necessary, he'd use the gun to kill anyone who dared get in his way.

The more he thought about it, the better he liked his chances if he eliminated Brick completely. He was obviously obsessed with the bitch, and taking him out would be the smartest option. The others would be so shocked and alarmed by the death of their friend, it would probably take hours for them to discover Alaska was missing. If they even cared.

She was homelier than he'd thought. The Russian had lied a bit when describing her. But it didn't matter. Yong had paid for her, and he had way too many clients lined up and too much money on the line to abort his plan now. If needed, he'd just put a bag over her head so his clients couldn't see how average she was.

Yong grinned. He'd worked so hard, for so long, and the time was almost here. He'd been outraged when he'd found out his property had been intercepted. But this was the most fun he'd had in years.

"Soon," he murmured as he paced. "Soon you'll be mine."

CHAPTER EIGHTEEN

It was later than Brick wanted before he and Alaska had been able to get out into the forest. As soon as he arrived back at his place, Spike had called and said there was a water leak in one of the cabins. Brick had dealt with that, then a guest had reported seeing a bear close to the resort. It was possible, as black bears did inhabit the higher elevations where The Refuge was located, but in all the years they'd been open, there hadn't been one sighting.

Tonka and Brick went out to investigate anyway, then spent a good amount of time reassuring the guest that they wouldn't be eaten, the bear wouldn't break into their cabins, and even though guests weren't allowed to have weapons allowed on the property, Brick and the other owners did have them, and could deal with the threat if one occurred.

By the time Brick got back to the cabin, it was pretty much dinnertime. He didn't want to take Alaska out on a hike, even a short one, without eating first. So she'd volunteered to make them a quick meal while he showered.

It was silly for him to take a shower right before they went on a hike, but Alaska obviously knew he needed a moment to himself to decompress, so he gladly took her up on her offer and disappeared into the bathroom.

He took his time, letting the hot water beat on his back, neck, and shoulders. He felt much better afterward, even smiling a bit, knowing how much Alaska loved the way he smelled right after he'd showered.

They ate the sweet potatoes she'd nuked in the microwave and the roasted broccoli before heading out into the fresh evening air. The sun was just starting to set as they got on their way.

One of the best things about his woman was that she always seemed up for anything. Hiking in the dark? No problem. Trying a sexual position she hadn't heard of before? Bring it on. Tackling an issue with the website? She was up for the challenge. Brick had never been with a woman who was so willing to try new things.

"You know, most other women would balk at heading out for a hike knowing long before they turned around to go home, it would be dark," he told her.

Alaska laughed. "You forget that we hiked in the dark last night."

"True, but you didn't blink last night either."

"That's because I was still high from the sex," she said wryly.

Brick chuckled.

"But for the record, I'd go anywhere, and do anything, with you by my side."

Emotion made it impossible for Brick to respond for the longest time. Eventually, he said, "I'm terrified of you getting hurt on my watch."

But Alaska didn't tense at all. Brick was holding her hand as they walked and he didn't see or feel any change in her demeanor.

"You shouldn't be. You think I haven't noticed how you're constantly keeping an eye out for me? How you slip me an orange after lunch when you think I might need a snack? Or when you step in to mediate when I've got a challenging guest? Or how you make sure I'm warm enough when we sit outside on your back deck? Drake, you're more attuned to my needs than I am. Of course I trust you."

Her voice lowered as she continued. "You came when I needed you most. You didn't have to. You didn't even really know me. And yet you didn't hesitate. I love you because of who you are, but I'll never forget that as long as I live. You proved that you have my best interests at heart in the most extraordinary way a person could."

Brick's hand tightened around hers. "I wasn't there for my team," he said after a moment.

"Bullshit," Alaska said fiercely. "And what happened was through no fault of your own. I know me saying you shouldn't feel guilty doesn't make it so, but seriously, Drake—surviving that explosion was a gift. And every one of your friends would say the same thing. We both know you would've done anything to save even one of them."

She wasn't wrong. And Brick had been over and over this with therapists. Survivor's guilt was an insidious thing. Just when he thought he had it conquered, it would rear its ugly head again.

Alaska stopped in the middle of the trail and stepped into him. She put her hands on his cheeks and tilted his head down so he had no choice but to meet her gaze. "You deserve me," she said softly. "Just as I deserve you. This place, The Refuge, is your tribute to Vader, Monster, Bones, Rain, and Mad Dog. They'd be so damn proud of you. Just as I am."

The fact that she knew his friends' names, and wasn't afraid to talk about them, made his heart lighten. They didn't deserve to be forgotten.

He nodded, too emotional to speak.

But she didn't seem to expect him to. She went up on her tiptoes, kissed him oh so tenderly, then grabbed his hand once more and continued down the trail. They walked briskly for a while without talking.

Brick was relieved she didn't feel the need to fill the silence with chatter. He needed this. The quiet of the forest. Her hand in his. Alaska silently supporting him at his side. Some of the guilt would always be there, deep down, but he'd do his best to keep it at bay as much as possible. She was right. They deserved each other.

They walked with no real destination in mind. At one point, Brick steered them off the main path toward a lesser-used trail. There weren't as many good over-looks or views, as it took them through a thicker part of the forest, but Alaska didn't seem to mind.

They were probably about two miles from The

Refuge, the last of the day's light quickly waning, when Brick's phone vibrated in his pocket.

He sighed in frustration. He could've left his phone back at the cabin, or turned it off, but he felt too much responsibility to his friends to do that. Looking down, he saw it was Tiny calling.

"What's up?" he said as he answered.

"Where are you?" Tiny asked in lieu of a greeting.

The tone of his friend's voice had Brick immediately on alert. He stopped walking and could feel Alaska staring at him in concern, but all his attention was on his conversation with Tiny. "On trail number four. About two miles out. Why?"

"We heard back from Elizabeth about Choo," Tiny said. "First of all, his name's not Bolin Choo. It's Yong Chen. It's him, Brick."

"Him who?" he asked in confusion.

"*Him*. The person who bought Alaska from the Russian."

The whole world went black for a second or two. Then fury rose within Brick so intense, he thought his skin was on fire. "*What?*" he bit out.

"The guy's good. Really covered his tracks well. But Elizabeth's better. Her tenacity paid off and she found him. Apparently, he used the name Bolin Choo when he was first getting into sex trafficking. He's changed his name several times since then, but it was enough for Elizabeth to eventually find him. He bought Alaska from the Russian, and she wasn't his first purchase. Elizabeth has traced about twenty missing women back to him—so far. From all over the world. They literally disappeared without a trace and were never heard from again. I'm guessing Choo—sorry, *Chen*—was pissed when Alaska didn't arrive as scheduled, and he immediately began to make plans to get her back."

"He's here for her," Brick said. "So it was all a ruse."

"Looks that way. But that's not the worst," Tiny said.

"What?" Brick barked.

"He's lined up three million dollars' worth of clients who want a turn with her. From the messages and chat rooms Elizabeth found, he's sold time with her to over three dozen men. It looks like his plan is to take her to Los Angeles, stay there for a month or so, then head back to China with his bank account fat and happy...and without Alaska."

Brick knew without having to ask what that meant. The asshole had sold Alaska to other men and, when it was time for him to go home, he'd dispose of her without a second thought.

"Drake?" Alaska asked in a shaky voice as she put a hand on his arm.

"Give me a second," he told her, struggling to control his anger.

He hated when she took a step away at his tone, but at the moment, it was taking all of his control not to completely lose it. This was literally his worst nightmare come true.

"Where is he now?" he asked Tiny.

"We don't know. That's why I called you," Tiny said. "He's not at the hotel, but he hasn't checked out."

"He's coming for her," Brick said almost flatly. He'd tamped his emotions down so far, he was running on pure instinct at the moment.

"We think so," Tiny agreed.

"It's why he was so interested in touring the property," Brick went on. "He was casing the place."

"Right. So you need to get back here and hole up. We'll—"

Tiny's voice cut out when a massive boom sounded through the phone line.

"What the fuck was that? Tiny?" Brick yelled.

"Holy shit! *Fuck*! There was an explosion near the POW cabin. It's on fire. Thank fuck no one's in it right now," Tiny replied.

Brick's stomach clenched. This Chen guy wasn't fucking around. Then he heard more noise through the line. "What's that?"

"Fireworks. A shit ton of them. Going off all around the camp."

"Distraction," Brick said. All of a sudden, he felt utterly calm.

"Yup. The guests are freaking out."

"Lock 'em down," Brick ordered.

"Already in the process. Stone's putting the emergency procedures into place now. But the guests who're triggered by fireworks are going to be difficult to calm."

Brick had no doubt Chen knew that.

"We aren't coming back there," he told his friend.

He could hear Tiny breathing hard, as if he was running somewhere. "All right."

He was relieved his friend wasn't questioning him.

"I'm taking her to bunker one-eleven," Brick said.

"Ten-four."

What no one knew, except for the men who owned The Refuge, was that there were seven underground bunkers hidden on The Refuge property. In the woods.

316

They'd given them numbers, so they could be referred to in an emergency. If the lodge was at six o'clock on a standard clock face, the cabins were at nine o'clock through three o'clock on the property. They were named according to their position. Bunker one-oh-one was at one o'clock, just northeast of the lodge. Bunker one-o-nine was at the nine o'clock position. All of them spread out in the forest surrounding the main cabins.

Each bunker was stocked with about a month's worth of food and water. They were primitive, designed for the men to escape if necessary. And they were hidden so well, there was no way anyone would stumble upon them. In fact, they could walk right over them and have no idea the bunkers were there. When The Refuge was built, they'd been a necessity for the owners' peace of mind. Three years later, they were rarely given a second thought.

Until now.

Brick had never been so happy to have a bolt-hole as he was right this moment.

"Keep your head down. This guy's armed," Tiny said. "Just heard a gunshot. He's got three million dollars on the line. He obviously wants Alaska bad and will do anything it takes to get her. Including taking you out," Tiny warned.

"Not happening," Brick said sternly. "Keep me updated. You guys have the situation there under control?"

"Yes."

Brick didn't know if his friend was lying or not, but there was nothing he could do to help at the moment, and he had more important things on his mind—namely, keeping Alaska safe.

"You have Mutt with you?" Tiny asked.

Blinking, Brick looked down. His loyal and faithful dog seemed to be able to read his mood, because he was sitting at Alaska's side, practically on her foot, not taking his gaze from his master's face.

"Yes."

"Okay, I'll make sure Tonka knows he's safe."

In emergencies, when they had to implement lockdown procedures, Tonka was in charge of the animals, of course. And he took his job very seriously.

"Once I check in with everyone, I'm headed your way," Tiny told him. "I'll bring one of the others as well. We're gonna find this guy. This is our territory. Chen just made the biggest mistake of his life."

"I'll take Alaska to bunker one-eleven and meet you," Brick said.

"You're gonna leave her in there by herself? We haven't checked the batteries in the emergency lights in a while. We've let that slip," Tiny said.

"*Fuck.*"

"We've got this," Tiny reassured him.

Brick *wasn't* reassured. He'd had to watch his battle buddies die in front of him once; he didn't think he was capable of sitting back and letting his new friends take care of what he felt was his problem to deal with. But at the same time, he wasn't sure he could leave Alaska. Especially if the lights in the emergency bunker weren't working. He had a high-powered flashlight, but doubted it would be enough for either of their comfort.

"Keep me updated," Brick said, not agreeing or disagreeing with Tiny.

"Ten-four. Watch your six."

Brick disconnected the phone, shoved it in his pocket, and turned to Alaska.

The daylight was almost completely gone now, and soon it would be pitch dark in the woods. The previous evening, it hadn't worried him. He'd had no doubt he could get them back to his cabin safely. But now? When there was a man hunting them? The dark wasn't nearly as comforting.

"What's wrong?"

Brick didn't have time to explain everything that was happening, but he also respected Alaska too much not to make her aware. "Long story short, Choo is really Yong Chen. He's the man who bought you from the Russian."

Alaska rocked back on her feet in shock. Brick hated this. Fucking *hated* it, but knowing a threat existed was safer for her than *not* knowing.

"Oh my God," she whispered. She began to rub her right palm against her thigh over and over. "He touched me!"

Brick felt sick. He reached for her hand and held it tightly, even when she tried to wrench it out of his grasp. "He's not going to fucking touch you *ever* again," he growled.

It took Alaska a long moment, but even as he watched, she pulled herself together. "So what's the plan? I'm assuming he's here?"

"He set fire to the POW cabin and set off fireworks near the lodge," Brick told her.

"Oh, no! Our poor guests! They have to be so upset!"

Figures she'd be more concerned about others than knowing the man who'd bought her as if she were a piece of meat was on the property. "He's armed, and I'm assuming he's here for you," Brick said bluntly. "But he's not going to get you."

Alaska began to tremble, but asked, "So what now? Does he know where we are? Is he going to come out here to find me?"

"I'm assuming he'll go to our cabin, and when we aren't there, he'll know we're out here somewhere. We had a long conversation today about my love of hiking and which trails are my favorite. He's even seen a map of the entire property. He'll assume you're out here with me."

"Where can we go? Where can we hide?" she asked, her voice louder than it had been.

Cognizant of the fact a man who wanted to snatch Alaska for his own sick agenda was likely stalking the forest at that very moment, Brick stepped into her personal space. He pulled her against him so they were plastered together from hips to chest.

"I've got this. I've got *you*. I haven't just found you, only to lose you already. That asshole isn't going to get his hands on you. No fucking way."

His words seemed to calm her. Brick felt her take a deep breath, then let it out slowly. "Okay."

"Okay," Brick agreed. He took hold of her hand in an unbreakable grip, then stepped off the trail and headed east. He knew exactly where he was and where the closest bunker, the one they called one-eleven, was located. Mutt stayed right on their heels, never more than a few steps away.

Brick didn't want to use the flashlight but had no choice. It would be a beacon shining right on them if Chen was anywhere nearby, but he also needed it to get them to safety.

He walked quickly, holding onto Alaska when she stumbled. But she didn't complain once.

When they arrived at the spot where the bunker was located, he led Alaska over to a tree and said, "Stand right here. I'll be right back."

"Okay."

Brick hesitated. "We've got this, Al. Promise."

She nodded bravely.

"Mutt, stay," Brick told his dog. Mutt sat, once again nearly on Alaska's foot as he obeyed.

Brick clicked off the flashlight and closed his eyes for a beat, letting them adjust to the darkness. He heard Alaska's quick inhalation, but she managed to control her fear.

When he opened his eyes, he could just make out the trees around him. He walked toward a small grouping nearby. Just to the north of them was a flat area, which concealed the bunker. He leaned over and, after a few seconds of searching, found the ring on the circular lid to the bunker. It lifted straight up.

This particular bunker was one of the smallest on the property, which wasn't ideal, considering the circumstances. Brick would've preferred to be in bunker one-oh- seven It was more spacious, wouldn't bring back as many bad memories for Alaska. But he also didn't want to risk being out in the open for any longer than they had to be. Once she was inside, Chen wouldn't find her. And Brick could go hunting.

As he stared down into the blackness of what he knew was an eight-by-five-foot box, he had his first doubt that Alaska would be able to handle this. The bunkers weren't built for long-term living. They were more like hidey-holes, in case their demons ever got the best of them. Meant as a temporary place to regain their equilibrium, and to keep others safe, if need be.

"Drake?" Alaska whispered from behind him.

Brick immediately turned to go back to her. "I'm here," he said softly as he approached.

"What's going on? I don't understand why we're just standing here."

Brick put his arm around her waist and led her toward the hole in the forest floor. "I'm telling you something only seven people in the world know about. There are safe spaces out here. Places we built to escape to if needed. Bunkers."

"Oh! That's so smart," Alaska said, surprising him. He kind of thought she might be mad, offended, or hurt that he hadn't already told her about them. But he should've known better. His Alaska would understand why he and his friends needed to keep this a secret.

"Where is—oh!" she exclaimed as she stared down at the small manhole-size hole in the ground. Then she looked up at him and whispered, "It's underground."

"Yeah, hon." He didn't mention that a bunker implied it would be underground.

She stepped backward, out of his hold. "I...no. Drake...I can't."

"You *can*," he countered, trying to sound completely

relaxed. But he couldn't be nonchalant about this. He knew how big of a deal this was for her. Knew how hard it would be.

She shook her head frantically. "No, I can't! We can just hide behind some rocks or something. Maybe we can go to the Sitting Rock?"

The hair on the back of Brick's neck was standing straight up. He needed to get Alaska hidden. He didn't like standing out in the open like this. Not when a sick, desperate man was hunting for them. But he needed to soothe her. He couldn't just stuff her in the bunker and leave her there. She'd never forgive him, and her mental health couldn't take it.

He stepped toward her and whispered, "Breathe, Al."

"I'm trying," she said, practically panting.

"Slow down your breaths," Brick ordered. And then, clarity hit.

He wasn't going to leave her. There was no way he could do such a thing.

If he could get her into the bunker, he wouldn't leave her side. It went against everything he was, but he'd let his friends hunt Chen. They'd make sure he and Alaska were safe. They may not have been on missions together, may be a little bent around the edges, but they were as much a team as his SEAL teammates had been.

Brick pulled Alaska against him, surprised to realize he needed the body contact as much as she did. She clung to him, her fingers digging into his back.

"That's it. You're okay. I've got you," Brick soothed. "I'm not leaving you," he told her. "We're going to get into the bunker and hang out until Tiny gets in touch with me and tells me they've got Chen. It's going to be fine. I promise."

Alaska's body continued to tremble and Brick forced himself to give her time.

Sooner than he thought possible, she raised her head and took a deep breath. "You won't leave me?"

"No. Never."

"Okay. I can do this," she said, more to herself than him.

Brick had never been prouder of anyone in his entire life. He didn't disrespect her by asking if she was sure, he simply turned them back to the hole and walked toward it. "I'm going to send Mutt down first, then we'll go down together," he told her.

Alaska stared down into the hole. "Is that possible?"

Brick chuckled. "Well, you'll go down a few rungs, then I'll follow right behind you. I'd never send you down by yourself, and I'm not going to leave you up here by yourself either. So we'll figure it out one step at a time. Okay?"

Alaska nodded.

"Mutt, down, check it out."

As if the dog had done it a hundred times, Mutt lowered himself and went paw over paw down the wide rungs into the hole. There were only about six steps to the bottom. Clicking on his flashlight, Brick turned the beam so it was facing the hole. "Okay, Al, your turn."

He could see her hands shaking as she sat on the ground and put her feet on the first step. Then she eased herself forward, turning so she was facing the edge, and began to back down into the hole.

Brick was right behind her. He faced her, even

though the position was awkward. Her head was level with his belly as they made their way downward. Reaching up, Brick pulled the round lid shut behind them, the metal sound of it closing echoing in the small space.

Concerned, Brick looked into Alaska's eyes. She seemed like she was two seconds from completely losing it. The sound of the lid closing must've been too much for her psyche to handle. He quickly took the last two steps and pulled her into his arms once more.

"You're okay. You're good. I've got you," he murmured as she shook like a leaf against him. Brick went to his knees, as the bunker wasn't tall enough for him to stand upright, taking her with him. He scooted until his back was resting against the metal wall of the bunker.

"Don't let go!" she begged. "Oh my God, I don't think I can do this," she whispered.

"You can," he countered. "You're so brave. Alaska, you can do any-damn-thing you want. I know it."

"Not this. What if he finds me? He's going to hurt me. I can't...I can't do it!"

"He's not going to find you. This bunker is unfind-able." Brick was making words up, but he didn't care. "But the guys know where we are. I told Tiny, and he'll tell the others. It's not like that Conex container, Al. We have food, water, air...there's an air hole in the back that we can open and close as we need it. You think I'm going to let anything happen to you? No way in hell."

Brick had placed the flashlight so the beam was facing upward. It illuminated the space quite well, and he hoped when she was able to think clearer, Alaska would see that the space they were in wasn't anything like the Conex container she'd been forced to endure.

It took several minutes, but eventually Alaska stopped shaking quite so hard. She even turned her head and rested her cheek against his shoulder instead of having her face stuffed into his neck. She looked around them without letting him go.

Brick tried to see the bunker through her traumatized eyes. It was pretty austere. Water jugs and containers of MREs were against one wall. A sleeping bag was rolled up in an airtight container. A composting toilet was sitting near the other supplies as well. Brick flinched. Fuck, Alaska might not handle it well when she spotted it.

But to his surprise, he felt her relaxing against him even more.

"How you doin'?" he asked.

"I'm...I don't like this. But...the light, the food, you being here...it all helps."

Mutt chose that moment to nose his way between them, and he practically crawled onto Alaska's lap as she cuddled against him.

To his surprise, a small chuckle left her lips.

"Guess he wants in on the snuggling too," she said.

Brick had trained Mutt to recognize the signs of stress in him, and he figured the dog was pretty damn overwhelmed with those feelings at the moment, both from him and Alaska, and doing what he could to help.

With every minute that passed, Alaska relaxed further—but Brick got more and more tense. He couldn't help but wonder what was happening outside. Had his friends found Chen? Was he still out there stalking them? Had he shot any of the guests or his buddies?

Sitting around and letting others put themselves in danger wasn't something he was comfortable with. But he wasn't going to move an inch while Alaska needed him.

CHAPTER NINETEEN

Alaska's heart was beating so hard, she thought she was going to have a heart attack right then and there. The only thing holding her together was Drake.

When she'd first realized he wanted her to climb into the hole in the ground, she'd full-on panicked. It was too much like back in Russia, when she'd been enclosed in that metal box and realized what was happening.

But this wasn't Russia, and she wasn't alone. She wasn't being shipped off to an evil man for nefarious purposes. She was in New Mexico. With Drake. The man she'd loved all her life. And Mutt. And she had food and water. Even a soft place to sleep, if needed. She ignored the toilet she'd seen in the corner, not wanting to think about that. It was way too similar to last time for her comfort.

The longer she sat on the ground with Drake's arms around her, and with Mutt's warm body weight against her belly, the easier the situation got. She didn't like it in here, not in the least, but with the light, and Drake, it was bearable.

Though, as the minutes ticked by, she realized Drake wasn't relaxing. Not even a little. He was stiff as a board against her. A muscle in his jaw ticked, and every once in a while he let out a frustrated sigh.

It slowly dawned on her that he hated being in here just as much—but not because it was an enclosed space.

Drake was a SEAL. Maybe not on active duty anymore, but it was still who he was. A warrior. A righter of wrongs. And she knew without having to ask that being down here, hiding while his friends put themselves in danger, went against everything he believed in. Everything he was.

After being helpless to assist his teammates when he was hurt, having to watch them die...this had to be even more excruciating for him than it was for Alaska.

Drake had said he loved her. Only now did she understand she hadn't completely believed him.

But in this moment? Exactly *how* much he loved her sank deeply into her bones. He wanted to be out there. Hunting down the evil man who thought it was all right to buy and sell human beings. To rape them. To do whatever perverse things he could dream up.

Her Drake was a hero, and he was suppressing his own needs and instincts to make sure *she* felt safe.

She knew what she had to do...she just wasn't sure she was strong enough to do it.

It took another ten minutes or so for Alaska to get up the nerve to speak.

"You need to go," she said as firmly as she could.

Although she had a feeling she fell way short of the strong, confident woman she wanted to portray.

"What?"

"I'm okay. No one but you and your friends know about this place. That guy isn't going to find me. You need to be out there, tracking him down, making sure he isn't hurting anyone back at The Refuge."

"I'm not leaving you," Drake said resolutely.

His words made Alaska feel good, but she also knew it wasn't the right thing for his peace of mind. Taking a deep breath, she turned in his arms and shook her head. "It's okay, Drake. *I'm* okay."

He stared at her for so long, she felt trapped. As if he was staring into her soul. That he could somehow read her mind. See how badly she wanted him to stay with her. Know that, while she may have said the words, deep down, she was terrified to be left in this metal box by herself.

But while she might truly be terrified, she knew without a shred of doubt that she needed to let Drake be the man he was. The SEAL he'd trained to be for so many years. He wasn't the kind of person to hide when everything went to hell. He'd want to be in the middle of the chaos. He hadn't been able to save his SEAL teammates, and that still ate at him years later. Hiding here with her, while a man who'd duped him and his friends crept around in the forest, trying to find her, wasn't in his DNA.

And it would do his recovery far more harm if he stayed.

"I'll call one of the others to come stay with you," he said after another long moment.

But Alaska shook her head. "There's no time. We don't know where that guy is. The last thing you want is for one of your friends to be hurt or lead the guy right to me. Besides, it sounded as if they had their hands full back at the lodge with all the guests on lockdown. I've got Mutt. And I know you'll come back to me as soon as you can."

"I don't like this," he said fiercely.

Alaska couldn't stop the snort of laughter from escaping. "You think I do? Because of me, that guy terrorized all our guests. I'm sitting in a metal box scared out of my mind and there's a sex trafficker out there somewhere wanting to grab me. This *sucks*. But you aren't a simple hotel owner, Drake. You're a SEAL. If I can't trust you to keep me safe, who the hell *can* I trust?"

She could practically see the wheels turning in his head. "Are you sure?" he whispered.

"Yes," Alaska said, even though she was anything but sure. The one thing she *did* know was that she loved Drake exactly how he was. And making him stay with her was killing him. She had no doubt he'd willingly remain tucked away, just to keep her safe. But his innate need to fix what was wrong, to catch the guy *now* so he couldn't disappear and show up again at a later date, was more important than being coddled.

"All right. But I'm leaving the flashlight. And Mutt. And you aren't to come out, no matter what. I know that will be difficult, but it's important. As long as I know you're safe here, I can do what I need to do. If I have to worry about where you are or whether you'll get caught in whatever shit goes down out there, I won't be able to do my job as well."

Alaska nodded immediately. She didn't want to think about shit going down, but that was why she was sending Drake out there, right?

"I love you so much," he said, his voice sounding tortured. "You have no idea. You're the strongest person I know. You can do this."

The fact that he was giving her a pep talk when all she had to do was sit here, and he was going out there to try to find an armed man amongst hundreds of acres of forest, was almost laughable. "I can do this," she echoed.

Drake kissed her then. A long, deep kiss that told her without words how much she was loved.

If he stayed even a moment longer, Alaska would lose her nerve and beg him to stay. Tell him that she couldn't handle it. That this bunker reminded her too much of that Conex container. "Go," she whispered. "But please don't forget about me."

"Never," Drake vowed. "Once this is done. Once this asshole is caught, I'm coming straight back here. That's a promise. Mutt, stay. Guard."

Alaska nodded and swallowed back the cry that almost left her lips when he stood and made his way to the short ladder. She watched with wide eyes as he pushed up the circular lid and climbed out of the bunker.

Mutt put his head across Alaska's legs and let out a low whimper.

"I love you," Drake said, before closing the lid once more.

And then Alaska was alone. At least she had the light from the flashlight. It sucked that she was in another metal box. But she wasn't on her way to a fate worse than death.

"Drake knows what he's doing," she whispered. "He'll be back before I know it."

But her words didn't make her feel better. With every second she sat there alone, the more memories pressed down on her, making her feel as if the walls were closing in.

Then Mutt nudged her hand, and Alaska jerked. Right. She wasn't on a train. She was here in New Mexico. Drake loved her and he was going to come back as soon as he could.

Alaska repeated those words over and over again in her head.

Drake loves me and he's coming back for me as soon as he can.

The silence around her was eerie. She strained to hear something, anything, but the only sound in the bunker was her own fast breathing and Mutt's soft exhalations.

Drake loves me and he's coming back for me as soon as he can.

Drake loves me and he's coming back for me as soon as he can.

The words became her mantra. Alaska gripped Mutt's fur and held on for dear life. She could do this. She was the one who'd told Drake to leave...she couldn't fall apart now. The last thing she wanted was for him to come back and find she'd completely lost it.

* * *

Every step Brick took away from the bunker was painful. He knew Alaska was suffering. She'd been so damn brave, but it was costing her.

Even knowing that, he'd still left.

She wasn't wrong. Hiding away while his brothers-in-arms looked for Chen, knowing they could be in danger and he wasn't doing anything to help, was physically painful. Not only that, but mentally, it had threatened to send him back to the dark place he'd been in right after his SEAL teammates had been killed.

But this time was different. He needed to help track Chen not only because his psyche demanded it, but also because he knew without a shadow of a doubt, Chen would never stop coming for Alaska.

For whatever reason, he was obsessed. And obsessed men were the most dangerous type. If he didn't find her today, he'd escape and come up with a new plan. He'd send someone else after her. Maybe someone disguised as a guest. She'd have to constantly look over her shoulder. And Brick didn't want that for her.

He certainly didn't want to think about her being used as a sexual plaything for Chen and his dark web deviants.

No, the guy needed to be taken down—and Brick needed to have a hand in doing so.

The problem was, as soon as he left the bunker, everything within him screamed to go back. That Alaska needed him. That she was probably freaking out being alone in that metal box.

He was torn, and it pissed him off further. It was

Chen's fault Alaska was scared. Chen's fault Brick had to leave her. Chen's fault that she might have a relapse and retreat into her mind to protect herself.

The man was going to pay. For terrorizing Alaska. For scaring The Refuge's guests. For being an evil human being.

But first, Brick had to find him.

Doing what he could to quiet his worry about Alaska, Brick thought back to what he and Chen had discussed throughout the day. They'd spent a lot of time together. Making small talk...or so Brick had thought. Now he realized the man had been pumping him for information. Trying to figure out his routine, his schedule.

A conversation he'd mentioned to Alaska came to mind. Chen had asked Brick about his favorite spots on the property. At the time, he'd assumed the man was just trying to learn more about The Refuge in order to suggest improvements, but now he wondered...

He'd told Chen that Table Rock was one of the best places to have a picnic.

He'd described the not-so-difficult trail to get there, how the guests enjoyed the peace and quiet of the area, the view. How it was a great spot to decompress.

Chen had been full of questions. How far away was it from the lodge? Could people who weren't used to physical activity get there easily? Was it accessible in the dark?

Most importantly, Brick had readily admitted that he and Alaska hiked out there all the time—including at night, because it was one of the best places to see the stars.

Was it possible Chen would think that was where he and Alaska were tonight? That they didn't hear or know what was happening back at the lodge and cabins? Was he that stupid?

After everything else the man had done so stealthily—the dark web, coming to the States, booking all the clients—would he really assume when he didn't find Alaska at his cabin, that they'd be out at Table Rock?

It was worth a shot to find out. Otherwise, with no other idea where to start, Brick could search these woods for hours and still not find him.

He stopped briefly, listening, straining to hear any sign of human life in the trees around him. He heard nothing but the normal sounds of the forest at night.

Knowing he was taking a chance, but needing to find out what was going on back at the resort, Brick dialed Tiny's number.

"Tiny."

"It's Brick. What's the situation?"

"The fire at the POW cabin is out. Three of the guests assisted Stone and Owl and they were able to get it under control before we lost the entire thing."

"Good. How is everyone?"

"Nervous, but holding it together. Many of the guests have taken positions at their windows and are keeping watch for that asshole. Since the fireworks and the gunshots, it's been quiet. Tonka's down at the barn with the animals...and Henley."

"What's she doing here?" Brick asked. It was unusual for the therapist to be at The Refuge this late.

"She was in an unplanned session with one of the

guests when everything started. As soon as she realized what was happening, she left to go help Tonka."

"Um…Tonka doesn't need help," Brick couldn't help but say.

"You and I know that, but apparently, Henley doesn't. Or she didn't care. I'm assuming all is well down there, because I haven't heard from him."

"Good. No word on Chen's whereabouts? Wait— where are you right now?"

"I'm with Spike and Pipe. We're starting a grid search for this asshole. He has to have a car around here somewhere. He certainly didn't walk in from Los Alamos."

"Agreed."

"How's Alaska?"

Brick tensed. "She's freaked," he admitted. "Not because of Chen…but because I left her back in bunker one-eleven by herself."

"*Fuck*," Tiny breathed.

"Yeah. She practically pushed me out of there. She knows I need to be out here searching."

"Got any ideas on where he might go?" Tiny asked. "You spent more time with him than the rest of us."

"I'm going to start my hunt at Table Rock."

"Table Rock? Seriously?"

"He was oddly interested in the place today when we were talking, and I mentioned Alaska and I spent quite a bit of time out there."

"Right. Okay, we're on the other side of the property, but we can switch directions and head that way now."

Brick wouldn't mind the backup, but there was no

way he was waiting on his friends. "I'm not too far from there."

"He's armed," Tiny reminded him.

"I know. This asshole is not taking me down," he vowed. "But...in case something does happen, I need you to get to Alaska as soon as possible. Don't wait, Tiny. Get to her and get her out of there."

"I will," he promised without hesitation.

The vise that had been around Brick's heart loosened a fraction. Not all the way—that wouldn't happen until the threat against Alaska was eliminated and she was in his arms, and he could make sure she wasn't permanently damaged from having to hide out in the bunker.

"Thanks. I'm shutting my phone off so it doesn't alert the fucker to my presence if it rings or vibrates."

"Understood. We'll be there as soon as we can. Out."

Brick clicked off his phone and powered it down before shoving it in a pocket in his pants. Then he set off toward Table Rock. Chen probably thought his plan was foolproof. He'd made more than one telling comment that day about the guests who came to The Refuge. It was clear he thought they were damaged mentally, without overtly stating so. In fact, he'd suggested changing the name of The Refuge, and getting away from the impression it was a place only for those who suffered from PTSD.

Brick and his friends had dismissed the suggestion outright, but it was clear now that Chen didn't think the guests would be any kind of threat to him or his plans. He was wrong. They might've been startled by the cabin fire, fireworks, and the gunshots, but they were also strong as hell...and most likely pissed someone was purposely fucking with them.

The closer Brick got to Table Rock, the more his resolve strengthened. Chen couldn't be allowed to escape. He had to pay for the wrongs he'd done against women in the past, and for what he'd planned for Alaska. He was a menace to society—and literally no one was safe with him on the loose.

Brick didn't really have a plan. First, he needed to find the man. And there was only about a twenty-percent chance Chen would actually be anywhere near Table Rock. The only good thing about this situation was that there was no way—absolutely no way whatso-ever—he'd be able to get his hands on Alaska. She was safe where she was.

As long as she stayed put.

There was no guarantee she wouldn't panic and leave the bunker. Brick prayed she didn't attempt it. He needed her tucked away, so there was zero possibility Chen could get his hands on her. The only thing that could keep Brick away from the man was if he used Alaska as a shield. As a bargaining chip.

Brick did his best to slow his breathing as he neared the Table Rock area. He wasn't on any of the estab-lished trails, choosing instead to use the trees and undergrowth as cover as he approached. Each step was deliberate and silent as he crept forward. At one point, he crouched down and listened, as he'd done earlier. Alert for any indication he wasn't alone.

There.

It was faint, but the sound of a stick breaking might

as well have been a huge neon sign pointing toward his objective.

Brick slowly and methodically moved positions, closer to where he'd heard the noise. The moon gave just enough light for him to see where he was walking.

His first glimpse of Chen made him stiffen.

He'd been expecting the man he'd spent the day with. The city slicker who was out of his depth in the forest. But from what he could glean, Chen was well prepared. He was wearing black from head to toe and had what looked like night-vision goggles over his eyes. He was also carrying a pistol—his finger on the trigger. The pockets of his pants bulged with whatever he carried with him, and Brick had to assume the man was more than equipped for an abduction. He was probably carrying items to subdue Alaska... zip ties, handcuffs, maybe even some sort of drug to knock her out once he got her back to his car, wherever that was.

He might not have his own gun with him, but Brick was far from helpless. And the one thing Chen *didn't* account for was how noisy the forest could be. His every step announced his trajectory.

Keeping his eye on the man, Drake followed behind him stealthily as he made his way toward the huge, flat rock.

Brick knew his best chance was to take Chen off guard. To surprise him. Which would be difficult, since the man had night-vision goggles. For a brief moment, he thought of how useful his flashlight would be right now. But there was no way in hell he would've left Alaska in that bunker without a light.

He could wait until Tiny and the others caught up

with him, then they could surround Chen and force him to put down his weapon and surrender.

He swiftly tossed aside that plan. Chen wouldn't stand around waiting for someone to find him. He'd continue his search for Alaska, probably ending up back at the resort eventually—and who knew what he'd do then. Desperate men acted rashly, and the last thing Brick wanted was to involve the guests more than they already were.

An idea formed as he hid amongst the trees. It wouldn't be quite as effective without his powerful flashlight, but it should give him enough time to take Chen down, hopefully without the man getting off a shot.

Moving slowly so as not to make a sound, Brick pulled his phone back out of his pocket. He pressed the button to turn it on and waited impatiently for it to power up. He'd only have a split second at best. A single moment when he'd have the upper hand.

Chen had climbed onto Table Rock and was staring out into the blackness. Except, with those night-vision goggles, he could no doubt still see the same gorgeous view guests enjoyed in the daytime.

With the man's back to him, Brick moved.

He burst out from behind the trees and ran toward Chen.

The other man spun as soon as he heard the commotion behind him, but Brick was ready. Even as Chen raised the hand holding the pistol, Brick held up his phone, the light from the flashlight app hitting Chen square in the face.

With the night-vision goggles, it would be four hundred times brighter than normal.

Even as he turned his head away from the glaring light, Chen pulled the trigger. Once. Twice. Three times. He shot blindly in quick succession.

Pain bloomed on Brick's arm, but he didn't slow down. Didn't stop his advance. He was a split second from dropping his phone and tackling Chen when the man made a fatal mistake.

He took two giant steps backward.

Maybe to get away from the light shining in his eyes. Maybe to try to hide.

Probably because he knew he was fucked.

Whatever the reason, it would be the last thing the man ever did.

Brick watched as his arms pinwheeled frantically in the air as the rock disappeared from under him.

Table Rock was such a great place to sit and enjoy the peacefulness of the area because of where it was situated. On the edge of a drop-off. It wasn't as dramatic a cliff as where the sitting rock was located... but it was still a good ways up.

As Chen hurtled off the edge of the rock, Brick heard the loud grunts as the man bounced against jagged rocks on his way down. The sound his body made as he hit the first narrow ledge, then the second, then landed on the sharp field of boulders at the bottom, probably around twenty feet below, was unmistakable.

Brick's adrenaline was pumping through his bloodstream as he ran to the edge of the rock and carefully looked down. He could see nothing but darkness.

"Fuck," he muttered. He was pretty sure no one could survive a fall like Chen just had and walk away, but he'd witnessed more than one situation where a person should've been killed instantly and wasn't—including his own.

The darkness prevented him from seeing anything. Realizing he still had his phone in his hand, Brick pointed it over the edge of the rock through the shadows below. The light wasn't powerful enough to illuminate any farther than the first ledge.

A chilling satisfaction spread through Brick at seeing the dark stain on the rock, but an injured man could still be a danger. Brick knew that better than most people.

As he debated what to do next—make his way to the bottom to ensure Chen wouldn't be a threat to Alaska or anyone else, ever again, or head back to the bunker—he heard a sound behind him.

Without thought, Brick moved. He dove to the left, away from the ledge, and into the bushes. His first thought was that Chen had somehow made it back up and was about to ambush him.

Then he recognized the whispered command to "hold."

Reinforcements had arrived.

"Tiny?" he asked quietly, still not convinced Chen was really dead.

"It's us," his friend said. "Where are you?"

Brick emerged from the bushes.

"Are you all right?" Pipe asked. "We heard shots."

"I'm good," he said.

"Did he run off? Which way?" Spike asked urgently.

In response, Brick turned and pointed over the edge of Table Rock.

"Damn," Tiny breathed.

Brick quickly explained what happened. "Do you have a light? My flashlight app isn't strong enough to see all the way to the bottom."

Tiny stepped up to the edge of the rock and got down on his knees to be safe, clicking on his high-powered flashlight. The four men peered over the edge at the same time.

Brick sighed in relief at the sight that greeted him.

Yong Chen lay at the bottom of the drop-off. His body contorted in an unnatural position, his back obviously broken beyond repair. He still had the night-vision goggles over his eyes, and the pistol he'd been holding was lying about a dozen feet from his body, amongst the boulders.

They waited a heartbeat, trying to see if the man moved or made any kind of sound. After a minute or so, Pipe said, "He's dead."

"We need to go down there, make sure," Spike added.

"I'll contact the sheriff," Tiny offered as he got off his knees and turned to Brick. "Fuck, man, you're bleeding," he said with a frown.

Brick looked down at his arm, and in the light from the flashlight Tiny was holding, saw the sleeve of his shirt was soaked. Now that he'd noticed it, the pain began to register.

He ignored it. "I have to get back to Alaska."

"You need to get that arm looked at," Pipe disagreed.

"My woman's sitting in a metal box, exactly like the one she was forced into when she was kidnapped and endured for days. I need to get to Alaska," Brick bit out.

"Right, at least let me wrap it real quick," Spike said calmly.

He was already reaching for the hem of the T-shirt he was wearing. He cut off a wide strip with the KBAR knife he always carried and had it wrapped tightly around Brick's upper arm inside of two minutes.

"There. At least now you won't bleed to death on your way back to her," he said grimly.

"I'm coming with you," Pipe said.

"No," Brick said with a shake of his head. "I don't know what condition she's going to be in when I get there."

"All the more reason for me to go," Pipe argued.

"She's not going to want you to see her if she's freaked. She's got a lot of pride, and while I think she's the bravest person I know, I still don't want to do anything that might make her ashamed of her reaction."

Pipe sighed. "Fine. But you need to keep us updated. Call us the second you get there, and when you're on your way back to the lodge."

Brick didn't miss how Pipe hadn't insisted they return to Table Rock. It would be impossible to keep Alaska's name or Brick's role out of what happened here tonight. They'd have to explain why Chen was there, what his plans were. But thanks to Elizabeth and her very thorough research into the dark web—and the file of everything she'd found, which Brick had no doubt was already sitting in their email—they had more than enough evidence to prove that Chen wasn't the innocent potential investor he'd portrayed himself to be.

Not only that, all the men who'd paid Chen to spend time with Alaska needed to be tracked down and punished. It was likely the fallout from tonight would continue on for quite a while, and unfortunately, Alaska would most likely have to tell her story many times in the coming days and weeks.

But Tiny and the others would make sure the sheriff saw the situation for what it was. The night-vision goggles, the gun, the way Chen's body had landed, Brick's injury...it all pointed to self-defense on Brick's part.

He nodded at his friends, grateful they were there to have his back, and turned to make his way through the woods toward Alaska. He used the flashlight app and stayed on the trails, which allowed him to move much faster than before. When he got to the area of the bunker, Brick took the time to turn off the light and study the area with all his senses.

Everything was as he'd left it. The ground around the bunker hadn't been disturbed. No sounds came from either the bunker or the forest around him. But the pit in Brick's stomach didn't dissipate. He wouldn't be satisfied until he had Alaska in his arms and he knew she was all right, mentally and physically.

He hurried over to the lid and pried it open. He stared down into the hole—and the first thing he saw was Alaska's upturned face looking back at him.

The relief that coursed through his veins made him momentarily unable to move or speak.

Luckily, Alaska didn't have the same problem. She

scrambled to her feet and flew up the ladder so fast, it was all Brick could do to catch her when she threw herself at him. He went back on a foot, then his legs crumpled under him.

He vaguely heard Mutt's nails on the rungs, heard him running around them excitedly a moment later, but Brick's attention was on Alaska.

"Are you all right?" he asked, attempting to get her to look at him. Her face was buried in the crook of his neck and she was holding him with a death grip.

"Al? Talk to me. Was it awful? Shit, of course it was. I'm so sorry. I didn't want to leave you, but you were right. I needed to. Tell me you aren't scarred for life. I think Henley's still at The Refuge, we'll go get her and you can talk to her. This isn't going to break you, you're too strong for that."

He felt more than heard her take a long, deep inhalation, then she picked up her head and looked into his eyes. "You love me, and you came back for me as soon as you could."

"Damn straight, I do, and I did," he breathed. The relief he felt was almost overwhelming. He could see the panic in her eyes, but even as he watched, it began to fade.

"I kept saying that over and over. I'm not saying I want to spend time in one of your secret bunkers again anytime soon, but the longer I was in there, and the more I reminded myself that you were coming back, the better it got. I wasn't in a train car headed to who knows where. I was in a safe place. *Your* safe place. The situation was completely different."

It was and it wasn't, but Brick didn't contradict her. "You're amazing," he said. "I'm in awe of you."

She gave him a small smile and shook her head. "Don't be. More than once I contemplated leaving and trying to find you. Once, I even climbed up the ladder and cracked open the lid."

"But you didn't leave."

She shook her head. "No. One, because Mutt wasn't happy with me at all. He kept tugging at my pants and growling, trying to get me to sit back down."

"He takes his guarding seriously," Brick said, reaching out and petting the dog for the first time since returning. Mutt leaned forward and licked Brick's face, making Alaska giggle. Brick turned back to her. "What's the other reason you didn't leave?"

"Because I could open the lid to the bunker," she said simply. "When I was on that train, behind that false wall, there was no way out. I was trapped, no matter how much I kicked and pounded. As soon as that lid lifted...I realized that I wasn't stuck. Just having the option to leave if I wanted calmed me enough to sit back down. Again, I'm not saying I want to come out here and camp in that thing on a regular basis, but knowing I was able to get out was a huge game changer."

Brick closed his eyes and rested his forehead against hers. She was in his arms. Safe. And it didn't seem as if she'd had a huge mental setback because he'd left her alone. He couldn't put into words how much that meant to him.

"What happened?" she asked softly. "Did you find him?"

Brick took in a huge breath and lifted his head. "Yeah. He won't be a threat to you, or anyone else, ever again."

She closed her eyes and her breath hitched, but she quickly got control over her emotions. Her eyes popped open and she frowned. "Are you going to be in trouble?"

"In trouble?" he asked in confusion.

"Yeah, for killing him?"

"No. First of all, the asshole was armed and I wasn't. Second, he was trespassing with the intent of kidnapping you. Third...I didn't kill him."

Alaska frowned. "You didn't?"

"No. He fell off the edge of Table Rock. Backward. I didn't even touch him."

"Wow...um...are you *sure* he's dead?"

Brick wasn't surprised she asked. Hell, he'd wondered the same thing. "I'm sure," he replied. "But to be *one hundred percent* sure, Tiny and the others will hike down there and check things out."

"Okay."

The relief in that one word was easy to hear.

She started to wrap her arms around him once more, but froze when her hand brushed against his upper arm. "What's that...?" she asked, as she felt the wetness of his makeshift bandage.

"A graze. I'm fine," Brick reassured her.

"What? You were *shot*?" she asked.

"Yeah. Used my phone flashlight to blind him, since he was wearing night-vision goggles, and he got a few shots off as he was trying to get away from me. That's how he fell over the edge. But only one shot grazed me."

To his surprise, Alaska scrambled off his lap and stood. "Get up! We need to go! Get back to the cabin. Call an ambulance. Get you looked at!"

His heart melted. "I'm okay," he tried to reassure her.

"No. You were shot. *Shot*! You are *not* okay. You're bleeding, Drake. I felt it. We're going. Right now! Back home. Come on, get up!"

Brick slowly stood, but instead of moving, he put his hands on her face and tilted it up to his own. "I promise I'm okay, love. I barely even feel it. I was too worried about getting back here to you."

"Which is another reason we need to go. You could have a delayed reaction or something. Pass out on the trail. I can't exactly give you a blood transfusion in the middle of the forest, Drake. I'm fine. Can we please just go?"

"Yeah, Al, we can go."

Apparently worrying about him seemed to snap her out of whatever residual fear she might've had about being left behind in a big metal box like the one in her nightmares. Brick leaned down and kissed her softly. He knew when they got back to the lodge, they were in for a long night. The sheriff would want to talk to them both, he needed to make sure their guests were all okay, and Brick had no doubt Alaska would want to fuss over them as well.

He needed to check out the damage to the POW cabin and check in with the rest of his friends. And to make Alaska feel better, he'd even let the paramedics check out his arm...after they made sure *she* was all right.

So he took a minute to just be with Alaska. He hugged her to his chest and stood there for a long moment, more thankful than he could put into words that everything had turned out the way it had.

It was Alaska who stirred first. "Come on, Drake, I'm serious—we need to get you back."

He nodded, closed the lid to the bunker, made sure it was undetectable to anyone walking by once more, then wrapped his fingers around hers and started back in the direction of The Refuge.

CHAPTER TWENTY

It was four-thirty in the morning before Alaska and Drake were able to crawl into bed in their cabin.

Drake hadn't been wrong. The second they'd arrived back at the camp, they'd been busy. She'd learned all of Chen's evil plans from listening to Tiny talk to the sheriff. Drake knew, but he hadn't told her any of it when they'd been out in the woods and in the bunker. He'd been trying to protect her, as always.

It hit home how close of a call she'd had. It was hard to wrap her brain around the fact that there were men and women in the world who thought nothing about selling human beings. Not only selling them, but doing so with the knowledge of the horrific things that would befall them. It boggled her mind.

It might've sent her into a deep depression if it hadn't been for the seven men at The Refuge. They'd spent a large portion of their lives fighting for good. To do everything in their power to keep the evil forces from winning. And now, even after their own traumas, they were trying to help others move on with their lives. And they *did* help. A lot.

After Drake's arm had been looked at by a paramedic, Alaska found herself alone with Henley. There was no doubt in her mind that Drake had somehow arranged it. He couldn't seem to take his eyes off her, and it made her feel warm and fuzzy that he was so worried.

She couldn't blame him. For a while, she'd thought she was going to lose it. She'd gone so far as to open the lid to that metal box, but then, just as she'd told him, she realized that she wasn't locked in. She wasn't a prisoner. She could leave anytime she wanted. That was enough for her to get control over her emotions, push past the trauma that was attempting to overwhelm her, and wait for Drake to come back.

Henley had wanted to talk about what happened. To make sure she was all right. But Alaska realized she didn't *need* to talk about it. At least not with the therapist. She might at some point, but for now, all she needed was Drake.

The guests all seemed to be on edge, but were handling the situation remarkably well. They'd been happy to report to the sheriff what they'd seen... including Chen lurking around the cabins right before the gunshots went off and the fireworks sounded.

When they'd finally gotten back to their own cabin, Mutt had immediately collapsed with exhaustion on his dog bed in the living area. He'd stuck right by Alaska's side throughout the night, refusing to budge, no matter what.

She'd helped Drake shower so his arm wouldn't get

wet and now they were finally in bed together. Neither had dressed after drying off, and the feel of his hot, hard body against her own was as much a balm to her soul as anything else.

"I'm sorry I had to leave you," Drake said softly.

"I'm not," she told him. "I mean, here's the deal. It's impossible for you to be by my side every second of every day. I needed that. To know that I could deal with the situation on my own. Not that I wouldn't have preferred for you to be there with me, but knowing that I *could* do it on my own was...a relief. I don't want to be a burden to you, Drake. Ever. If that time comes, I expect you to let me go."

"I'm never letting you go," Drake told her fiercely. "And you could *never* be a burden to me. I have no doubt you can do anything you want to do...you don't need me. It's a gift to be by your side. Your love is a gift I'm still pinching myself that I've been given."

"Drake," Alaska said softly, on the verge of tears.

"No crying," he ordered gently. "We're having a happy moment here," he told her with a smile.

"Sorry," she said, wiping her cheek on his shoulder.

Drake's hand eased into her hair, holding her against him even as the fingers on his other hand gently caressed her arm, which was thrown across his body. "You were right before—I deserve you, Alaska. After all I've said and done and been through, you're my reason for living through that explosion. I'll spend the rest of my days proving that my life being spared wasn't wasted. For Vader, Monster, Bones, Rain, and Mad Dog, and for myself."

"And I deserve you," Alaska told him. "We deserve each other."

"Yes, we do," he agreed. "Now, on a slightly different topic...I'm gonna need to call my mom tomorrow. Let her know what's up," Drake said. "I wouldn't put it past her to find out somehow about the shit that went on here through her many connections. I want to be the one to tell her so she doesn't worry. But I'm guessing she'll want to come and see for herself that we're both okay."

"Oh, wow. I haven't seen your mom since graduation day."

"I know. That's why I wanted to warn you. And you haven't tried to get in touch with your own mom. You want to do that?"

"No," she said immediately. "I have no idea where I'd even start...and if she hasn't cared where I am or what's going on in my life for the last two decades, she's not going to start now. Besides, if I do manage to find her, I'm guessing all she'll do is try to get money out of me. That's what happened last time I found her."

Drake sighed. "That's what I figured, but I had to ask."

"It's okay, Drake," Alaska told him. "I came to terms with our relationship a long time ago. I'm better off without her in my life. I promise."

"All right. But if you ever change your mind, all you have to do is say the word and I'll get Elizabeth on finding her."

"She's pretty amazing," Alaska said. "I'm impressed she was able to find out all that info on Chen. What's her story?"

"She works with Tex...who I'm sure you'll meet one of these days. Anyway, she was a kidnapping victim herself. A serial killer nabbed her and another woman. He physically tortured Elizabeth while mentally torturing the other woman. That was in California. She moved to Texas to try to deal with everything that happened, became agoraphobic, then a firebug...and eventually married a firefighter. She's the best hacker, IT person, computer genius, whatever you want to call it, I've ever worked with...except maybe for Tex."

"Wow. Okay," Alaska said. "I was kind of expecting you to tell me she was just a chick who worked with the police or something."

"Or something," Drake agreed.

"We owe her a lot," Alaska told him.

"Yup. She's already got an open invitation to come to The Refuge anytime she wants."

"Good. Drake?"

"Yeah, Al?"

"I'm happy."

He chuckled. "Only you could say that after the day —or night, morning, whatever—you've had."

"I'm alive. I'm naked with the man I love. I didn't completely lose it when confronted with my worst nightmare, and I get to see your mom again soon...I've always admired and liked her. What's not to be happy about?"

"One of these days, I'm gonna ask you to marry me," Drake said.

Alaska lifted her head to stare at him. "What?"

His hand tightened in her hair, and he gently pressed her head back down against his shoulder. "Not right now. Not tomorrow. But it's gonna happen. I'm just warning you so you can get used to the idea."

"Yes!" she blurted.

It was Drake's turn to lift his head. "What?"

"Yes," she said with a small smile. "When you ask me, that'll be my answer. Just so *you* know, so you can get used to the idea."

Drake chuckled. "Right. Good to know."

Alaska opened her mouth to say something else, but a huge yawn came out instead.

"Sleep, Al."

"We've got stuff to do in the morning. Don't let us sleep too long," she mumbled.

"Okay."

She sighed. "You're totally gonna let us sleep until noon, aren't you?"

"Yup," Drake said without apology. "It's been a long fucking night, Al. It's nearly dawn already. We're both exhausted. All I want to do is sleep with you in my arms and not think about all the shit we have to do for a while. When we wake up, I want to make love to the woman I adore and admire more than anyone in the world. Then we'll shower, eat, and *then* we'll wander over to the lodge to check out what's happening."

Alaska sighed in contentment. "Okay."

"Okay," Drake agreed. "And for the record...I'm happy too."

His words meant the world to Alaska. Because she knew for a long time, he *hadn't* been happy. He'd been devastated about losing his friends, and then he'd been too busy battling his demons, and getting The Refuge up and running, to even think about his own wants and desires. Knowing he was happy, with *her*, plain ol' Alaska, was a feeling she couldn't even begin to put into words.

"Good night. Thanks for being you," she whispered.

Drake's lips brushed across her forehead. "Thanks for being you," he echoed.

To her surprise, Drake fell asleep almost immediately. It took her a bit longer, as the events of the evening replayed through her head. But eventually, she relaxed further into Drake and felt herself drifting off.

If someone had told her four years ago—hell, twenty-five years ago—that this was where she'd be today, she never would've believed them. She'd held Drake on a pedestal in her mind for so long, had seen him as completely unattainable. But time had a way of changing perspective, and Alaska knew without a doubt that the man in her arms needed her just as badly as she needed him.

* * *

Henley McClure took a deep breath and forced herself to turn back toward the barn. It had been a long night for everyone, and she'd done her best to be there for the guests who'd suffered flashbacks after the incidents of the evening.

During the height of the confusion, she'd gone to the barn. She wasn't supposed to. She knew the procedures. She was supposed to stay put in the lodge. But knowing Tonka—no, *Finn*—was by himself in the barn, trying to calm the animals, had nagged at her. So she'd left to help him.

Of course, Finn had *never* wanted her help. Not in a professional way, and not in a personal way. She was the stupid one who wouldn't give up on him.

Finn was different from the other men who owned The Refuge. He was more...broken...than the others.

But even after all the time she'd been working at The Refuge, she hadn't made any headway with his therapy, despite the fact he attended group sessions semi-regularly. It was heartbreaking because he was such a good man. When the bedlam erupted tonight, he'd headed straight for the animals, to make sure they were safe and calm. Yes, it was his job, but Henley knew it was more than that. He had a connection with every four-legged creature at The Refuge that went beyond what most people had with pets and farm animals.

She hadn't been able to stop herself from going to him. She was drawn to Finn. As a therapist, she knew it was a slippery slope. It wasn't professional to have feelings for a client...but then again, Finn had never, not once, participated in any of her sessions. He attended but didn't speak, simply watching her with those all-seeing eyes of his. Being the focus of his attention was uncomfortable...and exciting at the same time.

From the moment she stepped into the barn, it was obvious Finn had his work cut out for him. The fire coming from the POW cabin had all the animals on edge. And the firecrackers weren't helping the situation. The horses were snorting and stomping in their stalls, even banging against the gates, trying to get out.

Melba was mooing nonstop. It was a terrified sound, one that instantly made tears spring to Henley's eyes. The chickens were agitated and running around, the goats were bleating, and she even saw a cat dart from one end of the barn to the other as it tried to find a safe place to hide.

She immediately waded into the chaos, eager to help in any way she could. She went to Melba's stall and began to pet the petrified cow. She knew the beast's story as well as anyone, knew Melba had been trapped in a barn fire. She stroked her head and put an arm around her giant neck. She murmured calmly to the creature, doing her best to keep her voice low and composed. To her surprise, one of the dogs Finn and the rest of the guys at The Refuge had adopted joined her in the stall. As did two of the goats. They all hunkered down, taking solace from each other.

All the while, Finn walked around doing the same thing with the horses and the other animals. Henley could hear his deep voice reassuring the anxious animals that they were all right. That they were safe. That he wouldn't let anyone or anything hurt them.

The noise from the firecrackers finally faded and the crackling of the nearby fire stopped.

She'd just stood up when Finn appeared in front of Melba's stall. But instead of looking calm and controlled, as she'd assumed by his voice, his eyes were wide, he was breathing hard, and he looked as if he was on the verge of a nervous breakdown.

She moved before thinking about what she was doing. She took hold of his arm and steered him out of the stall, making sure to latch the door behind her so Melba wouldn't take it upon herself to go on a midnight walk around the property.

She escorted Finn to a small office, surprised when

he let her. She sat him on the small couch and, to her utter shock, he immediately leaned into her, burying his face in her neck and holding her as if he'd never let go.

Henley wrapped her arms around him and simply held him back as his large body shook.

Something had triggered him tonight, but she wasn't exactly sure what. The firecrackers and fire and gunshots could've set him off...but she didn't think so. She hadn't seen him flinch with any of those sounds. He'd been completely focused on the animals.

In the two years she'd been working at The Refuge, she'd locked down her attraction to this man. Just as she suspected he'd done with her. Despite that...when they were in the same room, their eyes always seemed to meet. When he sat in on sessions, she got the peculiar feeling he was there to protect her from anyone saying or doing anything offensive. He'd even escorted a guest or two out of sessions in the past, when he or she got too angry or worked up.

And the few times she'd recounted what had happened to her when she was a girl, he'd gripped the arms of his chair so tightly, Henley was sure he'd break the wood.

But neither of them had ever acted on their attraction. Hadn't crossed that line. They were co-workers, and while it made Henley unbearably sad, she understood that Finn wasn't ready for a relationship. If he ever made it back to a place where he was ready for companionship, he very likely wouldn't start anything with *her*. Not only because they worked together, but because she was a psychologist. He wouldn't be the first man too afraid she'd probe into his psyche and want to know all his secrets.

She *did* want to know his secrets...but only because she cared about him.

And now here they were, holding each other as if they were each other's lifeline.

How long Finn sat with her, shaking and holding on for dear life, Henley didn't know. She didn't encourage him to talk, to tell her what was wrong. She simply held him.

When he finally loosened his hold, Henley braced. To her utter surprise, he didn't pull away abruptly and leave without a word, as she'd expected. He stared at her for a long moment before saying, "Thank you. I... needed that."

Henley nodded. "Me too."

"You okay?" he asked quietly.

"Yes. Are you?"

He thought about her question for a few seconds before saying, "I think I am now. I need to check on the others. Make sure Brick and Alaska are all right."

Henley nodded again.

Finn stood and held his hand out for her to take.

She took it, shivering as electricity seemed to shoot down her arm. He dropped her hand as soon as she was on her feet, but Henley could somehow still feel it.

The rest of the night was exhausting, as Finn left to check on his friends and Henley did what she could to help the guests who were on edge.

She was happy that everything had turned out all right. That no one was seriously injured, animal and human alike, and the man who'd come after Alaska was no longer a threat. Now she was tired. Drained, really.

"You look beat," Pipe told her. "Why don't you stay the night? We've got a cot we can put in one of the meeting rooms here at the lodge."

She smiled at him. "Thanks, but I need to get home."

"Are you sure? It's very late."

"I'm sure. My daughter is at my neighbor's, and she's a nurse and has to go to work at five in the morning."

Pipe stared at her for a moment. "You have a daughter?"

Henley nodded. "Yeah."

"I didn't know that. Did you know that, Stone?" Pipe asked, turning to his friend standing nearby.

"Nope."

Henley merely shrugged. "It hasn't come up," she told them.

"All right then, well...drive safe. And you're definitely going to be paid overtime for the hours you were here tonight. We appreciate all you did, more than we could ever say," Pipe said.

"There's no place I would've rather been," Henley reassured them. Her eyes swept the room once more, making sure all the guests had gone and no one was left who might need an ear to listen. Her gaze caught on Finn's. He was standing near the front desk—staring straight at her. She couldn't read the look in his eyes. She hoped their time in the barn tonight would perhaps bring them closer, would make him at least willing to talk to her.

When he turned and headed for the door, she knew that wouldn't be the case.

She sighed heavily.

"Drive safe," Stone reiterated.

"Please text when you get home," Pipe added.

Henley couldn't help but wish it was another man who'd made the request, who was worried about her, but she nodded at Pipe anyway. "I will. Thanks."

She gathered up her coat and purse and headed for the door. It had been a long, hard day, but she couldn't help but be pleased with the assistance she'd been able to give the guests. Being a single mother and working the odd hours she did made her life tough, but she wouldn't change anything about it. Her daughter was her entire world, and she'd do whatever was necessary to provide a safe, happy, stable life for her.

* * *

Tonka was so tired he could barely see straight...yet he couldn't stop thinking about Henley. She'd done everything right tonight. Had stepped in to help him with the animals. Hadn't asked him a million questions. Her instincts had simply kicked in and she'd done what he needed her to do.

And after the animals were settled? When he'd remembered *another* animal, in another time and place, that he hadn't been able to help...allowing his demons to creep in? An animal he'd had to watch suffer? She'd simply let him work through the worst of the memories in silence while holding him tightly so he didn't explode into a million pieces.

From the moment he'd met the psychologist Brick had hired to work with the guests, Tonka had known she was special. She didn't force anyone to tell their stories. Didn't make anyone feel as if they were broken or fragile. She treated clients as if they were close friends, creating a feeling of calm, quiet intimacy in her sessions that made people feel safe enough to speak freely. To admit fears and traumas from their pasts.

And when he'd heard what she'd been through as a child? It took everything within Tonka not to demand information about who the assholes were who'd killed her mom. He wanted to make sure they wouldn't hurt anyone ever again. It had been decades since she'd been that ten-year-old girl, scared out of her mind and hiding under her bed, and for all he knew, the men were in jail or dead. But that event still affected her. Tonka could tell.

He felt a pull toward her. Probably because they'd experienced a trauma that was surprisingly similar. They'd both had to watch and listen as a loved one was tortured and killed. But while Tonka had allowed his experience to break him, Henley turned hers into a life-long crusade.

He had a hard time relating to people now, preferring the company of animals. But when Tonka had heard Henley mention a daughter, something inside him shifted.

Unreasonably, he didn't like knowing Henley had kept something as important as a child from them. She wasn't married; he knew that unequivocally. There was also no mention of an ex—and her daughter was with a neighbor—which meant she was likely the sole parent.

Were they doing all right? Was she making enough money? Were they struggling at all? Did she have a regular babysitter? The hours she worked at The Refuge weren't exactly steady.

How old was her daughter? What was her name?

His curiosity almost overwhelmed him. All of a sudden, Tonka wanted to know *everything* about Henley McClure. Everything she'd been keeping to herself.

It was an odd feeling, this curiosity. Tonka hadn't really cared about almost anything for a long while now, ever since he'd gotten out of the Coast Guard. He'd been living his life one day at a time and concentrating on the ins and outs of running The Refuge with his friends.

But tonight, Henley had snuck beneath his very high, thick walls. He wasn't sure if that was good or bad, but he acknowledged that something had changed.

He *wanted* to care again. Wanted to act on the interest he saw in her eyes, which he'd done his best to ignore for two years. Wanted to admit that her interest wasn't one-sided.

He'd have to move slowly. For his sake as well as hers. He wasn't at all sure he was ready to be in any kind of romantic relationship. She'd want him to open up. To talk about his past.

He had a feeling Henley would understand better than anyone why he couldn't talk about what happened on that fateful day so many years ago. It wasn't fair to want to know all her secrets while sharing none of his... still, he didn't know if he could.

As he finally settled into bed, Tonka's mind continued to whirl. It wouldn't be easy for him to open up to Henley, but he couldn't deny the urge to get closer. To see if the connection they seemed to share might be strong enough to withstand the trauma of his past.

For the first time in what felt like forever, Tonka was cautiously excited about the future. He drifted to sleep...looking forward to tomorrow.

* * *

Find out what demons are in Tonka's head and if Henley can break through his shields to get to his heart in *Deserving Henley!*

Want to talk to other Susan Stoker fans? Join my reader group, Susan Stoker's Stalkers, on Facebook!

Scan the QR code below for signed books, swag, T-shirts and more!

Also by Susan Stoker

The Refuge Series
Deserving Alaska
Deserving Henley (Jan 2023)
Deserving Reese (May 2023)
Deserving Cora (TBA)
Deserving Lara (TBA)
Deserving Maisy (TBA)
Deserving Ryleigh (TBA)

Eagle Point Search & Rescue
Searching for Lilly
Searching for Elsie
Searching for Bristol (Nov)
Searching for Caryn (April 2023)
Searching for Finley (TBA)
Searching for Heather (TBA)
Searching for Khloe (TBA)

SEAL Team Hawaii Series
Finding Elodie
Finding Lexie
Finding Kenna
Finding Monica
Finding Carly (Oct)
Finding Ashlyn (Feb 2023)
Finding Jodelle (July 2023)

SEAL of Protection: Legacy Series
Securing Caite

Delta Force Heroes Series

Rescuing Rayne

Rescuing Aimee (novella)

Rescuing Emily

Rescuing Harley

Marrying Emily (novella)

Rescuing Kassie

Rescuing Bryn

Rescuing Casey

Rescuing Sadie (novella)

Rescuing Wendy

Rescuing Mary

Rescuing Macie (novella)

Rescuing Annie

Badge of Honor: Texas Heroes Series

Justice for Mackenzie

Justice for Mickie

Justice for Corrie

Justice for Laine (novella)

Shelter for Elizabeth

Justice for Boone

Shelter for Adeline

Shelter for Sophie

Justice for Erin

Justice for Milena

Shelter for Blythe

Justice for Hope

Shelter for Quinn

Shelter for Koren

Shelter for Penelope

Ace Security Series

Claiming Grace
Claiming Alexis
Claiming Bailey
Claiming Felicity
Claiming Sarah

Mountain Mercenaries Series

Defending Allye
Defending Chloe
Defending Morgan
Defending Harlow
Defending Everly
Defending Zara
Defending Raven

Silverstone Series

Trusting Skylar
Trusting Taylor
Trusting Molly
Trusting Cassidy

Stand Alone

Falling for the Delta
The Guardian Mist
Nature's Rift
A Princess for Cale
A Moment in Time- A Collection of Short Stories
Another Moment in Time- A Collection of Short Stories
Lambert's Lady

Special Operations Fan Fiction

ABOUT THE AUTHOR

New York Times, *USA Today* and *Wall Street Journal* Bestselling Author Susan Stoker has a heart as big as the state of Tennessee where she lives, but this all American girl has also spent the last fourteen years living in Missouri, California, Colorado, Indiana, and Texas. She's married to a retired Army man who now gets to follow *her* around the country.

She debuted her first series in 2014 and quickly followed that up with the SEAL of Protection Series, which solidified her love of writing and creating stories readers can get lost in.

If you enjoyed this book, or any book, please consider leaving a review. It's appreciated by authors more than you'll know.

www.stokeraces.com
www.AcesPress.com
susan@stokeraces.com

facebook.com/authorsusanstoker

twitter.com/Susan_Stoker

instagram.com/authorsusanstoker

goodreads.com/SusanStoker

bookbub.com/authors/susan-stoker

amazon.com/author/susanstoker